From the Worlds of Andre Norton

The Sorcerer's Conspectus I

Witch World Saga Explored

by

"Lotsawatts"

Witch World © A Series by Andre Norton

Edited by: Jay P. Watts
Creator of
Andre-Norton-Books.com
The Official website of
The Estate of Andre Norton

The Sorcerer's Conspectus I Witch World Saga Explored

By Lotsawatts

Witch World © A Series by Andre Norton

Compiled and Edited by Jay P. Watts   aka: Lotsawatts since 1980
Creator of Andre-Norton-Books.com   aka: Andre-Norton.com since 2004

ISBN 13: 979-849-18642-87

1st HC edition published October 2021

Dedication:

To Andre Norton
May She Rest in Peace

I wish to thank several people by name for without their help I
would have never attempted such a project.

Mike Brenner and Jay Demetrick for all their work on the
timelines and detailed information and then letting me have it.

Irene Harrison and Sandy Larkey for helping with the synopsis
on some of these stories.

Michael Martinez for letting me copy his
Glossary of Witch World.

And last but not least – Sue Stewart for giving me the
Jaunita Coulson Index and maintaining the Legacy that is
Andre Norton's.

Table of Contents of Volume I WW Saga

Biography of Andre Norton
by Maciej Zaleski - Ejgierd

Andre Norton in her Office: Winter Park, Florida in the 1990's

Alice Mary Norton was born on February 17, 1912 in Cleveland, Ohio, USA. She was the second daughter of Adalbert Freely Norton, owner of a rug company, and Bertha Stemm. Being a late child, born seventeen years after her sister, she never developed close relationships with her siblings or contemporaries and was influenced primarily by her parents, especially her mother, who later on did all her proofreading and served as a critic-in-residence.

Much attention was paid in Ms. Norton's family to books, the visible sign of which was the weekly visit to a public library. Even before she could read herself, her mother would read to her and recite poetry as she went about various household chores. Even the good grades at school were rewarded by books, namely by copies of Ruth Plumly Thompson's Oz novels. It was this fondness of her parents that marked her whole life. She started writing at the Collinwood High School in Cleveland, under the tutelage and guidance of Miss Sylvia Cochrane. She became an editor of a literary page in the school's paper, called *The Collinwood Spotlight*. As such, she had to write many short stories. It was at the school hall, where she wrote her first book - "Ralestone Luck", which was finally published as the second in 1938 (the first one was "The Prince Commands" in 1934). Also in 1934, she legally changed her name to Andre Norton (Andre Alice Norton, to be exact). She was expected to be writing for young boys, and the male name was expected to increase her marketability.

After graduating from the High School, she continued her education at the Flora Stone Mather College of Western Reserve University (now Case

Western Reserve) for a year from the autumn of 1930 to the spring of 1931, intending to become a history teacher. Then, due to the economical depression, she was forced to find work in order to support the household. She took evening courses in journalism and writing that were offered by Cleveland College, the adult division of the same university.

In 1932 she was employed by the Cleveland Library System. Most of her time was spent as an assistant librarian in the children's section of the Nottingham Branch Library in Cleveland. Although she became something of a troubleshooter for the entire system, the lack of a degree prevented her from advancing as her ability might have dictated. She couldn't change jobs, because there weren't many employment opportunities during the depression.

In 1941, for a short period of time she owned and managed a bookstore and lending library called the Mystery House, situated in Mount Ranier, Maryland. Unfortunately it was a failure. At much the same time, from 1940 to 1941, she worked as a special librarian in the cataloguing department of the Library of the Congress, involved in a project related to alien citizenship, which was abruptly terminated by the beginning of the World War II. After Ms. Norton left the Cleveland Library System, she began working as a reader for Martin Greenberg at Gnome Press. After 8 years she left, totally devoting herself to writing.

On March 17, 2005 at 2:23am Andre Norton passed away at her home in Murfreesboro, Tennessee. Since middle February she had been fighting with a combination of flu and pneumonia and has at last succumbed to a congestive heart failure.

She often said she never wished to be more than a storyteller, and that skill she has mastered to perfection. Writing was her calling and she has not abandoned it till the very end. She was a prolific author and leaves a legacy of over 200 books and short stories.

Her writing, always uplifting and positive in its message, has touched the lives of many people - she has received numerous letters and emails from people who told her how her stories helped them find strength to overcome the obstacles they faced in real life. She will be sorely missed by us all.

She requested before her death that she not have a funeral service, but instead asked to be cremated along with a copy of her first and last novels.

She asks that memorials be made in her honor to:

St. Jude's Children's Hospital (Memorial and Honor Program), 501 St. Jude Place, Memphis, TN 38105

Or Veterinary Services (c/o the Noah Fund) P.O. Box 10128, Murfreesboro, TN 37129.

The Scribe Explains his Work

By Lotsawatts

In futures past and on worlds across the galaxy there exists a phenomenon called Story-Telling. For most of history the galaxies' stories were passed down verbally and only in the most recent of times have we learned to make marks on paper and record these stories. Almost every sentient being on these worlds thinks they can be a Story-Teller. Now, on most of these worlds being a Story-Teller is a great honor but the history of story-telling has not always been so honorable.

From the beginning of time to this day this talent has been in the control of men. It is the task of the Wise-Man, the Sorcerer, the Warlock, the Shaman, the Medicine Man and many other labels to be the Story-Tellers. The only stories the females can tell are for the benefit of the children. For the men can't be bothered with the children. But that in itself is a whole other story all on its own.

Even on this world, in some societies, to be caught telling stories as a female is punishable by all manner of deeds including death. The female Story-Teller is labeled a Witch, Sorceress, Enchantress, Occultist, Necromancer, Wiccan, Beldam, a Pythoness and many others. Only to be cast out, if not stoned or burned at the stake. And in modern times in a lot of societies it's still illegal for females to learn how to read and write.

On most of the worlds in the galaxy and in most of the societies on this world the females tell the children how the world works and how they should behave. This type of Story-Telling is told to both the boys and the girls in the village until the boy is ready to be a man. Then the boy is allowed to join in the story-telling of the men but only if they sit quietly and behave. Never are they to interrupt or ask questions unless they are taken on as an apprentice Story-Teller.

What the men don't know is that throughout history the women have been hiding in the shadows listening to these stories and learning on their own. Which turns out to be a wondrous thing, for females or women if you prefer, are often the better story-teller. The sad thing is that it has taken centuries for the people of this world to recognize this fact.

My name is Lotsawatts and I once thought that even I could be a Story-Teller but soon learned that I was better suited to be a lowly scribe. Being a scribe is not such a bad lot in life. You not only get to hear the story but you get to work with the Story-Teller and record it for prosperity. You often get to follow the Story-Teller into places forbidden and best of all, go unnoticed.

Like I said, in the society that I am a member of, we have finally come out of the dark ages and let the females share their stories instead of hiding them. On this world one of the greatest female Story-Tellers was a Sorceress by the name of Andre Norton. She lived from the Year of Our Lord 1912 until 2005. She told stories not only of this world but of many others and thanks to the fact that she was also taught to be a scribe, many of these stories have been recorded exactly as she intended.

Her stories have been so great that many people have spent countless hours composing their own stories about this Sorceress or about her stories. Yes, you read that right, stories about her stories. What better praise can you receive than to have Story-Tellers create stories about your story? This piece of work is an attempt at just that. You see, one of Andre's stories has morphed into a super-story. In that it is made up of a hundred separate stories both by her and other Sorceress' and Sorcerers. It is known as "Witch World".

This lowly scribe has spent years gathering up all the stories by and about Andre Norton, who he thinks is the best Story-Teller ever, and put them on a relatively new technology called the internet. And now, using stories by other Story-Tellers, I am going to attempt to show the world how all of these stories in "Witch World" fit together.

The first four stories in volume 1 are fiction and are somewhat obscure because of the limited places that they have appeared. The first one is written by Andre herself in 1971, explaining the art of Story-Telling called "On Writing Fantasy". And then there are three by Story-Tellers that excel in explaining other peoples stories, for I could never produce work as good as these. We have one from 1971 by Rick Brooks explaining why he thinks Andre has had a "Loss of Faith". Then one from 1977 by Sandra Miesel discussing Andre's stories from the beginning and winding up with "Witch World" and last but not least is one from 1983 by Roger Schlobin that is all about "The Witch World Series". The later three will give the reader of this great 2 volume tome three different views on the work of Andre Norton. I am still searching for stories about "Witch World" from the years 1984 until today but I have yet to find any suitable for your eyes, just the stories themselves.

Then we get to the "Witch World" stories within volume 2. Each story meticulously explained by a master in Story-Telling and Three Sorcerers Apprentices'. The Story-Teller being Juanita Coulson best known for her series "Children of the Stars" Juanita Coulson told her story in the form of an index of the "Witch World" stories in the mid 1990s for Andre's use in writing other stories.

A fan of Andre's started to put together an explanation about "Witch World" on a website called Elwher.wikidot.com[1] under the username "Elwher" in 2009 and then in 2013 he turned over that work to two Sorcerer's Apprentices, "Metaldragon" (Jay Demetrick) and "Indagare" (Mike Brenner) who then greatly expanded it. The work by all of these people can be found throughout the website pages of Andre-Norton-Books.com. It should be noted that we have yet to identify the real name for "Elwher".

I have included some work by Master Sorcerer - Michael Martinez of the website Xenite.org. He has put together a glossary of names, places and races of "Witch World" that will also help the reader with their exploration of this world.

I'm going to attempt to combine the work done by each of these people while maintaining the integrity of their work. At times it may seem repetitive but it is really important to show the different views of the story. I tried putting it all into one volume but it became so massive that you would not want to hold it for long. If you have only picked up this volume you are going to want to get the other for they complement each other. There are only 16 pages that are duplicated in each volume.

 It is recommended that you read all the stories of Witch World in the Expanded Reading Order that includes the stories by other authors. If you start with *S'Olcarion's Sons* and then follow the recommendations at the end of each of the stories' write-up in volume 2 you will experience the whole Saga in the order of the timeline.

~ Lotsawatts

NOTE: The following Anthologies are not included in this tome but ALL the stories within each are covered.

Spell of the Witch World ~ 1972
Trey of Swords ~ 1977
Lore of the Witch World ~ 1980
Tales of the Witch World 1 ~ 1987
Four from the Witch World ~ 1988
Tales of the Witch World 2 ~ 1989
Tales of the Witch World 3 ~ 1990

---

[1] Wikidot pages in 2009-13 were is my opinion an achward grouping of webpages that sort of resemble a Library File Card system. I still find myself kind of discombobulated when navigating the site.

On Writing Fantasy
by Andre Norton

Original in *The Dipple Chronicles*, November/December 1971
Reprinted in: <u>The Many Worlds of Andre Norton</u> 1974 (p.61)
And then in: <u>The Book of Andre Norton</u> 1975 (p.71)

ONE of the first and most common questions put to any writer is: "Where do you get your ideas?" That is sometimes difficult to answer in particulars, but in general, the one source one must rely on is reading. In fact, the writer must read widely in many fields. For my own books (unless I am dealing with some specific period of history when research becomes highly concentrated) I read anthropology, folklore, history, travel, natural history, archeology, legends, studies in magic, and similar material, taking notes throughout.

Andre in Her Office 1980

But the first requirement for writing heroic or sword and sorcery fantasy must be a deep interest in and a love for history itself. Not the history of dates, of sweeps and empires---but the kind of history which deals with daily life, the beliefs, and aspirations of people long since dust. (And it is amazing to find such telling parallels between a more ancient world and ours, as in the letter from the young Roman officer, quoted by Jack Lindsay in *The Romans Were Here*, who was writing home for money in much the same terms as be used by a modern G.I.) While there are many things we can readily accept in these delvings into other times, there are others we must use imagination to translate.

There we can find aids in novels the novels of those inspired writers who seem, by some touch of magic, to have actually visited a world of the past. There are flashes of brilliance in such novels, illuminating strange landscapes and ideas. To bring to life the firelit interior of a Pictish broch (about whose inhabitants even the most industrious of modern archeologists can tell us little) is, for example, a feat of real magic.

Read such books as Price's *Made In the Middle Ages*---then turn from her accounts of the great medieval fairs to the colorful description of the Thieves' Market in Van Arnan's *The Players of Hell*.

Renault's *The King Must Die*: here is Crete, and something within the reader is satisfied that this must be close to reality. Joan Grant's Egypt of *The Eyes of*

Horus and *The Lord of The Horizon*, Mundy's *Tros of Samothrace* and the *Purple Pirate*---Rome at the height of its arrogant power but as seen by a non-Roman---the wharves of Alexandria in the torchlight of night, the great sea battles, a clash of arms loud enough to stir any reader.

Turn from those to the muted despair and dogged determination against odds in Rosemary Sutcliff's Britain after the withdrawal of the last legion---the beginning of the Dark Ages---as described in *The Lantern Bearers* and *Swords in the Sunset*. This lives, moves, involves the reader in emotion.

Davis's Winter *Serpent* presents the Viking coastal raids, makes very clear what it meant to live under the shadow of the "Winged Hats." And, a little later, the glories and the grim cruelties of the Middle Ages are a flaming tapestry of color in such novels as Barringer's *Gerfalcon* and its sequel, *Joris of the Rock*; Adam's *Desert Leopard* and Graham's *Vows of the Peacock* are also excellent.

There are "historical" novels, but their history is all sensuous color, heroic action raised to the point where the reader is thoroughly ensorcelled and involved.

So history is the base, and from there to imagination, rooted in fact, sun-warmed by inspired fiction, can flower into new patterns. And those can certainly be ingenious and exciting.

The very atmosphere of some portion of the past can be carried into fantasy in a telling fashion, Take Meade's *Sword of Morningstar*, which gathers in the telling validity from the author's interest and research into the history of the Robber Barons of Germany and the Black Forest region. Beam Piper's *Lord Kacin of Otherwhen* envisions a world in which the sweep of the migrating Aryan peoples---the People of the Axe---turned east instead of west, flowing through Asia, China, to eventually colonize this continent from the west instead of the east, with an entirely different affect on history.

Though historical novels can furnish impetus for story growth, the basic need is still history. General history can be mined at will, but there are various byways which are very rich in background material.

Herrmann's *Conquest of Man*, a fat volume to open new vistas as it discusses the far range of those Bronze Age traders who set out in their small ships hugging unknown coastlines in the Atlantic, or the North Seas, or went on foot with their trains of laden donkeys into new lands. Thus he presents a wealth of new knowledge barely touched upon by the usual history book.

Four Thousand Years Ago by Bibby---a world spread of history at a single date. What were the Chinese doing when pharaohs held the throne of Egypt? And what then was going on in Peru, Central America?

Lewis Spense's careful studies of near forgotten legend and lore in his native British Isles, *Magic Arts in Celtic Britain* and the like, are very rich in nuggets to be used.

Rees gives us *Celtic Heritage*, Uden the beautifully illustrated *Dictionary of Chivalry*, Oakeshott's *Archeology of Weapons*---page after page of information on swords, shields, any other armament your hero needs.

Desire a new godling to squat in some shadowed temple? *Try Everyman's Dictionary of Non-Classical Mythology* and be straightway amazed at all the diverse gods the men of this world bowed head to down the ages.

For the layout of a castle, plus the numeration of a proper staff to man it, try Byfield's delightful *The Glass Harmonica* (Which also goes into careful detail on such matters as trolls, ogres, and the training of sorcerers); it is indispensable. And Thompson's *The Folktale*, a careful listing of the basic plot of every known tale and its many variations, is a book to keep to hand.

The professional writer does have to build up his or her own library, though the rich shelves of the public libraries await. Unfortunately, many of the volumes one wishes the most for reference are also the most expensive. But there is an answer---the remainder houses which send out at monthly or six-weeks periods catalogues of their stock. For one half, one third of the original price one can pick up such volumes when dealing with Marboro or Publishers Central Bureau. And, in recent years, the paperback house of Dover has been reissuing long out of print works in folklore, history and natural history.

So, one has the material, one has the plot---now comes the presentation. One must make come alive for the reader what one has created in one's mind.

Rider Haggard, who was the master of the romantic action adventure at its birth, stated firmly that those who write such books must themselves live in their creations, share every hope and care of their people. And this is the truth; you cannot write fantasy unless you love it, unless you yourself can believe in what you are telling. (Unfortunately, as every writer learns, that which goes on paper, in spite of all one's struggles, is never the bright and shining vision which appeared in one's mind and led one to get to work. At times a scene, a page---if one is exceedingly lucky, a chapter---may draw close to the dream, but one is always left unsatisfied with the whole.)

The approach may be direct in the use of ancient saga or legendary material without much alteration. And this can result in excellence if done by a skillful craftsman who has steeped him or herself in the subject. In this category are such outstanding books as Walton's *Island of the Mighty*, those books by Thomas Swan based on classical myths, Garner's two stories based on ancient legends of Britain; *Weirdstone of Brisinggamen* and *Moon of Gomrath*. While Poul Anderson drew first on Scandinavian sources for *The Broken Sword*, and then on the Charlemagne cycle for *Three Hearts and Three Lions*, Emil Petaja works from a classic lesser known to the general American public when he draws from the Finish Kalevala for a series of adventures. And Sprague de Camp has given us *The Incomplete Inchanter* with its roots in Spencer's *Faerie Queen: The Land of Unreason*---Oberon's kingdom plus the legend of Barbarossa; and *The Wall of Serpents*, another presentation from the Kalevala. Nicholas Gray has turned directly to fairy tales, writing the haunting and memorable *Seventh Swan* and the amusing *Stone Cage*. The former "what happened after" in the fairy tale of the Seven Swans wherein the hero, the seventh brother of that story, is forced to adjust to living with a swan's wing in place of his arm. While in the latter, he gives a new and sprightly version of Rapunzel.

From that background of general legend comes the work of masters who are so well read in such lore that they create their own gods and sagas, heroes and mysteries. Tolkein's Middle Earth is now so deeply embedded in our realm that his name need only be mentioned to provide a mountain-tall standard against which other works will be measured perhaps for generations to come.

Lord Dunsay is another of the masters. Eddison's *Worm Oroborous* is perhaps a little mannered in style for modern taste, but his descriptions are, like Merritt's, so overflowing in color and vivid beauty they flash across one's mind in sweeps of hues and forms one readily remembers.

To sample some of these earlier writers one can at present easily turn to the series of books under the editorship of Lin Carter--- issued by Ballantine--- where for the first time in many years some of the older, and to this generation perhaps even unknown, writers are introduced again. Such books as *Dragons, Elves and Heroes*, *The Young Magicians*, *Golden Cities, Far* provide small tastes. But this series also reprints in full length the works of Wilbam Morris, Dunsay, Cabell and kindred writers.

Those modern writers who create their own worlds stand well when measured to these pioneers, with some pruning of the dated flourishes of another day.

Hannes Bok, who was an artist with paint and brush, as well as with pen, produced *The Sorcerer's Ship*. Using the classic saga approach of the quest we have such treats as Van Arnan's *Players of Hell* and its sequel *Wizard of Storms*. David Mason gives us two excellent examples of the careful building of an entire world detailed to the full in *Kavin's World* and *The Sorcerer's Skull*. Ursula Le Guin has *Wizard of Earthsea*, an offering which not only presents a strange island-sea planet but makes clear the training of a would-be sorcerer, and the need for self-control in handling great forces. Jack Vance explores a far future in which our almost exhausted world turns to magic in its last days in his *Dying Earth*. And Katherine Kurtz with *Deryni Rising* pictures a dramatic meeting of alien forces in a strange setting loosely based on Welsh myths.

The common pattern of most sword and sorcery tales which incline to action-adventure is a super-man hero, generally a wandering mercenary (which is an excellent device for moving your hero about). Of this company

Robert Howard's Conan is perhaps the best known---unless one may list Burroughs's John Carter thus. Howard's plots may have been but his descriptions of sinister ruins and sharp of action move the stories into leadership in the field. We now have John Jakes's Brak, a Viking type wanderer whose adventures tend to get better with each book. There is also Lin Carter's Thonger of Lemuria. And the unbeatable Grey Mouser and Ffahrd whom Fritz Leiber moves about an ancient world seeming to have some parts in common With our own middle east, but highly alien in others.

From the super-man we come to Moorcock's flawed heroes who tend to have massive faults as well as abilities, swinging sometimes to evil. The Elric of the demon-souled sword, and he of the four Runestaff stories are ambivalent.

There are moments of humor in the adventures of the Grey Mouser and his companion in arms, the great northerner Ffahrd. But Sprague de Camp, almost alone of the writers of fantasy, can handle the humorous element as a continued and integrated part of the adventure itself. His teller of tales who is also a doughty fighting man, the hero of *The Goblin Tower*, is something quite different from the humorless Conan or the stormy men of Moorcock. Only the much put-upon magician of Bellairs's *Face in the Frost* can compare with him.

Brunner's *Traveller in Black* is still another type. A troubler of the status quo, he does not fight, merely uses his own form of magic to adjust the scales of alien gods in many lands. Wandering by the demands of some strange pattern he does not understand, on a timeless mission decreed by something beyond the human, he seems to drift, and yet his adventures have all the power of straight action.

These are the heroes, but what of the heroines? In the Conan tales there are generally beautiful slave girls, one pirate queen, one woman mercenary. Conan lusts, not loves, in the romantic sense, and moves on without remembering face or person. This is the pattern followed by the majority of the wandering heroes. Witches exist, so do queens (always in need of having their lost thrones regained or shored up by the hero), and a few Come alive. As do de Camp's women, the thief-heroine of *Wizard of Storm*, the young girl in the Garner books, the *Sorceress of Island of the Mighty*. But still they remain props of the hero.

Only C. L Moore, almost a generation ago, produced a heroine who was as self-sufficient, as deadly with a sword, as dominate a character as any of the swordsmen she faced. In the series of stories recently published as *Jirel of Joiry* we meet the heroine in her own right, and not to be down-cried before any armed company.

When I came to write <u>Year of the Unicorn</u>, it was my wish to spin a story distantly based on the old tale of Beauty and the Beast. I had already experimented with some heroines who interested me, the Witch Jaelithe and Loyse of Verlane. But to write a full book from the feminine point of view was a departure. I found it fascinating to write, but the reception was oddly mixed. In the years now since it was first published I have had many letters from women readers who accepted Gillan with open arms, and I have had masculine readers who hotly resented her.

But I was encouraged enough to present a second heroine, the Sorceress Kaththea. And since then I have written several more shorter stories, both laid in Witch World and elsewhere, spun about a heroine instead of a hero. Perhaps now will come a shift in an old pattern; it will be most interesting to watch and see. At any rate, there is no more imagination stretching form of writing, nor reading, than the world of fantasy. The heroes, heroines, colors, action, linger in one's mind long after the book is laid aside. And how wonderful it would be if world gates did exist and one could walk into Middle Earth, Kavin's World, the Land of Unreason, Atlantis, and all the other never-nevers! We have the windows to such worlds and must be content with those.

To offer a complete reference list would be a librarian's and run for more pages than space allows. so the following bibliography is a restricted and personal one. In the non-fiction I list books which I found particularly rich in ideas for my own writing, and yet, I believe, would interest the browsing reader, too. In the fiction you will find the fantasy books mentioned as good examples and worthy yardsticks to measure by.

BIBLIOGRAPHY
NON-FICTION REFERENCE BOOKS
Paul Herrmann, *Conquest by Man*, Harper & Row.
John Campbell, *Hero with 1000 Faces*, Meridian Books.
Peter Lum, *Fabulous Beasts*, Pantheon.
Basil Davidson. *Lost Cities of Africa*, Atlantic-Little Brown.
Geoffrey Bibby, *Four Thousand Years Ago*, Knopf.
Myles Dillan and Nora Chadwick, *The Celtic Realms*, New American Library.
E. A. Wallis Budge, *Amulets and Talismen*, University Books.
Stuart Piggott, *The Druids*, Thames Hudson.
Lewis Spense, *Fairy Traditions in Britain*, Rider.
Lewis Spense, *Magic Arts in Celtic Britain*, Rider.
Lewis Spense, *Minor Traditions of British Mythology*, Rider.
Alwyn Rees and Brisley Rees, *Celtic Heritage*, Grove Press.
Grant Uden, *Dictionary of Chivalry*, Longmans.
R. Ewart Oakst hott, *Archeology of Weapons*, Lutterworth.
Ed. by publisher, *Everyman 's Dictionary of Non-Classical Mythology*, Dent-Dutton.
Ed. by publisher, *Crowell's Handbook for Readers and Writers*, Crowell.
Barbara Byfield, *The Glass Harmonica*, Macmillan.
Smith Thompson, *The Folktale*, Dryden press.
Sprague de Camp, *Science-Fiction Handbook*, Hermitage.
Sprague de Camp, *Conan Swordbook*, Hermitage.
Sprague de Camp, *Conan Reader*, Hermitage.
Christine Price, *Made in the Middle Ages*, Bodley Head.

Isaac Asimov, *Dark Ages*, MiHin.

FICTION

Elizabeth Walton, *Island of the Mighty*, Ballantine.
David Mason, *Kavin's World*, Lancer.
David Mason, *Sorcerer's Skull*, Lancer.
David Van Arnan, *Players of Hell*, Belmont.
David Van Arnan, *Wizard of Storm*, Belmont.
Michael Moorcock, *Swords of Dawn*, Lancer.
Michael Moorcock, *Jewel in the Skull*, Lancer.
Michael Moorcock, *Sorcerer's Amulet*, Lancer.
Michael Moorcock, *Secret of The Runestaff*, Lancer.
Michael Moorcock, *Stormbringer*, Lancer.
Michael Moorcock, *Stealer of Souls*, Lancer.
Fritz Leiber, *Swords of Lankhamar*, Ace.
Fritz Leiber, *Swords Against Death*, Ace.
Fritz Leiber, *Swords and Deviltry*, Ace.
Fritz Leiber, *Swords in the Mist*, Ace.
Fritz Leiber, *Swords Against Wizardy*, Ace.
Richard Meade, *Sword of Morningstar*, Belmont.
Sprague de Camp, *Tritonian Ring,* Pyramid.
Syrague de Camp, *Incomplete Inchanter*, Pyramid.
Sprague de Camp, *Wall of Serpents*, Pyramid.
Sprague de Camp, *Land of Unreason*, Pyramid.
Sprague de Camp, *Castle of Iron*, Pyramid.
Sprague de Camp, *Goblin Tower*, Pyramid.
C. L Moore, *Jirel of Joiry*, Paperback Library.
John Jakes, *Brak the Barbarian*, Avon.
John Jakes, *Brak and the Mark of Demons*, Paperback Library.
John Jakes, *Brak and the Sorceress*, Paperback Library.
John Brunner, *Traveler in Black*, Ace.
Robert Howard, *Conan series*, Lancer.
Robert Howard, *King Kull*, Lancer.
Alan Garner, *Weirdstone of Brisinggamen*, Ace.
Alan Garner, *Moon of Gomrath*, Ace.
Ursula Le Guin, *Wizard of Earthsea*, Ace.
John Bellairs, *Face in the Frost*, Macmillan.
Poul Anderson, *Broken Sword*.
Poul Anderson, *Three Hearts and Three Lions*, Avon.
Nicholas Stuart Grey, *Stone Cage*, Dobson.
Nicholas Stuart Grey, *Seventh Swan*, Dobson.
Lin Carter, ed., *Golden Cities, Far*, Ballantine.
Lin Carter, ed., *Dragons, Elves and Heroes*, Ballantine.
Lin Carter, ed., *Young Magicians*, Ballantine.

Andre Norton: Loss of Faith

by Rick Brooks

Original in *The Dipple Chronicles*, November/December 1971
Reprinted in: *The Many Worlds of Andre Norton* 1974 (p.178)
And then in: *The Book of Andre Norton* 1975 (p.187)

The impression that a regular reader of Andre Norton's books might have is that of growing pessimism. From light hearted adventure stories like *Star Rangers* and *Sargasso of Space*, she has gone to books like *Dread Companion* and *Dark Piper* that give the feeling at the conclusion that it is best not to see or even guess what lies ahead.

While Miss Norton has never seemed too comfortable in the here-and-now, it seems that now the future that once beckoned has become another area for distrust. Even the latest Solar Queen story, *Postmarked the Stars*, is more subdued and grim in tone. The Patrol, a largely unsullied organization, comes in for its lumps in *The Zero Stone* and its sequel, *Uncharted Stars*. In *Ice Crown*, the Service makes no move to help those under a planet-wide conditioning program. As a correspondent, children's librarian Devra Langsam remarked:

> more and more it is the organized cultural groups, like the Patrol, and in this case, the Service (cultural-anthropology?) who are the villains ...I suppose that this was foreshadowed in her *Solar Queen* stories, but it's still surprising. . . and she's a bit old to be getting, this anti-establishment thing.

But are these impressions correct? Has Miss Norton lost faith in the future? After reading her books over the last few weeks, I see the answer as yes...and no. She has definitely lost some of her optimism--but haven't we all? In novels like *Dread Companion* and *Dark Piper*, she is trying for deeper characterization. This slows down the action and gives one more time to spot her usual lack of blind faith in the future.

Star Man's Son, her first science fiction novel, was written after warming up with a couple of short stories (as *Andrew North*) in *Fantasy Book*, two historical novels, and "Adapting" the myth of *Huon of the Horn*. Since Miss Norton "wastes" little in previous writings, in 1965, *Steel Magic*, a juvenile sequel to *Huon of the Horn*, came out.

Star Man's Son takes place in a post-nuclear-war world. While the ending is upbeat with the hope of a rebirth of civilization, most of the story is rather bleak. This novel sees the birth of a theme that runs through all Norton's books--tolerance for other races.

Star Rangers (her first of many Ace Books, published in 1955) extends this theme to non-humans and introduces the reptilian race of Zacan (the Zacathans) which have become almost a fixture in her later far future novels. The mighty stellar empire of Central Control seen at a much earlier stage is collapsing later in *Star Guard*, and a battered Patrol ship limps back to Terra, now long forgotten, to start anew. The upbeat ending again overshadows the brutal future pictured with a hardening of hereditary stratification in all groups, even the Patrol, and bloody power struggles in which entire worlds with all their people are burnt off with little apparent concern. The character's rather matter of fact acceptance of the latter is quite chilling.

The Stars Are Ours! starts on another post-destruction Terra, this time by a satellite burn-off which triggers a program against Free Scientists. A few escape to Astra under cold sleep. The bleak repressive Terra miraculously gives way to the vividly drawn Astra. With this, Miss Norton comes into her major strength, the portrayal of other worlds. The switch between bleak winter on Terra and the verdant growing season on Astra also seems to mark a turning point in Norton's writing.

She now has a more optimistic tone as she explores the glory of other worlds. In *Sargasso of Space*, the planet Limbo has been partially burnt off, but in a long gone Forerunner war. *Star Guard* sees an attempt to set human mercenaries against each other, but no killings of non-combatants. *The Crossroads of Time* does show some brutal alternate presents. *Plague Ship* features a run-in with the Patrol and the danger of being shot on sight as plague carriers. *Sea Siege* is a downbeat near-future tale where radioactive mutated sea life and a nuclear war endanger humanity. *Star Born* features a clash with Those Others, the vicious native race of Astra. While there still is a lot of violence, the characters' attitude has changed from passive acceptance of it as a part of life to downright loathing.

Star Gate is a rather unique book as it concerns the alternate histories of another world. With the exception of Norton's later *Toys of Tamisan* (ss), this is the only science fiction that comes to mind covering both star travel and travel sideways in time. Creating an alien world is usually considered enough, without creating a history to go with it.

Andre Norton seems to have suffered a rough period in 1961-62. _Star Hunter_ has the Patrol ignoring the mental conditioning of a young drifter so that a Veep can be nabbed. In _The Defiant Agents_, a group of Indians are mentally conditioned and sent off to occupy Topaz before the Reds can. The optimism of _Galactic Derelict_, where the universe and its wonders had been opened to man, have in its sequel turned to dread of the weapons of the earlier galactic empire in human hands. _Eye of the Monster_ is Norton's most xenophobic story by far. The previous _Storm Over Warlock_ had a very nasty portrayal of the Throgs, but humans still try to make peace. Here there is no thought of peace. In all other stories, evil aliens are the result of forbidden researches. Here the crocs are vicious barbarians that suddenly start butchering all off-worlders. Several racial characteristics are adversely mentioned, especially odor. In all other Norton novels, aliens are evil for what they do, not what they are. Despite provocation, no other Norton hero has reacted by a hatred that could be classified as racial. This momentary failure underlines her usual tolerance for living beings.

Outside of these three novels, not much distinguished one Norton novel from another during the late fifties and most of the sixties except a little more polish in the writing of later ones. With _Dark Piper_ (1968), a lessening of optimism is again visible.

One of the most fascinating things about Andre Norton has been her consistency with respect to certain ideas and themes while totally ignoring consistency where most authors wouldn't. As Ralph Waldo Emerson said:

> A foolish consistency is the hobgoblin of little minds...with consistency a great soul has simply nothing to do...Speak what you think today in words as hard as cannon-balls, and to-morrow speak what to-morrow thinks in hard words again, though it contradict everything you said today.

At least one fan has waged a titanic struggle in trying to sort out a consistent "future history" from Norton's books when she never has bothered with one. However, most of her stories do fall within a loose framework. It is almost like such terms as _Free Traders, Forerunners, First Ship, Patrol, jack, Veep, First-in Scout_, and _Combine_ fit so well that she doesn't bother to coin others. Races such as the Zacathans and planets such as Astra receive mention in many stories, as does the game of Stars and Comets. Whether this is a matter of sentiment, laziness, or practicality (it is work to create an entire world for just one story, let along several worlds) is a point that can be argued.

Miss Norton, instead of being bound by a future history, has created a series of alternate universes that largely overlap. All her interplanetary stories, with the exception of _Star Gate_ (though a planet Gorth is mentioned in _Moon of_

Three Rings), *Secret of the Lost Race*, *Long Live Lord Kor!* (ss) and *Dark Piper* have interlocking references. The latter is probably to emphasize the isolation of the research planet of Beltane from the rest of the galaxy. I think that it is significant that the two novels date from 1958 and 1959, while the other is a novelette. Since Miss Norton's references to previous books have become more numerous in her last group of books, it would seem that certain races, planets, and things have become touchstones for her.

In *Uncharted Stars*, the sequel to *The Zero Stone*, she runs wild with references to *The Zero Stone*, a Salarik (pp. 13, 72; the feline race of Sargol in *Plague Ship*), a male Wyvern of Warlock (p. 114; *Ordeal In Otherwhere*), a Trystian (p. 117), Zacathans (pp. 117, 176), a Faltharian (p. 166; three races prominent in *Star Rangers*), "...the Caverns of Arzor and of that Sargasso planet of Limbo..." (p. 140; *The Beast Master* and *Sargasso of Space*), and koro stones (p. 173; *Plague Ship*). References to many other races and many other gem stones are mentioned in passing.

This is a good thing and gives depth to a story, but occasionally Miss Norton goofs in choosing a "spear-carrier" from an earlier story. The worst example is the Salarik who tended bar in *Star Hunter*. He could not have taken the odors of the place without protection.

Miss Norton's stories are born in many ways. *Star Rangers* started from the story of the Roman Emperor who ordered a legion eastward across Asia to the end of the world. Childe Roland and *The Dark Tower* became *Warlock of the Witch World*. The *Year of the Unicorn* owed its origin to the folk tale of "Beauty and the Beast." Even more obvious are the links between *Dark Piper* and the *Pied Piper*. However, few would realize that *Night of Masks* was sparked by the "powerful descriptions" of William Hope Hodgson's classic *The Night Land*.

Long Live Lord Kor! (ss) was written around an unused cover that showed the couple mounted on a giant fire worm firing at a flying thing. The title was originally *Worm Walk*. Running things--by human default was a giant super computer called ZAT "...whose limitations had yet to be discovered." (*Worlds of Fantasy* No. 2, p. 53). The *X Factor* is dedicated to "Helen Hoover whose weasel-fisher people gave me the *Brothers-In-Fur*." Helen has a series of excellent nature books illustrated by her husband Adrian (whose illustrations remind me of Ernest Thompson Seton's, who was a very early idol of mine. But Adrian's are much better.)

The stories are shaped by references to an "extensive personal library of natural history, archaeology, anthropology, native religions, folklore, and travel in off-beat sections of the world." The "...forests of Janus and *The Zero Stone* are both taken from the great forests of the Matto Grosso." And of course history plays an important part.

History, by the way, is not weapons (which are again a form of machines) but human beings--the fact that some ruler was ill on a certain day and so made a decision he might not have done otherwise--the fact that some personal animosity moved action can be seen over and over again. Until we read it from the viewpoint of the people, who were worked upon by the strains and stresses of their times which again may be alien to our present thinking, we do not read real history. I wish the students in school would study diaries and the volumes of contemporary letters of the period they are seeking to study rather than read the texts (which cannot help but be influenced by the personal tastes of their writers). From such sources they would learn what moved these people three, four, five hundred years ago to behave as they did. One volume of Pepys' diary can give one a vivid impression of Restoration England of far more value to the student than any list of dates and decisions of Parliament of that period.

To which, I agree heartily. To create an alien culture, it is a big help to understand one. Which means just about all previous cultures as well as the present one. Our command of technology separates us from the cultures of the past. The Founding Fathers had more in common with the Classical civilization members of Greece and Rome than they do with us. But have we lost something?

Descartes' dicotomy had given modern man a philosophical basis for getting rid of the belief in witches, and this contributed considerably to the actual overcoming of witchcraft in the eighteenth century. Everyone would agree that this was a great gain. But we likewise got rid of the fairies, elves, trolls, and all of the demicreatures of the woods and earth. It is generally assumed that this, too, was a gain, since it helped sweep man's mind clear of 'superstition' and 'magic'. But I believe that this is an error. Actually what we did in getting rid of the fairies and the elves and their ilk was to impoverish our lives; and impoverishment is not the lasting way to clear men's minds of superstition. There is a sound truth in the old parable of the man who swept the evil spirit out of his house, but the spirit, noticing that the house stood clean and vacant, returned, bringing seven more evil spirits with him; and the second state of the man was worse than the first. For it is the empty and vacant people who seize on the new and more destructive forms of our latter-day superstitions, such as beliefs in the totalitarian mythologies, engrams, miracles like the day the sun stood still, and so on. Our world has become disenchanted, and it leaves us not only out of tune with nature but with ourselves as well. (*Man's Search for Himself* by Rollo May, Signet, pp. 62-3)

So in the end, the chief value of Andre Norton's writing may not lie in entertainment or social commentary, but in her "re-enchanting" us with her creations that renew our linkages to all life. One might say of her writing that

There was much she said beyond my understanding, references to events and people unknown, such hints only making me wistful to go through the doors they represented and see what lay on the far side. (*Moon of Three Rings*, Ace, p. 103)

But Norton falls into a much more rigid pattern in her view of the complex technological future that largely ignores the individual. Her sympathies can be easily seen as the Norton hero or heroine never seems to fit into their society and often are outright misfits. In *Night of Masks*, Nik Kolkerne has a badly mutilated face and a personality to match. Diskan Fentress is a clumsy oaf crashing through the faerie world of Vaanchard in *The X Factor*. Ross Murdock is an alienated criminal when he becomes part of a time traveling team in *The Time Traders*. Roane Hume in *Ice Crown* finds the medieval life of Clio draws her from her relatives who treat her like an extra pair of hands.

Miss Norton seems to be fond of the medieval period. *Moon of Three Rings* was deliberately based on the culture of the European Middle Ages. (Dark Ages is a misnomer, for an age that saw the inventions of the horse collar, the windmill, and stirrups. These allowed men to harness horsepower and windpower for the first time and to weld man and horse into a battle unit. See Lynn White's book on medieval technology. Miss Norton would stress the Guilds and other human factors.) All six Witch World novels, *Key Out of Time*, *Star Gate*, *Star Guard*, *Toys of Tamisan* (ss), *Wizard's Worlds* (ss), and to some extent *Plague Ship* feature a medieval-like culture. Some writers use such a culture regularly because they are too lazy to work out another, but Miss Norton sees important values that we have bypassed in the medieval period.

Another major feature is the stressing of the bond between man and animal (and Iftin and tree in the *Janus series*). In *Star Man's Son*, Fors of the Puma clan had Lura, the mutant cat, as a companion. In *Star Rangers* occurs the following:

> Fylh's crest lifted. He raised his face to the sky and poured out a liquid run of notes, so pure and heart tearing a melody that Kartr held his breath in wonder. Was this Fylh's form of happy release from emotion?
>
> Then came the birds, wheeling and fluttering. Kartr stiffened into statue stillness, afraid to break the spell. As Fylh's carols rose, died, rose again, more and more of the fliers gathered, with flashes of red feathers, blue, yellow, white, green. They hopped before the Trystian's feet, perched on his shoulders, his arms, circled around his head.
>
> Kartr had seen Fylh entice Winged things to him before but never just this way. It appeared to his bewildered eyes that the whole campsite was a maze of fluttering wings and rainbow feathers.
>
> The trills of Song died away and the birds arose, a flock of color. Three times they circled Fylh, hiding his head and shoulders from sight with the tapestry of tints they wove in flight. Then they were gone--up into the morning. Kartr could not move, his eyes remained fixed on Fylh. For the Trystian was on his feet, his arms outstretched, straining upward as if he would have followed the others up and out. And for the first time, dimly, the sergeant sensed what longings must be born in Fylh's people since they

had lost their wings. Had that loss been good--should they have traded wings for intelligence? Did Fylh wonder about that? (Ace, 1955, p. 166)

In view of this, it is also hardly surprising that the survivors of the Patrol choose to go out into the wilderness and live off nature instead of seeking another abandoned city to live in at the book's end. *Star Rangers* also introduces the theme of telepathy. In *The Beast Master* (1959) the two are fused together and we have Hosteen Storm, the Beast Master, and his team of African Black Eagle, Meerkats, and dune cat are telepathically linked. But like Diskan Fentress in *The X Factor*, his talent just covers animals. Kartr in *Star Rangers* as well as Zinga the Zacacathan can communicate telepathically with animals, but do not try for an emotional bond or work with them.

Murray Leinster's "Exploration Team" (Astounding ScienceFiction magazine, March 1956, "Combat Team" in *Colonial Survey*) had a team of man, eagle, and giant bears. They manage to save a colony that was supposed to be protected by robots. It could have influenced Norton, but since she was heading that way anyway, I doubt it. Besides, she makes a point of not reading other sf when she is writing so it won't influence her. The treatment of robots is about the same (the robots in Leinster's story were computer controlled as I remember). Andre Norton's only favorable mention of robots is in *Star Rangers* where one had been a member of the crew and "...he was good with engines-being one himself." (Ace, 1955, p. 20)

In *Moon of Three Rings*, Maelen the Moon Singer can telepathically communicate with her animals that work together for her traveling show. Travis Fox and the mutant coyotes work together and communicate on Topaz in *The Defiant Agents*. *Key Out of Time* features Karara Trehern telepathically linked with dolphins. Shann Lantree and his wolverines mentally share information and work together in *Storm Over Warlock*.

Catseye carries the idea the next logical step. Troy Horan, once son of a Range Master on Norden, becomes an equal partner with a kinkajou, two foxes and two cats that have been mutated for greater intelligence. Rerne, the ranger of the wilds, asks:

> "Always we. Why, Horan?" Rerne rubbed his wrists.
>
> "Men have used animals as tools." Troy said slowly, trying to fit into words something he did not wholly understand himself. "Now some men, somewhere, have made better tools, tools so good that they can turn and cut the maker. But that is not the fault of the tools--that they are no longer tools but--"
>
> "Perhaps companions?" Rerne ended for him, his fingers still stroking his ridged flesh, but his eyes very intent on Troy.
>
> "How did you know?" the younger man was startled into demanding.
>
> "Let me say that I am also a workman who can admire fine tools, even when they have ceased, as you point out, to be any longer tools."

> Troy grasped at that hint of sympathy. "You understand--"

> "Only too well. Most of our breed want tools, not companions. And the age-old fear of man, that he will lose his supremacy, will bring down all the hawks and hunters of the galaxy down on your trail, Horan. Do not expect any aid from your own species when it is threatened by powers it cannot and does not want to understand..." (Ace, pp. 141-2)

In Eric Frank Russell's *The Undecided* (ss) (Astounding ScienceFiction magazine, April 1949, *Deep Space*) he handles the same theme of equality between man and our "little brothers." As he sums it up:

> For all had passed through the many eons. Some had leaped ahead, some lagged behind. But several of the laggers had put on last moment spurts-- because of late functioning of natural laws--and the impact upon their various kinds of the one kind called Man.

> Until they had breasted the tape together. (Bantam, p. 53)

Or, as Miss Norton puts it in *Catseye*:

"We are of one kind, plains rider." Then Rerne looked beyond the man to the animals. "So shall we all be in the end." (Ace, p.176)

Judgment on Janus (which begins in the Dipple of Korwar, as does *Catseye*) has a working agreement between the Iftin and the quarrin, a vaguely owl-like bird that can communicate mentally with the Iftin. In *The X Factor*, Diskan Fentress seems to almost fall under the domination of the "Brothers—in-Fur," and their communication is rather uncertain.

Ordeal In Otherwhere, the sequel to *Storm Over Warlock*, takes things a step further than equality. Shann Lantee and the wolverine Taggi (Togi is busy with the kids) are joined by Charis Nordholm and Tsstu, the curl-cat. Together they form a unit (almost the same as the mental fusion in Doc Smith's *The Children of The Lens*, Astounding ScienceFiction magazine, November, December 1947, January, February 1948) that can withstand all that the Power of the Wyverns can throw at them. (But even in the unit, the man is still "first among equals")

In places, Norton's consistency is disturbing as she insists on attacking the computer of ten or fifteen years ago. But Miss Norton's true to her daemon wherever it leads her. She sees a nuclear war as our probable future and it or the threat of it is a part of all her near future stories except *The Stars Are Ours!*. The Crosstime series, the Time Trader series, and *Operation Time Search* take place in the calm before the storm and this blights *The Defiant Agents*. Both *Star Guard* and *Plague Ship* note the changes wrought on Terra by such a war several hundred years past.

But her afterview is much too optimistic. Our civilization has delved deeply into the earth for the resources we now use. Let civilization collapse for very long and some of the resources needed to rebuild it will be out of reach. This is our main chance. Muff it, and most likely the stars will forever remain no more than points of light in the night sky.

However, Miss Norton's main thrust is not in the area of science and technology, but in that of human society. While all her stories are good entertainment, most contain more. Most of the writers now considered great, from Shakespeare on, have considered it necessary to entertain as well as say something, but for some reason that is out of style today.

> No writer writes out of his having found the answer to the problem; he writes rather out of his having the problem and wanting a solution. The solution consists not of a resolution. It consists of the deeper and wider dimensions of conscience to which the writer is carried by virtue of his wrestling with the problem. We create out of a problem; the writer and the artist are not presenting answers but creating as an experience of something in themselves trying to work--'to seek, to find and not to yield.' The contribution which is given to the world by the painting or the book is the process of the search. (*Love and Will*, Rollo May, pp. 170-1)

Miss Norton's main problem seems to be that of the relationship between man and his machines. And her attitude is fairly obvious. I'd hardly expect a Norton story featuring a planet-bound misfit who finally realizes his dream of becoming a star ship mechanic. There have been sympathetic characters that have dealt with machines, but not recently. Since _Galactic Derelict_ (1959) only Ali Kamil from the engine room of the Solar Queen in _Postmarked the Stars_ comes to mind. And he had played a strong part in the first two books of the series.

Miss Norton is rather unacquainted with the "hard sciences" and her earlier books suffer a bit with her attempts to go into detail. This was especially true of astronomy. Sol is off the charts, yet the "Sirius Worlds" are mentioned as a familiar part of history (_The Last Planet_ /_Star Rangers_, Ace, 1955, pp. 158, 170) while the ship is the "Vegan Star fire" (p. 183) and the Hall of Leave-Taking was supposed to be on Alpha Centauri (p. 171). Norton's Star Atlas gives Vega as 26 light years away, Sirius 9, and Alpha Centauri 4.3. With a galaxy around 100,000 light years wide, these are literally in our lap. And only Proxima Centauri is now closer than Alpha Centauri.

By _The Stars Are Ours!_ and following books, Miss Norton avoids the trap most beginning sf writers fall into, and coins most of her planet names, mostly from mythology.

Even this early, Miss Norton showed a marked distrust of what Gene Marine in _America the Raped_ termed the engineering mentality. Those Others who inhabit a part of Astra and almost wiped themselves out were rather evil. In _Star Born_ (1957), Astra is visited by Terran space travelers generations after the events of the first book.

> To Raf, the straight highways suggested something else. Master engineering, certainly. But a ruthlessness too, as if the builders, who

refused to accept any modifications of their original plans from nature, might be as arrogant in other ways. (Ace, p. 39)

In the battle between technology and nature, Miss Norton took a stand long before the great majority of us had any doubts. Miss Norton has little knowledge of technology and rarely tries to explain the scientific wonders in her stories. John Campbell, whose death has left us all the poorer, once said something like, "If we really could explain it, we'd patent it." The less explanation, the less likely the science of the story is to date. But Andre Norton doesn't go into detail because she doesn't care. Technology is a necessary evil to get there for the adventure and to get some of the story to work. And the adventure is as much to mold her universe to her views as to entertain.

Two of the most extreme nature vs. technology novels are _Judgment on Janus_ and its sequel, _Victory on Janus_. In this story the Iftin race have left "traps" that change humans sympathetic to nature into Iftin. Their lives are bound with nature and the massive trees. Technology becomes very distasteful. The chief villain turns out to be an alien computer.

The same type of villain turns up in _Star Hunter_, while a human built computer is the main evil in _Ice Crown_. In both _The Stars Are Ours!_ and _Dark Piper_ where the computer performs a useful function, it isn't allowed any more scope than yesterday's model. In _Star Rangers_, a city computer directs a robot to destroy the heroes.

No, Norton does not like computers. Which is really a pity. Out of all the tools that man has created, the computer may well prove to be even better than the scientific method. Its potential is barely scratched today.

In Florida, Miss Norton lives on the border of two counties. She has been charged by both for local taxes due to a "computer error" (a term used to cover a computer operator or computer programmer error). She was told that it was too much trouble to correct the programming and to ignore the wrong tax. Which could have led to legal problems. "... It is this sort of thing which arouses hatred of having a machine in control."

But the point is that the machine is in control only in the way that it is told to be. In _Star Rangers_, the computer was programmed to shoot any trespassers (Ace, 1955, p. 68). All that people blame on the computer, which is getting to be a symbol of technological oppression, is due to lazy programming. A computer can be made responsive enough so that every child can have a private tutor to supplement his teacher. But the programming barring a breakthrough would take a vast effort. Is the machine to blame for our refusing to take the time and expense to make it responsive?

Miss Norton sees no marriage of science and human powers. "One had to be anti-tech to be a Beast Master." (_Lord of Thunder_, p. 120) "But even so much a modification as a dart gun--that meant careful preparation in thinking patterns. We could not ally with a machine!" (*Sorceress of the Witch World*, p. 126) So it should not be a surprise after traversing all the magical horrors the Witch World universe has to offer to find that the ultimate depth is a world from an environmentalist's nightmare where a degenerate humanity fights against men incorporated with machines both using weapons of advanced technology.

An interesting treatment of the theme occurs in Roger Zelazny's *Jack of Shadows* where technology is relatively untainted and human powers largely harnessed to evil ends. Jack of Shadows runs afoul of the Lord of Bats and he retreats to tap dayside technology (again, a computer) and harness it to his magic. In doing so, he destroys his world so that a better one can be rebuilt on its foundations, utilizing technology.

Even the biological technologies are usually not for Miss Norton. In *Three Against the Witch World*, delving too deeply in magic (?) to create humanoid races and to gain knowledge is condemned. In *Warlock of the Witch World*, one of the characters is still considered within the pale since he "... had for a tutor in his childhood one of the few remaining miracle workers who had set a limit on his own studies." (p. 27) But Dinzil went on from there and he turns out to be the chief villain of the story.

In her only fall from grace, *Star Guard* (1955) has the bodies of the mercenary group being adapted to the conditions of the Planet Fronn while in flight to that world. Yet they show no discomfort on returning to Terra, despite no mention of reverse conditioning. After this, she ignores adverse planetary conditions.

After considering the possibilities set forth in Gordon Rattray Taylor's *The Biological Time Bomb*, one is tempted to agree that there are things the human race shouldn't mess with at its present level of maturity.

> Science and our social habits are out of step. And the cure is no deeper either. We must learn to match them. And there is no way of learning this unless we learn to understand both...So however we might sigh for Samuel Butler's panacea in *Erewhon*, simply to give up all machines, there is no point in talking about it...It is just not practical, nationally or internationally. (*Science, the Destroyer or Creator* (essay) by J. Bronowski in *Man Alone: Alienation in Modern Society*, edited by Eric & Mary Josephson, p. 284)

Going back to nature has its temptations. But it would mean that at present 2 or 2 ½ billion people would probably starve--most of them in the cities. That is a rather high price to pay. Miss Norton's reasons for disliking machines tie in with her liking for medieval settings. In her words:

> Yes, I am anti-machine. The more research I do, the more I am convinced that when western civilization turned to machines so heartily with the Industrial Revolution in the early nineteenth century, they threw away some parts of life which are now missing and which the lack of leads to much of our present frustration. When a man had pride in the work of his

own hands, when he could see the complete product he had made before him, he had a satisfaction which no joys of easier machine existence could or can give.

Why all the accent on hobbies and do-it-yourself projects now--so many of them futile? Simply because in his productive work a man can no longer take any pride. Read some of the accounts of the old Guilds and I think you can see what I mean. Before a man could practice any trade then, he had to prove to his peers that he could do it. Very few people now have any pride in what they do--they are slip-shod in a piece of labor because they cannot see that good worksmanship in the day of the machine means anything more than poor.

This extends on now from the work itself--there is a wave of bad manners, of outright discourtesy in stores and businesses--no worker identifies with his job enough to actually want to produce something better--he feels a part of a machine, vast, impersonal, not the master of it. And the more we deal so with machines--for example the more computers are brought in to rule our lives--with their horrible mistakes and no one to appeal to to correct them--then the more alienated man will become.

So I make my machines the villains--because I believe that they are so; that man was happier--if less geared to a swift overproductive life--when he used his own personal skills and did not depend upon a machine. And I fear what is going to happen if more and more computers take over ruling us.

This will doubtless seem like rank heresy to you who are training to use such machines--but with the growth of the impersonal attitude towards life which these foster, there is going to be more and more anger and frustration. And where it will all end perhaps not even a writer of sf can foresee.

This is indeed a damning indictment of our age, and there is enough truth in it so that it bites deeply. It is over-reacting and placing the blame in the wrong place. We have definitely lost something, but this is the fault of those who lacked foresight and took the easy way of fitting the much more adaptable man to the machine. "Now some men….have made better tools, tools so good that they can turn and cut the maker. But that is not the fault of the tools…" (*Catseye*, Ace, p. 141)

"The enemy is not a devil out there called technology—He is Man, the creature we are trying to save. Only because he has become more conscious of his powers is he capable of so much folly and evil." (*The Children of Frankenstein: A Primer on Modem Technology and Human Values* by Herbert Muller, p. 331)

The Third Force by Frank Goble concerns the theories of "humanistic psychology," mainly those of Abraham Maslow. Behaviorism and Freudian psychology are both looks at a limited part of man; humanistic psychology tries to view the whole man. Instead of studying people who have mental problems, Maslow started with "self-actualizing" people whom he felt had adjusted the best to living. The second part of this excellent popularization is concerned with proof of these theories.

> The President of an electronic manufacturing company challenged Dr. Argyris to prove his contention that the average worker was giving the company only about a third of his full capability. Argyris set up a one year experiment in which twelve female electronics assemblers were given individual responsibility for assembling an entire electronic unit. Instead of efficiency experts telling the assemblers how to do the job, they were free to develop their own methods. Furthermore, each of the twelve girls was to inspect the finished product, sign her name to the product, and then handle related correspondence and complaints from customers.

> The first month of the experiment was not encouraging. Productivity dropped 30% below that of the traditional assembly-line method, and worker morale was also low. It was not until the end of the eighth week that production started up. But by the end of the fifteenth week production was higher than ever before, and overhead costs of inspection, packing, supervision, and engineering were way down. Production continued significantly higher than that of assembly-line methods for the balance of the one year experiment. Re-work costs dropped 94%, and customer complaints dropped from 75% a year to only 3%

> When the twelve girls were returned to the routine assembly line, three of them were relieved by the decrease in responsibility. The remaining nine found it hard to adjust to the old routine; they missed the challenge of greater freedom with greater responsibility. (Pocket Books, p. 186-7)

Other cases with about the same results were also covered. The most significant point is not the economic factors--our culture vastly overstresses economic values--but the improvement in workmanship. With almost complete control over what they were doing and the faith in them showed by giving them responsibility for the product, the women seemed to care about what they were doing and felt that it--and they--were of value. Of course, this will not work with very complex products. But they can and probably should be broken into sub-assemblies. One auto plant is totally automated at the moment. All should be.

While the Society for Creative Anachronism wastes most of their energy on costuming and mock duels, they have the right idea in trying to select out of that bygone era what we need today. "Time was and it was all time up to 200 years ago, when the whole of life went forward in the family, in a circle of loved, familiar faces, known and fondled objects, all to human size. That time has gone forever. It makes us very different from our ancestors." (*The Worlds We Have Lost* (essay) by Peter Laslett in *Man Alone*, p. 93) (While overstated and overlooking the brutality of the period, and "tyranny of the family," the point is certainly valid.)

> In a society of hereditary privilege, an individual of humble position might not have been wholly happy with his lot, but he had never had reason to look forward to any other fate. Never having had prospects of betterment,

he could hardly be disillusioned. He entertained no hopes, but neither was he nagged by ambition. When the new democracies removed the ceiling on expectations, nothing could have been more satisfying for those with the energy, ability and emotional balance to meet the challenge. But to the individual lacking in these qualities, the new system was fraught with danger. Lack of ability, lack of energy or lack of aggressiveness led to frustration and failure. Obsessive ambition led to emotional breakdown. Unrealistic ambitions led to bitter defeats.

No system which issues an open invitation to every youngster to 'shoot high' can avoid facing the fact that room at the top is limited. Donald Paterson reports that four-fifths of our young people aspire to high-level jobs, of which there are only enough to occupy one-fifth of our labor force. Such figures conceal a tremendous amount of human disappointment. (*Excellence: Can We Be Equal an Excellent Too?* by John Gardner (now head of Common Cause}, pp. 19-20)

Here is a major social problem that has little to do with machines. Worrying about machines is worrying about an effect rather than a cause. The answer is remodeling society. Gardner's solution to the problem he stated above is for our society to cultivate excellence in all walks of life.

An excellent plumber is infinitely more admirable than an incompetent philosopher. The society which scorns excellence in plumbing because plumbing is a humble activity and tolerates shoddiness in philosophy because it is an exalted activity will have neither good plumbing nor good philosophy. Neither its pipes nor its theories will hold water. (*Excellence*, p.86)

Our culture is also burdened by what Alvin Toffler called "Future Shock" in the book of the same name. Just the rate of change that an individual faces will have an adverse effect on his health if it increases (pp. 291-6). He also points out that technology can free man. "This is the point that our social critics--most of whom are technologically naïve--fail to understand: It is only primitive technology that imposes standardization. Automation, in contrast, frees the path to endless, blinding, mind-numbing diversity" (p.236). For example, the computer designed apartment house, Watergate East, in Washington, D.C., has no continuous straight lines, no two floors alike and 167 different floor plans for 240 apartments (p. 237).

Just as Norton's computers are a parody of the ones we now have, so are the people of the future's attitude toward machines.

The assigner sent him and it was supposed to be always right in its selection (Troy Horan in <u>Catseye</u>, p. 9)

All his life, he had relied on machines operating, of course, under the competent domination of men trained to use them properly. He understood the process of the verifier, had seen it at work. At the Guild headquarters there were no records of its failure; he was willing to believe it was infallible. (Ras Hume in *Star Hunter*, p. 29)

Naturally with that kind of build-up, the verifier fouls up royally.

Star Hunter, while just apparently written so that Ace would have a short novel to fit opposite the abridged *The Beast Master*, is a meaty book for attitudes. Besides rubbing our noses in the fallibility of "infallible" machines, we get her feelings on computers. Such phrases as "Mechanical life of a computer tender" (page15) and "but to sit pressing buttons when a light flashed hour after hour--" (page 85) bring out her limited view. There is another reference to button pushing in response to flashing lights in the ultra-scientific hell of the *Witch World*. (pp. 131.-2)

Star Hunter also has the Patrol winking at the mental conditioning of Vye Lansor so that they can net the Veep, Wass. Afterward, of course, he is offered Compensation. In *Ice Crown*, morality extends to not interfering with the conditioned people of Clio, but no attempt is made to release them from conditioning. In this the successors of the Psychocrats are as bad since they also keep the people of Clio for observation. In *The Zero Stone*, Murdoc Jern notes that "the Patrol ever takes the view that the good of many is superior to the good of the individual." (Ace, p.155)

Norton Consistently views the future as one where the complexity of science and technology have reduced the value of the individual. But the good of many is in the long run the good of the individual. As John Gardner points out in *Self-Renewal: The Individual and The Innovative Society*, our cultures become rigid and decay when they cease to allow a wide range of freedom to the individual.

So Miss Norton is actually wrestling with the prime problem, that of human worth and purpose. The question of human purpose has led to reams and reams of prose, most of it junk. Miss Norton's right in saying that it is not to be machine tenders, but she is vague on what human purpose should be. Arthur C. Clarke in his "beautiful vision" of the future in *Profiles of the Future* feels that "...in the long run the only human activities really worthwhile are the search for knowledge, and the creation of beauty. This is beyond argument; the only point of debate is which comes first."(Bantam, p. 87)

Margaret Mead would certainly disagree. She states that automation should result in people doing only "...Human tasks--caring for children, caring for plants and trees and animals, caring for the sick and the aged, the traveler and the stranger." (*The Challenge of Automation to Education and Human Values* (essay) in *Automation, Education, and Human Values*, edited by W. W. Brickman and S. Lehrer, p. 69)

And I have little doubt which Miss Norton would side with. But either is too restrictive; we need a synthesis of the two. The important thing is to establish a society where all individuals can realize as much of their potential as possible. Since our society comes the closest--despite its many faults--we should start improving it.

As Herbert J. Muller points out (*The Children of Frankenstein*, pp. 369-83], utopias are out of style in this era as they tend to be too simplistic and too rigid. We get glimpses of a Norton utopia in *Judgment on Janus* and *Victory on Janus* as well as scattered places throughout her books. The most appealing might well be the Valley of Green Silences which we see very little considering that parts of three Witch World novels take place there. While all her desirable places are those of nature, it is well to remember that man might not be man as we know him without his links to nature.

In *Star Rangers*, they ponder the reason why the cities are deserted.

> "It seems to me," began Fylh, "that on this world there was once a decision to be made. And some men made it one way, and some another. Some went out"--his claws indicated the sky--"while others chose to remain--to live close to the earth and allow little to come between them and the Wilds--"
>
> "Decadence—degeneracy--" broke in Smitt.
>
> But Zacita shook her head. "If one lives by machines, by the quest for power, for movement, yes. But perhaps to these it was only a moving on to what they thought a better Way of life." (Ace, 1955, p. 169)

The question today is not whether we can do without technology, but how much we can compromise with nature. Like the Orbsleon in *Uncharted Stars* (p. 165), we shall have to learn to live by using technology to assist nature.

As Charis Nordholm explains to the Wyvern Gidaya in *Ordeal In Otherwhere*,

> Four have become one at will, and each time we so will it, that one made of four is stronger. Could you break the barrier we raised here while we were one, even though you must have sent against us the full Power? You are an old people, Wise One, and with much learning. Can it not be that sometime, far and long ago, you took a turning into a road which limited your power in truth? Peoples are strong and grow when they search for new roads. When they say, "There is no road but this one which we know well, and always must we travel it," then they weaken themselves and dim their future.
>
> Four have made one and yet each of that four is unlike another. You are all of a kind in your Power. Have you never thought that it takes different threads to weave a real pattern--that you use different shapes to make the design of Power? (Ace, p. 188)

It is impossible as far as we are along the way of the machine to leave it without untold human misery and suffering. But we must traverse the byways that will make the most of our humanity.

In her horror at the machine forcing men to be its tenders, she overlooks that machines have taken much drudgery off our shoulders and can free us from much more routine labor. When she turns her back on the machine, she ignores all the potential good that it can do us.

> The point was brought home to me recently when I visited an academic friend. He sat in an air-conditioned study. Behind him was a high-fidelity phonograph and record library that brought him the choicest music of three centuries. On his desk before him was the microfilm of an ancient Egyptian papyrus that he had obtained by a routine request through his university library. He described a ten day trip he had just taken to London, Paris and Cairo to confer on recent archaeological discoveries. In short, modern technology and social organization were serving him in spectacular ways. And what was he working on at the moment? An essay for a literary journal on the undiluted evil of modern technology and large-scale organization. (*Self-Renewal*, p. 62)

We must face the fact that while much of what we have is tainted, it is also much more on the positive side than any age before us has had. The potential is almost limitless. If we fail, it will not be because "...science, too, had its demons and dark powers," (*Victory on Janus*, Ace, p. 190), but because our nerve has failed us and we let technology run wild.

Even Arthur C. Clarke pauses in his optimistic view of the future to admit that

> Sir George Darwin's prediction that ours would be a golden age compared with the aeons of poverty to follow, may well be perfectly correct. In this inconceivably enormous universe, we can never run out of energy or matter. But we can all too easily run out of brains. (*Profiles of the Future*, Bantam, p. 155)

And just as the potential exists for a heaven beyond our wildest dreams, so does the potential for a hell worse than our bleakest nightmares. Science and technology are amoral and we must fit the morals to them. If we fail, not only we will foot the bill but many generations to follow.

> If there is a long chance that we can replace brutality with reason, inequality with justice, ignorance with enlightenment, we must try. And our chances are better if we have not convinced ourselves that the cause is hopeless. All effective action is fueled by hope. Pessimism may be an acceptable attitude in literary and artistic circles, but in the world of action it is the soil in which desperate and extreme solutions germinate, among them reaction and brutal oppression.
>
> It is not given to man to know the worth of his efforts. It is arrogant of the individual to imagine that he has grasped the larger design of life and discovered that effort is worthless, especially if that effort is calculated to accomplish some immediate increment in the dignity of a fellow human. Who is he to say it is useless? His business as a man is to try. (*The Recovery of Confidence* by John W. Gardner, Pocket Books, pp. 84-5)

But no matter how deeply Miss Norton's despair in the present and the future is germinating, she never councils quitting or even considering it. "It is better not to he met by pessimism when the situation already looks dark."

(*Uncharted Stars*, p. 230) Her heroes and heroines do not tamely bow their heads and accept their lot in a society that does not fit them. Some, like Diskan Fentress, may not seem to be concerned with others, but come through when the chips are down. Even if Norton's future societies do not value the individual, her sympathetic characters do.

Norton's future societies usually combine high ideals with a lack of concern for the people in it, an extrapolation of today's society that seems to be more comfortable treating men largely as interchangeable parts. And as our society worsens, so does her view of the future. *Catseye* (1961) marked the rise of organized crime. By *Night of Masks* (1964), crime syndicates had gone inter-stellar. *The Zero Stone*, (1968) and *Uncharted Stars* (1969) show the Patrol reacting by trampling individual rights in their efforts to stamp out crime.

In *Sargasso of Space* (1955), the Free Traders were recruited from the trainees that the Combines depended upon, too. By *Dread Companion* (1970) and *Exiles of the Stars* (1971), the Free Traders are almost a separate race, rigidly controlling themselves on the planets, with their women and the declining feline race kept on their asteroid bases. It is almost as though the cats began to die out as their masters became less human, less linked to nature.

In the future, most of Miss Norton's work will probably be mainly the more aware and less hopeful novels such as *Dark Piper* and *Dread Companion*. But I shall miss seeing more light-hearted optimistic adventures. After all, anyone can be aware. But few can give us an Astra or a Witch World.

Dread Companion Poland 1997

Introduction to Witch World

By Sandra Miesel

Published by Gregg Press, HC, 0-838-92355-X, LCCN 77023209, 222pg

THE REMARKABLY broad and steady popularity of Andre Norton's science fiction is a largely unexamined phenomenon. Indeed, so silent have the science fiction critics been that any discussion of Norton must begin with comments on her neglect.

The sheer number of Norton's books and their impressive sales by themselves should have sufficed to attract notice. Her first novel, _The Prince Commands_, appeared in 1934 before the author was twenty-one. Her initial venture into SF came in the 1930s. By now she has produced more than 75 books, about two dozen pieces of short fiction, and edited six anthologies. The majority of her output is SF, but the list of her writings also includes historical, mystery, suspense, and gothic novels. Her books have sold by the millions here and abroad. They have been frequently reprinted and reissued. Three of her works have been honored with Hugo Award nominations: _Star Hunter_ (1961), _Witch World_ (1963), and "_Wizard's World_" (1967), A 1966 Analog popularity poll listed her as eleventh of seventeen all-time favorite authors. She is, in short, a "saleable name" as an author of SF.

The "young adult" classification given to Norton's SF novels for trade purposes partly explains, but does not justify their critical neglect---Robert A. Heinlein's juveniles have not been ignored. Moreover, although her hardcover editions are usually packaged for the teenage or young adult market, the paperbacks are directed to all ages, (DAW Books even released her children's book _Dragon Magic_ as part of its general list.) But her work has sometimes been dismissed as naive. It would be fairer to describe it as unpretentious.

Many of today's SF readers grew up on Norton, yet she has never become the object of a cult as have Edgar Rice Burroughs, Robert E. Howard, J. R. R. Tolkien, and Marion Zimmer Bradley. Nor do personal ties stimulate interest. Norton, a retired Cleveland librarian now living in Florida, does not indulge in self-advertisement. Her public appearances have been rare and her contacts with either fans or fellow professionals have been private.

Finally, instead of reaping some benefit from the current vogue for women writers, she has drawn petty criticism for using a masculine pen name. The critics who have made this charge fail to realize that "Andre" is now Alice Mary Norton's legal name. Commercial pressures existing in the historical and suspense genres when her career began dictated this pen name. (Norton also used the pseudonym "Andrew North" on three early SF books because of simultaneous editorial ties to the publisher.) Once the label was established it would have been imprudent to change it.

Overall, little attention has been given to Norton for her exceptional entertainment skills, nor have the characteristics of her work been explored. Color, emotional appeal, and romanticism are the bases of her adventure tales' popularity. Their alien, far future settings do not date easily. Emphasis on soft rather than hard science makes them more humane and comprehensible. There is a special---and addicting---flavor to a Norton book.

This flavor can be analyzed in terms of Norton's distinctive motifs and themes. First of all, it should be noted that she reiterates certain backgrounds as well as ideas. Repetition of institutions (Patrol, Service, Combines, Thieves' Guild, Free Traders, the Dipple) and planet names (Korwar, Warlock, Sargol, Astra) form a of interlocking cross-references so that the majority of her science fiction novels occur in the same loosely-structured imaginary universe. Short series of two, three, or four directly related books fall within the overall pattern (e.g., _Storm Over Warlock_, _Ordeal in Otherwhere_, and _Forerunner Foray_ constitute the Warlock series), but this is in no sense an organized future history.

Not surprisingly, major motifs reflect her personal interests: parapsychology, animals, archeology, folklore, anthropology, and history. Norton often describes psi powers or alien sciences that function like magic (_Merlin's Mirror_, _Key Out of Time_, _Android at Arms_, "Wizard's World"). This allows her to blend fantasy with fiction. She treats affinity bonds and telepathic links between humans and animals as well as among humans (_Star Rangers_, _The X Factor_, Time Trader series, Warlock series, Beast Master series, Moonsinger series). And the animals are often as intelligent as the humans (_Catseye_, _The Zero Stone_, _Uncharted Stars_, _Iron Cage_, and _Breed to Come_, which was dedicated to her own pets).

Norton likes to equip her alien worlds with archaeologies, Recurring mention of the Forerunners, a vanished Elder Race, brings the antique and the futuristic together (_Lord of Thunder_, _Forerunner Foray_). Believing that objects acquire historical impressions, Norton uses artifacts as keys to adventure (_Forerunner Foray_, _Dragon Magic_, _The Zero Stone_).

She applies her knowledge of anthropology and folklore to create vivid primitive cultures. She has put Amerindian protagonists and settings to good use (_The Sioux Spaceman_, _The Defiant Agents_, _Fur Magic_, the Beast Master series). _Android at Arms_ is an unprecedented SF application of African culture. (She was depicting blacks sympathetically as far back as 1952 in _Star Man's Son_.)

Time travel, interdimensional gates, and parallel worlds are favorite devices of Norton's (_Here Abide Monsters_, Time Traders series, Crosstime series). One of her original innovations is the alternative histories of alien planets (_Star Gate_, _Perilous Dreams_).

Her paramount themes are: the freedom and integrity of the individual (_The Defiant Agents_), the perils of technology (Janus series, _Star Hunter_, _Star Rangers_), and temptations of elite power groups (_Ice Crown_, Warlock series).

These concepts and themes are always incorporated into the framework of a heroic story. Norton's plots follow the humble branch of Joseph Campbell's mono-myth in which a deprived, powerless, unwanted misfit who is usually young, sometimes an orphan or cripple, struggles against enormous odds to find a place for himself. At the same time, his deeds also benefit others. (_Night of Masks_ and _Dread Companion_ exemplify this for a boy and girl respectively.) The adventure is usually structured in chase-capture-escape-ordeal sequences. Success, in the final confrontation, often hinges on some past moral choice, kindness, or an accidentally-discovered talisman. This maturation formula is obviously ideal for juvenile novels, but its appeal is by no means limited to one age group, for it is a fine means of enlisting audience identification and sympathy.

To Norton, the _story_ is always uppermost. She modestly describes herself as "a very staid teller of old-fashioned stories" and cites the influence of H. Rider Haggard, Talbot Mundy, and the like upon her work. As a writer she is fascinated by situations rather than words. Connoisseurs of clever metaphors will have to seek their quarry elsewhere.

Her colorful alien worlds are rendered as series of impressions. They are never totally explained, and thus they create a pleasing ambiguity, a sense of mystery, which stimulates the reader's imagination. A Norton story leads one down a glittering road but does not permit distracting ventures down byways glimpsed passing.

The dominant note of her wonder-tales is wholesomeness. Hers is a hopeful, ecumenical vision of different races, cultures, life-forms cooperating so that the good may prevail.

The epitome of Norton's SF is her acclaimed Witch World series. The first volume, _Witch World_, was originally inspired by research on the medieval crusaders' kingdoms overseas. It was finally published in paperback by Ace Books in 1963 after several fruitless years' search for a publisher. The fantasy market was depressed in those days before the Tolkien boom, yet _Witch World_ was so warmly received it won a Hugo nomination for best novel of the year. Seven more novels and eleven shorter works have been completed thus far in this growing series as Norton fills in the details of her world. (Readers are urged to consult the table at the end of this article to sort out geographical and historical relationships.)

The Witch World---a descriptive, not a proper designation---is an Earth-like alien planet where magic works. It is far removed in time and space from our globe, yet linked to it and others by interdimensional "gates." _Past intrusions_ through those gates have peopled the world with a variety of human cultures superimposed on primordial non-human ones. These layers of peoples stretching farther and farther back into fabulous antiquity is reminiscent of the legendary Irish _Book of Invasions_ and real British history.

On the eastern continent dwells the Old Race of Estcarp, a dark-haired, dwindling breed ruled by a Council of Witches and, to the north and south, their foes, the rude younger nations of Alizon and Karsten. The Old Race is in the position of Britons beset by Anglo-Saxons and Normans. These peoples plus the Nordic Sulcarmen of the Western Ocean are at a medieval stage of development, but the Spartan Falconers of the south and the Vupsall of the southeast are far more primitive. (The latter tribe resembles a blend of Plains Indian and Scythian.)

East of Estcarp lies Escore, the forgotten original homeland of the Old Race. It is inhabited by a variety of fascinating creatures: the Green people of mixed Old and superhuman blood whose nature magic controls vegetation; the amphibious Krogan and Merfays; the reptilian Vrang; the avian Flannan; the subterranean Thas; the cervine Renthan; the lupine Gray Ones; the Mosswives; and a whole bestiary of bizarre fauna. The odder species resulted from genetic experiments by powerful magicians long since departed for other planes of existence.

Westward, overseas from Estcarp, is High Hallack, a mountainous land held by ordinary humans modeled on medieval Anglo-Normans. They are suspicious of magic and wary of the enchanted relics left behind by the Old Ones. It is implied that these Old Ones are akin to the vanished adepts of Escore, but on this continent most have retreated to Arvon, their own spell-guarded country in the north. This development resembles the withdrawal of the Sidhe in Ireland. Popular religion in both High Hallack and Arvon centers on personified natural forces who may have originally been super-human beings---older Old Ones.

Norton's chief inspiration in these books has been British myth and folklore: the perilous quests and otherworld journeys; the mystic signs and names; the charms and superstitions; the blurring of barriers between man and nature; the mountains and wasteland studded with mysterious towers, ruined strongholds, and ancient megaliths.

However, despite the British flavor of the Witch World's magic, the theory behind the practice comes from other sources. Norton's "power" is surely an ex- ample of *mana*, the Melanesian term for the essence of the "really real" (the same concept is found under other names among the natives of Oceania, North America, and Africa). Like *mana*, power grants the ability to function. It is present in all that exists but is especially manifest in anything strong, holy, or extraordinary. Its intensity varies. Certain people, places, or things are more richly endowed with it than others. In addition to power that a gifted person can tap in performing magic (weaving illusions, foretelling the future, reading minds, healing injuries, and so forth), there are also The Powers, beings possessing fabulous degrees of essence who can respond when summoned. One such is Gunnora, the fertility goddess of High Hallack, who lingers as a merciful presence in her shrines.

Norton emphasizes the mysterious and erratic nature of power. In Estcarp, the ability to wield it exists only in females and is apparently conferred by a recessive gene. Witches undergo years of rigorous training before receiving their jewel of office. They remain virgins for life because they believe that loss of their virginity would deprive them of their power. (This is not strictly true, as Jaelithe demonstrates, but is the result of politically-motivated conditioning.) Other general rules of magic hold all over the Witch World. Power may fail when it is most ardently needed. An adept must recuperate after excessive usage. Power can be lost or ruined by abuse. Having power begets the desire for more (only the most moral and carefully disciplined practitioners can withstand this insidious temptation). Too great a concentration of power is inherently dangerous---visitations by the Light can be as damaging as those by the Dark.

Such is the background against which Norton spins her tales of the Witch World.

Witch World is the story of Simon Tregarth, a disgraced American army officer driven outside the law after World War II. He escapes certain death by passage through an interdimensional gate, in this case the Arthurian Seige Perilous. (The author hints at earlier links between the worlds in Arthurian times, and it is Simon's Cornish blood that qualifies him for the Witch World.) He arrives in Estcarp and joins the Old Race's death-struggle against the combined might of Alizon, Karsten, and the Kolder. The Kolder are technologically-advanced but utterly inhuman invaders from another world---alien Nazis, as it were. They are bent on exterminating the Old Race by war or by massacre because they cannot mentally enslave anyone of that blood. Simon's understanding of technology and his latent talent for the power make him a uniquely effective champion against the Kolder. Aided by Jaelithe, a young witch; Koris, an exiled lord; and Loyse, a run-away heiress, he drives the enemy from their stronghold and saves Estcarp temporarily from the Kolder menace.

Web of the Witch World completes the account of the Kolder war and ties up loose ends from the preceding novel. Simon has married Jaelithe and thereby cost her her witch's jewel. However, they learn how to exercise a new form of power together. Using this, they discover the overseas base of the Kolder and permanently seal the invaders' gate.

Three Against the Witch World introduces the next generation of Tregarths and is told from the viewpoint of Kyllan, the eldest. Gratitude for the victory won by Simon and Jaelithe does not soften the attitude of the Witches towards them. They cannot accept a male with the power and despise Jaelithe for cancelling her witch's vows. Tregarths plan to rear their children---Kyllan the warrior, Kemoc the seer, and Kaththea the sorceress--- away from the Witches' influence. Both parents disappear while investigating new threats to Estcarp, and the triplets are brought up by foster parents. Kaththea is forced into witch training, but her brothers are able to rescue her because of the unique psychic bond they all share. The young Tregarths flee over the accursed eastern mountains and come into Escore. Their coming disturbs the long-standing stalemate there between the forces of Light and Shadow, but at the same time also provides the means to cleanse the land.

In *Warlock of the Witch World*, Kaththea suffers an acute case of *hubris* (overconfidence) and falls prey to the designs of Dinzil, an evil magician posing as a servant of the Light. Kemoc relates his struggle to save her. (His adventures were suggested by the story of Childe Roland and the Dark Tower.) He succeeds with the help of Orsya, a Krogan girl, but Kaththea forfeits her power for her sins.

Sorceress of the Witch World is Kaththea's story. She attempts to return to Estcarp for healing but on the way she is separated from her family and captured by the savage Vupsall. She is forced to become their tribal seeress but fails to forsee an enemy attack. She manages to escape the carnage and passes through another gate into a sterile world inhabited by remnants of a Kolder-like civilization. There she rescues the gate's fashioner, a might adept from Escore's past, and solves the mystery of her parents' disappearance.

Meanwhile, on the opposite continent, another cycle of adventures has been taking place.

"*Dream Smith*" occurs at an undetermined point in High Hallack's past. It is the poignant love story of a maimed silversmith and a crippled heiress united by the Old Ones' magic. (A similar enchanted instrument appears in Norton's non-series juvenile, *Octagon Magic*.)

After Estcarp defeated the Kolder, the forces of Alizon turn their attention elsewhere and invade High Hallack. They cause immense destruction but are eventually repulsed after years of bitter warfare. The psychotic ruthlessness of the aggressors is again reminiscent of Nazism and the defenders suffer as badly as the Dutch did in World War II. The next three stories are set during or after the conflict.

"*Dragon Scale Silver*" is based on the outraged fairy bride folktale motif. Elys and Elyn are the twin children of Estcarp refugees. Elys, the daughter, is treated like a boy and trained as both warrior and Wise Woman. She helps the people of her village survive the Alizon invasion and rescues her brother from the near-fatal spell of a female Dark Old One.

Year of the Unicorn retells "*Beauty and the Beast*." It is narrated by Gillan, an orphaned Estcarp girl who has grown up in a convent in High Hallack. She marries the Were Rider Herrel, one of the Old Ones who had aided in the war against Alizon. She and her husband endure terrible physical and psychic ordeals because of his kinfolk's hatred. They finally prevail and go to make their home in Arvon.

The fantasy gothic "*Amber out of Quayth*" is notable for its wonderful romanticized descriptions of amber stones. This story describes the postwar marriage of convenience between the unwanted daughter of an impoverished noble house and a Dark Old One. On learning her husband's true nature Ysmay helps the rightful lord and lady of the castle he usurped free themselves and punish him.

The major concerns of the Witch World series exemplify all the characteristics of Norton's work described earlier. All her misfit heroes and heroines find appropriate niches after enduring grave perils and making some kind of exodus. Their personal struggles mirror issues confronting their societies.

War has thrown Estcarp, Escore, and High Hallack into chaos while Arvon is beginning to feel the first stirrings of future conflict. Old orders are under attack on every hand. New social balances are being struck after much shaking and leveling. The violence of the changes, the stakes involved, and the consequent reversals of fortune border on the apocalyptic.

Simon Tregarth "was always a man standing apart watching others occupied with the business of living" (*Witch World*, p. 169). Marrying Jaelithe gives him psychological wholeness but at the cost of dislocating her. The special power they share together sets them apart from the accepted order in Estcarp. It is implied that they will find the situation there more favorable after returning from exile.

Their triple birth would be enough to make the Tregarth children curiosities in Estcarp. They flee their homeland to protect their shared powers from the control of the Witches. Ignorance and imprudence hamper them initially in Escore, but they eventually establish new homes there with suitable mates.

Gillan, and to a milder degree Elys, are marked off from their associates by blood, personality, and talents but are fortunate enough to find understanding men.

The handicapped lovers in "*Dream Smith*" and unwanted Ysmay in "*Amber Out of Quayth*" must leave the familiar world to find happiness.

A Norton protagonist is not looking for a place to be comfortable but for a place to be free. She or he will suffer the sharpest agonies, cut ties to home and kindred, wrestle with fate itself in order to find freedom. The author admits her fascination with this theme. As she says, "Loss of control over one's body or mind seems to be the ultimate in horror for me." Throughout the series, forces based on freely bonded unions vanquish those that depend on the compulsion of body, mind, or spirit.

The Kolder are the first such threat encountered. Their monstrous science can turn men into automatons or control selectively the wills and bodies of the living. At the climax of *Web of the Witch World*, Simon and Jaelithe act in concert to take over the Kolder leader's mind and do unto him as he had done unto others. *Sorceress of the Witch World* parallels this when the Kolder-like villains who had turned Hilarion into a living computer component and attempt to harness Kaththea are bested by a psychic gestalt.

Magic rather than technology is the chief hazard in Escore and High Hallack. The mind barrier between Estcarp and Escore has affected the Old Race for centuries, but the Tregarths are able to penetrate it and encourage others to do the same. Illusions---a stallion for Kyllan, a woman for Eryn---are deadly lures. There are spells which bind victims to one place and haunted sites from which there is no escape. Dinzil regards all other beings as his tools. His magic deforms the body while disfiguring the soul, but self-sacrificing cooperation by Kemoc and Orsya annihilates him.

The note of mutual support as a shield against evil is sounded again and again in this series. Gillan's Were Rider in-laws try to destroy her because they cannot control her mind, but she and Herrel reinforce each other and survive. No Norton protagonist finishes his adventures alone. He always finds loved ones with whom he can form a corporate identity that is stronger than any of its parts.

Social pressures pose a different sort of danger to personal integrity. The series emphasizes those pertaining to marriage. Women are reduced to political bargaining counters (*Witch World*, *Web of the Witch World*, "Dream Smith," *Year of the Unicorn*) or marry in haste to escape unhappy environments ("*Amber Out of Quayth*") or are denied marriage to suit the plans of others (*Three Against the Witch World*). Institutionalized female virginity among the Witches and seasonal male promiscuity among the Falconers taint those societies because they deprive some members of free choice.

Of course the most extreme example of dictated sex is rape. This is the method of choice for neutralizing a witch's power. Jaelithe, Loyse, and Kaththea are rescued from rapists, but Gillan saves herself. Women in "*Legacy from Sorn Fen*" and "*The Toads of Grimmerdale*" are less fortunate. There is also the multi-level seduction attempt in *Sorceress of the Witch World*, beguilement of men in "*Dragon Scale Magic*," and a love charm in *Witch World*. The prevalence of attempted rape in this series has to be considered more than a realistic presentation of medieval conditions. It is the author's loudest cry against compulsion...

Norton treats the impact of advanced technology as a rape of reality. She shudders in disgust at the dreary, sterile tyranny of the Kolder. They are masters of death-in-life, but living powers outlast minds welded to soulless machines. *Sorceress of the Witch World* treats a comparable situation with heavy irony when the Kolder-like leader boasts of his superiority to cyborgs: "They wrought worse than they thought, those builders of towers, giving themselves to the machines. We knew better! Man'---he beat one fist into the palm of his other hand---'Man exists, man abides!' " (p. 142). He, too, is overcome by magic. Alizon's technology likewise fails in High Hallack. The enchantments of the Were Riders are more effective weapons for the defenders than borrowed Kolder war engines are for the invaders.

Even when survival is not at issue, the Old Race has its reservations about mechanical devices. How might the use of such things affect the user? Even wielding a simple spring-operated dart gun "meant careful preparation in thinking patterns. We could not ally with a machine!" (*Sorceress of the Witch World*, p. 126). Norton's utopia is the Green Valley in Escore where the fundamental powers of nature reign supreme.

The conception behind the series lets the author describe both the mad scientist and his gothic prototype, the overambitious magician. The villainous alchemist Hylle in "*Amber Out of Quayth*" combines traits of both. Kaththea compares the menacing alien scientist to her false lover: "He had taken Dinzil's road, seduced by the thought of the victory so badly needed, or by the smell of power, which, as he handled it, became more and more sweet and needful" (*Sorceress of the Witch World*, p. 143).

The lust for ever-greater occult learning is a corrosive temptation for the Wise. Some adepts in Escore succumbed: "A handful of seekers after knowledge experimented with Powers they thought they understood. And their discoveries, feeding upon them in turn, altered subtly spirit, mind, and sometimes even body. Power for its results was what they sought, but then, inevitably, it was Power for the sake of Power alone" (*Three Against the Witch World*, p. 130). As a result, Escore became an ecological disaster area, a polluted country infested with loathsome animals and plants. (Arvon once faced a similar crisis but dealt with it more efficiently and suffered no grave harm.)

The power's attractions can ensnare lesser folk as well. *The Crystal Gryphon* and *The Jargoon Pard* involve people of limited abilities turned thoroughly evil by their craving for magical expertise. The people of High Hallack ordinarily shun works of the Old Ones because those who meddle are usually harmed. Smelting ancient metal proves calamitous in "*Dream Smith*" but is safely accomplished by a fore-warned craftsman in "*Dragon Scale Silver.*"

Kaththea, misled by a Faustian man, is a novel example of a Faustian woman. She consistently overrates her skills in *Three Against the Witch World* and uses her powers recklessly. Her desire for more power at any price nearly drives her to commit heinous crimes and costs her the use of her original gifts. Her behavior is contrasted with Orsya's admirable curiosity and boldness.

The least discussed aspect of the Witch World series is its feminist viewpoint. All the stories chronicle the struggles of independent women. The consistently unflattering portraits of conventional women make the virtues of the nonconformists shine more brightly.

For example, Jaelithe is differentiated first by having a witch's power and then by surrendering it. Afterwards she does not settle for cozy domesticity but accompanies Simon to war as vice-warder of Estcarp's southern border. One might regard Jaelithe as a career woman who leaves her children in day care while pursuing her business interests. (Her substitute is a Falconer woman who rebelled against the brutal laws of that people.) The image of Jaelithe saluting her children and riding away to rescue her husband is strikingly gallant.

An even less conventional heroine is Jaelithe's friend Loyse, the drab, scrawny daughter of a lusty baron. Oppression has shaped her into a creature of immense determination and fortitude. "Happiness! Loyse had no conception of that. She wanted only her freedom" (*Witch World*, p. 89). She abhors the usual trappings of feminity and is hypersensitive about her independence. As she warns her future husband: " 'I fight with my Own sword and wield my own shield in this or any other battle' " (*Witch World*, p. 203), Her neuroses do not hamper her effectiveness in action.

The contrast between Loyse and the coolly wanton beauty of Aldis, her first husband's mistress, is the most extreme example of a Norton heroine's typical predicament. Norton's heroines are never especially beautiful--- their attractiveness lies in character and personality--- and they often suffer at the hands of comelier ladies. The author mocks foolish men like the brothers of Elys and Ysmay who fall prey to empty charms.

The Witch World's intrepid and resourceful heroines are superior to their men in some ways. Kyllan is simply not on the same level as his superhuman bride (unless we are to see in their union a happier version of Diana and Endymion). Kemoc lacks certain of Orsya's occult and physical attributes, but they make an even match overall.

Norton emphasizes marriage as an equal partnership: " 'Between us there must never be ruler or ruled,' " says Hilarion to Kaththea (*Sorceress of the Witch World*, p. 217). The serene companionship between Simon and Jaelithe illustrates this marriage of equals splendidly. This is wholly unlike the utilitarian policy of Dinzil toward Kaththea and of Hylle toward Ysmay. It likewise offers a healthy corrective to the antimarital prejudices of the Witches and Falconers and to the plain misogyny of the Kolder.

Expectations of individual men and women clash in "*Dragon Scale Silver*," a feminist variation on fantasy conventions. Proud Elys the shieldmaiden is annoyed by a soldier's offer to accompany her in her quest for her brother. She feels that Jervon would prove a hindrance because he lacks magical talent, but he manages to resist the enticements of the Dark Old One who had beguiled Elys' brother and lends his strength to break the spell. Elyn is unappreciative of Elys' efforts because he is ashamed of the lust that lured him from the bed of his gorgeous but vapid wife. He hates and fears Elys' witch powers. His wife resents her mastery of arms and is anxious to get her safely into skirts. Recognizing the futility of further contact, Elys rides back to the wars with Jervon.

Elys' self-reliance is interesting enough but the noteworthy touch in this story is Jervon's attitude. Here is that singular being---a liberated man. His ego is secure; his opinions are unbigoted. He does not feel threatened by anything Elys can do. "Why should one learning be less or more than any other when they are from different sources?" (*Spell of the Witch World*, p. 78). Their companionship rests on mutual respect.

Even stronger feminist sentiments are expressed in *Year of the Unicorn*, the most artistically satisfying book of the series and, indeed, of all Norton's work. This was the author's first attempt to tell a story completely from the heroine's viewpoint, and she found it an exciting challenge to write. She remarks that "in the years since it was first published [1965] have had many letters from women readers who accepted Gillan with open arms, and I have had masculine readers who hotly resented her." ["On Writing Fantasy," The Book of Andre Norton, ed, Roger Elwood (New York: Ace Books, 1976), p. 77.]

Gillan has been fighting all her young life to control her own destiny. She resists pressures to become a nun and chooses to marry a Were Rider partly to spare a weak girl that destiny and partly to seek adventure. Her groom Herrel is the least promising of the Riders, a half-blood scorned by his pack-brothers. Her resistance to illusion and latent witch powers arouse the Riders' enmity. These are wonderworkers who cannot appreciate any wonders save their own.

However, Gillan's indomitable will nearly proves her undoing. She has to suffer incredible hardships before she becomes humble enough to ask for help: "Pride is a great deceiver. We who choose to walk apart from our fellows wear it, not as a cloak, but as an enshelling armor. I who have asked nothing from my fellows--- or thought I asked nothing---in that moment I was stripped of a pride which broke and fell from me, leaving me naked and alone" (p. 210).

The Riders' strategem is to imprison her intransigent soul in another dimension while bending her body to their will, but she and Herrel, acting together, rout them. Imagery and incident match her identity crises perfectly as she moves from "Who was I?" to "Truly I am Gillan" to "We are Gillan and Herrel." Once again full self-realization comes in the loving union of equals. They seek their own path unfettered by family or society.

Color, action, and sympathetic characters make Norton's stories entertaining but it is their vision of personal integrity combined with organic wholeness that especially commends them to our attention. She has a unique gift for " 're-enchanting' us with her creations that renew our linkages to all life." [Rick Brooks, "Andre Norton: Loss of Faith" in The Book of Andre Norton, p. 193.]

Bibliography of Andre Norton's Witch World
"Amber Out of Quayth" in *Spell of the Witch World*.
The Crystal Gryphon, New York: Atheneum, 1972.
"Dragon Scale Silver" in *Spell of the Witch World*.
"Dream Smith" in *Spell of the Witch World*.
The Jargoon Pard, New York: Atheneum, 1974.
"Legacy from Sorn Fen" in *Garan the Eternal* (New York: DAW Books, 1972).
"One Spell Magician" in *Garan the Eternal*. {Actually "One Spell Wizard"}]
Sorceress of the Witch World. New York: Ace Books, 1968.

The Witch World Series
By Roger Schlobin 1983

Published *in Survey of Modern Fantasy Literature, Volume 5*, Edited by Frank N. Magill and Keith Neilson, Published by Salem Press, (pgs. 2139-2149)

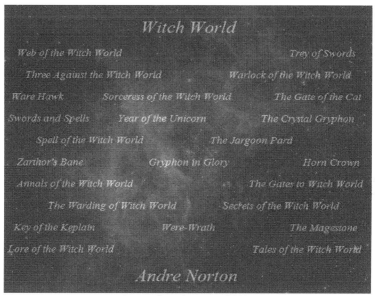

Image from internet 2008

Author: Andre Norton (Alice Mary Norton, 1912-2005)
First book publications: *Witch World* (1963); *Web of the Witch World* (1964); *Three Against the Witch World* (1965); *Year of the Unicorn* (1965); *Warlock of the Witch World* (1967); *Sorceress of the Witch World* (1968); *The Crystal Gryphon* (1972); *Spell of the Witch World* (1972); *The Jargoon Pard* (1974); *Trey of Swords* (1977); *Zarsthor's Bane* (1978); *Lore of the Witch World* (1980); *Gryphon in Glory* (1981); *Horn Crown* (1981)
Type of work: Novel and short stories
Time: Undetermined, but preindustrial
Locale: The Witch World, an alternate universe

Various heroic characters use magic to combat evil and science while finding themselves and their destinies

Principal characters :
ELRON THE CLANLESS
GATHEA THE WISE WOMAN
SIMON
JAELITHE THE WITCH

KYLLAN
KEMOC
KATHTHEA THE WITCH
KEROVAN OF ULM
JOISAN OF ITHKRYPT
HERREL
GILLAN
BRIXIA

When compared to authors of any type of literature, Andre Norton is considered prolific, and as a predominantly science-fiction and fantasy writer, she is particularly unusual. Her career, which began in 1934 with the publication of _The Prince Commands_: _Being the Sundry Adventures of Michael, Sometime Crown Prince & Pretender to the Throne of Morvania_ (a juvenile historical novel) and her legal name change from "Mary Alice" to "Andre," has almost spanned five decades. During this time, she has published more than ninety-eight novels, thirty short stories, numerous book reviews and pieces of nonfiction, and three poems; she has edited seven anthologies as well. In addition to her science fiction and fantasy, she has written adventure stories, historical novels, Gothic novels, mysteries, Westerns, and biographies. Mistakenly labeled in the past as purely a writer for children and young people, her fiction has actually entertained and delighted numerous readers of all ages.

Without doubt, Andre Norton is one of the five to ten major luminaries of modern speculative fiction, and her work must be considered in this context. Nowhere is this clearer than in her acclaimed Witch World series. It can justifiably be judged the crown of her career and belongs with such major fantasy series as Fritz Leiber's Fafhrd and the Gray Mouser, Roger Zelazny's Amber, Patricia A. McKillip's Riddle Master of Hed, and Michael Moorcock's Elric. Unlike many of these, the Witch World series is not the linear presentation of the adventures of one hero; instead, it is the chronicle of one world and all its diversities, and it moves among a wide variety of locations and social groups and focuses on far more than one character.

The Witch World series evolved without initial intention. In a brief article in the short-lived fanzine _The Norton Newsletter_ (1979), Norton explains that _Witch World_, the first novel published, was to have been a single effort, not the first in a series. It arose from the ongoing and in-depth research that has been one of her career trademarks. She had become interested in the Norman holdings in medieval Outremer; these were a group of small "baronies which were carved out and held by landless knights who did not wish to return to Europe after their long travel to the Middle East." Using information about these baronies as her basis, Norton added material from the Arthurian legends, such as the Siege Perilous, and then based two of the novels on specific folktales: _Warlock of the Witch World_ on the Saxon version of Child Roland and _Year of the Unicorn_ on Beauty and the Beast. In addition, _The Jargoon Pard_ is based in part on a special reading of the tarot cards for the protagonist. The series continued as the result of numerous inquiries from readers and of her own continuing fascination with the material.

To keep the series coherent, she has maintained a group of notebooks in which she keeps track of characters and their traits, time sequence, geography and places, plot intricacies, series interconnections, customs and beliefs, dates, fauna and flora, and much more. Stories are listed in order and cross-referenced to their times and settings. There is even a glossary of colloquial expressions. This meticulousness is one of the results of Norton's fascination with history, speculative archaeology, and psychometry; her love of the past leads her to create highly detailed histories of her own in most of her fiction. The sweeping history of the Witch World series is divided into four major divisions, listed here in reading order. The first is composed only of the recent background novel, _Horn Crown_ (1981), which is the account of how humanity came to the alternate universe through one of the magical "gates" and how the various areas were initially settled. The second and original branch is based in Estcarp and Escore (the geography of the Witch World is well illustrated by Barbi Johnson's map on the end papers of the 1977 Gregg Press reprints) and focuses on the transported earthling, Simon Tregarth; his wife, Jaelithe; their two sons, Kyllan the warrior and Kemoc the seer/warlock; and their daughter, Kaththea the Witch. All of them are featured at one time or another in _Witch World_, _Web of the Witch World_, (1964), _Three Against the Witch World_ (1965), and _Warlock of the Witch World_ (1967).

The third branch is set across the sea from Estcarp and Escore in Arvon and High Halleck. It features a group of "beasts"---hooved Kerovan and the Were Riders (shapechangers) --- and is composed of _The Crystal Gryphon_ (1972) and its immediate sequel, _Gryphon in Glory_ (1981); The _Year of the Unicorn_ (1965); and _The Jargoon Pard_ (1974). The last, miscellaneous branch is set in various places in High Halleck, Estcarp, and Escore and features a variety of characters. The first five High Halleck stories are set before the great wars, the remaining ones during the chaos of reconstruction. Most of these tales are in three short-story collections---_Spell of the Witch World_ (1972); _Trey of Swords_ (1977), and _Lore of the Witch World_ (1980)---and one novel, _Zarsthor's Bane_ (1978). Other parts are scattered about in various collections and anthologies.

The Witch World series is an example of "rationalized" fantasy because of the way _Witch World_, Norton's first book, begins. The protagonist, Colonel Simon Tregarth, is fleeing both the authorities and the underworld. A man at the end of his rope, he chooses an unusual form of escape and dares the Siege Perilous. This ancient stone chair transports people to the alternate worlds they deserve. Simon finds himself in the matriarchal state of Estcarp on the Witch World. The reason this is "rationalized" is that the Siege

Perilous provides the reader with a way to enter the fantasy realm, a bridge to help promote the "willing suspension of disbelief," the psychological identification so critical to effective fantasy.

The "sword-and-sorcery" designation is more obvious. Sword-and-sorcery fantasy is primarily involved with feats of arms and magic and tends to echo strongly the epic and romance forms, the *chansons de geste*. It tends to be a highly egotistic fiction that focuses on the achievements of single individuals and their abilities to alter and shape environments and circumstances. Almost without exception, the virtuous characters struggle against the forces of evil and seek to restore things to their natural condition and order. Norton's Witch World series does all of this exceedingly well. While magic on the Witch World appears initially to be only the province of virgin women, her characters must work in harmonious consort, not individually, to be successful. This is a major divergence from the severely "macho" and singular creations of such traditional sword-and-sorcery authors as Robert E. Howard and Michael Moorcock. Also, as with Fred Saberhagen's Empire of the East or Broken Lands trilogy (1968-1973) and Roger Zelazny's *Jack of Shadows* (1971), the Witch World tales include both magic and science, evoking the ambiguous label of "science fantasy." For Norton, however, science and technology can only be evils. The mechanistic Kolder in *Witch World* and *Web of the Witch World* and the superscientist Zandur in *Sorceress of the Witch World*, both from other universes, are presented as abominations. This aversion to science, which borders on phobia, is a common characteristic in Norton's fiction.

Other equally important themes and dispositions enrich the Witch World beyond run-of-the-mill sword-and-sorcery. While the characters dare the usual physical ordeals, they must also cope with two additional burdens: the brooding presence of the "Old Ones," the amoral, sorcerous remnants of the world's original inhabitants, and the personal agonies that Norton calls the "seeking and searching of thought and spirit." These two burdens are evident in *Sorceress of the Witch World*, the fifth volume in the main Simon Tregarth branch of the series. Kaththea---the daughter of Simon and his wife, the witch Jaelithe---is nearly destroyed when she ignores her brother Kemoc's misgivings and mistakenly places her love and magic in the hands of an evil adept, Dinzil of the Dark Tower, the "Warlock" of the Witch World. To restore herself and save her parents and brothers, she must pass through the agonizing darkness of her own fear. She undergoes a rite of passage and passes from a degenerate state into a generate one, the archetypal pattern of rebirth. She is then able to open herself to Hilarion, one of the virtuous Old Ones.

In Norton's fiction, there is a reliance on intuition and humanity, which is no surprise considering the author's aversion to science. There is mythopoesis, "myth-making," which Joseph Campbell describes as the ability to stir centers of humanity beyond the reach of mere language and reason. On a more social and political level, Norton is a pioneer in the use of strong, effective, and real female protagonists; there is Dairine in "*Spider Silk*"; Jaelithe throughout the series' main sections; Kaththea and Utta of the Vulpalls in _Sorceress of the Witch World_; and Orsaya of the water-bound Krogan, Loskeetha the sand reader, Fubbi the Mosswife, and Duhaun of the Green People in _Warlock of the Witch World_, among numerous others. These women fulfill functional and absolutely critical roles in the Norton canon, and it is not at all uncommon to find men depending on their powers and sensitivities. Yet Norton's women are not ultimately alone. They find, sometimes without seeking, generative relationships that preserve their integrity and their identities. One of the more striking examples of this is the androgynous relationship between Kaththea and Hilarion, which echoes that of Simon and Jaelithe in _Witch World_. When Jaelithe marries, it is expected that her powers will vanish with her virginity, but she retains them---to everyone's amazement, including her own. She does have to relinquish the special jewel that the witches use to focus their powers, but through their union she and Simon find a stronger and more personal means to use both their powers. While Norton's characters may agonize before they commit themselves, there are rewards for those who can find unselfish unions.

Looking more closely at the four branches of the series, _Horn Crown_ has been a long-awaited addition, and it answers some of the questions that series readers have had over the years; however, in true Norton fashion, it also does not answer many, leaving the series with its predominant tone of mystery and the unknown. As the background novel, _Horn Crown_ explains that mankind comes to the Witch World through the magic of the portal. The tribes that come are exiles from their own world, and they reflect Norton's frequent use of the outcast and sometimes the scapegoat as character models. The Witch World does not seem to be hostile to the pioneers at first. Scattered about are the ancient, twisted ruins of the "Old Ones," and there are no initial indications of intelligent life. A portion of the novel is devoted to the settlements that are more fully developed in later books.

Yet if the novel were only concerned with the march of humanity into the Witch World, Norton would be violating her own rule for the creation of history in heroic fantasy---that it should be human in its orientation. There is no inconsistency here, however; _Horn Crown_ is centered on the quests of Elron the Clanless and Gathea the young wise woman (who is a forerunner of the witches of Estcarp). Elron seeks his kinswoman, who has foolishly gone in pursuit of "Moon Magic," a task for which she is ill prepared. Gathea also pursues her "Power," and she is joined in her travels by a very large, native, telepathic feline who reflects Norton's frequent use of sentient and psychic animals, particularly cats. Both protagonists become embroiled in an ancient struggle between two divine trinities, one good, the other evil. Elron becomes linked to Kurnous the Horn God, Norton's version of the British Herne the Hunter and the Celtic Cernunnos (the god of the underworld).

Gathea is bound to dual aspects of the moon goddess Diana, one the generous mother, the other the virgin huntress. As they pass through psychological and physical travails, the two must continually struggle with the choice between the awesome powers offered by the dark and light deities and the preservation of their own humanity.

The second and main branch of the series focuses on Simon, Jaelithe, and the triplets: Kyllan, Kemoc, and Kaththea (who are introduced in _Three Against the Witch World_, the third book). These five novels are dominated by conflict, both internal and external, and legions of fascinating secondary characters (such as Koris, the acrobatic and immensely strong dwarf in _Witch World_) and intriguing events (such as the healing mud of the Edenic valley of Dahaun and the Green People). The first two novels, _Witch World_ and _Web of the Witch World_, center on the awesome struggle against the scientific offworlders, the Kolder, and on the problems of Simon and Jaelithe as they discover their love. The latter is further complicated by the resistance of Jaelithe's fellow witches to Simon; they simply cannot accept his special powers (thought to be only the prerogative of women), and they see Jaelithe's affection for him as a great danger. Simon and Jaelithe's adventures unite the forces of Estcarp against a common enemy from the outside; however, internal Conflict and the enmity of the Witch Women are challenges that the three "single-birthed" children must accept.

With the witches' distrust and antipathy in mind, Simon and Jaelithe decide to rear their three children away from the witches' center of power in _Three Against the Witch World_, which is narrated by the eldest, Kyllan, the most military and most adept at psychic communication of the three. While the parents are away and the children are in the care of their nurse, Anghart of the Falconers (a tribe repugnant to the witches, which is featured in "_Falcon Blood_"), Simon and Jaelithe's fears are confirmed. Kaththea is stolen by the witches, and they attempt to train her as a witch and draw her into their power. Through the unique psychic bond of the three children, however, a linking that produces power far beyond their individual abilities, the brothers are able to defeat the assembled witches and rescue Kaththea before she takes her final, irrevocable vows.

The three flee into Escore, a land to the northwest of Estcarp where the legendary past of the Witch World lives and walks. To get there, they must pass through a "mind barrier," a psychic wall that has long separated the two countries. To put it simply, there was no East until the three young people fled in that direction. Once in Escore, Kaththea's use of the power disturbs an ancient balance between the Light and the Shadow, and they become involved with varied remains of the Old Ones; the dread "Shadow" (Norton's personification of evil); Dahaun, the Lady of Green Silence, a member of a race more ancient than even the Old Ones; and strikingly unusual beasts, some benevolent like the winged Vrangs and Hannan, some deeply evil like the Wolf-Men and the subterranean Thas. Since this is Kyllan's book, it focuses on his ability to supply the virtuous with military unity and open communication, the powers he was given before his birth by the strange wise woman who gave gifts to all three children.

Warlock of the Witch World is Kemoc's Story, and he is perhaps the most intricate of Norton's male characters. He is based on the Celtic god Nuada of the Silver Hand, who was king of the *Tuatha*, a model also used by Michael Moorcock for his Prince Corum Jhalen Irsei series. Nuada carried an invincible golden sword through his battles, which he wielded with his artificial limb. Like him and the Fisher King of the Arthurian legends, Kemoc is an example of the archetype of the Maimed God, for his right hand is twisted to apparent uselessness. While he becomes moderately proficient with his left hand, he becomes an effective force against Dinzil and the Shadow only after he receives a golden talisman, a wand in the shape of a sword, from a blueshrouded figure in suspended animation in a forgotten tomb. (Blue and green are colors used throughout the Witch World as indications of virtue.) Interestingly, the sword talisman "fits" best in the deformed hand. As is typical in the Witch World, Kemoc also assumes something of the giver's persona and power when he accepts the weapon. Thus, he later is capable of more than merely his own abilities would permit when he calls on the power of Sytry, the sword's original owner.

Unlike Kyllan, however, and despite his effective use of the magical sword, Kemoc's special ability is mental, and of the three Tregarth offspring, he is the seer/sorcerer. Like most genuine intellectuals, Kemoc doubts his own ability, and his learning of the arcane knowledge in the Crypts of Lormt brings him humility rather than the self-defeating smugness of Dinzil. He is able to communicate and join with such strange beings as Orsya and Krogan and Fubbi the Mosswife without prejudice, a vital disposition since it is Orsya who is his major ally in his quest to rescue Kaththea. Kaththea has been taken by Dinzil through another magical gate into a weird realm that transforms its inhabitants into monsters. While Dinzil's dark magic protects him, neither Kemoc nor Kaththea is as fortunate and both become hideous reptilian creatures. Kemoc's rescue is made all the more difficult by Kaththea's poisoned power; Dinzil, like Shakespeare's Iago, had made her believe that fair is foul and foul is fair. Moreover, Kaththea's return to normal form demands a blood cure, and her twisted values see Orsya's death as her salvation. Thus, Kemoc must decide between the lives of two women he loves and respects. His solution and other decisions he has had to make identify him as the archetypal alchemist (the Magician in the tarot) who must join the old and the new worlds, provide the bridge between the seen and the unseen, and forge the necessary bond between the abstract and the real. His successes with the world of the mind join with Kyllan's abilities in the social world to prepare the way for Kaththea's ultimate triumph in *Sorceress of the Witch World*.

At the opening of _Sorceress of the Witch World_, Kaththea is helpless. Her union with Dinzil has left her with no power, and she fears that her emptiness makes her an open vessel for the Shadow to fill and use to attack her friends and family. Depressed, she thinks little of life, and her restoration parallels the healing of the Witch World's past and present. After she is rescued, she is separated from the family and becomes the unwilling pupil of the aged Utta, an untrained wise woman who serves a primitive tribe. When Utta dies, Kaththea takes her place, but when the tribe is attacked and destroyed, she and a young tribeswoman flee into the keep of an ancient and long-departed adept, Hilarion. After being transported into a sterile, mechanistic world through yet another portal, Kaththea discovers that Hilarion is not dead but a prisoner of the evil scientist Zandur, who is using Hilarion's power to run his war machines in an ugly and pointless war.

With the support of her mother and father, who have followed her, and using the barbarian girl as a tool, Kaththea succeeds in freeing Hilarion from his crystal prison. All return to the Witch World, and after Hilarion seeks solitude to consider the enormous time and changes that have occurred since his imprisonment, the family is threatened by the unified forces of the Shadow and by an unnamed force that is so powerful that none of them can even confront it. It is at this moment that Kaththea must overcome the deep guilt of bringing a friend into the perilous battle and call upon Hilarion to save them all. It is this resolution that identifies Kaththea as the final force that unifies the strength of Kyllan and the mind of Kemoc. Her ultimate power, then, is the ability to harmonize all the positive aspects of humanity through trust and respect, the only true form of love and the ultimate exaltation of the female principle of generation.

The third branch of the Witch World series focuses on a group of people with beastlike features who dwell in Arvon and High Halleck, lands across a small sea to the west of Estcarp. Its action is simultaneous with that of the main branch. The major theme that connects these two branches is appearance and reality. Just as Kemoc and Kaththea had to overcome their hideous appearances in _Warlock of the Witch World_, so too the characters in this branch who encounter those with hooves or those who can change into animals must understand that virtue lies underneath bestial forms. This "true seeing" and freedom from prejudice is a major philosophy that permeates all of Norton's fiction, and it is crucial to the "Beast" branch of the series, which begins with _The Crystal Gryphon_ and its immediate sequel, _Gryphon in Glory_.

These two novels center on the bittersweet and tempestuous marriage of Kerovan of Ulm and Joisan of Ithkrypt, apparent victims of an arranged "axe marriage" when he is only ten and she eight. Their initial psychic bond is a crystal sphere that contains a small white gryphon which Kerovan had found in the barren Waste among the ruined places of the Old Ones and sent to Joisan as a gift. The interesting twist here is that Kerovan does not have feet and normal eyes; instead, he has cloven hooves and amber-colored eyes with slit pupils, supposedly the results of a curse upon his forebears and family because they had looted "glowing" treasures from one of the sealed vaults of the Old Ones. Kerovan's deformity makes him an outcast even among his own kind, and his own mother and half-brother successfully plot against his proper succession to the lordship of Ulmsdale. In fact, his mother has refused to look at him since his birth even though his deformities are the result of her call to the dark powers for a changeling at his birth (the actual cause of his difference). She also spreads numerous rumors about the nature of Kerovan's deviations with appropriate hints that they are evil and have poisoned his mind. This contributes to Kerovan's restlessness, although his questing for self and arcane knowledge are also general characteristics of Norton's protagonists.

When both Kerovan and Joisan are bereft of their homes through the invasions of the evil Alizons with their sickly white, wraithlike hunting dogs, they embark on a series of trials that finally bring them together. While Kerovan has seen a painted likeness of Joisan, however, she has no idea what he looks like. Thus, when she first sees his eyes and hooves, she thinks that he is an Old One and calls him Lord Amber. Fearing her revulsion, he remains anonymous even when his half-brother arrives pretending to be him. Of course, what Norton is doing here is allowing Kerovan and Joisan to develop a true relationship beyond the bonds of the axe marriage, which Joisan has honored even when assailed by Toross (a childhood friend who, Norton hints, has been joined to Joisan in a previous life). In the final confrontation, both protagonists must call upon powers beyond themselves and accept the aid of a true Old One, Neevor, to defeat the dark power that Kerovan's mother Summons. The dark antagonist, Galkur, echoes the nature of the Greek Typhon and drinks life force. While this climax brings Kerovan an understanding of his kinship to the Old Ones, reveals some of the power of the globe, and confirms Joisan's love for Kerovan, it is in _Gryphon in Glory_ (which includes the two protagonists of "_Dragon Scale Silver_" as minor characters) that all of these issues are resolved.

Kerovan never grows comfortable with Joisan's acceptance of his cloven hooves and amber eyes and her love for him, and in _Gryphon in Glory_ he and Joisan are separated. Again they find each other through different routes. Initially, Kerovan's guilt and destructive self-concept prevent true union, but their ties to the power draw them both to the road in the Waste that he had discovered earlier and that ends flush at a cliff face. At the moment of most dire need, Joisan releases the Gryphon from the globe; it swells to enormous size and opens a magic doorway in the cliff. The two unrequited lovers are drawn to a mythopoeic meeting with Landisl, a benevolent Old One who has slept for eons and who is half-human, half-gryphon. As the three turn to face the dread that seeks to exploit them all, they are joined by Neevor, and it becomes clear that Kerovan's fortunes have been tied to matters far beyond the fortunes of individuals and small settlements. Kerovan's mother's dark calling at the moment of his birth has seemingly made him the son of Galkur, a Pan-like creature, and Kerovan's hooves are his mark. In a titanic psychomachia, good prevails. More important to Norton's view of the aesthetics of heroic fantasy, the two lovers are finally joined through mutual strength.

In *Year of the Unicorn*, the focus switches to the Were Riders and to Herrel the were-mountain cat and Gillan the latent witch. Norton draws here, as mentioned earlier, on the folktale of the *Beauty and the Beast*. Gillan is one of thirteen brides sent by the rulers of High Halleck to the feared Were Riders as payment for their aid in the wars that have shaken the Witch World. In a betrothal ceremony involving enchanted capes, Gillan is drawn to Herrel. Like so many of Norton's characters, however, he is an outcast, the object of his companions' contempt because he is a half-breed, and he draws their jealousy because of Gillan's choice. They contrive to separate the two, and when their revelation of Herrel's shapechanging does not deter Gillan's affection, they split her spirit from her body and leave the essential Gillan behind when they journey back to their home in Arvon. Gillan draws upon her undeveloped powers, however, and follows Herrel and her empty body. Unfortunately, she does not have the power to rejoin her body, and Herrel must force his comrades to send him into the spirit realm after her. Together, they are able to defeat its denizens and win their way back to the real world. Herrel denounces the insensitivity of his fellows, and he and Gillan leave to build a new life together.

The Jargoon Pard (its title reflecting the Norton love for jewelry and animals) is a semisequel to *Year of the Unicorn*. Its main character, Kethan, is the son of Gillan and Herrel from the earlier book. He has been stolen as an infant to replace the daughter of Lady Heroise of Car Do Prawn, who needs a male heir for her political machinations; however, as seen throughout the Witch World series, quality always expresses itself. After an attempted ensorcellment by his evil cousins, Kethan flees into the wilderness and struggles with his heritage as a were-leopard. At times more beast than man, he is pursued by the feuding forces of Car Do Prawn, who seek to exploit him and use him as a pawn. Amid his struggle to remain a man, he is discovered by his true parents, who defeat Heroise's pet witch, Ursilla, in a sorcerous duel that involves the use of the gates among worlds and a variation of the *Doppelganger* theme (the splitting of spirits from bodies). Their success results in Kethan's possible return to the clan of Were Riders, his control and understanding of his shapechanging, and, of course, his reunion with his parents. Thus, the recurrent themes of rebirth and regeneration are again primary focuses.

The miscellaneous portions of the Witch World series are scattered through the many dales, societies, and ages of this magical realm, and most are set in the chaos following the great wars. The one novel, *Zarsthor's Bane*, is set in High Halleck, and its protagonist, Brixia, is drawn into the lost city of AnYak to play a pivotal role in the transformation of an ancient malevolent curse and spirit by the power of Green Magic. As would be expected, she is joined by a number of worthy comrades, including an extraordinary cat named Uta. Also of note are the three Sword stories---"*Sword of Lost Battles*," "*Sword of Ice*," and "*Sword of Shadow*"---which are in <u>*Trey of Swords*</u>. These exciting stories tie the fates of their characters to an awesomely powerful force that draws them into the past to battle the forces of evil. One of the particular delights of all the Witch World short stories is that they multiply the number of the fascinating characters and magical events that have made the series what it is.

Amid the vast literary concerns involved in Norton's large canon, the Witch World series presents its own intricacies and convolutions, only some of which have been discussed here. In general, however, the series is dominated by its carefully constructed settings, its inventive magic, and its human characters. The figures who move through its physical and psychological dilemmas elicit reader empathy because of their humanity; they offer pathways to wondrous mysteries that could be shared if only readers could get to the Witch World and its mystical revelations and great challenges. The tension and suspense of their adventures allows any sensitive soul to stand at the focal point of matters both majestically cosmic and deeply intimate.

Roger C. Schlobin

Bibliography

(Bankier, Amanda). "Women in the Fiction of Andre Norton," in *The Witch and the Chameleon*. (August, 1974), pp. 3-5.
Brooks, Rick. "Andre Norton: Loss of Faith," in *The Dipple Chronicle*. (October/December, 1971), pp. 12-30.
McGhan, Barry. "Andre Norton: Why Has She Been Neglected," in *Riverside Quarterly*. IV (January, 1970), pp. 128-131.
Miesel, Sandra. "Introduction," in <u>*Witch World*</u>, 1977.
Norton, Andre. "On-Writing Fantasy," in *The Dipple Chronicle*. (October/ December, 1971), pp. 8-11, 30.
    "The Origins of the Witch World," in *The Norton Newsletter*. No. 1 (March, 1979), p. 2.
Schlobin, Roger C. *Andre Norton: A Primary and Secondary Bibliography*, 1980.
    "Andre Norton and Her Sources," in *The Norton Newsletter*. No. 3 (December, 1979), pp. 5-6.
Walker, Paul. "An Interview with Andre Norton," in *Luna Monthly*. No. 40 (September, 1972), pp. 1-4.
Wollheim, Donald A. "Introduction," in <u>*The Many Worlds of Andre Norton,*</u> 1974. Edited by Roger Elwood.
Yoke , Carl B. *Roger Zelazny and Andre Norton: Proponents of Individualism*, 1979.

Publication Order of Stories by Andre Norton

Note: Andre didn't write her stories chronologically. In some later books, she went back to fill in details of events mentioned in earlier stories.

Trey of Swords contains 3 novellas ~ *Sword of Ice, Sword of Lost Battles* and *Sword of Shadow* ~ they are treated as one within *The Sorcerer's Conspectus*

* Denotes Short Story

Witch World 1974

1 *Witch World* (1963)
2 *Web of the Witch World* (1964)
3 *Year of the Unicorn* (1965)
4 *Three Against the Witch World* (1965)
5 *Warlock of the Witch World* (1967)
6 *Sorceress of the Witch World* (1968)
*   *Ully the Piper* (1970) in *High Sorcery*
*   *One Spell Wizard* (1972) in *Garan the Eternal*
7 *The Crystal Gryphon* (1972)
8 Spell of the Witch World (1972)
*   *Legacy from Sorn Fen* (1972) in *Lore of the Witch World*
*   *The Toads of Grimmerdale* (1973) in *Lore of the Witch World*
9 *The Jargoon Pard* (1974)
*   *Spider Silk* (1976) in *Lore of the Witch World*
10 *Trey of Swords* (1977)
*   *Sword of Unbelief* (1977) in *Lore of the Witch World*
11 *Zarsthor's Bane* (1978)

* *Sand Sister* (1979) in *Lore of the Witch World*
* *Falcon Blood* (1979) in *Lore of the Witch World*
12 *Lore of the Witch World* (1980)
* *Changeling* (1980) in *Lore of the Witch World*
13 *Gryphon in Glory* (1981)
14 *Horn Crown* (1981)
15 *Ware Hawk* (1983)
16 *Gryphon's Eyrie* (1984)
* Were-Wrath (1984) in *Wizards' Worlds*
17 *The Gate of the Cat* (1987)
18 *Tales of the Witch World 1* (1987)
19 *Tales of the Witch World 2* (1988)
GURPS: Roleplaying Guide (1989)
20 *Four from the Witch World* (1989)
21 *Tales of the Witch World 3* (1990)
22 *Storms of Victory* (1991)
23 *Flight of Vengeance* (1992)
24 *Songsmith* (1992)
25 *On Wings of Magic* (1994)
* *The Way Wind* (1995) in *Tales from High Hallack 1*
26 *The Key of the Keplian* (1995)
27 *The Magestone* (1996)
28 *The Warding of Witch World* (1996)
29 *Ciara's Song* (1998)
* *Earthborne* (2004) in *Tales from High Hallack 1*
30 *The Duke's Ballad* (2005)
31 *Silver May Tarnish* (2005)

Suggested Reading Order of Stories by Andre Norton

Note: *Trey of Swords* contains 3 novellas ~ *Sword of Ice*, *Sword of Lost Battles* and *Sword of Shadow* ~ they are treated as one within The Sorcerer's Conspectus

* Denotes Short Story

The Settling of High Hallack
Horn Crown (1981)
* *One Spell Wizard* (1972) in Garan the Eternal
* *Dream Smith* (1972) in Spell of the Witch World
* *Of the Shaping of Ulm's Heir* (1987) in Tales of the Witch World 1
* *Heir Apparent* (1987) in Tales of the Witch World 1

The Fall of Sulcarkeep, The Horning of the Old Race in Karsten & The Defeat of the Kolder

Witch World (1963)
Web of the Witch World (1964)

The Crystal Gryphon 1976

The Invasion of High Hallack by the Hounds of Alizon & The Great Bargain with the Were-Riders

The Crystal Gryphon (1972)
*   *Dragon Scale Silver* (1972) in *Spell of the Witch World*
Gryphon in Glory (1981)
*   *Were-Wrath* (1984) in *Wizards' Worlds*
Zarsthor's Bane (1978)
*   *Sword of Unbelief* (1977) in *Lore of the Witch World*
*   *The Toads of Grimmerdale* (1973) in *Lore of the Witch World*
Year of the Unicorn (1965)
*   *Changeling* (1980) in *Lore of the Witch World*
Gryphon's Eyrie (1984)
*   *Amber Out of Quayth* (1972) in *Spell of the Witch World*
*   *Legacy from Sorn Fen* (1972) in *Lore of the Witch World*
*   *Ully the Piper* (1970) in *High Sorcery*
Silver May Tarnish (2005)

The Turning & The Battle for Escore

Three Against the Witch World (1965)
Warlock of the Witch World (1967)
Trey of Swords (1977)

Sorceress of the Witch World (1968)
Ware Hawk (1983)
Ciara's Song (1998)
The Gate of the Cat (1987)
The Duke's Ballad (2005)
Tales of the Witch World 1 (1987)
Tales of the Witch World 2 (1988)
\#   _GURPS: Roleplaying Guide_ (1989)
Four from the Witch World (1989)
Tales of the Witch World 3 (1990)

Witch World: The Turning trilogy
Storms of Victory (1991)
Flight of Vengeance (1992)
On Wings of Magic (1994)
The Jargoon Pard (1974)
*   _Spider Silk_ (1976) in _Lore of the Witch World_
*   _Sand Sister_ (1979) in _Lore of the Witch World_
*   _Falcon Blood_ (1979) in _Lore of the Witch World_
Songsmith (1992)
*   _The Way Wind_ (1995) in _Tales of High Hallack 1_

The Secrets of the Witch World trilogy
The Key of the Keplian (1995)
The Magestone (1996)
The Warding of Witch World (1996)
*   _Earthborne_ (2004) in _Tales of High Hallack 1_

Contains - Earthborne 2004

Expanded Reading Order Includes Other Authors

Note: *Trey of Swords* contains 3 novellas ~ *Sword of Ice*, *Sword of Lost Battles* and *Sword of Shadow* ~ they are treated as one within The Sorcerer's Conspectus

* Denotes Short Story

The Arrival of the Sulcar
*   *S'Olcarios's Sons* (Legendary oral tradition of origin of the Sulcar, Krogan appear) in *Tales of the Witch World 2*

The Turning (Estcarp/Escore)
*   *Futures Yet Unseen* (ends with the Turning of the mountains between Estcarp & Escore) in *Tales of the Witch World 2*

The Settling of the Dales of High Hallack

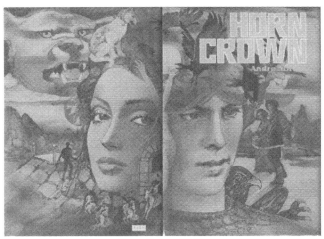

Horn Crown 1981

Horn Crown (people from High Hallack arrive in the Dales)
*   *Peacock Eyes* (Origin of Neevor & Volt, set in High Hallack) in *Tales of the Witch World 2*
*   *Plumduff Potato-Eye* (When Herrel or Kethan was a child, set in Arvon) in *Tales of the Witch World 3*
*   *Bloodspell* (Were-Riders banished from Arvon, Neevor & Ibycus appear as 2 different people) in *Tales of the Witch World 1*
*   *The Judgement of Neave* (A Daleswoman becomes Neave's Votary in

Arvon only a few generations after arriving in the Dales) in *Tales of the Witch World 2*

*   *Gunnora's Gift* (Could go anytime, set in High Hallack) in *Tales of the Witch World 3*
*   *Rite of Failure* (Were-Rider shaman's apprentice fails his rite of passage sometime after *Bloodspell*, set in The Waste) in *Tales of the Witch World 2*
*   *One Spell Wizard* (Becomes a tale/song by the time of *Songsmith*, set in High Hallack) in *Garen the Eternal*
*   *The Sentinal at the Edge of the World* (Sometime before Simon Tregarth arrives, set in Estcarp & Escore) in *Tales of the Witch World 2*
*   *Tall Dames Go Walking* (Set on Earth, origin of Jorge Petronius, Witches from Estcarp) in *Tales of the Witch World 2*
*   *Dream Smith* (Sometime before the invasion of High Hallack) in *Spell of the Witch World*
*   *Fortune's Children* (Sometime before the invasion of High Hallack. This may be one of the attacks from the Waste mentioned in *Dream Smith*) in *Tales of the Witch World 3*
*   *Of the Shaping of Ulm's Heir* & *Heir Apparent* (Kerovan's birth, set in High Hallack) in *Tales of the Witch World 1*
*   *Rampion* (Ends just after Kolder invade Gorm, set in High Hallack) in *Four from the Witch World*

The Horning/The Invasion of High Hallack

Witch World (Simon enters *Witch World*, Fall of Sulcarkeep, the Horning, the re-taking of Gorm from the Kolder)
*   *Neither Rest Nor Refuge* (The Horning in Karsten) in *Tales of the Witch World 1*
Web of the Witch World (Death of Yvian, destruction of the Kolder Gate)
*   *Sea Serpents of Domnudale* (Ends in Year of the Moss Wife, set in High Hallack) in *Tales of the Witch World 2*
The Crystal Gryphon (The Hounds of Alizon invade High Hallack 2 years after the fall of Sulcarkeep)
*   *A Question of Magic* (The Invasion of High Hallack just begun) in *Tales of the Witch World 3*
*   *Stormbirds* (Probably takes place in Year of the Leopard in High Hallack) in *Four from the Witch World*
*   *Wolfhead* (During the Invasion after alliance of northern lords probably during the Year of the Leopard) in *Tales of the Witch World 3*
*   *Fenneca* (Sometime during the Invasion) in *Tales of the Witch World 1*
*   *Dragon Scale Silver* (The invasion of High Hallack) in *Spell of the Witch World*
*   *Of Ancient Swords and Evil Mist* (Sulcar raiding Alizon, probably sometime during the Invasion of High Hallack) in *Tales of the Witch World 1*
*   *Night Hound's Moon* (GURPS: timeline placement) in *Tales of the Witch*

World 1
Gryphon in Glory (The Were-Riders join the war in the Year of the Gryphon)
Were-Wrath (Thra fleeing invasion, destruction of her keep, set in The Waste in the forest of the Were-Riders?)
*   *Green in High Hallack* (Set a year after the Hounds pass through their Dale, after the turning point of the Invasion?) in *Tales of the Witch World 1*

Zarsthor's Bane 1978

After the Invasion in High Hallack
Zarsthor's Bane (Just after Hounds defeated, late summer Year of the Hornet)
*   *Whispering Cane* (Shortly after the Hounds defeated, Year of the Hornet) in *Tales of the Witch World 3*
*   *Sword of Unbelief* (Late autumn of Year of the Hornet) in *Lore of the Witch World*
*   *The Toads of Grimmerdale* (Early winter of Year of the Hornet) in *Lore of the Witch World*
Year of the Unicorn (End of Year of the Hornet & beginning of the *Year of the Unicorn*)
*   *Changeling* (After *The Toads of Grimmerdale*, spring of the *Year of the Unicorn*) in *Lore of the Witch World*
Gryphon's Eyrie (Spring/summer of the *Year of the Unicorn*)
*   *Amber Out of Quayth* (From late summer to Midwinter of the *Year of the Unicorn*) in *Spell of the Witch World*
*   *Legacy from Sorn Fen* (After Hounds defeated) in *Lore of the Witch World*
Silver May Tarnish (During Invasion & after Hounds defeated)
*   *The Sword Seller* (4 years after *Amber out of Quayth*) in *Tales of the Witch World 3*
*   *Ully the Piper* (After Hounds defeated) in *High Sorcery*

Tales of the Witch World 1 UK 1989

* _Nine Words in Winter_ (After Hounds defeated, around time of _Ully the Piper_) in _Tales of the Witch World 1_
* _The White Road_ (Sometime after Hounds defeated) in _Tales of the Witch World 1_
* _The Road of Dreams and Death_ (Sometime after Hounds defeated and _Amber Out of Quayth_) in _Tales of the Witch World 1_
* _The Salt Garden_ (10 years after home destroyed during Invasion) in _Tales of the Witch World 2_
* _Candletrap_ (18 years after Year of the Crowned Swan) in _Tales of the Witch World 3_
* _Knowledge_ (Lormt before Turning) in _Tales of the Witch World 3_

Three Against the Witch World UK 1987

The Turning (Estcarp/Karsten) [24 years after The Horning]

Three Against the Witch World (The Turning and the opening of Escore)

* *Old Toad* (Witch protects a Gate from the Turning in the border mountains near Escore) in *Tales of the Witch World 2*

* *An Account of the Turning* (The witches council at the moment of the Turning) in *GURPS: Witch World: Roleplaying Guide*

Trey of Swords (Ends in chapter 6 of Warlock in Escore)

Warlock of the Witch World (Light vs Dark in Escore)

* *The Stones of Sharnon* (Probably shortly after Old Race from Karsten resettle Escore) in *Tales of the Witch World 2*

Sorceress of the Witch World (Light vs Dark, return of Simon & Jaelithe, Hilarion)

* *The Scent of Magic* (Probably during *Sorceress of the Witch World*, in Escore) in *Tales of the Witch World 3*

Ware Hawk (Shortly after *Sorceress of the Witch World*, set in Karsten & Escore)

* *Voice of Memory* (17 years after Year of the Hornet) in *Tales of the Witch World 3*

* *Were-Flight* (18 years after Year of the Fire Drake, set in High Hallack & The Waste) in *Tales of the Witch World 3*

* *Were-Hunter* (Roughly 20 years after *Year of the Unicorn*, in High Hallack) in *Tales of the Witch World 1*

* *To Rebuild the Eyrie* (After the destruction of the Eyrie in the Turning, in Estcarp) in *Tales of the Witch World 1*

* *Oath-Bound* (Falconer knows of Escore, no new Eyrie mentioned) in *Tales of the Witch World 1*

* *Falcon's Chick* (The Turning-after the Turning, in Estcarp, before *Falcon Blood*) in *Tales of the Witch World 3*

* *Milk from a Maiden's Breast* (Three years since Tregarth triplets entered Escore) in *Tales of the Witch World 1*

Ciara's Song (Ends sometime after the Turning in Karsten)

The Gate of the Cat (After 'Ware Hawk, the cleansing of Escore)

The Duke's Ballad (Begins three years after *Ciara's Song*, events of *Gate of the Cat* mentioned taking place during this, in Karsten)

* *Isle of Illusion* (Anytime after *Amber Out of Quayth*, near Arvon) in *Tales of the Witch World 1*

* *Through the Moon Gate* (Could go anytime, in High Hallack) in *Tales of the Witch World 2*

* *The Circle of Sleep* (around the same time as *Stillborn Heritage* or *Voice of Memory*, in The Waste) in *Tales of the Witch World 3*

* *Strait of Storms* (sometime after *Gate of the Cat*, in Escore) in *Tales of the Witch World 3*

* *The Hunting of Lord Etsalian's Daughter* (at least 6 years after the Turning, in Estcarp) in *Tales of the Witch World 2*

* *The Stillborn Heritage* (around the same time as *Falcon Magic*, in High

Hallack) in *Four from the Witch World*

* *Falcon Blood* (after the destruction of the Eyrie in the Turning, Salzarat the former home of the Falconers rediscovered, curse of Jonkara broken) in *Lore of the Witch World*

Storms of Victory 1991

Witch World: The Turning trilogy

Storms of Victory (after *Sorceress of the Witch World*) contains *Port of Dead Ships* and *Seakeep*

Flight of Vengeance (probably around the same time as *Falcon Blood*) contains *Exile* and *Falcon Hope*

On Wings of Magic (after *Falcon's Chick*/6 years after *To Rebuild the Eyrie*, around the same time as *Stilborn Heritage*) contains *We, the Women* and *Falcon Magic*

* *La Verdad: The Magic Sword* (Anytime after *Changeling* and *We, the Women*, probably before *The Warding of Witch World*, in High Hallack) in *Tales of the Witch World 2*

* *Darkness Over Mirhold* (probably after *Port of Dead Ships* in *Storms of Victory*, before T*he Warding of Witch World*) in *Tales of the Witch World 2*

The Jargoon Pard (After the Turning, set in Arvon)

* *Falcon Law* (after *Falcon Blood* and *Falcon Hope*, in the border mountains between Estcarp & Karsten) in *Four from the Witch World*

* *Spider Silk* (8 years after the Turning, in Estcarp) in *Lore of the Witch World*

* *Sand Sister* (Tursla & Simond shortly before the *The Warding of Witch World*, in Tor Marsh) in *Lore of the Witch World*

Songsmith (Alon & Eydryth shortly before the *The Warding of Witch World*, in Escore & Arvon)

* *The Way Wind* (Anytime, if in *Witch World*, published same year as *The Key of the Keplian*) in *Tales from High Hallack 1*

The Secrets of the Witch World trilogy

The Key of the Keplian (set in Escore)

The Magestone (set mostly in Alizon)

The Warding of Witch World

* *Dream Pirates' Jewel* (long after Invasion, possibly around *The Warding of Witch World*, in High Hallack) in *Tales of the Witch World 2*

* *The Root of All Evil* (anytime after *Gate of the Cat*, in Escore) in *Tales of the Witch World 3*

* *Earthborne* (after the *The Warding of Wirch World* in Estcarp) in *Tales of High Hallack 1*

* *Heroes* (17 years after Old Race from Karsten resettle Escore) in *Tales of the Witch World 2*

* *The Weavers* (Anytime after *Gate of the Cat*, in Escore) in *Tales of the Witch World 3*

* *Godron's Daughter* (17 years after Stones of Sharnon, in Estcarp) in *Tales of the Witch World 3*

* *Cat and the Other* (around the time of *Heartspell*? in Estcarp) in *Tales of the Witch World 1*

* *Yellow Eyes* (new lands introduced, after *Cat and the Other*) in *Catfantastic 1*

* *Shado* (some years after *Cat and the Other*) in *Catfantastic 2*

* *Heartspell* (30 years after the Turning in Estcarp) in *Tales of the Witch World 3*

* *Gate of the Kittens* (Simon Tregarth's grandson in Escore) in *Catfantastic 1*

Tales of the Witch World 2 UK 1989

A Glossary of the Witch World

by Michael Martinez
Sorcerer and Creator of Xenite.org,
Master of Ceremonies at SF Fandom.com

Sorceress of the Witch World 1987 by John Pound

Aleeth

Daleswoman of High Hallack. She was one of the Were Rider brides, and
came from a southern family. Her family emblem was a salamander curled
among leaping flames. (*Year of the Unicorn*).

Aldis

Woman of Karsten. Mistress of Yvian. She tried to procure a Wise Woman's
aid to ensure Yvian's fidelity to her bed after his ax-marriage, but she was
enticed into becoming Jaelithe's puppet. She became an agent of the Kolder
and when escaping with Loyse from the Kars Castle she created total chaos,
skilfully spreading rumors that someone whom Duke Yvian trusted was a
traitor. (*Witch World* & *Web of the Witch World*).

Aliz

Chief port and city of Alizon, capitol of the nation. (*Witch World*, *The Magestone* & *Warding of Witch World*).

Alizon

Nation to the north of Estcarp, situated on the western coast. The land was cool and harsh. The Alinzondern were led through a gate by two Adepts of Escore who discovered their own world was dying. The Alizondern had a pack society modelled after the packs of their vicious hounds. Their nobles were scheming and jealous, and after the gate was closed before all their people could be brought through the Alizondern eschewed all users of Power. They made war upon Estcarp and allied themselves with the Kolder. Using Kolder machines the Alizondern invaded High Hallack but when their war with Estcarp turned against them they had to abandon the expeditionary force. The descendants of Elsenar, one of the Adepts who brought the Alizondern to Witch World, eventually established contact with Estcarp through Lormt and began a process of reconciliation. Aliz was the largest city of Alizon, serving as both seaport and capitol. (*Witch World*, *The Magestone* & *Warding of Witch World*).

Alousan

Daleswoman of High Hallack, a Dame of Norstead. She was a gifted healer and herbalist. (*Year of the Unicorn* & *The Crystal Gryphon*).

Alovin or Alavin

A seaman serving on the Wave Cleaver. (*Web of the Witch World*).

Alwin

Dalesman of High Hallack. Son of the village headman in Ithkrypt. He married Martine the year before the invasion but he perished when Ithdale was invaded. (*The Crystal Gryphon*).

Alwin

Dalesman of High Hallack. Son of Alwin and Martine, born after Martine and others escaped from the ruin of Ithdale. (*The Crystal Gryphon*).

Alys

Daleswoman of High Hallack, wife of Randor. She bore him four children, of whom the first was stillborn. Cyart was their second child, Math their third, and Islaugha the fourth. Alys apparently died sometime after the birth of Islaugha. (*The Crystal Gryphon*).

An-Yak

Zarsthor's domain in greater Arvon, cursed by the Bane. When Brixia converted the Bane to a talisma of power, releasing the spirits of Zarsthor and Eldor to seek their peace, Marbon planted the bane and the former lands of An-Yak recovered. (*Zarsthor's Bane*).

Angarl

Dalesman of High Hallack. He was an armsman from Toross' dale who went to Ithdale with Toross, Islaugha, and Yngilda. (*The Crystal Gryphon*).

Annet

Daleslady of High Hallack, wife of Gyrerd. She was the daughter of Urian of Langsdale. After the war with Alizon Annet assumed control over Gyrerd's household in Uppsdale, displacing his sister Ysmay, of whom she was apparently jealous. Annet was unable to grow herbs. (*Spell of the Witch World*).

Archan

Dalesman of High Hallack. Cyart's scribe in Ithdale. He made an image of Joisan that was sent to Kerovan. (*The Crystal Gryphon*).

Arnar

Dalesman of High Hallack. Elder son of Broson, smith of Ghyll. (*Spell of the Witch World*).

Asper, the Waves of

The Sulcar seamen swear on them. Perhaps this was the name of their homeworld, long-forgotten except in curses and oaths. (*Web of the Witch World*).

Bethora

Woman of Karsten. Agent of the Kolder in Kars City who lured Loyse of Verlaine into a trap set by the Kolder. (*Web of the Witch World*).

Bettris

Woman of Karsten. Mistress of Fulk. She apparently came from Verlaine's coastal folk and had scoured the shores for salvage before rising to Fulk's attention and bed. (*Witch World*).

Blank Shield

Term applied to mercenaries or men whose lords had been killed. It was apparently the custom for soldiers to paint the emblem of their lord on their shields. Estcarp hired blank shields when its forces were diminished or insufficient to meet immediate needs. (*Witch World*).

Boldre

Town in High Hallack, possibly ruled by Vescys before the war with Alizon. (*Spell of the Witch World*).

Borderers

Dalespeople of northwestern High Hallack, said to be of mixed blood. (*The Crystal Gryphon*).

Border Warder of the South
One of the highest ranks, apart from the Guards Commander and Marshal, a man in Estcarp could achieve in Estcarp's armed forces. His duties were to protect the southern border of Estcarp from Karsten's attacks. Simon Tregarth was Border Warder of the South. (*Web of the Witch World*).

Borderers
Soldiers of Estcarp who warded the borderlands with Karsten and Alizon. Many were recruited from the Old Race exiles of Karsten as they fled north into Estcarp. Originally Koris of Gorm commanded the Borderers with Simon as his lieutenant, but Koris was recalled to Estcarp, leaving Simon in command of the growing force. Simon eventually became Captain of the Borderers. (*Witch World*, *Web of the Witch World* & *Three Against the Witch World*).

Borstal
Dalesman of High Hallack, forester of Ithdale. He led one band of survivors out of the dale. (*The Crystal Gryphon*).

Briant
The name Loyse took when she escaped from Verlaine, posing as blank shield. (*Witch World*).

Brixia
Daleswoman of High Hallack. Daughter of the House of Torgus in southern High Hallack, Brixia escaped the ruin of her family's keep during the war with Alizon. Brixia's mother died in childbirth and her father died in one of the earliest battles of the war with Alizon. (*Zarsthor's Bane*).

Broc
Man of the Old Race, lord of Quayth. Broc was deposde and imprisoned by Hylle the Usurper. Ysmay freed Broc and Yaal, his lady, and they restored Quayth to its former beauty. Broc invited Ysmay to stay with him and Yaal after Hylle was destroyed. (*Spell of the Witch World*).

Broken Sword
The emblem of Ithdale and the House of Harb. (*The Crystal Gryphon*).

Broson
Dalesman of High Hallack. He was the smith of Ghyll during Vescys' time. (*Spell of the Witch World*).

Calder
A river in southern High Hallack. Kerovan discovered the Alizonders advancing along this route during his last scouting mission for Lord Imgry. (*The Crystal Gryphon*).

Caluf

Man of the Old Race of Karsten. He joined the Borderers under Simon Tregarth after escaping from Karsten. (*Witch World*).

Cape of Black Winds

A cape between Vestdale and Ulmsport. (*The Crystal Gryphon*).

Cargo bottom

Sulcar ship, built for haulling cargo or making long voyages. (*Witch World*).

Casterbrook

Town or dale of High Hallack, apparently bordering Dimdale on the north. North of Casterbrook lay the Gorge of Ravenswell, marking a northern boundary of High Hallack. (*Year of the Unicorn*).

Collard

Dalesman of High Hallack. Younger son of Broson, smith of Ghyll. (*Spell of the Witch World*).

Coomb Frome

A keep or fortress, probably in Edale (q.v.). (*Spell of the Witch World*).

Croffkeep

A mountain fort of High Hallack, situated near the border with the Waste and depleted of men for the war with Alizon. Croffkeep may have stood in or near Hockerdale or Dimdale. (*Year of the Unicorn*).

Cup and Flame

Religious tradition in High Hallack, associated with marriage. (*The Crystal Gryphon*).

Cyart

Dalesman, lord of Ithdale before the war with Alizon. Cyart had no clear heir and he concluded a marriage for his niece Joisan with Kerovan of Ulmsdale. Cyart apparently respected Ulric of Ulmsdale enough to back him politically, and was keenly aware of the connivings of Ulric's relatives. Cyart was killed during the war with Alizon. Cyart was given a foreseeing gift while he was still in his mother's womb. If he prophetically dreamed twice he could escape misfortune, but if he had the same dream a third time he could not avoid the consequences. Cyart dreamed when his wife would die, but he was far to the south of Ithdale and though he killed a horse trying to reach her, he arrived too late to save her. (*The Crystal Gryphon*).

Dagale

Dalesman of High Hallack, Marshal of Menie under Cyart. He was left by Cyart to protect Ithdale with only a small force of men, and he sacrificed himself to save Joisan and other refugees when the Alizonders attacked Ithkrypt. (*The Crystal Gryphon*).

Dairine

Daleswoman of High Hallack, daughter of the lord of Marchpoint. She briefly befriended Ysmay of Uppsdale while travelling to the fair at Fyndale five years after the war with Alizon. Dairine's parents met at a fair in Ulmsport. (*Spell of the Witch World*).

Dart gun

weapons, apparently in large and small form, used by the soldiers of Witch World. Their spring mechanisms were apparently powerful enough to launch darts with deadly force.

Deep Chill

An affliction or illness suffered by the Dalesfolk of High Hallack. (*Zarsthor's Bane*).

Delta Island

Name not used in the books for an island just beyond the mouth of the Kars river. Yvian sent men there to be sold as slaves to the Kolder. (*Witch World*).

Demons

Creatures feared by the inhabitants of Witch World. Harb defeated the demon of Irr Waste. Gillan warned Herrel that she knew how to deal with demons. When Jaelithe's illusionary fleet vanished by the shore of Verlaine, the common folk of that land decided it had been a demon fleet. (*Witch World*, *Year of the Unicorn* & *The Crystal Gryphon*).

Dimdale

Dale of High Hallack. Bordered Hockerdale on the north. Casterbrook stood on the northern side of Dimdale. (*Year of the Unicorn*).

Donnar

Man of Karsten. Bodyguard for Lady Aldis. (*Witch World*).

Duarte

Man of Karsten. A member of the old nobility, Duarte was one of three envoys sent by Yvian to the ax-marriahe ceremony with Loyse in Verlaine. His house appears to have been the oldest established noble family of Karsten. Duarte was probably murdered by Fulk after Loyse escaped with Jaelithe. (*Witch World*).

Durstan

Man of the Old Race of Karsten. A borderer under Simon Tregarth. His company, which consisted of twenty soldiers, was supposed to patrol the hills near SouthKeep the day when Loyse of Verlaine was kidnapped by the Kolder. Together with Simon Tregarth they set forth to free her but only managed to learn that she had been taken on board a ship bound for Kars city. (*Web of the Witch World*).

Dwed

Dalesman of High Hallack. Son of the Marshal of Itsford. His family was related to Marbon's mother and they held a small border watch-tower. Dwed was the third son in the family. Marbon took him into his service. After Marbon lost his wits, Dwed took him back to Eggarsdale. (*Zarsthor's Bane*).

Eggarsdale

Dale of High Hallack, located near the waste somewhere in the upper dales. Eggarsdale had a keep with twenty cottages in its main village. A road ran through the dale down to the lowlands. (*Zarsthor's Bane*).

Eldor

Man of the Old Race of Arvon, lord of Varr in Kathal. He was Zarsthor's brother-in-law and apparently schemed to gain power or to become a Dark Adept. Their spirits were trapped after Zarsthor confronted Eldor. (*Zarsthor's Bane*).

Elvan

Dalesman, lord of Rishdale. He was middle-age and either widowed or divorced when he concluded a marriage with Yngilda, daughter of Islaugha. Elvan was killed during the war with Alizon when he retreated to his keep and attempted to withstand the war machines. (*The Crystal Gryphon*).

Enkere

An underground river crossing the Tor Marsh which was used by the Kolder submarine to reach the Tormen village to pick up Simon Tregarth and Loyse of Verlaine. Its estuary was situated north to the Es city. (*Web of the Witch World*).

Es City

Capitol of Estcarp. Largest city of Estcarp. Es was surrounded by a high wall and its largest building was Es Castle, a citadel where the Guards of Estcarp had their main base. Es was an active trading center and the heart of Estcarpian society. (*Witch World*, *Web of the Witch World* & *Warding of Witch World*).

Es Port

Small city on the coast of Estcarp at the mouth of the Es River. The Sulcar ships gathered here to trade their wares. Anner Osberic established a Sulcar community there after Sulcarkeep was destroyed by his father, Magnis Osberic. (*Web of the Witch World*).

Estcarp

Domain of the Old Race in the eastern continent. Estcarp was founded by refugees from Escore, families of the Old Race who fled the devastating wars unleashed by the Dark Adepts. At first protected by the few remaining Adepts of the Light, the Old Race of Estcarp were left undefended when the

Adepts accidentally destroyed themselves (or were drawn irretrievably through an immense gate they had tried to open in Lormt). The Witches arose from the ruin and established order, raising up a high chain of mountains between Estcarp and Escore. The Old Race then slowly forgot their origins and built a new civilization. Their capitol was at Es City on the Es River, and there they built the mighty Citadel. They established borders with Alizon and the Tor-men and some clans gradually spred south to settle in the lands that later became known as Karsten. When the Sulcar ships first appeared the Old Race of Estcarp welcomed them, accepting their trade in port cities such as Es Port at the mouth of the river. In time Estcarp was drawn into wars with the adventurous Hounds of Alizon, but shielded by the power of the Witches and the strength of their own doughty warriors the Old Race came to dominate the western coasts, trading with the younger races of men who settled in Gorm, Karsten, and Var. Eventually, however, the Kolder entered the Witch World and realizing the potential threat of the Old Race tried to eradicate them. Gorm and Karsten were turned against Estcarp as Alizon launched a new war. When Karsten turned against its own Old Race clans, Estcarp welcomed them home and eventually the Witches destroyed Karsten's army by turning the mountains between the two nations. The Falconers, allies of Estcarp who had settled in the mountains, for a time took refuge in Estcarp but their customs were too foreign and offensive to the Old Race for the two peoples to live close together. Some of the Sulcar also settled in Estcarp after their chief fortress, Sulcarkeep, was destroyed in the war with the Kolder. After the Witches lost much of their power, Koris of Gorm assumed control of Estcarp, governing wisely. He led the nation in re-establishing its influence and opening new ties with Alizon after a young Alizonder lord entered Lormt through a gate. Lormt was the oldest city of Estcarp, having been established by the Adepts of the Light before Estcarp was itself founded. Many ancient records were preserved or partially preserved there and after a thousand years a small community of scholars dug through the crypts and chambers of Lormt looking for clues to their past and to the power their race had once commanded. (_Witch World_, _Web of the Witch World_, _Three Against the Witch World_, _Sorceress of the Witch World_, Witch World: The Turning, _The Magestone_ & _Warding of Witch World_).

Ewald

Dalesman of High Hallack, from Uppsdale, brother of Gyrerd. Ewald was killed during the war with Alizon. Savron was probably their father. (_Spell of the Witch World_).

Exiles of Arvon

Members of the Old Race who were sent out from Arvon after the Great Struggle in which peace was restored to the ancient realm of the Old Race. Many of the Exiles settled or wandered in the Waste, but some lingered near the sea in the ruins of the old places where Arvon's people had dwelt before taking the Road of Memory back to Arvon. Some of the Exiles interbred or at least interacted with the Dalesmen of High Hallack. (*The Crystal Gryphon*, *Year of the Unicorn* & *The Jargoon Pard*).

Three Against the Witch World 1986 by John Pound

Falcon-Fist
Mountain to the east of Norsdale. (*Year of the Unicorn*).

Falconers
Men who served as mercenaries on Sulcar ships, or fought as allies with Estcarp. Their race originally came from Salzarat, a land apparently far to the south of Karsten. Koris tells Simon that they fled over sea to Estcarp after their land was invaded by barbarians, but in Lore of the Witch World we learn that Jonkara had tried to enslave their race. About 2,000 Falconers (2/3 of them men) escaped in Sulcar ships. Settling in Estcarp, their custom of keeping the women in separate villages offended the Witches, so the Falconers moved into the mountainous lands south of Estcarp, north of Karsten. There they established the Eyrie and new villages for their women and children. Each year young men were selected to visit the villages and breed with the women. Deformed babies were killed. When the boys reached a certain age they were taken to the Eyrie and trained to be warriors. The Dukes of Karsten tried three times in the hundred years before Simon Tregarth entered the Witch World to defeat the Falconers, but the Falconers won all three wars. The ruler of the Eyrie was called the Lord of Wings. Although the Witches of Estcarp eschewed a formal alliance with the

Eyrie, they did not watch closely the relationship between their Guards and the Falconers. The unacknowledged alliance therefore served both peoples well. And when the Witches turned the mountains to stop Duke Pagar's army, the Falconers were welcomed into Estcarp. However, their culture was too alien. Too many of their women fled their villages to ensure the survival of the Falconers. Several companies settled in High Hallack, where they forged a new alliance with the Dalesfolk, agreeing to give up some of their customs. The Falconers developed close bonds with their birds, from which their tribal name was taken. They were able to communicate with the creatures better than other men. In the mountains they used sturdy ponies capable of bearing two men. Falconers had reddish hair and brown-yellow eyes. (*Witch World*, *Lore of the Witch World* & Witch World: The Turning).

Falthingdale

Dale of High Hallack, situated to the west of Norsdale. Falthingdale was heavily forested. (*Year of the Unicorn*).

Faltjar

Falconer. Assigned to the southern gate of the Eyrie. He met Koris, Simon, Jaelithe, and Loyse and took Simon and Koris to meet with the Lord of Wings after they showed him a false falcon apparently built and used by the Kolder. Faltjar was later sent by the Lord of Wings to investigate reports of ships setting into coves near the Eyrie's domain, and he was captured with his men by the Kolder. (*Witch World*).

Farseeing

A method of divinition, shorned by adherents of the Flame but typically used by Wisewomen, Witches, Adepts, and other users of Power. (*The Crystal Gryphon*).

Farthom

Man of Karsten. A hill lord, father of Fulk. Farthom's holding was in the northern hill of Karsten, apparently near the border with Estcarp. (*Witch World*).

Fast Ridge

A mountain or chain of high hills visible from the bell tower of Norstead Abbey. (*Year of the Unicorn*).

Firtha

Woman of Karsten. Maid to Lady Aldis. She visited Jaelithe's house in Kars City and persuaded Aldia the Wise Woman of Kars would help her retain Yvian's attentions. (*Witch World*).

Flame Oath

A sacred oath of High Hallack, considered to be unbreakable. (*The Crystal Gryphon*).

Flathingdale

Dale of High Hallack, north of Ulmsdale. (*The Crystal Gryphon*).

Floating Weed

Seaweed which grows on the surface of warm seas near the Lost Trace. The Kolder used mutated Floating Weed as a first line of defence for their base. Merely a touch of the red-russet plant caused fast spreading scalds and in consequence a painful death. The mutated weeds would attach themselves to ships and grow around them. They also formed large floating barrier islands, and only the submarines of the Kolder could get past them until Jaelithe and Koityi Stymir discovered that the weeds could be burned. (*Web of the Witch World*).

Fold Gather

Possibly another name for a fair. Gillan speculated that Marimme's uncle (Lord Imgry) would take her to the next Fold Gather immediately after the war to find a husband for her. (*Year of the Unicorn*).

Fortal

Dalesman of High Hallack, lord of Paltendale prior to the war with Alizon. He was the father of Tephana, who married Ulric of Ulmsdale after her first husband died. (*The Crystal Gryphon*).

Freeza

Daleswoman of High Hallack, wife of Furlo. She became Gillan's foster mother and fled with her to Norstead Abbey during the war with Alizon, eight years prior to the Year of the Unicorn. Freeze died at the abbey. (*Year of the Unicorn*).

Fulk

Man of Karsten. Second son of Farthom, he became Lord of Verlaine through marriage but had only one child, a daughter, Loyse. Fulk was a shore baron in Karsten's hierarchy, not of much account in Loyse's reckoning. Fulk preyed on the ships which were wrecked on the coast of Verlaine, scheming to build his wealth and power. Fulk apparently also raided the lands of his neighbors, as Loyse privately hoped he might perish on one of these raids. He arranged for Loyse to be ax-wedded to Duke Yvian, ruler of Karsten, but was then killed by Simon, Jaelithe, and Koris. (*Witch World*).

Fulk's Hold

A name not used in the books. Fulk's fortress is referred to as a hold. The fortress sat atop a rise on a cliff. Between the hold and the cliff's edge there was a natural pasture where Fulk kept horses penned in. One or more paths led down the side of the cliffs to the rocky shores where Fulk's gleeners gathered up the debris of ship-wrecks caused by the storms off Verlaine's coast. (*Witch World*).

Furlo

Dalesman of High Hallack, lord of Thantop. He fostered Gillan. Furlo died in the war with Alizon. (*Year of the Unicorn*).

Fyndale

Dale in High Hallack, located to the south of Uppsdale. Fyndale held small fairs every year before the war with Alizon and restored the practice five years after the war.

Hagon

Dalesman of High Hallack. A trader who ventured into the Wastes, and perhaps an outlaw. He refused to divulge the sources of his finds to Riwal. (*The Crystal Gryphon*).

Halse

Were Rider. He tried to take Gillan away from Herrel. His totem was a bear. (*Year of the Unicorn*).

Halsfric

Man of Karsten. Bodyguard for Lady Aldis. (*Witch World*).

Hamel

Dalesman of High Hallack. Probably a kinsman or rival of Lord Marbon. (*Zarsthor's Bane*).

Harb

Dalesman of High Hallack, founder of Ithdale. Called Harb of the Broken Sword after he defeated the Demon of Irr Waste. (*The Crystal Gryphon*)

Harl

Were Rider. He married Kildas. (*Year of the Unicorn*).

Harrowdale

Dale of High Hallack, between Norsdale and Hockerdale. (*Year of the Unicorn*).

Herlwin

Man of Gorm, once known to Koris. Koris said he could hunt dangerous spear fish with only a knife. He was converted to a zombie-like warrior by the Kolder and used to attack the company of Magnis, Koris, Simon, and Jaelithe on their road to Sulcarkeep. Koris put his body to death. (*Witch World*).

Hilder

Man of Gorm. Lord Defender of Gorm and father of Koris. Hilder married a Tor woman, who bore him a son. After his Tor wife left him Hilder took another wife, Orna, a daughter of a trading family. She bore Hilder a second son, Uryan. When Koris was a grown man Hilder fell ill and after a long lingering died. (*Witch World*).

Hisin
Were Rider. Solfinna's husband. (*Year of the Unicorn*).

Hlymer
Dalesman of High Hallack, elder son of Tephana. He tried to murder Kerovan upon his return to Ulmsdale after Ulric's death. Hlymer was killed when Tephana called upon Dark power to stop Kerovan. (*The Crystal Gryphon*).

Hockerdale
Dale of High Hallack. Bordered Harrowdale on the borth. A stream or small river ran through the dale. Imgry had stationed a guard post in this dale at the end of the war with Alizon. (*Year of the Unicorn*).

Honey Brew
A name not used in the books. The villagers in Verlaine made a strong liqueur from honey and herbs which was so potent even a hard-drinking man like Fulk would fall asleep after the third tankard. (*Witch World*).

Hour of Great Silence, Last Light & Fifth Flame
Time markings in Abbey Norstead. (*Year of the Unicorn*).

Hulor
Were Rider. (*Year of the Unicorn*).

Hunold
Man of Karsten. Mercenary companion of Yvian. Lord Commander of Karsten under Yvian. He was one of three emissaries sent by Yvian to Verlaine for the Ax-marriage ceremony with Loyse. Jaelithe forced him to kill himself with his own dart pistol. (*Witch World*).

Huthart
Dalesman of High Hallack, Gwennan's brother. (*Spell of the Witch World*).

Hylle
Man of the Old Race, usurper of Quayth. He was an astrologer and alchemist who used amber to create a false amber that he used in his dealings with the Dark. He apparently desired Yaal, mistress of Quayth, and imprisoned her and Broc her lord. Hylle then assumed control over Quayth. He ventured into High Hallack after the war with Alizon, seeking new sources of amber. He married Ysmay of Uppsdale after he learned that the closed amber mine there was her dowry. Hylle returned to Quayth but in time was defeated by Ysmay, Broc, and Yaal. (*Spell of the Witch World*).

Hyron
Were Rider. Captain of the company, father of Herrel. Hyron's totem was an eagle. (*Year of the Unicorn*).

Ibycus

Man of the Old Race of Arvon. A user of Power, an Adept or near-Adept who served the Voices of Arvon and worked to maintain a balance between the forces of Light and Dark, or to tilt the balance in favor of Light. In High Hallack he was known as Neevor, and there he met and advised Kerovan. (*The Crystal Gryphon*).

Imgry

Dalesman of High Hallack. One of the Four Lords from southern High Hallack who led the defense of the Dales against Alizon. Imgry was ambitious and he eventually emerged as the most powerful of the Dales lords after the war. He reluctantly accepted Gillan as a bride for the Were Riders after learning of her deception (pretending to be Marimme, Imgry's niece. (*Year of the Unicorn* & *The Crystal Gryphon*).

Ingaret

First lord of Edale. (*Spell of the Witch World*).

Ingaret, House of

Descendants of Ingaret, the first lord of Edale. Franklyn and his daughter Brunissende (Elys' wife) were of the House of Ingaret. One of the Lords of Edale married a woman of the Old Race but spurned her. In retribution she cursed the house and drew off many men over the generations to their doom. (*Spell of the Witch World*).

Ingvald

Man of the Old Race of Karsten. Formerly a nobleman of Karsten, he took service with the Borderers under Simon Tregarth, rising to become an officer or Simon's Lieutenant. Ingvald perceived an alien intelligence behind the slaughter of the Old Race, which conclusion led Simon to document infiltration among Karsten's commanders. Ingvald's father and brother were slain in Karsten. Ingvald accompanied Simon on the mission to rescue Loyse from Duke Yvian. (*Witch World* & *Web of the Witch World*).

Insfar

Dalesman of High Hallack, shepherd in the Fourth Section of Ithdale. He escaped when the dale was invaded but was wounded. (*The Crystal Gryphon*).

Invincible, the

A sobriquet of Yvian, the prince of Karsten. (*Web of the Witch World*).

Islaugha

Daleswoman of High Hallack. Younger sister of Cyart. She married a daleslord and bore him two children, Toross and Yngilda. Although both Islaugha's husband and his dale are unnamed, he lived close enough to Ulmsdale to be familiar with the legends surrounding the House of Ulm. (*The Crystal Gryphon*).

Ithdale

Dale of High Hallack, located in the middle or low northern coastands. Ithdale was founded by Harb of the Broken Sword and was a pleasant, prosperous dale until Alizon invaded it. The inhabitants fled and dispersed throughout High Hallack. Ithdale was close to Trevamper and apparently was either located directly on the coast or on a navigable river. Ithdale was probably not as far north as Vestdale, which Ulric approached before he approached Cyart in warning High Hallack about the Alizonders. (*The Crystal Gryphon*).

Ithondale

Westernmost dale ruled by Vescys. (*Spell of the Witch World*).

Itsford

Dale of High Hallack, overrun by Alizon during the war. Dwed's father was the Marshal of Itsford. (*Zarsthor's Bane*).

Jacinda

Daleslady of High Hallack, daughter of Vescys. (*Spell of the Witch World*).

Jago

Dalesman of High Hallack, master of menie for Ulric of Ulmsdale until he was injured. Jago was given the task of teaching and warding Kerovan during his youth. (*The Crystal Gryphon*).

Jappon

Man of Karsten. Yvian's chef, who mastered the art of making boar in red wine, Yvian's favourite. (Web of the Witch World)

Jartar

Dalesman of High Hallack, Marbon's foster-brother. He fell in the Battle of Ungo Pass. He may have been of mixed blood, and was apparently a Wise Man. (*Zarsthor's Bane*).

Jivin

Guardsman of Estcarp. Said by Koris to be an excellent riding master. He rode to Sulcarkeep with Koris and survived the battle there, accompanying Koris and Simon to the Eyrie. From there he returned to Estcarp with Tunston. Jivin was able to catch fish with his bare hands. (*Witch World*).

Joisan

Daleswoman of High Hallack and Arvon. Niece of Cyart of Ithdale by his younger half-brother, Joisan was axe-wedded to Kerovan of Ulmsdale. (*The Crystal Gryphon*, *Gryphon's Eyrie* & *Warding of Witch World*).

Jokul
Man of unknown country. A seaman serving on the Wave Cleaver. Small, hunched man with brown, with brown, sunburnt and weather-beaten face, who was called by the captain, Koityi Stymir, to confirm the direction the ship headed. (*Web of the Witch World*).

Jothen
Man of Karsten. One of Hunold's armsmen. He aided in the capture of Jaelithe. (*Witch World*).

Kantha Twice Born, House of
An Abbey of the Flame in High Hallack. The abbey was overrun by Alizon during the war. Dame Wirtha (see Ulrica) came from this Abbey. (*Spell of the Witch World*).

Kantha Twice Born
Some personage, historical or imaginary, for whom one of the Abbeys of the Flame was named. The tradition may very well have been brought with the Dalesmen from their original world.

Karn
Man of the Old Race of Karsten. He joined the Borderers under Simon Tregarth after escaping from Karsten and proved to be one of Simon's best scouts. (*Witch World*).

Kars City
Chief city and capitol of Karsten, situated on the Kars river. The city had a port to which ships sailed up the river. (*Witch World*).

Kars River
Large river running west through Karsten toward the sea. A great deal of trade passed along the river, at least between Kars City and the sea. (*Witch World*).

Kathal
City, Eldor's stronghold in Varr. (*Zarsthor's Bane*).

Kerovan
Dalesman of High Hallack, warrior of the House from which Ulm and his descendants came. He was the namesake for Kerovan, son of Ulric. (*The Crystal Gryphon*).

Kerovan
Dalesman of High Hallack and Arvon, last rightful lord of Ulmsdale from Ulm's House. He was cursed through both parents' lines, and walked upon cloven hooves and had amber eyes. Kerovan was axe-wedded to Joisan of Ithkrypt before the war with Alizon. Tutored by a master armsman, Jago, raised by a forester, Kerovan was befriended by Riwal, an adventurer related

to Ulric's Head Forester, who often took Kerovan into the Wastes. Kerovan served in the war for several years, earning the respect of Lord Imgry. When Ulric died, Kerovan returned to Ulmsdale but was deposed by Tephana, Hlymer, and their kinsman Rogear of Paltendale. Kerovan went on to rescue Joisan, at first pretending to be one of the Old Ones. Eventually he earned her love and revealed his true identity to her. They travelled to Arvon, where they met Alyn and Jervon, reviving Landisl and working with Ibycus against the Dark. (*The Crystal Gryphon*, *Gryphon's Eyrie* & *Warding of Witch World*).

Kildas

Daleswoman of High Hallack, sister of Gralya. Sent to be one of the Were Rider brides. She married Harl. (*Year of the Unicorn*).

Witch World 1984 by John Pound

Koris

Man of Gorm. Commander of the Guards, Marshal and Seneschal of Estcarp. Son of Hilder by a Tor wife, Koris was not allowed by his step-mother Orna to succeed his father. Instead, he barely escaped from Gorm alive when the Kolder arrived to take over his land. Koris found his way to Estcarp, taking service with the Guards and rising to become their Captain. He befriended Simon Tregarth and took Simon with him when he went to Sulcarkeep to help defend the fortress against the Kolder. After Sulcarkeep was destroyed Koris and his men took ship with Simon and Jaelithe, but Koris and Simon's vessel was caught in a wild storm and dragged toward the coast north of Verlaine in Karsten. There Koris found and claimed the Axe of Volt, a great

81

weapon and talisman. He also met Loyse, daughter of Fulk, lord of Verlaine. Loyse joined Koris, Simon, and Jaelithe in their travels and she eventually married Koris. They had one son, Simond. After Simon and Jaelithe disappeared from Estcarp, Koris and Loyse protected their children, preventing the Witches from taking Kaththea to the Place of Wisdom. But eventually Koris was wounded and the Witches seized Kaththea after Loyse went to be with Koris. Koris in time recovered from his wounds but he could no longer bear the Axe of Volt. It was beieved among the Estcarpians that he made a special trip to Verlaine to return the Axe to Volt's tomb. Koris then returned to Estcarp, resumed command of the Guards, and eventually restored order to Estcarp after the Witches' nearly destroyed themselves in bringing about the Turning. Koris then became effective ruler of Estcarp, and he helped to establish relations with people in Escore, Alizon, High Hallack, and Arvon. Koris convened the great council that decided to destroy all the gates and he oversaw the progress of the various missions from Es City. (*Witch World*, *Web of the Witch World*, *Three Against the Witch World* & *Warding of Witch World*).

Kuniggod

Daleswoman of High Hallack. Brixia's nurse. After the death of Brixia's mother, Kuniggod ruled the household of the Lord of Morrachdale, and governed the dale after his death. She was sick with the Deep Chill when Moorachdale fell to the Alizonders, but she and Brixia escaped from the keep of Torgus before it was destroyed. Kuniggod was apparently a Wise Woman who was familiar with some places of the Old Ones in or near Moorachdale. She died soon after getting Brixia to safety. (*Zarsthor's Bane*).

Lalana

Woman of the Old Race or some other ancient kindred of Arvon. A guest at Eldor's table when Zarsthor confronted him over the Bane. (*Zarsthor's Bane*).

Langmar

Plant of unknown region and origin. When the stems were boiled they would give off a burnable oily substance that the Sulcar used for lamps during storms at sea. The oil was therefore highly flammable and did not mix well with water. (*Web of the Witch World*).

Langsdale

Dale, probably in northern High Hallack close to Uppsdale. Urian was lord of Langsdale during and after the war with Alizon. He gave his daughter in marriage to Gyrerd of Uppsdale. (*Spell of the Witch World*).

Lathor

Man of the Old Race of Karsten. He joined the Borderers under Simon Tregarth after escaping from Karsten and proved to be one of Simon's best scouts. (*Witch World*).

Lisana

Daleswoman of High Hallack, youngest child of Ulric. She was raised separately from Kerovan and supported her mother, Tephana, in her schemes. Lisana was destroyed when they tried to call upon Galkur to destroy Kerovan. (*The Crystal Gryphon*).

Llan, Challenge

A song celebrating the deeds of Torgus. Perhaps synonymous with the Song of Torgus. (*Zarsthor's Bane*).

Lonan

Dalesman of High Hallack. A soldier in Marbon's service. He suffered a wound that would not heal until Jartar brought herbs out of the wild to treat it. (*Zarsthor's Bane*).

Loquths

Reddish-purple plant whose flowers became bolls filled with a silk-like fiber. The plants were used by Estcarp's cloth-makers. Simon and Loyse found a field of Loquths in the Tor Marsh. (*Web of the Witch World*).

Lorlias

Daleswoman of High Hallack. A Dame of Norstead Abbey, she read the stars. (*The Crystal Gryphon*).

Lost Trace

An area of the southern seas filled with Floating Weed. Sulcar ships came to avoid the region after the weed was altered by the Kolder to attack ships. (*Web of the Witch World*).

Loyse

Woman of Karsten. Daughter of Fulk, lord of Verlaine. Loyse was unhappy in her father's household. She was axe-wedded to Duke Yvian, but managed to escape from the castle under the disguise of Briant, a blank-shield, setting free Jaelithe, with whom she went to Kars City and whom she assisted in a mission against Yvian. She met Koris while helping Jaelithe and she fell in love with him. Refusing to claim rule over the Duchy, Loyse forsook her homeland and went with Koris to Estcarp where they were married. She bore Koris a son, Simond, and assisted Koris in governing Estcarp and watching over the Tregarth children after Simon and Jaelithe vanished. But when Koris was wounded Loyse went to be with him and so left the Tregarth children unwarded. The Witches took Kaththea and Koris and Loyse were unable to retrieve her from the Place of Wisdom. (*Witch World*, *Web of the Witch World* & *Three Against the Witch World*).

Malwinna

Daleswoman of High Hallack. Former abbess of Norstead. She had learned the ways of Power and performed a Farseeing for Joisan. She also befriended

Gillan, and guessed at Gillan's heritage, but died three years before the Year of the Unicorn. (*The Crystal Gryphon*).

Mamer
Dalesman of High Hallack, merchant who sold ale at Fyndale's fair five years after the war with Alizon. (*Spell of the Witch World*).

Marbon
Dalesman of High Hallack, last lord of Eggarsdale. Marbon inherited some of the power of the Old Race and could speak with birds, calm horses, and sing wounded men to sleep. (*Zarsthor's Bane*).

Marc
Man of Karsten. One of Hunold's armsmen. He aided in the capture of Jaelithe. (*Witch World*).

Marchpoint
Town or dale in northern High Hallack, located near Uppsdale and Fyndale, possibly to the west. (*Spell of the Witch World*).

Marimme
Daleswoman of High Hallack, niece of Lord Imgry. She was to be sent as one of the thirteen brides of the Were Riders, but Sussia and Gillan arranged to have Gillan take her place. (*Year of the Unicorn*).

Martine
Daleswoman of High Hallack. She had married Alwin, the son of Ithkrypt's village headman, the year before Ithdale was invaded. She bore a son soon after escaping. (*The Crystal Gryphon*).

Master Trader
Title among the Sulcar. Magnis Osberic bore this title and it may be there was only one Master Trader at any time. (*Witch World*).

Math
Daleswoman of High Hallack. Sister of Cyart, lord of Ithdale. She was axe-wedded in her youth to a lord of the southern Dales, but he died before they met. Math then entered Abbey Nortsead but before taking the final vows of a Dame Cyart's wife died. Math returned to Ithdale to become mistress of the household. She oversaw Joisan's education. (*The Crystal Gryphon*).

Matild
Daleswoman of High Hallack, Dame in Ghyll. (*Spell of the Witch World*).

Midir
Man of Gorm, once known to Koris. Midir was a recruit in the Bodyguard of the Lord Defender of Gorm when the Kolder invaded the island. He was converted to a zombie-like warrior by the Kolder and used to attack the

company of Magnis, Koris, Simon, and Jaelithe on their road to Sulcarkeep. Koris put his body to death. (*Witch World*).

Midwinter Feast

A feast in High Hallack. Betrothals were sometimes celebrated at this feast. (*Spell of the Witch World*).

Moorachdale

Dale of High Hallack, located in the south. Ruled by the House of Torgus until the war with Alizon, when the dale was overrun. Although in southern High Hallack, Moorachdale was close enough to Norsdale for Kuniggod to visit the Abbey twice a year. (*Zarsthor's Bane*).

Moycroft

Dale of northern High Hallack. Moycroft was abandoned during the war with Alizon because of a lack of manpower. (*Spell of the Witch World*).

Nalda

Daleswoman of High Hallack. Wife of Stark, Ithdale's miller. She escaped with a small party of survivors when Ithdale was overrun. (*The Crystal Gryphon*).

Nalin

Falconer. He was a sentry on the border between the lands of the Eyrie and Karsten, and he encountered Koris, Simon, Jivin, and Tunston, giving them safe passage to the Eyrie. (*Witch World*).

Name-day

Personal anniversary in High Hallack, apparently celebrating the day of a child's naming. It was customary (at least among the noble families) to give gifts to loved ones on their name-days. (*The Crystal Gryphon*).

Neevor

See, Ibycus.

Nicala

Daleswoman of High Hallack, wife of Arnar. She is referred to as a mill-woman. (*Spell of the Witch World*).

Ninque

Woman of the Old Race, sorceress in Quayth, ally and servant of Hylle. (*Spell of the Witch World*).

Nolon

Dalesman of High Hallack. Apparently a nobleman, his house is not mentioned. He served Ulric of Ulmsdale, negotiating the marriage of Kerovan and Joisan and standing in as Kerovan's proxy at the axe-wedding. (*The Crystal Gryphon*).

Nornan

A name by which Koris swore he would not seek to rule in Gorm. (*Witch World*).

Norsdale

Dale of High Hallack. Located five days west of Ithdale, it was east of Falthingdale and bordered on the north by Harrowdale. The Arm of Sparn, a rock outcropping, marked the northern border. Abbey Norstead was located in this dale. Many refugees from the coastal Dales fled to Norsdale and Abbey Norstead during the war with Alizon. (*Year of the Unicorn* & *The Crystal Gryphon*).

Norsdale, Village of

Unnamed village with an inn where men visiting Abbey Norstead were accustomed to stay. (*Year of the Unicorn*).

Norstead

Abbey of the Flame in High Hallack. Probably the largest and most renowned of the Abbeys. Being far removed from the sea, Norstead was a popular refuge for the wives and daughters of many of the noble houses of High Hallack during the war with Alizon. Lord Imgry assembled the thirteen brides there who were to be given to the Were Riders in payment for their service against Alizon. (*Year of the Unicorn* & *The Crystal Gryphon*).

Oath of Sword and Shield, Blood and Bread

An oath Koris called upon to win acceptance and hospitality from among the Falconers. This was apparently a warrior's oath sworn between friends or allies. (*Witch World*).

Orna

Woman of Gorm. Second wife of Hilder, mother of Uryan. She conspired with the nobles of Gorm to supplant Koris and put Uryan in his place as Lord Defender. Because Uryan was still a child when Orna assumed control of Gorm she was able to impose her will, but eventually she saw the need for powerful allies and summoned the Kolder to back her. She and all her people were then enslaved by the Kolder. (*Witch World*).

Osberic Anner

Man of the Sulcar. Leader of the Sulcarmen after the death of his father, Magnis, who died defending the Sulcarkeep. (*Web of the Witch World*).

Osberic, Magnis

Man of the Sulcar. Master Trader, leader of the Sulcar and lord of Sulcarkeep when Simon Tregarth first entered the Witch World. Magnis rode to Estcarp to get help from the Witches, but when he returned to Sulcarkeep the Kolder invaded from the air. Magnis ordered his people to abandon their home. He set off the explosives which destroyed the fortress and prevented the Kolder from using it as a base against Estcarp. (*Witch World*).

Over Guardian

A mystical force, perhaps, referred to by Jaelithe when she said to Simon, "...our two strands of life stuff have been caught up together by the Hand of the Over Guardian." Perhaps a euphemism for God, a supreme being. (*Witch World*).

Oxtor, Fangs of

Named in a curse or oath. Perhaps a reference to a demon, real or mythical, in High Hallack's folklore. (*Zarsthor's Bane*).

Paltendale

Dale of northwestern High Hallack, home to people of mixed blood (see Borderers). The Dalesmen of this land were often shunned by other men of High Hallack. (*The Crystal Gryphon*).

Peace of the Highways

Custom by which Sulcar traders were allowed free travel through foreign lands unmolested. The peace was most established in stable lands such as Estcarp and probably High Hallack, but was less certain in lands such as Alizon and Karsten. (*Witch World*).

Pole of Proclamation

Decrees were given by messengers from the Duke of Karsten in the shadow of these poles. The thrice horning of the Old Race was performed by Poles of Proclamation. (*Witch World*).

Power Projector

The source of light and heat for Sulcarkeep, and the means by which Magnis Osberic destroyed the city. It apparently had a core of pure energy, or something which radiated energy. (*Witch World*).

Quayth

Coastal domain north of High Hallack, apparently a remnant of the ancient Arvonic culture. Broc and Yaal ruled Quaythy until Hylle trapped them and seized power. After he brought Ysmay back as his wife, Hylle was overcome by Ysmay, Broc, and Yaal (whom Ysmay freed). (*Spell of the Witch World*).

Randor

Dalesman of High Hallack, lord of Ithdale. He was the father of Cyart, Math, Islaugha, and Joisan's father. He harbored a Wise Woman who journeyed through the Waste and roused the fear of Ithdale's people. When Randor went off to Trevamper his people tried to burn out the Wise Woman, but he returned in time to save her. In gratitude she blessed Randor's unborn child (Cyart) with a foreseeing ability to aid him in times of trouble. (*The Crystal Gryphon*).

Rangers
Men of Karsten, servants of Fulk. Their duties are not certain, but they required horses. (*Witch World*).

Rathkas
Were Rider's horse, given by Herrel to Gillan. (*Year of the Unicorn*).

Renston
Man of the Old Race of Karsten. He had been blood brothers with Garnit and his brother. They were captured by Yvian's men, the leader of whom killed Renston since he could not be sold as a slave to the Kolder. (*Witch World*).

Rishdale
Dale of High Hallack, apparently in the southern mountains, called an upper dale. Rishdale specialized in wool. Rishdale was one of the first dales invaded and overrun by Alizon. (*The Crystal Gryphon*).

Rishdale, House of
Lords of Rishdale. Their emblem was a serpent. (*The Crystal Gryphon*).

Riwal
Dalesman of High Hallack. A Wiseman from Ulmsdale, Riwal was related to Ulric's Head Forester. Riwal raised herbs and helped the farmers of Ulmsdale raise good crops. The countryfold went to Riwal with all their illnesses, as he was an herbmaster of superb skill and lore. He befriended Kerovan and took him into the Wastes, where Kerovan eventualy discovered the Crystal Grphon. (*The Crystal Gryphon*).

Rogear
Dalesman of High Hallack. A member of the House of Paltendale, Rogear was hand-fasted to Lisana, Ulric's daughter and youngest child. He schemed with Tephana to gain control of Ulmsdale by killing Kerovan and marrying Lisana. After destroying Ulmsport in an effort to defeat Alizon, he parted company with Tephana and the others and found his way to Joisan. Rogear briefly assumed Kerovan's identity, but Kerovan unmasked him. Stealing Joisan away, Rogear rejoined his kinsfolk but perished trying to destroy Kerovan. (*The Crystal Gryphon*).

Romsgarth
A small town of Estcarp with a marketplace for the local community. Situated a few miles from the cove where the Kolder ship which seized Loyse of Verlaine anchored. (*Web of the Witch World*).

Roshan
Were Rider's horse, Herrel's mount. (*Year of the Unicorn*).

Rudo

Dalesman of High Hallack. He was an armsman from Toross' dale who went to Ithdale with Toross, Islaugha, and Yngilda. (*The Crystal Gryphon*).

Runner

A type of Sulcar ship, apparently used for fast travelling. They could go armed or unarmed and were undoubtedly used for trade whenever possible. (*Witch World*).

Samian...

Magnis Osberic mentioned a "necklace of Samian fashioning" lying amid the hoard of Sulcarkeep. Samia may have been the name of a race or nation with whom the Sulcar traded. (*Witch World*).

Santu

Man of the Old Race of Karsten. He joined the Borderers under Simon Tregarth after escaping from Karsten. (*Witch World*).

Savron

Dalesman of High Hallack, lord of Uppsdale in Ulric's day. He was probably the father of Gyrerd, Ewald, and Ysmay. Savron heeded Ulric's warnings about Alizon and attended Kerovan's first arming, which event served as an excuse for the northern lords to meet without rousing suspicion among the Alizonder spies. Savron was killed during the war. (*The Crystal Gryphon*).

Sharvana

Wise Woman of High Hallack. She lived in Ghyll during Vescys' time.

Year of the Unicorn 1989 by John Pound

Shaver

Dalesman of High Hallack. Probably a kinsman or rival of Lord Marbon. (*Zarsthor's Bane*).

Shrine, the

Apparently an Abbey of the Flame, in or near Uppsdale. (*Spell of the Witch World*).

Sigrod

Man of the Sulcar. A marine serving on the Wave Cleaver, who together with his mate Ynglin transported Jaelithe to the island base of Kolder. (*Web of the Witch World*).

Sippar

Largest city and capitol of Gorm. Sippar had a large port and many warehouses, and the Lord Defender lived in a palace. (*Witch World*).

Siric

Man of Karsten, priest in the Temple of Fortune in Kars City. Siric was one of three envoys sent by Yvian to the ax-marriage ceremony with Loyse. Siric was probably murdered by Fulk after Loyse escaped with Jaelithe. (*Witch World*).

Skirkar

One of the Four Lords who united High Hallack against Alizon. He died heirless. Since the Four Lords came from the south, he was a southern Dales lord. (*Spell of the Witch World*).

Solfinna

Daleswoman of High Hallack, from Wasscot Keep. She came of an impoverished house that received favors from Imgry in exchange for her becoming one of the Were Rider brides. Solfinna had at least two sisters. She married the Were Rider Hisin. (*Year of the Unicorn*).

South Ridges

Hills or mountains in southern High Hallack where iron was mined. Savron of Uppsdale consulted with a miner from South Ridges in hopes of re-opening the amber mine of Uppsdale. (*Spell of the Witch World*).

SouthKeep

The fotress headquarters of the Border Warder of the South -- Simon Tregarth and his wife Jaelithe. SouthKeep was the chief garrison of the Borderers, who were recruited mostly from the Old Race refugees from Karsten. The keep was situated four hours by horse from the seashore. (*Web of the Witch World*).

Spearfish

Apparently a large, dangerous fish found near Gorm. It was considered dangerous or at least risky for a man to face one with only a knife. (*Witch World*).

Stark

Dalesman of High Hallack. Ithdale's miller. Apparently killed when the dale was overrun. (*The Crystal Gryphon*).

Stone of Engis

Talisman or ancient shrine named by Caluf in an oath to assure Simon he was certain of a report he had made. (*Witch World*).

Strange Place

A cavern underneath Fulk's clifftop fortress in Verlaine. Jaelithe identified it as a place of power where old gods had been worshipped a thousand years or more in the past. (*Witch World*).

Stymir, Koityi

Man of the Sulcar, captain of a Sulcar cruiser Wave Cleaver. Tall, well-built, with broad shoulders and light hair, young but already having some successes on his account. He agreed to follow the Kolder submarine in which Simon Tregarth and Loyse of Verlaine were imprisoned. (*Web of the Witch World*).

Sul

The name cried aloud by the Sulcar warriors when they went into battle. (*Witch World* & *Web of the Witch World*).

Sulcar

Seafaring men who entered Witch World through a gate in the northern seas. Their own world was used as a refuge by a race so foreign to them the Sulcar tried to destroy them. But the aliens were too powerful and the Sulcar were themselves nearly destroyed. An Adept of Witch World opened a gate for a small fleet of Sulcar ships to escape through. The Sulcar then established themselves as renowned traders throughout Witch World, earning respect and a repuation for fairness and bravery unmatched by other peoples. But they chose their friends carefully and entered into alliances with the Falconers, the Old Race of Estcarp, and the Dalesmen of High Hallack. Some of the Sulcar may have fallen into a barbaric or near-savage state, perhaps being cut off from their main enclaves. These groups seem to have harried the eastern coasts of Escore. The Sulcar eventually built Sulcarkeep on a peninsula to the west of Estcarp and from their conducted their trade throughout the world. When Sulcarkeep was destroyed new enclaves were established in other lands but the chief group seems to have settled under Anner Osberic in Es Port. The Sulcar assisted in searching for gates and destroying them. (*Witch World*, *Web of the Witch World* & *Warding of Witch World*).

Sulcarkeep

Vast fotress city situated on the peninsula to the west of Estcarp, built in the day of Magnis Osberic's great-grandfather to be a haven in time of storm and war for the Sulcar and their ships. Sulcarkeep was built of solid stone and masonry and took advantage of the natural outlines of a promontory jutting out into the sea. Gongs seem to have been positioned around the perimeter of the fortress to warn ships of impending peril during times of fog. Sulcarkeep was filled with many warehouses, and Magnis boasted that every pirate and lordling in Witch World dreamed of looting the city. The Sulcar always manned the fortress but had prepared its power projector (q.v.) against the need to destroy Sulcarkeep should it ever be taken. This proved to be the fate of Sulcarkeep during the Kolder War. Magnis Osberic destroyed Sulcarkeep when the Kolder overran it. (*Witch World*).

Sussia

Daleswoman of High Hallack, last of her immediate line. Sussia's homeland was situated on the coast of High Hallack and was one of the first to fall to Alizon. She was harbored in Abbey Norstead, but at war's end her surviving kinsmen betrothed her to prevent her being sent to the Were Riders. Sussia confided in Gillan as the time of payment grew near. (*Year of the Unicorn*).

Sword Bride

A Sulcar ship which brought provisions for Estcarp's army from the south to Es Port. Koityi Stymir took some of these provisions aboard the Wave Cleaver when he accepted Jaelithe's commission to follow the Kolder submarine carrying Simon Tregarth and Loyse. (*Web of the Witch World*).

Sym

Town in High Hallack, possibly ruled by Vescys before the war with Alizon. (*Spell of the Witch World*).

Talisman, Kolder

A device Aldis used to track Loyse and monitor her thoughts. (*Web of the Witch World*).

Tandis

Falconer. He served as a marine on Sulcar ships for five years. During the Kolder war he accompanied Faltjar on a mission to the coast and was captured by the same Kolder who took Simon Tregarth prisoner. (*Witch World*).

Temp of Fortune

Temple in Kars City. (*Witch World*).

Temple Brotherhood

A religious organization of Karsten. Siric was apparently a member of it. (*Witch World*).

Tephana

Daleswoman of High Hallack, third wife of Ulric. Tephana shunned Kerovan, her second son and first child by Ulric, because of his hooves. She had called upon the Darl Adept Galkur to give her a tool to fulfill her ambitions, but did not understand that Gunnora and Landisl interfered with the spell until too late. She bore a second child to Ulric, a daughter named Lisana. Tephana schemed to gain control of Ulmsdale for her kinsman Rogear, but the invasion by Alizon upset her plans. Tephana helped defeat the fleet of Alizonders threatening Ulmsdale but Ulmsport was destroyed in the process. Tephana was destroyed when she called upon Dark power to destroy Kerovan. (*The Crystal Gryphon*).

Thantop

Dale of High Hallack. Thantop was a small coastal dale ruled by Furlo before the war with Alizon. He traded with the Sulcar. Thantop was apparently overrun by Alizon. (*Year of the Unicorn*).

That Which Abides

Some power or powers to which Gillan made reference with respect to unseen movers and planners of the future fate of Men. (*Year of the Unicorn*).

Those Who Have Set The Flames

Whatever powers the Dalesfolk of High Hallack attributed as the source of their sacred Flames. (*Year of the Unicorn*).

Thrice Horning

A sentence of death, declaring an open warrant on anyone so designated. Duke Yvian had the Old Race thrice horned in vengeance for the loss of his envoys and bride. He was probably motivated by Kolder to do this. (*Witch World*).

Timon

Dalesman of High Hallack. Son of Nalda and Stark. He escaped when Ithdale was overrun by Alizon. (*The Crystal Gryphon*).

Tolfana

Daleswoman of High Hallack. She was sheltered in Abbey Norstead during the war with Alizon. (*Year of the Unicorn*).

Torgus

Dalesman, perhaps of High Hallack. Ancestor of Brixia. He defeated the Power of Llan's Stone, whatever that was. Also called Trogus. (*Zarsthor's Bane*).

Torgus, House of

Descendants of Torgus. Lords of Moorachdale, a small dale in southern High

Hallack. It appears that the family was wiped out in the war with Alizon, except for Brixia. (*Zarsthor's Bane*).

Torgus, Song of

Song celebrating the deeds of Torgus against the Power of Llan's Stone. (*Zarsthor's Bane*).

Toross

Dalesman of High Hallack. Son of Islaugha. He visited Ithdale in the autumn time, assisting in the hunts which helped build up the winter stores for Ithkrypt. He befriended Joisan and desired to inherit the lordship of Ithdale. Toross was killed in the war with Alizon. He was said to be very handsome and much admired by young women. (*The Crystal Gryphon*).

Tregarth, Jaelithe

*Jaelithe Tregarth
by Sally C. Fink*

Woman of the Old Race of Estcarp. A witch, one of the most powerful of the Estcarpian witches of her day. Jaelithe undertook dangerous missions against Estcarp's enemies and met Simon Tregarth while fleeing the Hounds of Alizon. She was paired up with him again later in actions the Witches took against Gorm and the Kolder, and went with Simon to Karsten, Gorm, and the Kolder Nest. Jaelithe eventually decided to give up her place among the Witches and marry Simon. For this she was cast out from their order and treated poorly. Jaelithe bore three children at one birth: Kyllan, Kemoc, and Kaththea, foretelling their fates: warrior, warlock, witch. Before the children were fully grown Jaelithe followed Simon out of Estcarp and into another world. Eventually they were reunited with the grown Kaththea, who had fled from the Witches, and they returned with her and the Adept Hilarion to the Witch World. Staying in Escore a short time to assist in the war against the rising Dark, Jaelithe and Simon eventually returned to Estcarp. There they assisted in the final great effort to close all the gates after while power started opening them.

Jaelithe was tall, slim, and had long black silky hair. (*Witch World*, *Web of the*

Witch World, *Three Against the Witch World*, *Sorceress of the Witch World*, *The Magestone* & *Warding of Witch World*).

Tregarth, Simon

Man from Earth. His family originally came from Cornwall, but Tregarth was born in Matacham, Pennsylvania. He served in the U.S. Army during World War II, rose to the rank of Lieutenant Colonel, but was discharged for dealing on the black market after the war. Simon worked for a man named Hanson, apparently in charge of a criminal organization, but eventually crossed him and had to flee for his life. He met George Petronius, keeper of the Siege Perilous, and used that device to open a gateway to the Witch World.

Simon Tregarth
by Sally C. Fink

Tregarth entered Estcarp through a gate in southern Alizon near the border. He took service with the Witches of Estcarp and fought against the Kolder, travelling to Gorm, Karsten, and eventually the island where the Kolder Nest was established. Simon married the witch Jaelithe, who bore him three children: Kyllan, Kemoc, and Kaththea. Tregarth was given a command over the Borderers, special forces watching the marches with Karsten. In time, Simon left Estcarp to investigate rumors of a Kolder base. When no word came back from Simon, Jaelithe followed him. They passed to another world and were eventually reunited with their grown daughter Kaththea, who had followed the Adept Hilarion to a technological world devastated by a terrible war. Simon, Jaelithe, Kaththea, and Hilarion returned to the Witch World through Hilarion's gate. There they became embroiled in Escore's ancient wars, but with aid from Hilarion they eventually helped turn the tide in favor of the Light and Simon and Jaelithe eventually returned to Estcarp.

When the Magestone was taken from the Witch World, and gates began opening wildly, Simon and Jaelithe assisted in locating and closing several gates. (*Witch World*, *Web of the Witch World*, *Three Against the Witch World*, *Sorceress of the Witch World*, *The Magestone* & *Warding of Witch World*).

Trevamper

Town or city in northern High Hallack. Merchants held fairs there every year which many people from the northern Dales attended. Trevamper was located at a crossing of a highway and a river. The river leading to Trevamper was navigable, and the trade there was of sufficient volume to attract Sulcar ships. (*Spell of the Witch World* & *The Crystal Gryphon*).

Tunston

Man of the Old Race of Estcarp. Koris' second-in-command over the Guards of Estcarp. He rode to Sulcarkeep with Koris, survived the battle for the city, and accompanied Koris and Simon to the Eyrie. From there he returned to Estcarp with Jivin. Tunston eventually served in the force which assaulted Gorm, and was one of the twenty Guards and Sulcar who accompanied Simon Tregarth on his assault of the fortress of Sippar. (*Witch World*).

Twyford

Town or trading place in Vescys' lands. Possibly a port. (*Spell of the Witch World*).

Ulm

Dalesman, founder and lord of Ulmsport. Called the Horn-handed. Father of Ulric. Ulm looted treasure from a place of the Old Ones. He and all the men with him on that expedition took sick, and most of them died. Ulm chartered the sea-rovers who founded Ulmsport, apparently merchants who needed a port-city of their own. (*The Crystal Gryphon*).

Ulm, House of

Lords of Ulmsdale, establied by Ulm, who was apparently a younger son of an older noble house. Their emblem was the Gryphon on a green field. (*The Crystal Gryphon*).

Ulmsdale

Dale in northern High Hallack, north of Vestdale, east of Fyndale, south of Flathingdale. Ulmsdale was first settled by Ulm, grandfather of Kerovan. The chief city was Ulmsport, which became a major trading center. Ulmsdale was one of the ports visited by Alizonder ships prior to the war, and a Wise Woman of Ulmsdale discovered the Alizonders were planning to invade High Hallack. During the war with Alizon, Ulmsdale was invaded and Tephana tried unsuccessfully to defend it with Dark power. Ulmsdale may have been resettled after the war with Alizaon. (*The Crystal Gryphon* & *Spell of the Witch World*).

Ulmsdale Keep

Fortress in Ulmsdale, home of the Lords of Ulmsdale. (*The Crystal Gryphon*).

Ulmsport

City of northern High Hallack, a major seaport, capitol of Ulmsdale. Founded by Ulm approximately fifty years before the war with Alizon. Ulmsport was destroyed during the war with Alizon. Before the war Ulmsport hosted fairs. The lord of Marchpoint (Dairine's father) met his wife at a fair in Ulmsport. Ulmsport may have been rebuilt after the war. (*Spell of the Witch World* & *The Crystal Gryphon*).

Ulric

Dalesman of High Hallack, lord of Ulmsdale. He was the son of Ulm. All of Ulric's children by his first two wives were either stillborn or died young. Ulric finally married Tephana of Paltendale about nineteen years before the war with Alizon (he was middle-aged). Their son was Kerovan, named for an ancestor or relative of a generation prior to Ulm's coming to Ulmsdale. Ulric tried to warn the lords of High Hallack of the impending invasion but he was unable to marshal sufficient forces to defeat the initial onsloughts of the Alizonders. Ulric was killed during the invasion. (*The Crystal Gryphon*).

Ulrica

Wise Woman of High Hallack. She served in the House of Kantha Twice Born, one of the Abbeys of the Flame. Also called Dame Wirtha. (*Spell of the Witch World*).

Uncar

Falconer. He accompanied Simon Tregarth and Koris when they captured Fulk of Verlaine. (*Web of the Witch World*).

Ungo, Pass of

Place in High Hallack where a battle was fought in the war with Alizon.

Uppsdale

Dale in northern High Hallack. About 40 years before the war with Alizon Uppsdale had an active amber mine, but a rock slide closed it. The mine was then passed through the daughters of the House of Uppsdale as a dowry, although it seemed to have no value. Hylle the Usurper from Quayth married Ysmay and re-opened the mine. See also Savron, Ysmay, Hylle, Quayth, Langsdale. (*Spell of the Witch World*).

Urian

Daleslord High Hallack, lord of Langsdale. He apparently fought against Alizon during the war, and married his daughter Annet to Gyrerd of Uppsdale. (*Spell of the Witch World*).

Uryan

Man of Gorm. Younger son of Hilder, only child of Orna. Uryan was set up in his brother's place by Orna after the death of Hilder but he did not live long enough to seize and enjoy the power for himself. (*Witch World*).

Uta

Cat, Brixia's companion. Probably the same Uta whom Kethan freed and married. (*Zarsthor's Bane*).

Varr

Domain of Eldor, situated in the lands which were abandoned by Arvon to become part of the Waste. (*Zarsthor's Bane*).

Verlaine

Coastal province of Karsten which grew rich on salvage from the sea. Fulk married into the Line of Verlaine and developed ambitions for increasing his power throughout Karsten by marrying his daughter, Loyse, to Duke Yvian. (*Witch World* & *Web of the Witch World*).

Vescys

Dales lord in High Hallack. He ruled many dales before the war with Alizon. (*Spell of the Witch World*).

Vestdale

Dale of High Hallack. Apparently located along the middle to northern coast. Vestdale, also called Vastdale, contained Jorby (also called Jurby), one of the chief trading cities of High Hallack. Vastdale was one of the first to be invased by Alizon. Wark was a client dale ruled by the lords of Vastdale. (*The Crystal Gryphon* & *Spell of the Witch World*).

Volt

Last survivor of a pre-human race on Witch World. He took pity on the primitive men of the Old Race and taught them wisdom and lore. Volt possessed great power and he warred against some human tribes or nations whom he deemed to be evil. His final resting place was a cave north of Verlaine where Simon and Koris found him. Volt's weapon was the ax, and Koris upon finding Volt's weapon intact claimed it. (*Witch World*).

Vortgin

Man of the Old Race. A servant or soldier in the service of Lord Vortimer, Estcarp's ambassador to Karsten. Vortimer sent Vortgin to warn Jaelithe of the thrice horning. Vortgin accompanied Jaelithe, Simon, Koris, and Loyse north out of Kars city. He helped rouse the Old Race into flight from Karsten. (*Witch World*).

Vortimer

Man of the Old Race of Estcarp. A nobleman from an ancient house, Vortimer was the last ambassador of Estcarp to Karsten. When Yvian was told that a raid from Estcarp was responsible for the deaths of his envoys and bride, he ordered the thrice-horning of all Estcarp's people in Karsten and Karsten's Old Race families. Vortimer gathered as many of Estcarp's people as he could into the tower that served as the embassy and he destroyed it with them all inside. (*Witch World*).

Wager discs

Coin-like objects with radiating markings used for gambling in Karsten. The mark pointing away from the thrower was used as the betting value. After one thrower established his value the discs would be passed to another thrower. The higher value won the wager. Fulk and Hunold used Wager discs to determine who would take Jaelithe's innocence. (*Witch World*).

Waldis

Man of the Old Race of Karsten. As a boy he served in Ingvald's household and escaped from Karsten, tracking down Ingvald and joining the Borderers under Simon Tregarth. He accompanied Simon Tregarth and Koris of Gorm when they followed Loyse to Verlaine. (*Witch World* & *Web of the Witch World*).

Wark

Dale of High Hallack, situated on the coast and subject to Vestdale. Truan and Almondia settled here after fleeing Estcarp. (*Spell of the Witch World*).

Warnings

In the mainland of Estcarp the warnings and alarm signals were transmitted by liaison-witches, who sent them by thoughts to their sisters in Es city. In the south-western part of the country, too distant from the centre, where the watch-towers were small and often provisional, light signals were used, passed on by a system of observation-towers established on top of the hills. (*Web of the Witch World*).

Wasscot Keep

Home of Solfinna, one of the thirteen Were Rider brides. Apparently Wasscot's dale was located in northern High Hallack, as the prospect of marrying a southern dales lord or captain would have meant much the same for Solfinna as leaving High Hallack: never seeing her kin again. (*Year of the Unicorn*).

Waste, the

Forbidding land to the west of High Hallack and the south of Arvon. Much of the Waste is arid semi-desert or scrub land, but there are some small woods and forests scattered across it. Once inhabited by the Old Race and others, the Waste appears to have been created by the effects of the ancient wars of the Adepts. Outlaws and adventurers, as well as some Exiles of Arvon, lived in the Waste. (*The Crystal Gryphon* & *Year of the Unicorn*).

Wave Cleaver

Sulcar cruiser, small, fast and manoeuvrable ship, whose captain was Koityi Stymir. The Wave Cleaver followed the Kolder submarine which had captured Simon Tregarth and Loyse of Verlaine, and it was the first ship to find a way through the Floating Weed surrounding the Kolder Nest. (*Web of the Witch World*).

Wintof

Dalesman of High Hallack, lord of Flathingdale in Ulric's day. He attended Kerovan's first arming. (*The Crystal Gryphon*).

Wise Woman of Kars

Persona assumed by Jaelithe on her missions to Karsten. She maintained a large house in of the seedier parts of the city, selling love potions and charms as a way of meeting people with the information she sought. In this persona Jaelithe gained access to Duke Yvian's chambers through Lady Aldis. (*Witch World*).

Witches

Women, usually of the Old Race, with Talent. The Witches of Estcarp were an ancient order, established after the Adepts of Escore nearly destroyed themselves and all others with their insane wars and gates. The Witches blamed the male Adepts for the disastrous war and forbade men to learn or use the Talent. They, however, used their own considerable powers to raise the mountains between Estcarp and Escore and to block the minds of their people so they would not think of the East and the ancient past. The Witches established a refuge, the Place of Wisdom, where they trained young girls of the Old Race. The restriction placed upon Witches was celibacy, and the slow extraction of women with Talent from the Old Race of Estcarp eventually resulted in a decline of Witch-stock among the Old Race of that land. They were reinforced by refugees from Karsten but when invasion from the south became eminent the Witches used their powers to again raise the mountains and destroy Pager's army. However this mighty deed devastated the Witches' ranks, as many died or became burned out husks incapable of using the Power again. Bereft of their great pool of strength and Talent, the Witches lost control of Estcarp to Koris of Gorm, their Seneschal, who assumed responsibility for governing Estcarp. The Witches recovered their numbers slowly and a new generation of leaders guided the councils in the Place of Wisdom to work with Hilarion, Simon and Jaelithe Tregarth, and other users of Power to help close the gates. The Witches of Estcarp were considered formiddable adversaries and were renowned throughout the Witch World for their great Talent. They concluded alliances with the Falconers and Sulcarmen which proved beneficial to both Estcarp and the allied races, especially as the Sulcar provded to be the only people with whom the Old Race could intermarry and produce children. (*Witch World*, *Web of the Witch World*, *Three Against the Witch World*, *Warlock of the Witch World*, *Sorceress of the Witch World*, Witch World: The Turning, *The Magestone* & *Warding of Witch World*).

Worship of the Cleansing Flame

the religion of the Dames of the Abbeys of High Hallack. This tradition was apparently brought by the Dalesfolk from their original world, and its adherents often clashed with the traditions taken up by the common people under the influence of the Exiles of Arvon. (*The Crystal Gryphon*).

Yaal

Lady of the Old Race, lady of Quayth. Yaal was desired by Hylle but she was faithful to Broc, her husband. Imprisoned with Broc by Hylle, Yaal hid a serpent talisman in the keep that Ysmay found and used to free them. She accepted Ysmay as a sister-in-spirit after Hylle was destroyed. (*Spell of the Witch World*).

Yle

Kolder city, situated on the southern shore of a peninsula dividing Estcarp from Karsten. After Sippar's defeat it became surrounded with a force field. Though built of native Estcarpian stone and not of metal, it was somehow separated from the land it stood on in Simon Tregarth's perception. (*Web of the Witch World*).

Yngilda

Daleswoman of High Hallack. Daughter of Cyart's youngest sister Islaugha, and was married to Elvan of Rishdale. She was impoverished by the war with Alizon after Rishdale was overrun. (*The Crystal Gryphon*).

Ynglin

Man of the Sulcar. A young marine serving at the Wave Cleaver who together with his mate Sigrod transported Jaelithe to the island base of Kolder. (*Web of the Witch World*).

Yonan

Lord of a southern dale in High Hallack. (*Spell of the Witch World*).

Yrugo

Dalesman of High Hallack, Marshal of Ulmsdale. He was Jago's successor and rode to war with Kerovan when Ulric sent a force to help the southern Dales. (*The Crystal Gryphon*).

Ysmay

Daleswoman of High Hallack, from Uppsdale, sister of Gyrerd and Ewald. Ysmay inherited an amber amulet and the amber mine of Uppsdale as her dowry. She governed Uppsdale during the war with Alizon but after Gyrerd returned with Annet Ysmay was relegated to meaningless tasks by Annet. Ysmay alone was made responsible for the herb garden in the keep since only she could raise the herbs properly. After five years she married Hylle the Usurper out of Quayth and went there to live with him, but in time freed

Broc and Yaal, the rightful rulers of Quayth. Ysmay stayed with Broc and Yaal after Hylle was destroyed. (*Spell of the Witch World*).

Yulianna

Daleswoman of High Hallack. Dame of Abbey Norstead, successor of Malwinna as Abbess. She presided over the Abbey in the Year of the Unicorn and allowed Gillan to accompany the Were Rider brides without protest. (*Year of the Unicorn*).

Yvian

Man of Karsten. An apparent orphan, he embarked upon a mercenary career that culminated in his seizing control of Karsten and proclaiming himself Duke. For ten years Yvian fought off resentful nobles until he arranged for a marriage with Loyse of Verlaine. Her maternal line was old and respected and he hoped to establish some legitimacy through the marriage. He also hoped to build a port in Verlaine to compete with Sulcarkeep for the northern trade. He was killed by Koris.

Yvian had a sharp, pointed chin and light, bushy eyebrows. (*Witch World* & *Web of the Witch World*).

Zarsthor

Dalesman, ancestor of the Lords of Eggarsdale. Formely lord of An-Yak, he married a woman of the Old Race and settled in Eggarsdale. But Zarsthor roused the anger of his brother-in-law, Eldor, who called upon the Dark Power to curse Zarsthor and all his line. Zarsthor had a powerful sword which was used against him to his undoing. When he learned that Eldor plotted against him, Zarsthor confronted his brother-in-law. An-Yak was cursed and Zarsthor appaently fled to High Hallack, but his spirit seems to have been irretrievably bound to Eldor's. (*Zarsthor's Bane*).

Web of the Witch World 1983 by John Pound

Natural Races
by Michael Martinez

Old Race

Appearance: Black hair, grey eyes, pale skin that tans but does not become ruddy

Living Area(s): Estcarp, Escore, Arvon

Other: The Old Race is very long-lived, not even showing outward signs of aging until death is only a few years away. They are naturally inclined to have Power which allows them a connection with the land around them. For the past thousand years only women were thought to have (or trained in) the ways of Power. With the coming of Simon Tregarth and the reopening of Escore, however, more and more males seem to be coming into the Power again. They are assumed to be among the natives of the world since they have no legends of coming through a Gate.

Latt

Appearance: Black hair, grey (?) eyes that slanted up on the edges, short, stocky bodies, pale skin that tans but does not become ruddy

Living Area(s): North of Alizon and Arvon

Other: The Latt are hunter-gatherers. They may be related to the Old race since their physical appearance is similar and they also do not have any lore of coming through a Gate. Both females and males seem able to wield Power, though not everyone in their society is a Power-wielder. Those north of Alizon were driven out of that land by the Alizonders.

Sulcar

Appearance: Blond to platinum hair, green, blue-green, blue or sea-colored eyes, pale skin that tans, tall and robust

Living Area(s): On their ships at sea. Current land base is Korinth, north of Alizon

Other: Sulcars are traders and fighters of some skill. They live with their families on their ships. Though most among them do not have the Power, some have the ability to read waves, find safe routes, and similar sea-related powers, though they seem unable to directly control wind or wave. They were chased from their home world by an invading alien force. Their gate was far to the north of the world and has been sealed. Some seem to have gotten lost or took a different route and ended up near Escore. These sea raiders seem to be more barbaric in nature.

Alizonder

Appearance: Silver-white hair, vivid blue or green eyes, sharp teeth, pale skin

Living Area(s): Alizon

Other: Alizonders have a barony that has constant bouts of treason and treachery. Poison is quite commonly used and most Alizonders take small doses of the more common poisons to develop immunity. They are very fond of their dogs, white creatures with lithe bodies and have termed themselves the 'Hounds of Alizon'. This trait seems to allow them to be easily tracked by Grey Ones and they could be forced into the Dark by a Master Power. Very, very few have natural Power and are usually of melding between other races. They were brought through a Gate by two Adepts, a Gate that was later sealed by one.

Dale Folk

Appearance: Blond to dark brown hair, green, blue, brown, or hazel eyes, pale skin that tans and becomes ruddy
Living Area(s): High Hallack, Karsten(?)
Other: Coming into the world by a Gate of their own making, those of High Hallack closed the Gate behind them once through. They have created many dales and are still recovering from the war brought to them by the Kolder and Alizonders. Some seem to have moved into Karsten prior to the war, given the description of the average Karstinian.

Falconers

Appearance: Red hair, amber eyes, pale skin that may be tan or ruddy.
Living Area(s): Eyrie
Other: The Falconers were one of the first peoples brought through the gates. It is assumed the Gate they were brought through was shut. They bond with falcons, black birds with a white 'v' on their chests, for the life of the bird. After the death of the bird the Falconer can die from shock. Barring this, a Falconer may bond again with another bird. Male Falconers bond most strongly with male falcons, though they can bond with females as well. Though they could bond as well, female Falconers, until recently, have not been allowed to bond since it helped keep them passive. This was due to the interference of the Dark One Jonkara, who enslaved Falconer men through the women they cared for (causing the women to become extensions of herself). It may be possible that Jonkara was not truly of the Dark but merely a Great One called upon for vengeance.

Varnian

Appearance: Tan or dark skin, black (?) hair, brown (?) eyes, very tall and skinny
Living Area(s): Var
Other: Varnians seem to have come through a Gate that is presumably closed. They are taller than any other known race and are exquisite glass-makers. They seem to have means of detecting Power, and females among them can use it. Despite (or perhaps because of) this females and children are kept within the deepest part of their houses when outsiders visit except for Power users.

Torfolk

Appearance: Downy hair, long, thick arms and short legs
Living Area(s): Tormarsh, Tormoor
Other: Those of the Tor seem to be very ancient and whether they came through a Gate or not is debatable. They worship the being known as Volt. They are quite lithe and graceful despite their ape-like appearance. It is not mentioned that they walk on all fours at any time, though potentially they could given the length and heaviness of their arms. It is not mentioned whether their feet are human or more ape-like in nature nor whether they may be of some avian decent or not.

Gormian

Appearance: Wheat blond hair, blue, blue-green or green eyes, pale skin
Living Area(s): Estcarp, presumably
Other: Those of the island of Gorm were overthrown by the Kolder, the population of their island home was decimated. How many of their race remains is debatable, though some seem to turn up now and again. It is possible that this race is now extinct or near extinct.

Vuspell

Appearance: red-yellow hair (possibly naturally black), dark brown skin, broad features
Living Area(s): Nomadic, Escore
Other: The Vuspell, or at least the band described, seem to have originated somewhere in the north-eastern part of Escore before their tribes were broken and scattered by sea raiders. They are primitive in many ways, but may have once had a more advanced civilization. They are extremely skilled with gems and metal-forging and practice elaborate burials. They paint their bodies and might also dye their hair. They may have come through a Gate. They seem to have large, wolf-like dogs that can be hitched to sleighs. These dogs have cream-colored bodies and brown legs with a brown stripe running down their backs to the tip of the tail.

Kioga

Appearance: Dark skin, hair and eyes. High bridge noses and cheekbones. Most ear braided hair. Men wear mustaches.
Living Area(s): Nomadic, Arvon.
Other: The Kioga Gated themselves in barely a generation ago when another race of their own world began enslaving them. They have a deep bond with their horses. They carry short, barbed spears as weapons. Worship the Mother of Mares and her Twins. Their horses are intelligent and strong and Choose their rider. They do not seem to have mind speech but could well have near-human intelligence.

Unknown

Appearance: Very dark brown skin, hair and eye color unstated

Living Area(s): Cliff areas, western Waste

Other: This race is very small, no larger than around 3 feet (91.44 centimeters) tall, and apparently very light boned. They have developed gliders, which probably serve them well due to their light mass. They may have been Gated in at some time in the past. The full extent of their Powers is not mentioned, though they seem to have both warding and communication technologies.

Kolder

Appearance: Pale skin: eyes and hair are not described.

Living Area(s): Kolder island base

Other: Once occupying the areas of Yle and Gorm as well as their overseas island base, the Kolder seem to be hyper technological in nature. They came through a Gate of their own making which was eventually destroyed as was their entire race. They left the world scarred and their strange technology as legacy. This technology has yet to be fully explored. None of the areas the Kolder once possessed have yet to be inhabited again.

Unknown

Appearance: Reddish hair, brown-yellow skin

Living Area(s): Unknown

Other: Some of this race appears as Kolder zombie slaves. Their origins are still unknown, though it can be presumed that they lived somewhere on the western continent.

Trey of Swords 1986 by John Pound

Created Races [Non Humanoids]
by Michael Martinez

Rethan

Appearance: Unicorn-like creatures with golden eyes, roan red body fur and creamy underbody. They have creamy tails and creamy manes with a single, backwards curving red horn.

Living Area(s): Escore

Other: Rethan are capable of speaking telepathically with others. They will not wear bridles or saddles, though they will carry supplies in cases of dire need. They seem to have other abilities as well, though to what extent they have Power beyond telepathy is not clearly defined.

Keplain

Appearance: Jet black horse with blue or red eyes

Living Area(s): Valley of the Keplain, Escore

Other: Keplains were originally created for the Light. Somehow they were corrupted and controlled by the Dark. They have since been released from this bondage and now serve the Light again. They can run very quickly and are able to communicate telepathically with others. They seem to have other Powers as well, though like with the Rethan these are not well-defined.

Vrang

Appearance: Bird-like form but with the head of a lizard. The head is covered with red scales that glitter the sun, but its feathers are blue-grey.

Living Area(s): Heights of Escore

Other: Vrang can work effectively both as scouts and as warriors.

Scaled Ones

Appearance: jewel-scaled lizard whose front feet work as hands

Living Area(s): Valley of Green Silences, Escore

Other: These lizards seem to serve as sentries to the Valley.

Falconer Falcon

Appearance: Black-feathered bird with a white 'v' on their chests. They have golden eyes.

Living Area(s): Heights of the former Eyrie on the boarder of Karsten and Estcarp, new Eyrie in the Dales.

Other: Though they are rarely separated from their human companions the Falcons are capable of advanced planning and can telepathically talk to those with the Power to read animal minds. Through gestures and actions they can also try to convey messages non-telepathically with others, though this requires non-telepaths to believe the bird is actually trying to communicate.

Created Races [Humanoid]
by Michael Martinez

Green People

Appearance: Variable hair, eyes, and skin. Males have two ivory horns on their heads

Living Area(s): Valley of the Green Silences, Escore

Other: The color of a male or female from the Green Valley varies on both mood and time of day, and perhaps on the person that views them. The degree to which these changes manifest themselves vary from individual to individual, but all change to some degree.

Were Riders

Appearance: Black hair, green eyes, pale skin that tans but does not become ruddy

Living Area(s): Arvon – the Grey Tower

Other: They seem related to the Old race in some way; the Were Riders are all male and can all shapeshift into animals, usually related to a heraldic image: pard, lion, hawk, eagle, horse, boar, wolf, fox, bear, badger, etc. They are also apparently able to assume other shapes as well, though they do so less often. Their children are through Dalesfolk, how much of their Power they retain is not clear, some seem to shift easily while others seem to need magic items to help them shift. It is possible the Were Riders will die out in another generation or two if the ability to shapeshift fades entirely.

Krogan

Appearance: Pale skin, silvery hair, green eyes with no whites, gilled, slightly webbed fingers and frog-like feet

Living Area(s): Lakes and streams of Escore

Other: The Krogan are humanoids dependant on living in or near water. They can live outside water for a while but must return to it occasionally or die. This limits their range of living area to those connected or close waterways in Escore, though at least one is known to have ranged further.

Flannan

Appearance: Feathered human-shaped body, spreading bird wings, clawed feet

Living Area(s): Heights of Escore

Other: Though they make excellent messengers, the Flannan lack the concentration to be able fighters. They are short of stature, possibly to allow them to fly in the first place. It is not mentioned whether their wings come from their backs or replace their arms.

Thas

Appearance: Short, fur-covered

Living Area(s): Underground areas, Escore

Other: Thas have very great powers over the earth. They have poisonous claws and have apparently allied themselves with the Dark.

Moss Woman

Appearance: Long, mossy hair, withered-looking body, green(?) eyes
Living Area(s): Forest of Mosswomen, Escore
Other: Mosswomen seem to stay within their forest home rarely if ever leaving it. They seem to have an affinity towards names beginning in 'F'. There have never been moss men sighted or reported, though the Mosswomen give birth to children.

Grey One

Appearance: Anthropomorphic wolf
Living Area(s): Escore, Estcarp, the Waste
Other: Creatures of the Dark, Grey ones hunt in packs like normal wolves. They are capable of both two-legged and four-legged locomotion. They are able to speak and a rare few have been shown to have minor Power. They seem particularly able to track down Alizonders, possibly due to the traits Alizonders may have absorbed from their hounds.

Sarn Riders

Appearance: Ambiguous
Living Area(s): Escore
Other: Sarn Riders are creatures of the Dark. Though they once took Keplain mounts they now seem to ride on lizard-like mounts. They seem to have an equivalent that rides in Arvon that is not necessarily of the Dark, but might serve it.

Winged Ones (Varks)

Appearance: They have heads of birds and the bodies of men and women. It is likely that they are also winged.
Living Area(s): Arvon, the Waste.
Other: The blood of a Winged One is dangerous to the living and seems to be acidic. They seem able to continue to fight even if dismembered or beheaded. Their numbers seem to be dwindling, however. They serve the Dark.

Creatures of the Witch World
by Michael Martinez

Web Riders

Appearance: Greenish-white phosphorescent creatures that seem half transparent. They are about a foot (30.48 cm) in diameter, looking like a mixture of crab and spider with many-jointed legs. They have pincers and fangs and are apparently slightly more crab-like than spider-like.

Living Area(s): Arvon, the Waste.

Other: Web Riders get their name from the purple filaments they ride on top of. Their bite is poisonous and their blood is acidic. They can ride the wind with their webs but cannot control the wind. It is possible to counter them by creating a strong enough breeze to blow them away. It is not stated that they are intelligent though they do seem able to plan ambushes.

Rasti

Appearance: 3 foot (91.44 centimeters) long weasel-like creatures.

Living Area(s): Nomadic, Escore, Estcarp.

Other: Rasti are usually servants of the Dark whether they were created for that purpose or not. They are driven by their hunger, though they seem to have some sort of society beyond this. They are described as having wonderfully soft fur that makes excellent clothing, which makes it unlikely they are truly intelligent since those of the Light wear rasti fur as clothing. It is mentioned that they have counterparts in Estcarp, though those rasti are no more than 3 inches (7.62 cm) in length.

Unknown (possibly Lizard Mounts)

Appearance: Long, narrow heads, necks, bodies, and legs. They have smooth, white to grey-scaled skins and sharp, curving teeth. Instead of hooves they have clawed talons.

Living Area(s): Arvon, possibly Escore.

Other: These mounts look like a cross between a lizard and a horse. They are ridden by servants of the Dark, though it is not explicitly stated that they are of the Dark themselves. It is not mentioned but they likely have long, lizard-like tails as well, though if seen from a distance they can be mistaken for normal horses.

Were Rider Mount

Appearance: Dappled grey, white and black horses with green pupilless eyes.

Living Area(s): Arvon: Grey Towers, Reeth

Other: The mounts of the were riders are trained to carry their riders in both human and animal forms. Normal horses tend to shy away from them, though they are not usually dangerous. They seem to have a measure of intelligence, though how sentient they are is debatable. They cannot shape shift.

Races of Witch World
By Metaldragon and Indagare

Alizonders

Alizonders (their warriors are known as the Hounds of Alizon or just the Hounds) are established as an old enemy of those of Estcarp. They have an affinity with their hounds. They were gated in a long time ago by the Adepts Shorrosh and Elsenar.[1] The Gate to their home world was sealed.

Appearance: Alizonders have silver-white hair, vivid blue or green eyes, sharp teeth, and pale skin.

Living Area(s): Alizon

Life Span: The exact length of an Alizonder life span is never covered, but they probably have a life span similar to an Earth humans - if they survive the various intrigues that are part of their lives.

Power: Alizonders do not normally possess any form of Power - in fact they have an aversion to it. In *Year of the Unicorn*, *Darkness Over Mirhold*, and *The Circle of Sleep*, though, there are implications they can use Power - though those able to seem to be a hybrid of Old Race and Alizonder.

Other: Alizonders have a barony that has constant bouts of treason and treachery. Poison is quite commonly used and most Alizonders take small doses of the more common poisons to develop immunity and are trained to detect the taste and smell of it at an early age. They are very fond of their dogs, white creatures with lithe bodies and cat-like, retractable claws. Their attachment to their dogs seems to allow them to be easily tracked by Grey Ones.

The Alizonders made a pact with the Kolder and agreed to fight in the Dales of High Hallack to keep the Sulcar forces distracted. Why the Kolder treated with Alizon rather than turning them into the soulless hordes as they did with those of Gorm is unknown. It is also unknown why the Kolder simply didn't have the Alizonders attack Estcarp with the powerful weapons used in the Dales instead of sitting off their coast or only using their flying vehicles. In *Gryphon in Glory* Galkur implies that he manipulated the Kolder and Hounds with his dark powers to unleash them upon the Dales and was leading them to The Waste in order to attack Arvon.

Footnotes:
1. *The Magestone*

Anakue

The Anakue appear in *Gryphon's Eyrie*.

Appearance: Anakue have dark blue eyes and dark hair. They seem to have a fair complexion as well.

Living Area(s): Anakue live in huts built on stone pillars on a large lake somewhere in the south west of Arvon.[1]

Life Span: The lifespans of the Anakue are not mentioned.

Power: Some Wise Women seem to hold the healing Power among the Anakue, but more than that is unknown.

Other: The village of the Anakue is set up entirely on large pillars of rock jutting out of a large lake. Their structures are wooden and the various stone platforms are connected by bridges or ladders that lead down to boats. It's possible they are an offshoot of the Old Race of Arvon.

Footnotes:

1. Whether this is the area is debatable. Car Re Dogan is next to the south-east boarder of The Waste, just north of High Hallack. Kar Garudwyn is next to Car Re Dogan and so should be similarly located. If Kerovan and Joisan are moving to the south-east they ought to be heading to The Waste based on most maps.

Dalesfolk

The Dalesfolk are first introduced in *Year of the Unicorn*. Their entry into the [Witch World] is covered in *Horn Crown*.

Appearance: Dalesfolk have blond to dark brown hair and green, blue, brown, or hazel eyes. They have pale skin that tans and becomes ruddy.[1] Some Dalesfolk have mated with the Old Ones and have unusual features as a result.

Living Area(s): High Hallack

Life Span: The exact life span of the Dalesfolk is not given, but they seem to live about the same length of time as an Earth human.

Power: Some Dalesfolk seem to occasionally have Power on their own but generally they treat it with wariness and suspicion. Most Wise Women healers seem to have some form of it and a few of the Dames of the Flame, but in general, the Dames eschew all worldly things (including magic) in favor of contemplation and veneration of the Flame. The Bards and Sword Brothers mentioned in *Horn Crown* also seem to have some form of Power.[2]

Other: The people of Hallack came into the Witch World by a Gate of their own making and the Bards closed the Gate behind them once through. They have created many dales and are still recovering from the war brought to them by the Kolder and Alizonders. In *Horn Crown* it is mentioned that the Bards both opened and closed the Gate to Hallack, their home world, erasing the memory of why they made that transit. It is also mentioned that a group known as the Sword Brothers were Dalesmen with a touch of Sight. What happened to this group and the Bards in later years is undocumented. It seems the sacred Flame was passed from the Bards to the newly formed order of the Dames at some point before they died out.

How many Dales there are, exactly, isn't mentioned though they extend from the eastern coast of the sea to the edge of The Waste in the west & north, and as far south as Sorn Fen.

Footnotes:

1. In *Year of the Unicorn* Gillan describes the differences: "I need only to look in the mirror within these walls to know that I was not of the breed of High Hallack. Whereas their womenkind were fair of skin, but with a fine color to their faces, their

hair as yellow as the small flowers bordering the garden walks in spring, or brown as the wings of the sweet singing birds in the stream gullies, I was of a flesh which burned brown under the sun, but held no color in cheek. And the hair I learned to plait tightly around my head, was of a black as deep as a starless night." p.345 *Annals of the Witch World*

2. In both *The Circle of Sleep* and *The Stillborn Heritage* it seems that many of the Old Ones are being reborn in the children of the Dalesfolk. Kerovan himself seems to also be involved in this somehow. So it's possible that the Dales will become a more magical place over time.

Falconers

Falconers are a mercenary race. They were apparently gated in some time back, but whether they gated themselves or were gated in or stumbled upon a Gate is unclear. It's possible Jonkara herself gated them into the Witch World since she refers to herself as "Opener of Gates".

Appearance: Falconers have dark, reddish hair and brown-yellow eyes[1]. Their skin color is not mentioned, though it probably is light and possibly ruddy.

Living Area(s): Eyrie. Originally they came from Salzarat, a land apparently to the south of Karsten somewhere.[2] In *Falcon Hope* Tarlach is trying to establish a new Eyrie in High Hallack. In *Falcon Law* another Eyrie is established somewhere in the mountains between Karsten and Estcarp again by a group of tradition bound Falconers.[3]

Lifespan: How long Falconers live is not mentioned directly, but presumably they live a good deal shorter lives than the Old Race.

Power: Falconers can bond with their falcons. They can also create talismans that cannot be removed from their owners without their free consent - a virtue that passes to anyone one it is gifted to.[4] It could be Falconers had more Power in the past but it is no longer practiced. This is supported in part by *Falcon Blood* where Jonkara, one of the Dark Old Ones, was partly defeated by a ritual Langward learned.

Other: In *Witch World* it is mentioned that there is a complex communication device attached to the Falcons they use. Later stories mention they actually bond with the falcons and imply that such devices were used to disguise their true bond and the intelligence of the falcons from other races. Each Falconer appears to have a different level of bond with their falcon. Some Falconers may only have an empathic bond and they may not be able to speak telepathically with their falcons which may be another reason for the communication devices. On the other hand, in *Witch World* one of the falcons seems to speak to Simon, so the devices could be used for long-distance communication and listening by Falconers or it could allow the falcons to express their thoughts aloud to non-Falconers. In any case, the devices are no longer mentioned after *Witch World*.

Similarly, in *Witch World* it is mentioned that the Falconers were chased out of their lands by barbarians, which is largely contradicted by other books. They are also mentioned as having come over and settled in some hundred years or more before the story.

The Falconers leader was called the Lord of Wings (see: *Witch World*) but he may have decided to fall with the Eyrie because he is not mentioned in later books when the Falconer race is divided between those who accept women as equals and those who remained separate, though the Warlord Varnel is mentioned as their leader in *Falcon Hope*. It could be that Varnel is the Lord of Wings but doesn't use the title outside the Eyrie.

Falconer falcons are black birds with a white 'v' on their chests[5], and Falconer males bond with the falcon for the life of the bird via some form of Power. After the death of the bird the Falconer can die from shock, though it may be less if the bird dies of natural causes like old age.[6] A Falconer may bond again with another bird. Male Falconers bond most strongly with male falcons, though they can bond with females as well.[7] This is fairly rare and almost never happened before the Turning.[8] The Falconers were one of the first peoples brought through the Gates (*Seakeep*). It is assumed the Gate they were brought through was shut.

Though they could bond as well, female Falconers, until recently, have not been allowed to bond since it helped keep them passive. This was due to the interference of the Dark One Jonkara, who enslaved Falconer men through the women they cared for (causing the women to become extensions of herself). It may be possible that Jonkara was not truly of the Dark but a Great One called upon for vengeance.[9]

The books make it unclear exactly how human-like the intelligence of the Falconer falcons are. They are certainly able spies and can report by mind-send to their partners. The falcons apparently die if their partners die, and vice versa (though it is easier for the Falconers to resist death). A notable exception is in *Songsmith* where the falcon accompanying Alon lives well over a year after his Falconer partner dies.

Sorcerer's Notes:

Because the falconer Falcons may be at least as intelligent as their human partners they might rightfully be called another race.

Another unclear point is what, if any, relationship Volt may have had with the Falconer race. He seems to be of avian decent and could, possibly, have been the one to gate them in.

Footnotes:

1. page 146, *Annals of the Witch World* specifically gives them reddish hair and brown-yellow eyes like their falcons. Other stories sometimes give them other colored hair or eyes. In *Falcon Blood*, Tanree describes Rivery's hair as dark, (looking black when wet), green eyes and paler skin than her Sulcar tan. In *Ware Hawk* Nirel the Falconer is described as having hair as dark as Tirtha's and a face not too far from that of the Old Race. He could possibly be mixed-blood. In *Seakeep* and *Falcon Hope* there are blue and silver eyes among the Falconers. Since they tend not to breed with outsiders variations in hair or eye color seems unlikely, though since the Turning it is more probable.

2. See *Falcon Blood*

3. However, several books and stories have the mountains between Estcarp and

Karsten be uninhabitable.

4. *Seakeep* and *Falcon Hope*

5. In *Falcon Law* the females are described as much larger than males and purely white. Though raptor females in real life do tend to be larger than raptor males, it seems odd the dichotomy would also include coloration - though this is also common in birds.

6. Except for in *Falcon Magic* it is unclear whether the lives of the falcons are extended to beyond normal falcon life spans. It seems more likely that a falcon would be given the life span of it's Falconer partner via Power, but it's also possible they just live a long time due to being well-treated and need to be replaced every so often.

7. *Falcon Hope*

8. See: *Falcon Law*

9. See: *Falcon's Chick* & *We the Women*. In *We, the Women* it is further implied that the women of Arona's Womens' Village were descended from the same race as the men who later became the Were-Riders and that they were captured by the Falconers when the Falconers arrived in the *Witch World*.

Flannon

The Flannan first appear in *Three Against the Witch World*.

Appearance: Flannan appear as small feathered human-shaped beings. They have wings on their backs as well as arms. They also have clawed feet.

Living Area(s): Heights of Escore

Life Span: It is not mentioned how long Flannan live.

Power: Flannan do not seem to have much in the way of Power.

Other: Though they make excellent messengers, the Flannan lack the concentration to be able fighters. They can also take on the shape of birds, though this shift seems mostly illusion and may not even be of their doing. The Flannan could have been gated or created. Given the Krogan have an affinity for water and the Thas have an affinity for earth, it seems logical a race with an affinity for air would be created, though given their lack of air-related Power they seem an unlikely fit for this.

Gormians

Gormians were one-time neighbors of the Old Race of Escore before they doomed themselves by calling on the Kolder.

Appearance: Gormians have/had wheat blond hair and blue, blue-green, or green eyes. Their skin color was described as pale.

Living Area(s): Originally, the island of Gorm, currently unknown but most likely Estcarp, Karsten and possibly among the Sulcar. One even turned up in Alizon.

Life Span: There is no mention of how long someone from Gorm lived.

Power: Koris and Gratch are the only two confirmed remainders of Gorm line and neither show any hints of Power.

Other: Those of the island of Gorm were overthrown by the Kolder, the population of their island home was decimated, those not killed in body were turned into zombies. How many of their race remains is debatable; it is possible that this race is now extinct or near extinct. There is no record of those from Gorm being Gated in.

Sorcerer's Notes:
It's likely those of Gorm came from oversea. It could be possible more of their race still exists somewhere on the western continent or other unexplored areas. They may be related to the Dalesfolk of High Hallack, Karstenians or the Sulcar.

Green People

Those living in the Valley of Green Silences first appear in *Three Against the Witch World*.

Appearance: The color of a male or female from the Green Valley varies on both mood and time of day, and perhaps on the person that views them. The degree to which these changes manifest themselves vary from individual to individual, but all change to some degree.[1] It appears to be a form of natural, defensive illusion they can dispel with concentration if they choose. Males have two short ivory horns on their heads like satyrs.

Living Area(s): The Valley of Green Silences, Escore.

Life Span: The life span of those in the Valley is unknown. They could live at least as long as the Old Race does, possibly even longer, and may actually be an offshoot of the Old Race.[2]

Power: Those of the Valley have a good deal of Power over growing, living things. They have a lot of wards around their valley and so are likely very skilled in that. The full extent of their possible Power is not mentioned.

Other: Those of the Valley live in 'houses' that are apparently grown. These structures are topped with blue-green feathers for thatch. The Valley is a stronghold for the Light in Escore but is not impenetrable. Their knowledge of the healing arts and uses of the healing mud pools is extensive. Their most common weapon is a short rod that produces a whip-like lash of Power that resembles lightning.

Footnotes:
1. Dahaun is the most obvious or most extreme.
2. It is implied that Dahaun may be over a thousand years old as the Old Race in Estcarp remember her name as a legend.

Grey Ones

Grey Ones are first introduced in *Three Against the Witch World*.

Appearance: Grey Ones look like humanoid wolves. They can speak and in *Wolfhead* are noted to have tails and digitigrade feet. In many stories they don't seem to take care of their fur very well, and it is sometimes missing or in patches (likely due to mange).

Living Area(s): Escore, Arvon, The Waste

Life Span: How long Grey Ones live is unknown. They could have been made humanoid from wolf stock, in which case they might have wolf-like life spans, though (as with the Keplian) they could have much extended lives thanks to the Power. They may have been humans transformed into something more wolf-like.

Power: Grey Ones are expert trackers and can thrice circle and bind. Following their trail directly leaves a person vulnerable to them. In _The Warding of Witch World_ a shaman seems to be able to call on some Power for illusion and they seem to be able to draw or track Alizonders, possibly due to the Alizonder canine affinity. Grey Ones could have additional abilities not mentioned in the books.

Other: Grey Ones hunt in packs like normal wolves. They are capable of both two-legged and four-legged locomotion. In _Wolfhead_ it is suggested that the Grey Ones once used metal weapons and were created as a tie to animals. They are not, perhaps, wholly of the Light and so may have corrupted into use by the Dark like the Keplian were.

Karstenians

Karstenians are one-time allies of the Old Race who turned on them due to Kolder manipulation. Their origins are unknown, except for the fact that they come from over seas "ten generations" ago.

Appearance: Fulk of Verlain is described as having red-gold hair, Hunnold's looks are described as foxy with hair colour to match, and Yvain has a sandier look of the same colors but whether this is true of all of Karsten blood is not mentioned. Loyse is described as having very pale blond hair, almost white. (See: _Witch World_) In _Ciara's Song_ and _The Duke's Ballad_ brown or hazel eyes seem to be common.

Living Area(s): Karsten

Life Span: The exact life span of Karstenians is not mentioned, but they have been in Karsten for some ten generations.

Power: Karstenians do not seem to have Power on their own. They do have a unique religion in the Temple of Fortune- a Brotherhood led by the obese "Reverend Voice" Siric. He wears yellow robes and has a servant priest.

Other: Karsten was thrown into turmoil after the Turning. They have an "old nobility" which may trace their lineage back to the first ships to arrive in Karsten or perhaps even older. It's important to them, as they consider mercenaries like Yvian as upstarts and this class division created much tension in the country that is explored in the _Witch World_, _Web of the Witch World_, _Ciara's Song_, and _The Duke's Ballad_.

Sorcerer's Notes:

It is possible the Karstenians are related to the Dalesfolk of High Hallack (and the people of Gorm?). They have axe-marriages like those in the Dales do. There is so little mentioned in most books about their overall culture, except in _Ciara's Song_ and _The Duke's Ballad_, that it's really hard to know. In those two books the ties to the Dales culture is strengthened. It seems strange that a great deal of time is spent in Karsten in the early books, yet so little is really mentioned about those living there.

Keplian

Keplian were first introduced in _Three Against the Witch World_.

Appearance: Keplian are pure black creatures that look like perfect horses. In earlier books they tend to have reddish eyes, signifying their allegiance to the Dark. After _The Key of the Keplian_, however, those serving the Light can have blue eyes.

Living Area(s): Escore, Arvon

Life Span: The lifespan of a Keplian is unknown. They might live as long as an Earth horse or their forming could have granted them a far longer lifespan.

Power: Keplian can seduce humans to ride them by appearing tame. They can run at supernaturally fast speeds and may be able to bind their riders to their backs so they can't escape. In _The Warding of Witch World_ the Keplians going on the southern mission were able to wall a Dark Gate by circling it, it is possible Keplians can do other things as well.

Other: Keplian can mind-send, though reading beyond the surface might be dangerous for an empowered individual - at least if they see the alien Keplian mind as evil. Eleeri proved in _The Key of the Keplian_ that a human can read thought below the surface, but she did not have the prejudice that many others have. The Keplian were apparently created by those of the Light but one was created by (or chose to be a servant for) the Dark, and that Dark one tainted their entire race for generations until he was defeated.

Keplians cannot mate with normal horses without powerful magical aid. In fact, the Keplians turned to the Light in _The Key of the Keplian_ consider the very idea disgusting. Monso, from _Songsmith_, seems to be the only hybrid of Keplian around. Whether Monso would have been affected by the events of _The Key of the Keplian_ is unknown. He does not appear in _The Warding of Witch World_, though the Keplian Eleeri helped do.

Kioga

The Kioga are first introduced in _Gryphon's Eyrie_

Appearance: The Kioga have dark skin, hair, and eyes.[1] Kioga have high bridge noses and cheekbones. Most wear braided hair. Men wear mustaches. Illustrations in the book make them look like Mongols.

Living Area(s): Originally the Kioga were a nomadic race in Arvon. They have since settled near Kar Garudwyn.

Life Span: The exact lifespan of a Kioga is unknown, but Nidu seems to have had a rather long lifespan.

Power: Kioga seem to have some way with their horses, though whether it's Power is a different question. Nidu certainly has some kind of Power with her drumming, and it could be there are talents of other sorts not displayed in the books.

Other: The Kioga gated themselves in barely a generation ago when another race of their own world began enslaving them. They have a deep bond with their horses. They carry short, barbed spears as weapons. Kioga worship the Mother of Mares (who seems a bit like Gunnora) and her Twins. Their horses are intelligent and strong and choose their rider. They do not seem to have mind speech but could well have near-human intelligence. Whether the Kioga would ever deal with the Keplian now that some have turned to the Light is unknown, but they seem to value their own horses too much for that.

Sorcerer's Notes:

The directions that are given in _Gryphon's Eyrie_ make little sense given the maps. Kerovan and the Kioga go south and slightly east in their searching for new mountainous places. Since Kar Garudwyn is next door to Car Re Dogan, and Car Re Dogan is close to the Gate near the boarder, they ought to be heading either into The Waste west of the Dales or back into the Dales themselves (especially since they've been traveling thirty days). Instead they find themselves in a seemingly endless prairie with only a wide river running through it. It seems far more likely they were heading either northwest or northeast.

Footnotes:

1. Though exact hair and eye color are not mentioned, it is not unreasonable to assume they have black hair and brown or hazel eyes.

Kolder

The Kolder first appear in _Witch World_.

Appearance: Kolder look like men that Simon knew from Earth, implying they have pale skin and look humanoid. Their eye color is not mentioned but they are described as large, they have flattened features, broad cheekbones, small noses with a low bridge, a small & narrow chin, and wear caps which block any showing of hair - if they have any hair. With some Kolder, metal helmets appear to be wired directly into their brains. Attempted removal of the helmets often kills the Kolder wearing it.

Living Area(s): Kolder island base, Yle, Gorm, with a few remaining in Alizon.

Life Span: The life span of a Kolder is unknown. They probably live at least as long as an Earth human (though with the technology they've shown they probably live a good deal longer).

Power: Kolder do not possess the Power per se. They can use a form of body and mind manipulation but they need their machines to do it. They seem to use forcefields like a form of telekinesis to immobilize & manipulate people and drugs, surgery & implants to turn people into their mindless slaves.

Other: Once occupying the areas of Yle and Gorm as well as their overseas island base, the Kolder seem to be hyper-technological in nature. They came through a Gate of their own making which was eventually destroyed as was their entire race. They left the world scarred and their strange technology as legacy. This technology has yet to be fully explored. None of the areas the Kolder once possessed have yet been inhabited again.

The Kolder are a mystery. They seem to have no qualms about turning people into zombies, but neither Dalesfolk nor Alizonders seem to ever be in their hordes. This might be partly explained, at least with the Dalesfolk, in the fact they only turned their attention to them later (though if their island base was really as close as maps show it to High Hallack it's still unclear why they couldn't have reached for the Dales first). When Simon Tregarth is captured and ends up on Gorm he does notice zombified people of different races, some he'd never seen before or heard of. Still, none of those match later descriptions of Dalesfolk. The majority of the Kolder's zombie army were of course from Gorm.

Instead of giving Alizon their weapons to directly attack Estcarp they instead have them attack the Dales. Even in the *Web of the Witch World* their motives for reopening their Gate - to get more men or more equipment - only leads to disaster as the skeleton-men from their own past come to attack them. Galkur's calling, possibly coupled with Witch manipulation on a more subtle level, is probably what kept them from striking more effectively against Estcarp.

The location of the Kolder island base is unclear. It is somewhere to the south in the ocean. Maps generally place it close to High Hallack, but this may not actually be the case.

Sorcerer's Notes:

Simon went to investigate some islands with suspected Kolder activities. These islands obviously had a Gate that lead to the machine world. Why this activity occurred was never explained, nor whether the Gate was closed behind Simon (he couldn't get back though it, but that doesn't mean it was closed permanently).

Krogan

The Krogan first appear in *Three Against the Witch World*. They are apparently known as myth in Estcarp.

Appearance: Krogan have silvery hair and green eyes with no whites. Their skin is pale skin and they have gills, slightly webbed fingers and frog-like feet.

Living Area(s): Escore (Lake of the Krogan)

Life Span: Their lifespan is unmentioned.

Power: The Krogan likely have water-related powers. It was seen that at least one work of theirs could produce far more water than one might expect. How far their influence over water goes is not covered, but if their Power is anything similar to that of the Thas over earth then they could quite probably control the flow and direction of water.

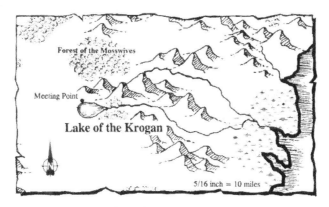

Forest of the Mosswives

Meeting Point

Lake of the Krogan

5/16 inch = 10 miles

GURPS: Witch World Roleplaying Guide 1989 p.28

Other: The Krogan are humanoids dependent on living in or near water. They can live outside water for a while but must return to it occasionally or die. This limits their range of living area to those connected or close to waterways in Escore, though water seem to flow in enough places that this is not normally a hindrance. They are also disinclined to explore far beyond their own lake.

Orsya was more curious than most of her race and explored areas they hadn't in some time. She was also somehow able to travel over the mountains with Kemoc and so was part of the crew in _Port of Dead Ships_. She has not had any children with Kemoc, though both his brother and sister have two. It could be that her kind cannot have children with any other races, at least not without magical aid. _S'Olcarios's Sons_ is the only time part-Krogans appear.

Krogan were likely the result of magical experimentation. Many races in Escore seem to have been created by Adepts in the past for some purpose, and the Krogan were likely created by some Adept with an interest in a race that could breathe and work under water.

What happened to the Krogan in Escore after _Warlock of the Witch World_ is unclear though they likely survived. They are known, in stories, in Arvon but their kind either died out there or are living in some remote area where they remain myth. Other races, like the Thas, Keplian, and Grey Ones seem to live in both Arvon and Escore so their absence is thought-provoking but unexplained.

Sorcerer's Notes:

In _Zarsthor's Bane_ there is a race of half-sized humanoids that wear shell armor. It is unclear if this is an actual aquatic race or just a race with a taste for sea-shells. It is also unclear if they are supposed to be related to the Krogan or not.

Latt

Latts are introduced in *The Warding of Witch World,* although in *Web of the Witch World* there is a reference to a northern race the Sulcar trade with.
Appearance: Latts have black hair and eyes that slanted up on the edges. They have short, stocky bodies. Their eye color is not mentioned but they could have gray eyes like those of the Old Race. In fact they seem almost to be an Inuit version of the Old Race.
Living Area(s): North of Alizon and (possibly) Arvon
Life Span: There is no reference to how old the Latt may live. If they are related to the Old Race, however, they could have a similarly long lifespan.
Power: Both females and males seem able to wield Power, though not everyone in their society is a Power-wielder. They can have prophetic or scrying dreams that show the future or where game is for hunters. Their shamans seem to be able to do other things as well. Whether there is a belief a female Power-wielder must remain virginal to retain her Power is not mentioned.
Other: The Latt are hunter-gatherers. They may be related to the Old Race since their physical appearance is similar and they also do not have any lore of coming through a Gate. In fact they've actually marked the constellations change shapes three times. Those North of Alizon were driven out of that land by the Alizonders.

Moss Wives

Moss Wives appear in *Warlock of the Witch World*
Appearance: Moss Wives have very long, mossy hair and short, withered-looking bodies.[1] Mosswives skin and hair blends in with the drab grays and browns of their moss covered forest giving them natural camouflage.
Living Area(s): Forest of Mosswomen, Escore. They might live in forests in Arvon, but this is unclear. On page 42 of *The Jargoon Pard* Kethan states: "I have seen the forest people come freely to our sowing feasts, our Harvest festivals. These we welcome, though they are closer to the plant world than to ours." Who or what the 'forest people' are is not really gone into, nor are they described, but if they aren't the Mosswives, they may be a kindred race.
Life Span: There's no indication how long Moss Wives live, but if they are anything like trees they could have very long lives indeed.
Power: It's unclear what exact power Moss Wives have. They can certainly manipulate plant life, but other Powers might be possible. Fyuru from *The Weavers* also seems to be able to cast an extremely powerful glamor (or possibly even shape shift) to appear as a beautiful woman. She is also so empathetic that she is overwhelmed by the emotions of anyone within the bounds of her woods.
Other: Moss Wives seem to stay within their forest home rarely, if ever, leaving it. They seem to have an affinity towards names beginning in 'F'. There have never been moss men sighted or reported, though the Moss Wives give birth to children. *Milk from a Maiden's Breast* explains their origins and why there are no males.

Footnotes:
1. Their eyes are not described, but could easily be gray, brown, green or even amber.

Old Race

The Old Race are among the first races thought to have inhabited the Witch World. In fact there are many races, both Light and Dark, that owe their existence (or at least their presence) to various Adepts of the Old Race. They are assumed to be among the natives of the world since they have no legends of coming through a Gate.

Appearance: The Old Race have black hair and gray eyes. Their faces are oval with high cheek bones. They have pale "ivory" skin that tans but does not become ruddy.

Living Area(s): Estcarp, Escore, Arvon and before the Horning, Karsten

Life Span: The Old Race is very long-lived, not even showing outward signs of aging until death is only a few years away. Exactly how long-lived the Old Race can be is never really stated, but Kaththea met Utta who had been with the Vupsall for several of their generations and Kethan's sword teacher in _The Jargoon Pard_ was among those who had walked into Arvon when the races retreated from the south (possibly a thousand years ago!). Strangely, none of the Old Race in Estcarp seem to share this same extreme longevity (or if they do they don't mention it). The constant attacks from Alizon seem to have taken their toll on the Old Race.

Power: They are naturally inclined to have the Power which allows them a connection with the land around them. Witches, in Estcarp, by far have the largest amount of training and talent (at least among females). They can cast illusions, cause shape-shifting and (quite literally) move mountains, though using the Power exerts a great cost. In Arvon and Escore both males and females are trained and use the Power. It is unclear how or why the Witches in Arvon became their sole magic users.

Other: For the past thousand years only women were thought to have (or trained in the ways of) Power, at least within Estcarp. With the coming of Simon Tregarth and the reopening of Escore, however, more and more males seem to be coming into the Power again.

In _Witch World_ the Old Race is noted to be able to mate with the Sulcar due to some tie with the sea (Yonan is a child of this pairing: _Trey of Swords_). In later books the Old Race is shown to be able to mate normally with those of the Dales (Elys & Jervon: _Songsmith_), Falconers (_Old Toad_), those of Karsten (Ciara's parents: _Ciara's Song_), Were-Riders (Hyron & Eldris, Herrel & Gillan: _The Jargoon Pard_), the Green People (_Songsmith_), and even Alizonders (_Darkness Over Mirhold_, _The Circle of Sleep_) and most famously, humans from Earth (Simon Tregarth & Jaelithe _Three Against the Witch World_). Of the Tregarth children only Kemoc has no offspring by his chosen mate, so it's possible the Krogan are too far removed for natural reproduction with the Old Race.

Renthans

Renthans were first introduced in *Three Against the Witch World*
Appearance: Renthans look like unicorns. They have golden eyes, roan red body fur and a creamy underbody. They have creamy tails and creamy, brush-like manes with a single, backwards-curving, red horn.
Living Area(s): Escore, particularly the Valley of Green Silences
Life Span: The lifespan of Renthans is unmentioned.
Power: Renthan are capable of speaking telepathically with others. They seem to have other abilities as well, though to what extent they have Power beyond telepathy is not clearly defined.
Other: They will not wear bridles or saddles, though they will carry supplies in cases of dire need. *The Warding of Witch World* suggests Renthans may be a created race.

Sarn Riders

Sarn Riders are involved in events in *Warlock of the Witch World*
Appearance: Though mentioned in many books and stories the exact appearance of a Sarn Rider tends not to be covered. Mostly because they tend to keep their features covered by helmets and hoods and seem to shun direct sunlight. Their very presence causes unease in people.
Living Area(s): Escore, possibly Arvon & The Waste. They appear to have been introduced by gates into the Witch World.
Life Span: It's not known how long a Sarn Rider lives.
Power: Sarn Riders do not tend to demonstrate Power overtly. That they might not have Power seems improbable. They have been seen to wield whips of black lightning, similar but opposite to the weapons of the Green People.
Other: Sarn Riders are creatures of the Dark. Though they once took Keplian mounts they now seem to ride on lizard-like mounts mainly. Songsmith seems to introduce an equivalent that rides in Arvon that is not necessarily of the Dark, but might serve it.
The lizard horses in *Songsmith* are described as having long, narrow heads, necks, bodies, and legs. They have smooth, white to grey-scaled skins and sharp, curving teeth. Instead of hooves they have clawed talons. Their tails are not mentioned, but since they resemble a cross between a lizard and a horse, they could well have a lizard-like tail.

Scaled Ones

Scaled Ones are first introduced in *Three Against the Witch World*.
Appearance: Scaled ones look like jewel-scaled or rainbow-scaled lizard whose front feet work as hands. In *Trey of Swords* Tsali is mentioned as having a crest and capable of both two-legged and four-legged movement.

Their heads are larger and more rounded than a normal lizard's to accommodate a larger brain.

Living Area(s): Valley of Green Silences, Escore and possibly The Waste

Life Span: It's unknown how long they live. They could have a fairly long lifespan, however.

Power: Scaled Ones can communicate telepathically, what else they can do is largely unmentioned.[1]

Other: Scaled Ones seem to serve as sentries to the Valley of Green Silences. It's mentioned in _Three Against the Witch World_ that they are led by a chieftain. Crytha in _Trey of Swords_ thinks of Tsali as a "Lizard man" and his people as "Lizard folk" which may also be an appropriate name for their race. It's possible they also live in the Were-Riders' forest in The Waste as Kerovan catches glimpses of lizard type creatures there (in _Gryphon in Glory_) who seem to act as sentries for the Weres.

Footnotes:

1. Tsali in _Trey of Swords_ can rune read and has a bag of glowing rocks, though whether the latter are directly connected to a specific Power of his is unclear.

Sky Ones

The Sky Ones first appear in _Gryphon in Glory_

Appearance: Sky Ones are humanoid gryphons. They have avian faces: a bill-like extension that serves as mouth and nose, a crest of feathers that goes down to the shoulders and arms. Their hands are bird-like claws. Their feet are like leonine paws.[1] The leonine paws may be exclusive to Landisl.

Living Area(s): None currently (they are apparently extinct on Witch World, Landisl being, perhaps, the last of his kind), formerly Arvon

Life Span: Unknown; Landisl survived for unknown centuries in a deep sleep, but the other three did not survive or had left the Witch World entirely.

Power: Landisl can teleport others. He was able to, without waking, alter the spell so Kerovan would be truly his father's son rather than of Galkur's get.

Other: Landisl, Matr, Yoer, and Rllene are mentioned as being of this race in _Gryphon in Glory_ but of these four Landisl is the only one left alive or with any connection to the world. A skull of a member of this race was found in The Waste in _Gryphon in Glory_ and Joisan has a vision of what he looked like when alive. Sylvya in _Gryphon's Eyrie_ is counted as kin to Landisl and is likely a member of this race. It is also likely Volt of the Ax from _Witch World_ and his sister Shallon from _Peacock Eyes_ may also be members of this race. Also, another pair of people resembling Sylvia's description appear in _Port of Dead Ships_ and Destree meets what appears to be the half-breed son of the avian woman and the human man who helped them escape the black cube gate there. There is some speculation that the inhabitants of Sorn Fen (_Legacy from Sorn Fen_) may be of this race since Volt settled in Tor Marsh for many generations raising the Torfolk out of savagery and the people of Sorn Fen have been described as "fey".

Footnotes:

1. This description is taken from Landisl in _Gryphon in Glory_, whether it applies to Matr, Yoer, and Rllene is unknowable.

Sulcar

The Sulcar are a seafaring race that first entered the Witch World somewhere in the north centuries ago. In _The Warding of Witch World_ they find their original Gate and seal it.

Appearance: The Sulcar have blond or reddish blond (tawny) colored hair and green, blue-green, blue or sea-colored eyes. They are much taller and more robust than most other Witch World Races. Their skin is light but tans easily.

Living Area(s): Sulcar families live on their ships, except for extremely dangerous missions. They once had a base at Sulcarkeep before the Kolder invasion, located at the tip of a peninsula in the south-western corner of Estcarp. In _Dream Pirates' Jewel_ a settlement called 'Osberic' is created somewhere to the south of the Dales. In _The Warding of Witch World_ 'Korinth', north of Alizon is mentioned as a recent base, as is 'End of the World', which is north of Arvon. They may have other bases as well.

Life Span: The lifespan of the Sulcar is not mentioned, but they likely have the life span of an average Earth human.

Power: Sulcar do not seem to have the Power per se, but 'wave readers' are mentioned in _The Warding of Witch World_ who have the ability to find safe routes. They seem unable to directly control wind or wave and may navigate the same way the Polynesians made their way across the Pacific Ocean.

Other: Sulcars are traders and fighters of some skill. They live with their families on their ships, which have dragon-like prows. They were chased from their home world by an invading alien force. Their Gate was far to the north of the world and has been sealed. Some seem to have gotten lost or took a different route and ended up near Escore. These sea raiders seem to be more barbaric in nature.

Sorcerer's Notes:

It could be possible that the Sulcar did not originally serve the Light. This is supported by the fact that the 'guardians' of legend found in _Port of Dead Ships_ seem to be of a darksome nature. When they confront one of their ancient, alien pursuers in the north she seems genuinely surprised that the Sulcar 'speak the truth as they know it'. Finally, the behavior of the sea raiders near Escore is one more similar to that of the Vikings of Earth (looting, plundering, enslaving) than the relatively more peaceful behavior of the Sulcar traders. Why this is the case may never be known.

The short story _S'Olcarios's Sons_ implies that in the distant past the Sulcar may have descended from the Krogan. This legendary story is an oral tradition passed down by Sulcar elders to their families to give comfort when the elder reaches an age where they feel the draw of the final gate. It's possible that S'Olcarias and Anatella's sons married Sulcar women sometime shortly after the Sulcar arrived on the Witch World and their bloodline and story was passed down through the generations.[1]

Footnotes:

[1]. Given that even in the first book it is established that the Sulcar come from the north, *S'Olcarios's Sons* seems apocryphal at best. The name S'Olcaris is an obvious play on 'Sulcar' and the story implies that S'Olcaris and Anatella are the 'Adam and Eve' of the whole race. Beyond this story it's not even clearly established that the Krogan can successfully interbreed with any other race.

Thas

Thas are beings that dwell in the underground realms in various places in the Witch World. They are creatures that serve the Dark, though they can be neutral when things go against them.

Appearance: Thas have small, wry bodies with bloated stomachs. Their bodies are completely covered by root-like hair. They have muzzle-like faces not unlike a hound's that show fangs of teeth. Their eyes are pits in rounded skulls. They have claws that may be poisonous.

Living Area(s): Escore, Arvon, The Waste

Life Span: The lifespan of a Thas is unknown.

Power: Thas have phenomenal power over the element of earth. In *Gryphon in Glory* they are literally able to churn the earth and suck in Joisan. Why they can't do this with *The White Road* is not explained, though the Road may be enchanted against their influence. They do not appear to be able to affect stone with their powers directly. They may be able to use their power over soil and their root-like plants to crack stone, undermine it and move it to create their tunnels but this probably takes time.

Other: Thas seem to be cowards unless driven by a more powerful evil force. They may have been created from human-stock by some Adept who was curious about what lay beneath the surface of the earth. It is unclear if they've always served the Dark or if they were created neutral and simply allied themselves with it, but given the possible age of the water trap found at the ruins in *Warlock of the Witch World* they've at least been direct enemies once before. They seem to have a strong aversion to water, though whether this is because of their nature or because they serve the Dark is unclear.

Torfolk

Torfolk live in the northern area of Estcarp on the boarder between it and Alizon. They have once aligned themselves with the Kolder but only under duress and truly seek to be neutral and left alone.

Appearance: Downy hair, long, thick arms, short neck, torso and legs. Women are more naturally proportioned than men.

Living Area(s): Tor Marsh, Tor Moor

Life Span: Their lifespan is unmentioned.

Power: The Torfolk seem to have their own form of Power. Simon, when held captive by them, sees them seemingly vanish from the building and reappear. They also summon Power in communal rituals filled with chanting and drumming led by the women. Some of their wise women have foresight and farsight and hold dreams as important. They could very well do other things, but it isn't mentioned. They were afraid of what the Kolder can do.

Other: Those of the Tor seem to be very ancient and whether they came through a Gate or not is debatable as they have no history mentioning it and claim to have seen other races rise and fall. They worship the being known as Volt who apparently found them when they were barely more than beasts[1]. They are quite lithe and graceful despite their ape-like appearance. It is not mentioned that they walk on all fours at any time, though potentially they could given the length and heaviness of their arms. It is not mentioned whether their feet are human or more ape-like in nature nor whether they may be of some avian decent or not.

In *Sand Sister* it is mentioned that those of Tor blood seem to be having trouble reproducing. Why this is the case is unknown, but it could be the race is slowly dying out. Torfolk live communally in clans, not taking husbands or wives. On certain times of the month/year, Tor women hold a fertility dance and choose a man to father a child with. It is up to the woman to declare the father of her child if she chooses but they don't form couples. Children are held as precious by all and the whole clan takes care of them, not just their birth mother. It's possible their fertility is dwindling due to inbreeding and need new blood to revive their race. They are able to produce children with other races; for example Koris is half Torfolk, half Gormians. He married Loyse who is Karstenians and they have a son, Simond. The Torfolk's infertility could also be some curse caused by their earlier actions with Simon and Loyse.

Footnotes:

1. p50. Midwife: 'For the Torfolk were very old indeed. They spoke in their Remember Chants of a day when they had been near unthinking beasts (even less than some of the beasts of this old land) and how Volt, The Old One (he who was not human at all but the last of a much older and greater race than man dared to aspire to equal) had come to be their guide and leader. For he was lonely and found in them some spark of near thought which intrigued him so he would see what he might make of them." With their "downy" hair, it's possible Volt may have joined their mating rituals and his bloodline runs through their race. This may be why Koris was able to wield the Axe.

Varks

Varks are first named in *Horn Crown*, though they first appear in *Zarsthor's Bane* where a bird-woman that could be a Winged One appears. They are also mentioned in *The Warding of Witch World*.

Appearance: Varks have heads of birds and the bodies of men and women. The one in *Zarsthor's Bane* was capable of flying over short distances, though whether she had true wings or just flapped her arms is unclear. The ones in *Horn Crown* appear to be able to fly and Sassfang in *The Warding of Witch World* also travelled in extended leaps aided by her winged arms.

Living Area(s): The Waste and Arvon.

Life Span: The lifespan of a Vark is unmentioned.

Power: In *Zarsthor's Bane* the bird-woman seems to be able to control some large, black birds. Varks seem able to continue to fight even if dismembered or beheaded. The blood of a Vark is dangerous to the living and seems to be acidic and venomous.

Other: The number of Varks seem to be dwindling. An Dark Old One adept of their race appears in *Horn Crown* allied with Raidhan and Cuntif. The one in *The Warding of Witch World* is named Sassfang and may be the same Vark woman to appear in *Zarsthor's Bane*. [1]

Footnotes:

[1]. It's possible the first Varks may have originally been of the same race as Sylvya, Shallon & Volt and at their time of Choice took the dark path like the Ravenlord did in *Peacock Eyes*

Vars

Vars are first introduced in *Port of Dead Ships*. They have their own enumeration of years, based on the founding of their city.

Appearance: Those of Varn are tan or dark skin, very tall and skinny. Their hair and eye color are not mentioned but they could have black hair and brown eyes, based on Earth humans with similar skin pigmentation. Most of the men wear small chin beards and pointed helmets with turban-like bands of cloth wrapped around the rim. Women and children are rarely seen outdoors by strangers and the women probably go out heavily cloaked if they must. Children probably never go outside unless they are under heavy supervision.

Living Area(s): Varn

Life Span: The life span of Varnians is unmentioned but it appears to be long and their population is fairly stable with birth rate steady with death rate. It's possible with birth rates so low it caused the men to be over-protective of their women and children. Many women and children were killed in the earthquake in *Port of Dead Ships* when buildings collapsed but with Gunnora's blessing rejuvenating the energy of the crystal of the Seated One and the destruction of the evil black cube gate in the *Port of Dead Ships*, they may recover and even prosper.

Power: They seem to have means of detecting Power and females among them can use it. Whether males can use Power is unknown. Despite (or perhaps because of) this females (except for Power users) and children are kept within the deepest part of their houses when outsiders visit. Their spiritual leader appears to be a powerful woman seer who is completely wrapped in bindings like a mummy (including her entire head and hands) who sits on a glass throne in their temple and holds a crystal orb of power. She has a cowled priestess who is the "Speaker for the Seated One" (who can use mindspeech, among other powers) as her voice to the people and representative in Council.

Other: The Vars may have come through a Gate that is presumably closed. Since the current year in *Port of Dead Ships* is the "Founding Years of Varn" 6810, they have been on the Witch World nearly seven thousand years and their city could be older than Es itself.

They are taller than any other known race and are exquisite glass-makers. They are also good fishermen and raise a unique breed of sheep which produce wool that is is highly sought after and rarely traded.

Their houses are brightly colored on the outside and are set in the cliffs facing a bay. Their temple is highly ornamented and contains many examples of their beautiful glass art.

Vrangs

Vrangs first appear in *Three Against the Witch World*

Appearance: Vrangs have a bird-like body but lizard-like head. Their heads are covered with red scales that glitter the sun, but its feathers are blue-grey. They are somewhat dragonlike in appearance.

Living Area(s): Heights of Escore

Life Span: It's unknown how long a Vrang lives. They could have the life span of a fairly long-lived bird.

Power: Vrangs are not mentioned to have Power though they can telepathically communicate. They could well have the Power to trice circle and bind opponents.

Other: Vrangs can work effectively both as scouts and as warriors.

Vupsall

The Vupsall are a race of nomads first mentioned in *Sorceress of the Witch World*. It is unclear whether or not they are a gated race though, given the sheer amount of races that were gated in by the adepts of old, they probably aren't native to the world.

Appearance: The Vupsall have red-yellow hair[1], dark brown skin, and broad features. Their eyes aren't described but, given their skin color, probably are brown (at least Kaththea makes no mention of their eyes being brightly colored).

Living Area(s): Escore (nomadic)

Life Span: The Vupsall life span is not mentioned directly, but Utta has outlived several generations of them by the time Kaththea shows up.

Power: Except for *The Scent of Magic* there is no mention of the Vupsall being able to use the Power, though their smiths and a few Wise Women might have something of it.

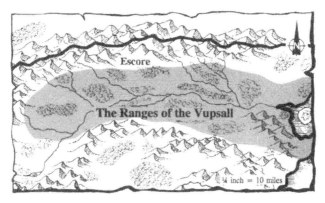

GURPS: Witch World Roleplaying Guide 1989 p.28

Other: The Vupsall, or at least the band described, seem to have originated somewhere in the north-eastern part of Escore before their tribes were broken and scattered by sea raiders. They are somewhat barbaric in many ways, but may have once had a more advanced civilization. They are extremely skilled with gems and metal-forging and practice elaborate burials. They paint their bodies and might also dye their hair. They seem to have large, wolf-like dogs that can be hitched to sleighs. These dogs have cream-colored bodies and brown legs with a brown stripe running down their backs to the tip of the tail.

The tribes of the Vupsall practice polygamy, with a chief having several wives. Raids on other tribes for supplies and slaves probably occur. They are no friends with the sea raiders.

Sorcerer's Notes:

Though they seem to enjoy the nomadic lifestyle they currently have it could be possible that the Vupsall once held a sea coast similar to the Dales, and like the Dales they were invaded. In their case, however, the tribes didn't unite to fight a common enemy and were broken and scattered. Whether they might ever settle again is unknowable since, aside from _Sorceress of the Witch World_ and _The Scent of Magic_, they are never mentioned again in any Witch World story. It's possible that after _Sorceress of the Witch World_, since Kaththea felt responsible for the Vupsall after the fate of the tribe she was forced to look after by Utta, she returned with Hilarion to rebuild his Tower and gathered the tribes under their protection.

Footnotes:

1. Kaththea, in the book, seems to think their hair color looks unnatural, especially since they have 'dark brows'. Given their habit of body painting, it's entirely possible the Vuspell have naturally black hair that they dye.

Were-Riders

The Were-Riders (sometimes written Were Riders or Wereriders) were first introduced in _Year of the Unicorn_.

Appearance: Were-Riders, as first introduced, have black hair and green eyes. They probably resemble the Old Race in other features.

Living Area(s): Grey Towers, Arvon. While they were in exile they lived in a Lodge in a protected forest in The Waste.[1]

Life Span: Though the life span of the Were-Riders is not mentioned, they have lived for centuries at least. This is backed up by Kethan's swordmaster mentioning having trained Herrel when he was young. In *Year of the Unicorn*, Herrel hints to Gillan that the Were-Riders are over a thousand years old.

Power: Were-Riders seem to have a lot of Power. Beyond their ability to shape shift they can easily cast very complicated illusions and separate a person into two entities. The exact limits of their powers is unknown. Herrel also implies to Gillan in *Year of the Unicorn* that they can bend time as it doesn't seem to flow at the same rate for them as it does for the Dalesmen of High Hallack. In fact this may be true of the defensive barrier around Arvon itself. They also demonstrate the ability to create powerful wards, seduction spells and travel into the spirit realm.

Other: How much of their shape shifting is illusion and how much is real is debatable. They can all shapeshift into animals, usually related to a heraldic image: pard, lion, hawk, eagle, horse, boar, wolf, fox, bear, badger, etc. They are also apparently able to assume other shapes as well, though they do so less often and these secondary forms seem more like an illusion than reality (their change into a beast seems to be real shape-shifting, not illusion).

Gryphon in Glory mentions there are twenty banners for the Were-Riders in their Lodge in The Waste. Whether this means there are twenty Were-Riders or merely twenty forms is unclear. Also possible is that only twenty were in residence at that time and the others were off on a mission of some kind. Though there are thirteen brides from the Dales, Herrel mentions there are nearly twice that number of Riders. *Bloodspell* mentions there are nearly forty Riders, though at least two die in that story. Given the length of time they traveled and any possible losses in their fight against the Alizonders during the invasion of High Hallack, it seems safe to say there are probably at least twenty-six Riders left.

Were-Riders seem to have an affinity for having names that begin with 'H'. Kethan is an exception, but he wasn't named by his true parents. Kethan's reliance on his pard belt seems to be due to the spells laid on him before he entered the Youth's Tower. Despite what is shown in *The Warding of Witch World* he has started to learn to transform without it by the end of *The Jargoon Pard* and with practice probably wouldn't need it at all.

The novella *Were-Wrath*, if set in the Witch World, shows Farne, whose mother was human and father Were, initially needing an animal fur belt to assist his transformation. When he fully accepts his heritage and takes up his sword of power, the belt disintegrated. His sword is similar to the sword Herrel uses to channel power in *The Jargoon Pard*. It's possible Farne is descended from Aurek & Derora from *Rite of Failure* as Greer and the northern lands mentioned in *Were-Wrath* are similar to High Hallack and

Arvon, though they are not named as such. It's possible they may be located in The Waste where *Rite of Failure* takes place.

There are no female shape shifters among the Riders, though both *Were-Hunter* and *Were-Flight* introduce female shifters. One is a young woman from Earth (Glenda) with a special ring that initiates her transformation after arriving in Arvon. The other (Khemrys) is the daughter of a Were-Rider (Herwydin) and a Daleswoman (Tirath). Both young women change into large cats and meet male Riders that also change into large cats (Harwin, son of Kildas & Harl, and Harlyn, whose parents names are unmentioned).

The Were-Riders were a created race, the Adept who built the Grey Tower fused his most loyal retainers with animals so they could transform into them at will. *We the Women* implies that the Were-Riders were originally men of a race the Falconers attacked when they entered the Witch World and drove from their land, their women taken as wives. The men eventually ended up in Arvon and took service with the Adept who made them into the Were-Riders.

It is unclear why the Were-Riders did not each have a bride. The number of "twelve and one" brides may have to do with the original geas of their banishment from and return to Arvon.

Names, forms, and brides

Despite the emphasis placed on the Brides, only five of them are mentioned by name in *Year of the Unicorn*: Kildas, Solfinna, Alianna, Aldeeth, and Marrime (whose place was taken by Gillan). The others are not mentioned in this book or any other.

Among the Were-Riders there are also only a few names and forms mentioned. Both *Year of the Unicorn* and *Bloodspell* have names and forms, though exactly how canonical *Bloodspell* is may be debated. *Were-Flight* and *Were-Hunter* also have some lineages (which, again, could be debated as to being cannonical or not). Names or forms in bold are from *Year of the Unicorn* & *Gryphon in Glory*, names or forms in italics are from "*Bloodspell*". Names and forms that are from "*Were-Hunter*", "*Were-Flight*", and "*Rite of Failure*" are noted when they appear:

Hyron [Horse]
Herrel [Snow Cat][2]
Harl [Eagle][3]
Halse [Bear]
Hisin [???][4]
Hulor [boar]
Hewlor **[Gray Wolf]**
Helder **[Black Wolf]**[5]
[Tawny red and black-spotted Cat]
Hessel **[Boar]**
[mountain cat]
["a snouted and armored lurker of the river"][6]
Hannon *[Black Bear]*[7]

Hathor [*Mountain Elk*]
[*Red Wolf*]
[*Desert Lion*]
Herwydin [???][8]
Harlyn [large cat with molted head and smoky-tipped tail][9]
Harwin [snow leopard][10]
Huran [???][11]
Aurek [golden pard][12]

Footnotes:

1. *Gryphon in Glory*
2. Marries Gillan. Son- Kethan, adopted daughter (niece)- Aylinn
3. Marries Kildas. Three children, youngest son- Harwin.
4. Marries Solfinna.
5. In "*Bloodspell*" the black wolf is killed, but in *Year of the Unicorn* is mentioned in passing as one of the Rider forms.
6. This, and the mountain cat, are mentioned in *Gryphon in Glory* as images on the banners at the lodge. Could this be describing a hippo?
7. Hannon was killed in "*Bloodspell*".
8. Mentioned in "*Were-Flight*". Separated from the other Riders, Herwydin meets and marries the lady Tirath. He dies, his form is unmentioned, but his daughter Khemrys can become a golden-furred pard.
9. Mentioned in "*Were-Flight*" his parentage and history seems out of sorts with the other Riders: page 430 "I sat musing near the fire, watching the twisting flames make patterns against the dark. Seeing them thus brought to mind my mother's face, bending her will to See what lay ahead in the scrying bowl" This seems to imply he was not born of one of the Dales Brides. Page 433 "The land I rode was familiar to me. Many times I had come this way hunting with my father and brothers. We were but a few leagues' distance from my childhood home". His age seems nearly the same as Khemrys in the story, and it's mentioned that the year of the Harpy moves into the year of the Orc - part of Kethan's childhood in *The Jargoon Pard* and he was, like Khemrys, born around the year of the Fire Drake. This causes some continuity errors, especially with *Year of the Unicorn* which states there are no more than thirteen Brides among the Riders. Also it's hard to reconcile the woman of Power his mother is given the treatment Gillan got. A possible solution to this would be that he, like Herrel, is half-breed and born before the Riders were forced to leave Arvon. Or, he is one of the Weres of the Waste like Farne and possibly descended from Aurek & Derora.
10. Mentioned in "*Were-Hunter*". He is the third child of Kildas & Harl.
11. He is mentioned in "*Rite of Failure*" as shaman to the Wereriders. Why they need a shaman is unclear since they all have Power.
12. In "*Rite of Failure*" he is the son of Huran. Why his name deviates from the usual is unknown but it's possible he was named by his mother and Huran honored her decision. Also unknown is why he and his father have blond hair when all other Riders are mentioned as having black hair.

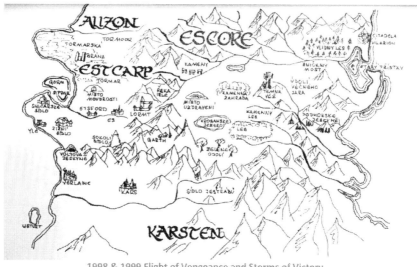

1998 & 1999 Flight of Vengeance and Storms of Victory
By Lubos Makarsky - Czechoslovakia

Genealogies:

House of Car Do Prawn

House of Car Do Prawn

House of Car Do Prawn										
Lied Kardisk	Lord ?	+	Lady Eldris			Lady Eldris	+	Hyron [Wererider]		
		=	=				=			
	=	=	=			=		**House of Reeth**		
Lady ¼	Lord Erach	Lady Heiroise		?	Herrel [Wererider]	Herrel [Wererider]	+	Gillan [Estcarp]
	=	=		=			=	
=	=	=		=			=	
Haughus	Thaney	Avginn (fostered by Herrel and Gillan)				Kethan (fostered by Heroise and Ursilla)		

-In *The Warding of Witch World* Aylinn is paired with Firdun of the House of Gryphon while Kethan is paired with Uta, a woman trapped in cat-form (implied to be a shapeshifter by the geneology of that book).

Footnotes:
1. The brother of Lady Eldris, gave Clan Right back to Eldris after her affair with Hyron, fell in the Battle of Thos.
2. Died of fever after Thaney's birth.
3. Who (or what...!) Ursilla brought to Heroise's bed to be the father of Aylinn is never mentioned and remains a mystery. One could speculate it might be Jakata the evil mage with steel coloured eyeballs from *The Warding of Witch World* considering Ursilla's connection with Garth Howell but there is no evidence either way.

House of Edale

House of Edale

House of Edale								
Lord Franklyn of Edale	+		Lady ?		Almondia [Estcarp]	+	Truan [Estcarp]	
	«							
	«		«		«	«	«	
	v		v				v	
	Brunissende	+1	Elyn				Elys	+	Jervon [Dorn]
							«	
						«	«	«
							v	v
				Alon	+	Eydryth		Trevon

Footnotes:

1. There is no reference to any children of Brunissende and Elyn, but there is no reason to think they don't have any, either.

House of Gryphon

House of Gryphon

	House of Gryphon				House of Paltendale		
	House of Ulmsdale						
	Ulm the Horn-Handed	+	Lady ?		Lord Fortal of Paltendale	«	Lady ?
		+				+	
		v				v	
Lady Elva1	«	Lord Ulric2	+1	Lady Tephana of Paltendale	Lady Tephana of Paltendale4	+	Lord ?
		«	«	«		«	
		v	v	v		v	
Joisan of Ithkrypt	+	Kerovan		Lisana		Hilmer	
«	«	«		+			
v		v		Rogear5			
Hivana		Firdun					

Footnotes:

1. Ulric's second wife. See the footnote for Ulric.
2. In *The Crystal Gryphon* it is mentioned that Ulric "...had taken two ladies before my mother and had of them children. But the children had been either born dead or had quitted this world in their early years, sickly creatures one and all. He had sworn, however, to get him a true, heir, and so he set aside his second lady in favor of my mother when it seemed as if he would get no son of her." His first wife died in childbirth and the name of his second wife was Elva, as told in *Of the Shaping of Ulm's Heir*.
3. In a way, Kerovan has 3 fathers. With her spells, Lady Tephana attempted to have Galkur possess Ulric while they were conceiving Kerovan which gave Kerovan cloven feet however, this awoke Landisl who became Kerovan's spiritual father, giving him amber eyes.
4. In *The Crystal Gryphon* she is mentioned as widowed (p 25). In *Heir Apparent* it is mentioned that her first husband was her cousin and was heir to the House of Fortal (even though Fortal is the name of her father in *The Crystal Gryphon* (p 26).) Her husband, however, has brothers who want to rule instead (p 27). It is mentioned that both of Lady Tephana's parents died in a plague shortly after her birth.
5. Rogear is "cousin-kin" to Kerovan p.16 *The Crystal Gryphon*. He's from the Lady Tephana's side of the family.

House of Ithkrypt

House of Ithkrypt

House of Ithkrypt[1]							
Lady Alys	+	Lord Randor			Lord Randor	+	Lady ?
"	"					"	
v	v	v				v	
Lord Cyart[2]	Dame Math	Lady Islaugha[3]	+	Lord ?	Lord ?[4]	+	Lady ?
+	+	"	"	"		"	
Lady ?[5]	Lord ?[6]	"	"	"		"	
		v	v			v	
		Toross	Yngilda			Joisan	(+ Kerovan of Ulmsdale)
			+				
		Lady ?	+[2] Lord Elvan of Rishdale				

Footnotes:

1. Founded by Harb, who defeated the Demon of Irr Waste with a broken sword.
2. There was a child before Cyart, but it died.
3. younger sister.
4. younger half-brother to Cyart.
5. Cyart's Lady died without providing him an heir.
6. Math "...had been axe-wed... to a lord of the south. But before he could claim her, the news came that he had died of a wasting fever."
7. "Yngilda... goes to one already wed once, a man old enough to be her father..." Presumably his first lady gave him no male heirs or he'd be risking trouble by remarrying.

House of Paltendale

House of Paltendale

House of Paltendale[1]										
Lord Parsen (founder)[2]										
First Generation[4]										
Second Generation										
Third Generation										
(First Son)				(Second Son)			Pletten the Wicked[3]			
First Generation since Pletten										
			Lord Fortal [4]		Second Generation since Pletten					
	+				"	"	"	"		
	"				v	v		v		
Lord Ulric of Ulmsdale	+	Lady Tephana[5]	+	Lord ?	Lord Hagar	+	Lady ?	Lord ?[8]	+	Lady?
"	v	"		"	"			"		
v		v	v	"	v			v		
Lord Kerovan of Ulmsdale		Lady Lisana of Ulmsdale	Heymer?	First Son	Halin	Hogeth	+	Lady ?[8]	Kogear?	
							v			
							Child			

Footnotes:

1. There is supposedly a curse on the line that every fourth generation one of the sons of the line will be evil and desire women whether they want him or not.
2. Paril of Paltendale, founder of Erondale, may be a younger son of Parsen since *Silver May Tarnish* says "He kept the badge of Paltendale, being a son of the House." p.23
3. Third son to the lord of Paltendale who raped Meive's ancestor.
4. Given that Lady Tephana is supposed to have married her cousin, her father or mother must be related to the Paltendale side as well.
5. In *The Crystal Gryphon* she is mentioned as widowed (p 25). In *Heir Apparent* it is mentioned that her first husband was her cousin and was heir to the House of Fortal even though Fortal is the name of her father in *The Crystal Gryphon* (p 26). Her

137

husband, however, has brothers who want to rule instead (p 27). It is mentioned that both of Lady Tephana's parents died in a plague shortly after her birth.

6. Since *Heir Apparent* mentioned "brothers", Lord Hogar can't be the only one - and is certainly not the eldest (since Lady Temphana's husband was heir). This actually fits in pretty well, since each generation tends to have three sons. It does raise the question of why Hlymer is not heir, though, since Dales tradition usually has it where the first son of the father inherits a given Dale. The third son being youngest makes sense - Hogar would inherit the Dale after his older brother died so Rogear would naturally be interested in marrying elsewhere.

7. Why Hlymer is not heir of Paltendale is never addressed. Since Dales tradition usually has it where the first son of the father inherits a given Dale there has to be something odd going on that the brothers are able to challenge Hlymer's inheritance or somehow force Lady Tephana out.

8. In *The Crystal Gryphon* it is mentioned Hogeth has a pregnant wife who would be better off without him.

9. Rogear is "cousin-kin" to Kerovan p.16 *The Crystal Gryphon*. He's from the Lady Tephana's side of the family (knowing and having Power). Since he's not Hogar's son he must be the son of the other brother.

House of Tregarth

House of Tregarth

House of Tregarth					
	Simon Tregarth	+	Jaelithe		
		=			
	v	v	v		
Dahaun	+	Kyllan	Kemoc	Kaththea	+	Hilarion
	=		+		=	
=	=	=	Orsya [Krogan]	=	=	=
v		v		v	v	
Eiona		Keris		???	???	Alon (adopted)

Houses of Erondale and Honeycoombe

House of Erondale and Honeycoombe

House of Erondale[1]					
Paril of Paltendale	+	Daughter of wealthy Sulcar			
	:				
	Lord Joros	+	Lady Ashera		
		=			
=	=	=	=	=	=
v	v	v	v	v	v
Merrion	Unnamed 1	Arila	Unnamed 2[2]	Lorcan[3]	Meera

		Honeycoombe[4]				
Meive's Great Grandmother	+	Pletten the Wicked				
	=					
	v					
	Meive's Grandmother	+	Meive's Grandfather			
	=					
	v					
	Meive's Mother	+	Meive's Father			
		=				
	=	=	=	=	=	=
	v		v	v	v	
Lorcan	+	Meive[5]		Welwyn[6]	Jenna	Saria
	=					
	v					
	Child					

Footnotes:

1. Cadet branch of Paltendale.

2. Two of Lorcan's older siblings die before he is born. When, exactly, they were born is not mentioned, but Merrion is seven years older than Loran and Anla is only three, so there could easily have been at least one between between Merrion and Anla.

3. Given the Paltendale connection, Lorcan and Kerovan must be related at some point as distant cousins.

4. Landale officially. Founded by the younger son of a lord four generations before. p51 *Silver May Tarnish*

5. Meive is pregnant by the end of the book and expecting by next summer.

6. Meive's older brother.

Hoses of Gorm and Verlaine

Houses of Gorm and Verlaine

House of Gorm						House of Verlaine			
Orna of Gorm[1]	+	Hilder, Lord Defender of Gorm	+	>[2] [Tor Marsh]		Lady ? of Verlaine	+	Fulk of Farthom[3]
	=		=				=	
	=				+	=	=	
	=				v			
	v		Korls of Gorm	+	Loyse of Verlaine	=[4]	Duke Yvian of Karsten
Uryan			=			
			v			
			Simond	+	Tursla [Tor Marsh]		

Footnotes:

1. Hilder's second wife.

2. Hilder's first wife is referred to as the "First Maiden" of the Torfolk in *Sand Sister*.

3. Fulk says he is "the younger son of Farthom in the northern hills" which makes it unclear if "Farthom" is his father's name or his family's home.

4. This was an Ax Marriage only and never consummated.

Abbreviations used in portions that follow.

REFERENCE ABBREVIATION	TITLE	REFERENCE ABBREVIATION	TITLE
Amb	Amber Out of Quayth	Oldt	Old Toad
Blood	Bloodspell	Peacock	Peacock Eyes
Candle	Candletrap	Plum	Plumduff Potato-Eye
Cat	Cat and the Other	Port	Port of Dead Ships
Change	Changeling	Que	A Question of Magic
Chron	The Chronicler	Ramp	Rampion
Circle	The Circle of Sleep	Rof	Rite of Failure
Crys	The Crystal Gryphon	Rodd	The Road of Dreams and Death
Dark	Darkness Over Mirhold	Root	The Root of All Evil
Dss	Dragon Scale Silver	Saltg	The Salt Garden
Dsm	Dream Smith	Sas	Sand Sister
Drpj	Dream Prirates' Jewel	Scent	The Scent of Magic
Exl	Exile	Seak	Seakeep
Falb	Falcon Blood	Seasd	Sea-Serpents of Domnudale
Falc	Falcon's Chick	Sentinel	The Sentinel at the Edge of the World
Falh	Falcon Hope	Shau	The Shaping of Ulm's Heir
Fallaw	Falcon Law	S'ol	S'Olcarias's Sons
Falm	Falcon Magic	Song	Songsmith
Fnca	Fenneca	Sorc	Sorceress of the Witch World
Fortune's	Fortune's Children	Sps	Spider Silk
Futures	Futures Yet Unseen	Stillborn	The Stillborn Heritage
Gate	The Gate of the Cat	Stones	The Stones of Sharnon
Godron's	Godron's Daughter	Storm	Stormbirds
Green	Green in High Hallack	Strait	Strait of Storms
Grye	Gryphon's Eyrie	Swseller	The Sword Seller
Gryg	Gryphon in Glory	Swou	Sword of Unbelief

Gunnora's	**Gunnora's Gift**	Tall	**Tall Dames Go Walking**
Heart	**Heartspell**	Three	**Three Against the Witch World**
Heir	**Heir Apparent**	Through	**Through the Moon Gate**
Heroes	**Heroes**	Tog	**The Toads of Grimmerdale**
Horn	**Horn Crown**	Torb	**To Rebuild the Eyrie**
Hue	**The Hunting of Lord Etsalian's Daughter**	Trey	**Trey of Swords**
Isle	**Isle of Illusion**	Voice	**Voice of Memory**
Jpard	**The Jargoon Pard**	Ware	**'Ware Hawk**
Judge	**The Judgment of Neave**	Warl	**Warlock of the Witch World**
Kep	**Key of the Keplain**	Wtw	**We the Women**
Know	**Knowledge**	Weavers	**The Weavers**
Lav	**La Verdad: The Magic Sword**	Web	**Web of the Witch World**
Legacy	**Legacy from Sorn Fen**	Were-f	**Were-Flight**
Mage	**The Magestone**	Were-h	**Were-Hunter**
Milk	**Milk from a Maiden's Breast**	Whisper	**Whispering Cane**
Nei	**Neither Rest Nor Refuge**	Whiter	**The White Road**
Nighth	**Night Hound's Moon**	WW	**Witch World**
Nine	**Nine Words in Winter**	Wolf	**Wolfhead**
Oath-b	**Oath- Bound**	Yofu	**Year of the Unicorn**
Ofas	**Of Ancient Swords and Evil Mist**	Zar	**Zarsthor's Bane**

The Warding of Witch World 1996

Calender

List of Years

The Witch World naming system originated in the Dales and was brought to the Eastern Continent by Sulcar traders.

Unnamed years: Refugees of Old Race fled from Escore and created a memory barrier re the eastern mountains. Approximately 600 unrecorded years then pass.

- *Year of the Cloven Hoof* = Dalesmen come to High Hallack. (Horn)

Approximately 400 more years pass, after which the following sequence begins:

YEAR OF THE...

- *Serpent King* = Kerovan is born in Ulmskeep   (Crys)
- *Ringed Dove* = Kerovan's sister Lisana is born.   (Crys)
- *Salamander* = Almondia and Truan are shipwrecked in Wark. (Dss)

         Joisan is born (Crys)   (Dsm?)
- *Phoenix / Fire Arrow*
- *Hippogriff / Bicorn* = Elys and Elyn born.   (Dss)
- *Roc / Hill Giant*
- *Basilisk / Sea Calf*

142

- *Black Adder / Kestrel*
- *Frost Giant*
- *Yellow Dwarf* = Dairine cast ashore at Rannock   (Sps)
- *Fox Maiden / Mandrake*
- *Spitting Toad* = Joisan and Kerovan axe married.   (Crys)
- *Kobold*
- *Snow Cat*
- *Horned Hunter*
- *Air Spirit*
- *Swordsmith*
- *Crowned Swan*
- *Moss Wife*
- *Fire Troll* = The Invasion   (Dss)
- *Leopard*
- *Falcon*
- *Raven*
- *Night Hound*
- *Gryphon* = Pact with Weres
- *Fire Drake* =   (Tog)
- *Hornet*
- *Unicorn* =   (Yofu)   (Grye)   (Amb)
- *Red Boar* =   (Legacy)   (Swou)   (Jpard = Kethan born)
- *Gargoyle* =   (Sps)
- *Mandrake*
- *Wyvern*
- *Winged Bull*
- *Horn Worm*
- *Dragon Horse* = Eydryth born   (?)(Song)
- *Gorgon*
- *Manticore* = Alon born   (?)
- *Barrow-Wight*
- *Cameleopard Firdun*
- *Sphinx*
- *Nix*
- *Lamia*
- *Chimera*
- *Harpy*
- *Orc*
- *Werewolf*
- *Horned Cat*
- *Pookaworm*

- *Weld*
- *Hydra*
- *Triton*
- *Centaur*
- *Opinicus*
- *Simurgh*
- *Remorhaz*

Months

Alizon	Season	Dales and Estcarp
Moon Of …….	Season	Month of the …….
	Winter	
Dart Venom (Nov.)		*Crested Owl*
Hunger Moon (Dec.)		*Fire Thorn*
The Knife (Jan.) (Extra calendar day, Veneration Day – falls between 9th and 10th days.)		*Ice Dragon*
First Welping Moon (Jan./Feb.)		*Snow Bird*
The Dire Wolf (Mid Feb. into March)		
	Spring	
		Hawk (First month of Spring)
Chordosh (March / April)		*Crooknecked Fern*
The Spotted Viper (April into May)		*Fringed Violet*
The Fever Leaf (May into June)		
	Summer	
		Willow Carp

144

The Split-tusked Boar (June / July)		_Golden Lac ewing_ (Their extra day, Midsummer's Day falls between the 14th and 15th.)
The Torgian Foals (July / August)		_Silver Crowned Bee_
The Second Welping Moon (August)		
	Autumn	
The Bloodwine (Sept.)		_Anda Wasp_ _Harvest Moon_
The Hooded Crow (Sept. / Oct.)		_Shredbark Tree_ (Oct. into early Nov.)

General Information

The following categories describe material which recurs throughout the series or is especially relevant.
Notes: An entry marked, for example, (Jpard) indicates the novel or story source of the information.

An entry marked, for example, -- See Jpard (no parentheses) indicates that further detail regarding the item in question will be found under its title in Section II. Consult the Alphabetical Listing for a complete key to abbreviations of novels and stories.

Locale Key

- (Arv) = **Arvon**
- (HH) = **High Hallack**
- (Tw) = **The Waste**
- (Est) = **Estcarp**
- (Alz) = **Alizon**
- (Kst) = **Karsten**
- (Esc) = **Escore**
- (Sul) = **Sulcar**

Geography

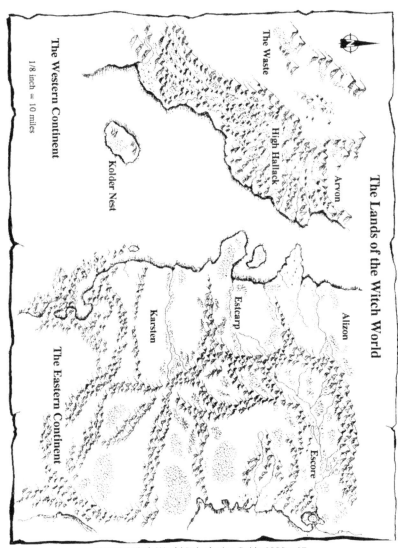

GURPS: Witch World Roleplaying Guide 1989 p.17

High Hallack

GURPS: Witch World Roleplaying Guide 1989 p.30

High Hallack is the sixth country introduced in the [Witch World] series and is one of the most widely chronicled. It first features in *Year of the Unicorn*.

Capitol: None. Each Dale has a Keep where the Lord resides.

Government: Each of the Dales of High Hallack has it's own Lord who rules from his Keep. Each Dale may have a number of small villages with a mayor who is responsible to the Lord. Until the invasion by the Hounds of Alizon, there was no formal central government. During the war an alliance of three (originally four) powerful Lords led by Lord Imgry organized the Dalesmen and finally drove the Hounds from High Hallack. After the war, it is unknown if this alliance was continued or eventually dissolved. Also present in the Dales are abbeys of the Dames who are led by an Abbess and council of Dames. The abbeys are autonomous refuges for women who are drawn to the veneration of the sacred Flame.

Geography: High Hallack is a country of many rolling hills and dales. There are a number of craggy areas as well as rivers that tend to run far inland. Most of the land tends to be very fertile.

Surrounding Areas: The Waste which forms the western and part of the northern border of High Hallack is a massive, mostly uncharted land littered with the remnants of Old Ones.[1] Much of the Waste appears devastated by powerful magic. Many strange and twisted creatures roam the Waste such as the Winged Ones and Thas. The Waste was also a temporary home for the exiled Were-Riders. Possibly in the north-west just inside the Waste is the small country of Greer. To the north lies Arvon, a country surrounded by a magic barrier that, unless one is admitted, the person may wander through the land without seeing any signs of occupation. Also to the north near the coast in the mountains which form the border of Arvon is Quayth. Further north west off the coast are some tiny island nations. (see: *Isle of Illusion* & *Rampion*) In the south, the Sorn Fen is a region populated by a fey and magical people who are known to reward acts of great kindness. Far to the east across the sea are the distant countries of Gorm, Estcarp, Karsten, the Tor Marsh and of course the home of the invading Hounds: Alizon. Somewhere (probably about a third of the way to Estcarp though maps mark it closer) is the island of the Kolder.

Since the Dales are covered in multiple books over the course of years, the Dales and places within the Dales are mentioned below in publishing order. It should be kept in mind that some Dales and places are mentioned in several books.

Year of the Unicorn [2]

Dales Mentioned
Norsdale
Dimdale (north past Arm of Sparn)
Falthingdale (west)
Harrowdale (north-west)
Hockerdale (north-west after Harrowdale)

Places Mentioned
Norstead Abby (in Norsdale)
Fast Ridge (can be seen from the bell tower of the abbey – may be to the south – there are Dales between)

Falcon Fist (to the east of Norsdale)
The Waste is to the north, past Arm of Sparn, Dimsdale, Gasterbrook, and Gorge of Ravenswell
Croffkeep (a mountain fort) - Croffkeep can be reached from Norstead Abby in winter by the night of the second day if there is a forced march. The Throat of the Hawk can be reached from Norstead Abbey by forced march in winter within three days' time.

The Crystal Gryphon [3]

Dales Mentioned

Ulmsdale – in the north; Gryphon is its symbol: when Kerovan leaves Imgry's camp it takes him about five days to ride to the dale, but he has to take a long, slow way: Ulmsdale is destroyed by the Power, flooded with the sea. It is northwest of Ithdale.
Paltendale – lies further northwest of Ulmsdale
Ithdale – famous for its fresh water pearls in its streams; Broken Sword of Harb is its symbol
Rishdale – ruled by Elvan. It is an upper dale that gets rich on wool. Serpent is its symbol.
Uppsdale – neighbors Ulmsdale ruled by Gyrerd and Annet of Langsdale. Formerly ruled by Savron[4]
Fyndale – neighbors Ulmsdale (has a fair)
Flathingdale – neighbors Ulmsdale and is ruled by Wintof[5]
Vastdale – has the port of Jorby (not a neighbor of Ulmsdale but is close-by): it falls during the war
Norsdale – five days' ride west of Ithdale

Places Mentioned

Ulmsport – port belonging to Ulmsdale
Ulmsdale Keep – two days ride away from the edge of the dale where Kerovan was raised
Shrine of Gunnora
Shrine of Galkur – a day's ride away from the Shrine of Gunnora
Ithkrypt – it takes ten days to go there from Ulmsdale; it is in Ithdale. There is a river that leads inland to it.
Trevamper – a town set at the meeting of highway and river where all the merchants of the north show their wares on occasion. Even Sulcar travel inland to trade there.
Moon Well – in the western portion of Ithdale. Under the full moon it is said to give good luck if a pin is dropped in and a spell-rhyme is canted. Its waters can be used for scrying. A plant with wide dark green leaves veined with white grows at the lip. The leaves when pinched give off a pleasant aroma.
Cape of Black Winds – Ulmsport is past this

Calder – one of the rivers the Alizonders were advancing on

Giant's Fist – on the crag on the southern edge of Ulm's dale. Under it is a smoothly flat platform with a gryphon deeply carved in it. There is a passage to Ulmskeep under it, and the passage also leads to a sea cave. In a south-eastern portion of Ithdale there is a woods with a place of the Old Ones in it. It has glowing white pavement with a star design and herbs.

Isle Keep – near Ithdale there is a Keep on an island.[6]

The Road of the Old Ones – one end is half a day's ride from Riwell's cottage. It runs strait west, and then makes a wide curve to the north. From there they can view mountains to the north and the land is more hospitable. It takes about two days to ride, but has a dead end.[7]

Spell of the Witch World [8]

"Dragon Scale Silver"

Dales Mentioned

Vestdale – where Wark and Jurby are located[9]

Haverdale – where Pell is from and Jervon took service

Dorn[10] – in the path of the first inward thrust. The keep was taken in five days. Haverdale is close by (within about three day's ride).

Edale - Where Coombe Frome is.

Places Mentioned

Wark – has a small, reef-guarded bay

Jurby Port – a larger port in Vestdale where taxes for the year are collected

A Place of Power lies in the hills above Wark[11]

Ford of Ingra – where, three days before they reached the inland dale the people of Wark inhabited, Jervon and Pell stood rear guard with others of Haverdale. Only Jervon and Pell survived, and Pell later died.

Inisheer – somewhere there was a last muster

Trevamper – a town south of the Ford of Ingra[12]

Keep of Coomb Frome – kept as a garrison but was once Edale's lord's house.[13]

House of Kantha Twice Born – overrun by the Hounds within the last year.[14] Kantha had the Old Learning.

Spiral Pillar Web – This was a trap of the Dark before being destroyed. The Old One in it would summon a lord of Edale from the Keep into her lair, leaving an empty husk.[15]

"Dream Smith"

Dales Mentioned
Ithondale - ruled by lord Vescys

Places Mentioned
Fos Tern – "one might as well try to empty Fos Tern with a kitchen ladle!"
Ghyll – lies at the river fork in Ithondale; westernmost holding of Lord Vescys
Twyford – where Bronson the smith travels twice a year with his wares
Sym and Boldre – far from Ghyll
Shrine of the Old One Talann high in the northern craigs.

"Amber Out of Quayth"

Dales Mentioned
Uppsdale – leaving it at dawn they reach the southern edge by noon and the outer rim of Fyndale by night
Fyndale – where annual fairs were held until the War and again after
Langsdale – Annet is the daughter of Urien of Langsdale[16]
Marchpoint - When Gyrerd, Annet, and Ysmay reach the edge of Fyndale they camp with the Lord of Marchpoint, his lady, and his daughter Dairine. (p.108)[17]

Places Mentioned
Ladies of the Shrine ruled by Abbess Grathulda
Ulmsport – where merchants would gather for great fairs.
Moycroft – a ruin abandoned during the War due to lack of manpower where Ysme, Hylle and company spend the first night from Uppsdale as they go north to Quayth.[18]
Silent Wood - By the third day of travel, Ysme, Hylle and company start to travel through a strange, silent woods[19] They travel through it for a day. By the end of the next they camp in hills. There are an unknown amount of days that pass after the hill camp until midmorning one day when they get a sea wind. On a ledge by the sea where there are three stone chairs. Shortly after they turn inland from them they reach Quayth.
Quayth – north; it is a large holding with four towers at its corners – two round, one square (which has the gate), and one angular (star-shaped)[20].

"Legacy from Sorn Fen" [21]

Dales Mentioned
None

Places Mentioned
Klavenport – located on the Sea of Autumn Mists. It is a Gate Keep.
Sea of Autumn Mists – where Klavenport is located; somewhere to the south.
Sorn Fen – to the southwest of Klavenport
Inn of the Forks – A road running north and south met there. It was Abandoned sometime before the Battle of Falcon Cut, some five or more winters back. Caleb restores it with the power of the ring and Higbold destroys it again with that same power. It is about a day's walk away from Sorn Fen.

Years Mentioned
None: It seems to take place immediately after the Invader's War so this story probably takes place either at the end of the Year of the Hornet and through the Year of the Unicorn or during the Year of the Unicorn and through the Year of the Red Boar.

"The Toads of Grimmerdale" [22]

Dales Mentioned
Landendale - Where Hertha had been sent two years before for safety and riding from it was raped by a Dalesman.
Trewsdale - ruled by Kuno, brother to Hertha. It escaped the Hounds, though a small, beaten group had stumbled in and had been defeated by Kuno.
Nordendale - Along the path Hertha is facing from Gunnora's Shrine.[23]
Grimmerdale - Past Nordendale.
Corrierdale - Wiped out by the Hounds of Alizon. The heir to it is drinking himself away at the inn in Grimmerdale.

Places Mentioned
Hola's Hold - in Landendale
Thunderer's Alter - where, if Hertha died from a failed abortion attempt her brother Kuno could pretend to be pious and say it was Fate.
Mulma's Needle and Wyvern's Wing - two landmarks Hertha uses on her journey to Gunnora's Shrine.
Gunnora's Shrine - This seems to be more or less a day's walk east away from Hola's Hold. It's among the heights and on an ancient road that also leads to the Circle of Toads.
Circle of Toads - In Grimmerdale. It is a place of ill repute.
Komm High - a marketplace for wool traders, though at the time of the story the market is no longer held.

Years Mentioned

"This was the last of the Year of the Hornet, next lay the Year of the Unicorn" (p.152)

"Changeling" [24]

Dales Mentioned

Lithendale

Places Mentioned

Years Mentioned

None: It was just about to turn from the year of the Hornet in the previous story, so this must be the Year of the Unicorn.

Horn Crown [25]

Dales Mentioned

Places Mentioned

Years Mentioned

Silver May Tarnish [26]

Dales Mentioned

Places Mentioned

Years Mentioned

Special Places:[27]

o Norsdale the dale on the northwestern border of High Hallack. (see: *Year of the Unicorn*, mentioned in *The Crystal Gryphon*)

o Norstead Abbey, an abbey of the Dames where many women and children took refuge from the invasion of the Hounds of Alizon. (see: *Year of the Unicorn*, *The Crystal Gryphon*, *Gryphon in Glory*, The Toads of Grimmerdale, & *Changeling*)

o Falthingdale, a mostly unoccupied forested dale west of Norsdale. (see: *Year of the Unicorn*)

o Dimdale, a mostly unoccupied dale north of Norsdale. The Arm of Sparn separates Norsdale from Dimdale. Casterbrook is in the north of Dimdale and the Gorge of Ravenswell is north of that on the border of the Waste. (see: *Year of the Unicorn*)

- o Fartherdale, a tiny north-western dale overlooked by the Hounds of Alizon. It's Lord died in the war. (see: *Ully the Piper*)
- o Coombe Brackett, a tiny village in Fartherdale where Ully is from. High Ridge Garth is a holding near Coombe Brackett. (see: *Ully the Piper*)
- o Ulmsdale, a northern coastal dale flooded during the Invasion. (see: *The Crystal Gryphon*)
- o Ulmsport, the port city of Ulsmdale also flooded during the Invasion. Beyond the cape of Black Winds, north of "Jorby". Nearby is the Giant's Fist, a beacon craig. (see: *The Crystal Gryphon*)
- o Paltendale, a dale north-west of Ulmsdale possibly the northern most dale of High Hallack where Kerovan's mother came from. Rumors of "Old Ones" blood running through their bloodline. (see: *The Crystal Gryphon*)
- o Ithdale, the dale where Joisan was born. Founded by Harb of the Broken Sword. (see: *The Crystal Gryphon*)
- o Ithkrypt, the keep where where Joisan grew up, now a ruins, destroyed during the Invasion. (see: *The Crystal Gryphon*)
- o Trevamper, a trading town near the Ford of Ingra. (see: *The Crystal Gryphon* & *Dragon Scale Silver*)
- o Rishdale, an "Upper Dale" near Ulmsdale known for it's wool trade, a serpent is it's House Badge. Joisan's cousin (her father's half-sister's daughter) Yngilda was to be married to Lord Elvan of Rishdale. (see: *The Crystal Gryphon*)
- o Flathingdale, a northern dale ruled by Lord Wintof. (see: *The Crystal Gryphon*)
- o Vestdale, an eastern coastal dale. (see: *Dragon Scale Silver*. Spelled Vastdale in *The Crystal Gryphon*)
- o Wark, a fishing village in Vestdale where Elys & Elyn grew up. (see: *Dragon Scale Silver*)
- o Jurby, a town in Vestdale where the tax from Wark was delivered to the Lord of Vesdale Keep. (see: *Dragon Scale Silver*. Spelled Jorby in *The Crystal Gryphon*)
- o Haverdale, an inland dale where Jervon was Master of Horse. (see: *Dragon Scale Silver*)
- o Dorn, a Keep neighbouring Haverdale (dale unmentioned). (see: *Dragon Scale Silver*)
- o Ford of Ingra, the location of a great battle against the Hounds (location unmentioned). (see: *Dragon Scale Silver*)
- o Edale, a western dale that escaped notice of the Hounds, where the Keep of Coomb Frome and the town of Inisheer are located. Also nearby is the House of Kantha Twice Born, an abbey of the Dames. (see: *Dragon Scale Silver*)
- o Coomb Frome, the original Keep of Edale, is infamous for Ingaret's Curse, where Elyn is Lord with his wife the Lady Brunissende. (see: *Dragon Scale Silver*)

- o Gastendale, a dale where the Lord (Myric) was wiped out by the Hounds (or assassinated) at the beginning of the Invasion. (see: *Dragon Scale Silver*)
- o Uppsdale is famous for it's amber and home to Lord Gyrerd. (see: *Amber Out of Quayth* also mentioned as a neighbouring dale to Ulmsdale in *The Crystal Gryphon*.)
- o Langsdale is home to Lord Urian who's daughter married Lord Gyrerd. (see: *Amber Out of Quayth*)
- o Fyndale a northern dale where a great fair is held in late summer. (see: *Amber Out of Quayth* also mentioned in *The Crystal Gryphon*.)
- o Grimmerdale infamous for it's circle of Toads. (see: *The Toads of Grimmerdale*, *Changeling* & *La Verdad: The Magic Sword*)
- o Lethendale where Hertha becomes Lady of Lord Trystan. (see: *Changeling*)
- o Shrine of Gunnora. (see: *The Toads of Grimmerdale*, *Changeling* & *La Verdad: The Magic Sword*)
- o The Inn of the Forks is a burned out inn at the intersection of two major roads just north of Sorn Fen. (see: *Legacy from Sorn Fen*)
- o The ruins of Eggarsdale, former home of Lord Marbon & Dwed, is on the western border of High Hallack, near the Waste. (see: *Zarsthor's Bane*)
- o Itsford, a town in Eggarsdale where Dwed is from. (see: *Zarsthor's Bane*)
- o The ruins of Moorachdale, former home of Brixia of the House of Trogus, is somewhere in the south. (see: *Zarsthor's Bane*)
- o The Pass of Ungo, location of one of the final battles against the Hounds of Alizon. Lord Jartar was slain and Lord Marbon received a serious head wound there. (see: *Zarsthor's Bane*)
- o Domnudale, a costal dale where it's rumoured there is a curse of a sea serpent.
- o Seakeep & Ravenfield [aka the new Eyrie of the Falconers] are located on the northern coast of High Hallack. (see: *Seakeep* & *Falcon Hope*)
- o Erondale is near Paltendale and was founded by a cadet branch of that house.(see: *Silver May Tarnish*)
- o Honeycoombe Dale (previously Landale) is a tiny hidden dale famous for it's honey. (see: *Silver May Tarnish*)
- o Merrowdale is two days wagons-ride from Honeycoombe. Both Dales are in the south. (see: *Silver May Tarnish*)
- o The new Sulcar port settlement of Osberic is located in the south on the coast of High Hallack. (see: *Dream Pirates' Jewel*)

Footnotes:
1. Though it often gets represented as a desert, in *Year of the Unicorn* the area of the Waste that Gillan and the others pass through does not look much different than the Dales, but there is a foreboding presence. It is also mentioned in other books that bits of the Waste are habitable and not simply a desert.
2. Published 1965
3. Published January 1st 1972

<u>4</u>. In *Amber Out of Quayth* he is mentioned as having died as did his son Ewald. Presumably Gyrerd is another son of Savron's since he inherited the dale and Annet calls Ysmay 'sister' (p.106). He is mentioned in *Wolfhead* as one of the three lords of the north.

<u>5</u>. He is mentioned in *Wolfhead* as one of the three lords of the north.

<u>6</u>. The lake empties into a shallow stream. There are two draw bridges leading to it. One is still usable while the other has its end melted into a glassy slag that is painful to Kerovan's touch. It has no windows on the bridge level but does have some on the next. The walls meet the water and there are two towers where part of the draw bridge is controlled. The inner court has a garden and a couple of trees.

<u>7</u>. By around noon of the first day they reach a point of rest, though they need to seek shelter a little further down the road which is a room with a partial roof. While in the shelter Kerovan has a vision of those withdrawing down the road. After turning north they come to an arched bridge that spans a stream of some size. They camp beside the running water for the night. By noon of the next day, they reach the foothills of the mountains. The road narrows and twists among the sharp ridges. There are faces and runes carved into the walls. Noon finds them in a narrow vale where they rest under the chin of a face. The carvings grow more complex until they see the Great Star. Shortly after there is a last turn in the Road and it ends at a flat surface of rock surrounded by two pillars. It is there that Kerovan finds the Crystal Gryphon.

<u>8</u>. Published April 1972

<u>9</u>. It's probable these are simply a one letter misspell of Vastdale and Jorby.

<u>10</u>. There is a lord of Dorn, so it's likely either part of an unnamed Dale or is a shortened form of Dorndale. The story implies that the lord of Dorn is either Jervon's grandfather or related through marriage.

<u>11</u>. It has walls about shoulder high and has a five-pointed star space within. At the center there was a star-shaped stone alter. Within the points of the star lay sand of red, blue, silver, green, and gold which is never disturbed. Outside the walls are the remains of an herb garden.

<u>12</u>. Also mentioned in *The Crystal Gryphon*

<u>13</u>. It is probably two or three day's ride from the Ford of Ingra since the cup goes from being 1/3 black at the Ford to having only two finger's width of clear left when Elys looks at it again there.

<u>14</u>. Either close to the beginning of the Year of the Gryphon or the end of the year before since it's now fall.

<u>15</u>. When leaving at dawn from Coomb Frome there is a day and a night of travel.

<u>16</u>. Since Gyrerd rode home from the south with her, Lansdale is presumably somewhere south of Uppsdale, though its exact distance is not stated.

<u>17</u>. Presumably the full name is Marchpointdale and the last bit is cut off much like how Seakeep's is.

<u>18</u>. They are presumably still in Uppsdale's territory. They are still in tilled lands by the second day of travel. They travel more north than west and angle towards the sea.

<u>19</u>. Tall, old trees with feathery lichens of green, rust, white and blood red and a hushed sense of someone watching. The path twists and turns but remains wide enough to accommodate a wagon.

<u>20</u>. This configuration would make the inner courtyard look like a diamond.

<u>21</u>. Originally published in 1972 and republished as part of *Lore of the Witch World* in 1980.

22. First published in 1973 and republished as part of _Lore of the Witch World_ in 1980.

23. The lord and his heir had fallen at Ruther's Pass two years ago. Hertha arrives there on the afternoon of the same day she leaves Gunnora's Shrine. It "had once been a regular halt for herdsmen with wool from mountain sheep on their way to the market at Komm High"p.156

24. _Lore of the Witch World_ 1980. Though _Sword of Unbelief_ was originally published before this story (in 1977) and republished as part of the _Lore of the Witch World_ anthology in 1980, it takes place completely in the Waste.

25. Published July 7th 1981. While both _Zarsthor's Bane_ and _Gryphon in Glory_ precede this book in terms of publication, the vast majority of those two books takes place in the Waste rather than in the Dales. Similarly _Gryphon's Eyrie_ takes place completely within Arvon. So while they are all generally considered part of the High Hallack cycle, they are not included here.

26. Published October 31st 2006. While _Songsmith_ precedes this book in terms of publication, that book takes place in Estcarp, Escore, and Arvon.

27. _GURPS: Witch World_, the following Dales are listed:

Uppsdale	Hockerdale
Paltendale	Lithendale
Rishdale	Corriedale
Ulsmdale Ulmsdale	Nordendale
Langsdale	Roxdale
Fyndale	Grimmerdale
Vastdale	Gastendale
Ithordale	Innerdale
Ithdale	Tryndale
Dorndale	Athendale
Haverdale	Bochsdale
Norsdale	Everdale
Dundale	Clewsdale
Harrowdale	Brimdale
Landendale	Durndale
Gastendale	Jensdale
Edale	Helmsdale
Vestdale	Smalldale
Tresdale	Mansdale
Garnsdale	Sutherdale
Summersdale	Lorndale
Fartherdale	Thromdale

Trey of Swords UK 1979

Gryphon in Glory Poland 1991

The Dales

GURPS: Witch World Roleplaying Guide 1989 p.33

- Corriedale
- Dimdale
- Domnudale
- Dorndale
- Dundale
- Edale
- Eggarsdale

159

- Ellsdale
- Estindale
- Falthingdale
- Ferndale
- Fyndale -- *Site of a large fair* (Amb)
- Garnsdale
- Gastendale
- Grimmerdale
- Harkendale
- Harrowdale
- Haverdale
- Hockerdale
- Ithondale
- Ithdale / Ithsdale
- Kylldale
- Langsdale
- Lethendale
- Menasdale
- Mistdale
- Moorachdale
- Nordendale
- Norrisdale
- Norsdale
- Paltendale
- Ravenfielddale
- Rimsdale
- Rhysdale
- Ronansdale
- Rosehilldale
- Roxdale
- Rozdale
- Seakeepdale
- Summersdale
- Syledale
- Trewsdale
- Tyrnsdale
- Ulmsdale
- Uppdale / Uppsdale
- Vastdale / Vestdale
- Ylsedale

Keeps and Holds
- Arnwold

- Birkhold
- Brettford
- Castle Van
- Coomb Frome
- Croffkeep
- Dorn
- Ellskeep
- Eroffkeep
- Faerwold
- Horla's Hold
- Ithkeep
- Ithkrygt
- Klavenport's Gatekeep
- Komlin's Keep
- Malmgarth
- Maryekeep
- Min's Hold
- Moycroft
- Paltenkeep
- Quayth
- Ravenfieldkeep
- Seakeep
- Sharoon Keep
- Thantog
- Traedwyth
- Trin
- Ulfmaer
- Ulmskeep
- Waleis
- Wealdmar

Abbeys
- Kantha Twice Born
- Landendale
- Lethendale
- Linna
- Meadowvale
- Norstead
- Rhystead
- Rishdale
- Ulmstead

Towns and Villages

- Boldre -- *Ithondale town* (Dsm)
- Casterbrook
- Colmera -- *Harkendale village* (Que)
- Coomb Brackett
- Ghyll -- *Ithondale* (Dsm)
- Greywold
- Handelsburg
- Itsford
- Inisheer -- *Interior town* (Dss)
- Komm High -- *Wool market* (Tog)
- Norstead
- Linna
- Lormill -- *village* (Wolf)
- Pessik -- *Harkendale fishing village destroyed by the invaders* (Que)
- Rannock -- *coastal Estcarp* (Sps)
- Sym -- *River village* (Dsm)
- Trevamger -- *Highway & river junction large fair*
- Twyford
- Wark -- *Fishing village* (Dss)

Ports
- Jorby/Jurby -- *in Vestdale*
- Kalaven Port
- KlavenPort -- *On the Sea of Autumn Mists* (Legacy)
- UlmsPort
- VennesPort

Bodies of Water
- Sea of Autumn Mists
- Komlin Sea

Landmarks
- The Cradle
- Emerald Cove
- Falcon Fist
- Falcon Pass
- Falcon Ridge
- Giant's Fist
- Gorge of Ravenswell
- Grayson Heights
- Hawk s Claw-- *Held by Silvermantle Clan and Voices of the Heights before their defeat in olden times* (Jpard)
- Mulma's Needle

- Salzarat
- Sorn Fen
- Throat of the Hawk
- Wyvern's wing

Battle Sites
- Arm of Sparn
- Falcon Cut
- Ingra Ford
- Inisheer
- Battle of Morlan
- Petthys
- Ruther's Pass
- Ungo Pass

Islands
- Lelanin
- Ulys

Inns
- Herdsman's Halt Inn of Nordendale
- Inn of the Forks -- *at a North-South road junction* (Legacy)

The Waste

The seventh region introduced in the [Witch World] series is the Waste.

Capitol: none

Government: none. Outlaws, prospectors for Quan iron and ancient artifacts from High Hallack, Winged-Ones, Thas, and more recently traders from Arvon to High Hallack travel the Waste.

Geography: The waste is a vast region, patchworked with areas of desert wasteland and lush greenery. Ancient ruins of the Old Race (and sometimes older races!) lie throughout it.

Surrounding Areas: To the east are the Dales of High Hallack. To the northeast is Arvon. To the southeast is Sorn Fen. To the far west is rumoured to be another ocean across which is the eastern shore of Escore. It is unknown how far north, south, and west the Waste extends.

Special Places:
1. There are many ruins throughout the Waste.

2. A forest where the Were-Riders made their home while in exile, "the lodge". (see: *Year of the Unicorn*, *Gryphon in Glory* & *Were-Wrath*)
3. The Road of Exile, an ancient road of the Old Ones Riwal & Kerovan discovered in the northern Waste. It leads to a cliff face where Kerovan discovers the crystal gryphon. (see: *The Crystal Gryphon*)
4. A grove of Laran trees which produce the White Heart blossoms. (see: *Zarsthor's Bane* & *The Warding of Witch World*)
5. The recently recovered ancient city of An-Yak, former home of Lord Zarsthor, now home to Brixia, Lord Marbon & Dwed. (See: *Zarsthor's Bane*)
6. The ancient land of Varr, where Kathal, the Keep of Lord Eldor used to be. Now there is nothing but ruins. (See: *Zarsthor's Bane*)
7. The White Road is an ancient highway of the Old Ones running from near the Were-Riders forest to the mountains which form the south-west border of Arvon. Like the Road of Exile, it too ends in a cliff face. (see: *Gryphon in Glory*)
8. The Range of Shifting Shadows, the mountain home of the <u>Thas</u>. (see: *Gryphon in Glory*)
9. Carfallin, a ruined keep where Joisan takes refuge. (see: *Gryphon in Glory*)
10. Possibly the tiny country of Greer. (see: *Were-Wrath*)
11. Vastar gate. (see: *The Warding of Witch World*)
12. The court of Gweytha. (see: *The Warding of Witch World*)
13. A nest of Rus. (see: *The Warding of Witch World*)
14. The Hold of Sassfang (a Winged One). (see: *The Warding of Witch World*)
15. The Web Lands, where Web Riders (giant spiders who float on the wind with their webs) and giant sand worms live. (see: *The Warding of Witch World*)
16. The Wing Ways, a hilly region where the tiny glider people live. (see: *The Warding of Witch World*)

Landmarks

- <u>The Black Tower</u>
- <u>The Horned One's Keep</u>
- <u>Narat</u>
- <u>Needle's Eye</u> -- *village* (Peacock)
- <u>Ravensmoore</u>

Enviroment

The Waste is not all desert. Many pockets of mountains, valleys, etc. unpredictable weather, with some dangerously harsh conditions, such as the: <u>Dune Moving Storm</u> (Swou)

Arvon

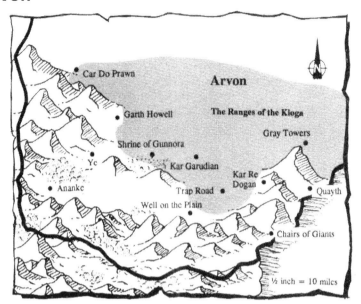

GURPS: Witch World Roleplaying Guide 1989 p.31

Arvon is the eighth country introduced in the [Witch World] series in *Year of the Unicorn*.

Government: The closest Arvon has to a central government are the Seven Lords (one of which is The High Lord Aidan[1]) and the Voices of the Heights (usually simply called "the Voices") who maintain the balance of power between the four Clans (Redmantle, Goldmantle, Bluemantle, & Silvermantle) of the Old Race and many other races and peoples of Arvon through prophecy and the Warders. House Lordship of the many Keeps is inherited through the mother's bloodline—the eldest son of the eldest daughter of the line becomes chieftain and his eldest sister's son becomes chieftain after him. House Lords of the Old Race give allegiance to one of the four Clan Overlords. The Were-Riders are led by Hyron.

Geography: Arvon is surrounded by mountains which (along with its powerful wards) cuts it off from the surrounding areas. Within the bordering mountains, the main of Arvon are rolling plains good for farming and wild forested areas. Time might flow differently in Arvon than elsewhere since many inhabitants are well over a thousand years old.

Surrounding Areas: To the southeast are the Dales of High Hallack. To the southwest begins The Waste which extends to an unknown distance up the western border. To the east is the sea (over which lies Alizon and the northern lands of the Latts). Just off the coast are some tiny island nations. (see: *Isle of Illusion* & *Rampion*) To the north is mainly unknown, though *The*

Warding of Witch World mentions a Sulcar settlement and possibly settlements of the Latts as well.

Special Places:

1. Car Do Prawn is home of Lord Erach and lies in the Redmantle Clan lands. (see: _The Jargoon Pard_)
2. Kar Garudwyn, the castle of the Gryphon lies near Car Re Dogan. (see: _Gryphon's Eyrie_, _Songsmith_ & _The Warding of Witch World_)
3. Car Re Dogan is the ruined home of Maleron, half-brother to Sylvya. It lies close to the Gate that blocks Arvon to the south near the Dales. The ruins have an odd visual effect on those traveling through them so that places that appeared clear a moment before seem suddenly blocked while other places that seemed blocked appear suddenly open. Anything that could be used as a marker seems to multiply in images. (see: _Year of the Unicorn_ & _Gryphon's Eyrie_)
4. Car Do Yelt "where there is said to be one favored by the Voices" (See: _The Jargoon Pard_)
5. The Setting Up of Kings is to the north of Car Re Dogan and serves as a place of advice and (possibly) judgment. (see: _Gryphon's Eyrie_ and _Year of the Unicorn_)
6. The Gray Towers is home to the Were-Riders. (see: _Year of the Unicorn_)
7. The Fane of Naeve (see: _Year of the Unicorn_, _The Jargoon Pard_, _The Judgement of Neave_ and _Songsmith_)
8. Quayth is in the south-east corner of Arvon, is famous for its amber and is home to Lady Yaal the Far Thoughted, a renowned healer, her Lord Broc, and Ysmay, formerly of Uppsdale. (see: _Amber Out of Quayth_)
9. The Shrine of Gunnora, where women wishing to conceive seek aid and those about to give birth find ease. (see: _The Jargoon Pard_)
10. Garth Howell, where magic is studied. (see: _The Jargoon Pard_, _Songsmith_ & _The Warding of Witch World_)
11. Linark, where Aylinn went to study moon magic. (see: _The Jargoon Pard_ & _The Warding of Witch World_)
12. Reeth is the Star Tower, home to Herrel, Gillan, Ayslinn and Kethan. (see: _The Jargoon Pard_ & _The Warding of Witch World_)
13. The Whiteflow (this is a river according to Andre's notes. See: _The Jargoon Pard_)
14. The Higher Land, home to the Wild Ones. (This may be the mountains bordering Arvon. Who the Wild Ones are isn't explained. See: _The Jargoon Pard_)

Clan Territories
- Bluemantle
- Goldmantle
- Silvermantle

- Redmantle
- Farmarsh -- *A village formerly in Silvermantle lands, but annexed by Goldmantle's Lord* (blood)
- Ford at Deepwater -- *In Redmantle lands* (Song)
- The White Flow -- *River boundary of Silvermantle territory* (Jpard)

Keeps and Holds
- Car of Prawn
- Car do Yelt
- Car re Dogan
- The Gray Towers
- Kar Garudwyn

Abbeys and Schools
- Garth Howell
- Halsted Abbey
- Linark

Landmarks
- The Fane of Neave
- Landisl's Valley
- Reeth / The Star Tower
- Valley of the Gryphon
- The White Highway -- *Runs from High Hallack across the Waste to Arvon*

Battle Sites
- Farthfell
- Thos

Footnotes:
1. see: *The Jargoon Pard*

Oceans Between Continents

North
- Islands of Ever Ice
- Northern Kingship
- Vellas Islands

South
- Bay of Dead Ships
- Point of the Hound -- *Landmark south of Estcarp / Karsten* (Port)
- Usturt -- *spiders' island* (Sps)
- Port of Varn

- Volcanic Island Chain

Alizon

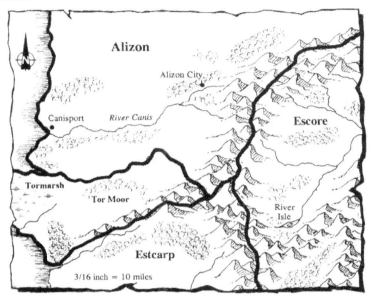

GURPS: Witch World Roleplaying Guide 1989 p.25

Alizon is the second country introduced in the [Witch World] series but the internal structure is not shown until later books. It is first mentioned in *Witch World* but isn't visited in any great detail until *Falcon Magic* & *The Magestone*.

Capital: Aliz (Alizon City?)

Government: Barony. Four Barons have ruled Alizon during the series, the previous probably murdered by his successor the moment he showed any weakness. Sandar (*Witch World*), Facellian (*Three Against the Witch World*), Mallandor (*Falcon Magic/The Magestone*), and Norandor (*The Magestone*).

Geography: The exact layout of Alizon is not generally stated, though it is likely flat in most places. There are some mountains in the south of the country, as well as a border with Tor Marsh and Tor Moor. To the west lies the ocean. The north and east of Alizon are uncharted. It's likely that there are mountains surrounding this country to the north and east, though it's also possible that (at least to the east) there could be no barriers at all.

Surrounding Areas: To the south are mountains and the Tor Marsh and Tor Moor and beyond them, Estcarp. To the south east lies Escore. To the south west, in the bay, lies the island nation of Gorm. Somewhere to the far north lie the land of the Latts. Far west across the ocean lies Arvon and High Hallack.

Special Places:

1. Alizon City.
2. Aliz is the main port city of Alizon. It lies on the western tip of the northern peninsula that forms the bay where lies Gorm and is due north from where Sulcarkeep was located. *Witch World*.
3. Alix is the town where Krevanel Hold is located. *The Warding of Witch World*.

Cities

- Aliz -- *On west coast, opposite Sulcarkeep across the bay* (WW)
- Alizon City -- *Capital, centrally located* (Falm & Mage)
- Canisport --*Western coast* (Mage)

Landmarks

- Alizon Gap -- *Between Tor Marsh and the mountains* (Falm)
- Alizon Ridge -- *On north side of the Forbidden Mountains* (Falm)
- Castle Krevonel -- *Kasarian's family holding: Alizon City* (Mage)
- Kennel of the Hounds -- *Royal castle, Alizon City* (Falm & Mage)
- The Long Sisters and the Hands -- *Shipwrecking rocks off Alizon's west coast* (Voice)

Inn

- The Hooded Crow Inn -- *in Alizon City* (Mage)

The Magestone 1996

Tor Marsh / Fen

GURPS: Witch World Roleplaying Guide 1989 p.26

Tor Marsh is the fifth country introduced in the [Witch World] series. It is first mentioned in _Witch World_, its border hidden by mists, and is visited in greater detail in _Web of the Witch World_ & _Sand Sister_.

Capital: The ruin of Volt's Hall where Volt's chair still remains.

Government: The villages are run by their wisewomen, the oldest having most seniority. The men form groups of hunters who are lead by the strongest and most successful.

Geography: The Tor Marsh is a large swamp bordered by a sandy beach.

Surrounding Areas: To the north is Alizon. To the west is the Tor Moor. To the South is Estcarp and to the east is the bay with the island of Gorm. Across the sea lies High Hallack.

Special Places:

- Besides the scattered villages of the Torfolk, there are ancient stone ruins hidden throughout the swamp. The most important being the Hall of Volt where his chair still remains. (see: _Sand Sister_)
- Near the shore is the hidden pool of Xactol, known only to Tursla. (see: _Sand Sister_)
- Enkere -- _Where the river draining Tor Marsh reaches the sea_ (Web)
- Volt's Shrine
- Xactol's Sand Pool

Karsten

South Keep

Estcarp

Eyrie

Cave of
Volt

Hawkholme

Verlaine

Kars

River Kars

Karsten

Stone of
Knowledge

¼ inch = 10 miles

GURPS: Witch World Roleplaying Guide 1989 p.23

Karsten is the third country introduced in the [Witch World] series. After Estcarp and the Dales, it is the country most often dealt with. It first appears in *Witch World*.

Capital: Kars

Government: Dutchy. There have been 3 Dukes of Karsten during the series: Yvian (*Witch World*/*Web of the Witch World*), Pagar of Geen (*Three Against the Witch World*) and Shandro (*Ciara's Song* / *The Duke's Ballad*).[1]

Geography: Karsten seems to be mostly plains. There are mountains to the north and to the east and ocean to the west. There are also mountains to the far south, though these are introduced in later books and only shown on later maps. In the south-east corner is a portion of coast of the eastern sea.

Surrounding Areas: To the north are mountains and the Eyrie and women's villages of the Falconers (at least pre-Turning). Beyond these lies Estcarp. To the north-west is the peninsula with Yle and Sulcarkeep (later, their ruins). To the north-east are more mountains and the land of Escore. To the east are mountains, though these appear to be purely coastal and only a small section of the east coast is easily accessible by Cynan's Hold. Somewhere to the far south is Salzarat, the former homeland of the Falconers. (see: *Falcon Blood*) To the south-west, somewhere off the coast, is the isle of Usturt, (in)famous for its spider silk. (see: *Spider Silk*) On the southern border is the ancient nation of Varn and the Port of Dead Ships. (see: *Port of Dead Ships*, *The Warding of Witch World*)

Special Places:

1. Kars is the capital city of Karsten and where much of the action in the country tends to take place. (see: *Witch World*)
2. Verlaine is a coastal holding famous (or infamous) for its location and gaining off of the wrecks of ships. (see: *Witch World*)
3. The Cave of Volt is located somewhere in the northern mountains of Karsten on the coast between Verlaine and Yle. (see: *Witch World*) Whether the Cave still exists after the Turning is unknown though it is mentioned in *Three Against the Witch World* that Koris returned the ax which is a good indication that it probably does.
4. Garthholm is a town on the north bank of the river across from Kars. (see: *Witch World*)
5. There is a small island at the mouth of Kars' river where Karsten prisoners were traded to the Kolder. (See: *Witch World*)
6. Yost is near the west coast where they mine iron and trade it with the Sulcar. (see: *Ware Hawk*)
7. Yar is near the west coast where they mine silver and trade it with the Sulcar. (see: *Ware Hawk*)
8. The ruined keep of Hawkholme is located somewhere in the east near the mountains that forms the border to Escore. (see: *Ware Hawk*)
9. Eleeri's Gate was somewhere in the far east of Karsten not far from Cynan's Hold. On the map included in *The Key of the Keplian* she arrived near the east coast of Karsten, south of the mountain border of Escore.
10. Cynan's Hold is in the far south east of Karsten near the coast of the eastern sea and south of the mountain border to Escore. (see: *The Key of the Keplian*)
11. Garthholm on the River (see: *Witch World*)
12. Hawkholme (see: *Ware Hawk*)
13. Kars -- *Capital, river city* (see: *Witch World*)
14. Verlaine Keep -- (see: *Witch World* and *Web of the Witch World*)

Footnotes:

1. There is also a fourth Duke, Asfrid, mentioned in The Sentinel at the Edge of the World who was sometime before Yvian. And a fifth, named Louvain, mentioned in Darkness Over Mirhold who takes power sometime after Pagar and Shandro, as it's mentioned that the wars between Karsten & Escarp are over by that point).

Gorm

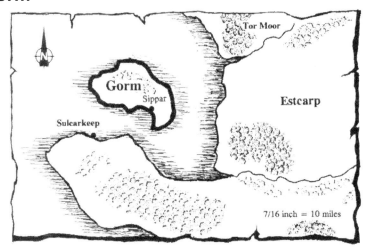

GURPS: Witch World Roleplaying Guide 1989 p.22

Gorm is the fourth country introduced in the [Witch World] series. Little is known about this island nation before it was invaded by the Kolder. It is visited in *Witch World* where they roust the Kolder.

Capital: Sippar

Government: Lord Defender. Hilder was the last (Koris's father, died just before the Kolder invasion).

Geography: Gorm is a large island off the coast of Estcarp.

Surrounding Areas: To the east is the coast of Estcarp. To the northeast is the shore of the Tor Marsh. To the south is the bay formed by the peninsula which had Sulcarkeep at it's tip. To the north is the peninsula that forms the northern side of the bay, that is part of Alizon, with the port city of Aliz at it's tip. Far to the west across the sea is the coast of High Hallack.

Special Places:

1. All that remains on Gorm is a small outpost of Borderers from Estcarp who keep anyone from contact with the Kolder tech that remains. The rest of the island has been left as a monument to the horror of what the Kolder did there. (see: *Witch World*)

- Sippar -- *Capital and port* -- See WW & Web

Estcarp

GURPS: Witch World Roleplaying Guide 1989 p.19

Estcarp is the first country introduced in the [Witch World] series and where readers first learn about the world. (see: *Witch World*)

Capital: Es City

Government: Formerly a matriarchal thaumarchy (ruled by the Council of Witches) led by the Guardian, currently ruled by Koris of Gorm until the Witches have recovered enough to resume their duties.

Geography: Estcarp is mostly plains with mountains surrounding it on the north, south, and east. To the west is the ocean. To the northwest is the Tor Marsh, which also occupies part of its northern boundaries.

Surrounding Areas: To the north is Alizon. To the northwest is the Tor Marsh and Tor Moor. To the east are the Barrier Mountains and, beyond them, Escore. To the south are mountains, and former home of the Falconers- the Eyrie and it's surrounding Falconer Women's Villages (possibly current home as well if the events of *Falcon Law*, where they've created a new Eyrie, are correct). Also in these mountains, closer to the coast is the tomb of Volt. Past the southern mountains is Karsten. To the immediate west lies the island of Gorm, currently abandoned except for a small garrison of guards from Estcarp.

Special Places:

1. The Gate of Simon Tregarth is located somewhere to the north and east on the Tor Moor close to Tor Marsh, south of the Alizon border. (see: *Witch World*)
2. Es City is located along the River Es and is probably close to the heart of the country. It surrounds Es Castle, the governmental centre of the Guardian and Guardians' Council of Estcarp.
3. The ruins of Sulcarkeep are located on a peninsula which forms the southern rim of the bay where the island of Gorm is located. For some reason the Sulcar decided not to rebuild their old keep by Estcarp after the Kolder War ended. (see: *Witch World*)
4. Just inland from the ruins of Sulcarkeep are the ruins of Yle, the Kolder outpost on the arm of the peninsula between Sulcarkeep and Estcarp that forms part of the Karsten border. (see: *Witch World*)
5. South Keep was the home of Simon Tregarth, Jaelithe, Koris of Gorm and Lloyse of Verlaine. Located near the junction of the mountains that form the border between Estcarp & Karsten, and the peninsula where Sulcarkeep & the Kolder settlement of Yle used to be. (see: *Web of the Witch World* & *Three Against the Witch World*)
6. Romsgarth, a town south-west of South Keep. (see: *Web of the Witch World* and *Ware Hawk*)
7. Es Port is on the mouth of the River Es opening out into the great bay. (see: *Web of the Witch World*)
8. The Place of Wisdom is the training place for all Witches. This holding is apparently a couple days ride west of the eastern mountains if *Three Against the Witch World* is accurate. Given the haste with which the Tregarth triplets were traveling it could be this distance actually might be a week or more if traveling at a more reasonable pace.
9. Lormt is a place of scholarship, long derided by the Witches due to its primarily (old) male population. Lormt seems to be gaining a wider population as its reputation spreads post Turning. Lormt is about ten days ride at a leisurely pace away from Es City. (see: *Three Against the Witch World*)
10. Just south of Tor Marsh on the coast of Estcarp lies the tiny fishing village of Rannock. (see: *Spider Silk*)
11. Esland, a farming community probably somewhere north-east of Romsgarth where they grow grain. (see: *Ware Hawk*)
12. Gottem is a farming village some ways away from Es City. (Mentioned in *The Warding of Witch World*)

Cities and Ports
- Es City
- Esland – *South; grain exporting town* (Ware)
- Eslee Port -- *Also called Estee Port and Es Port where River Es empties into the bay* (Song)

- Romsgarth -- *South Central town noted as a hiring center* (Ware)

Keeps
- Dhulmat Manor -- *East* (Three)
- Es Castle -- *Witches' Headquarters*
- Etsford -- *South Central; Loyse's Keep, where the triplets were fostered* (Three)
- Falcon's Eyrie -- *South*
- Gweddawl Garth -- *South; apprentice witch's home* (falm)
- Ravenhold Keep -- *South* (Fallaw)
- Sulcarkeep
- Keep of Trin
- Yle

Towns and Villages
- Blagden -- *Southeastern village* (Falm)
- Cedar Crest -- *Southeastern village* (Wtw)
- Kastryn --*North Central village* (Song)
- Mountain Gate -- *Southeastern village* (Oldt)
- Pethiel -- *North Central village* (Exl)
- Rannock -- *Coastal village* (Sps)
- Ravensmere -- *Northwest* (Heart)
- Riveredge – *South Women's village* (Wtw)
- Rylon's Corner -- *village famous for horse race and fair* (Song)
- South Wending -- *Village between Kastryn and Lormt* (Song)
- Torview -- *Northwest village* (Heart)
- Twin Valleys -- *South Central village* (Wtw)

Places of Interest
- Dame Cavern – *Southeast, A Place of Old Ones between Riveredge and Lormt* (Wtw)
- Lormt -- *Southeast* (Exl & Mage)
- Place of Wisdom --*Northwest Witch school* (Falm)

Landmarks
- Barrier Mountains -- *Between Estcarp and Alizon*
- Falcon Crag
- Falcon's Eyrie -- *Fane of Wings*
- Great Mountains -- *Notheast, between Estcarp / Alizon and Escore*
- Karsten Gap -- *Destroyed in the Turning*
- The Keyhole -- *Near Karsten Gap*
- Serpent Teeth -- *Rocks off Rannock*

Inns and Taverns

- The Bold Falcon -- *Eastern* (Sentinel)
- The Dancing Dolphin -- *In Eslee Port* (Song)
- Silver Horseshoe
- Silver Spur
- Wayfarer's Inn -- *Adjacent to the Silver Spur* (Heart)

Escore

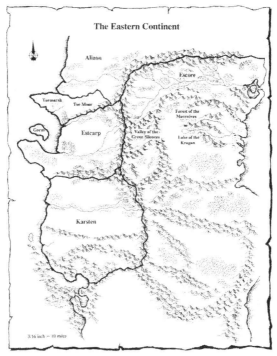

GURPS: Witch World Roleplaying Guide 1989 p.18

Escore is the ninth country introduced in the [Witch World] series in *Three Against the Witch World*.

Capital: None.

Government: There is no central government. The People of the Valley of Green Silences are lead by Ethutur, Dahaun & her husband Kyllan Tregarth. The Krogan are led by Orais. The Renthans are led by Shapurn. The Flannon are led by Farfar. The Vrang are led by Vorlong, the Wing Beater. The Old Race exiles from Karsten are led by Lord Hervon. The Scaled Ones also have an (unnamed) chieftain. Dinzil was the leader of the Old Race who did not flee to Estcarp. All these races but the Krogan have formed an alliance against the Dark. It's possible that after *The Gate of the Cat* the Krogan may have finally allied with the others. Otherwise, the different races and peoples of Escore generally keep to themselves. The Vupsall form tribes led by a

Chief that often war with each other and are preyed upon by the Sea Raiders. Herds of Keplian are ruled by a stallion but sometimes by the strongest, most senior mare if there is no adult stallion.

Geography: Escore has a range of geographical features. To the west are the Barrier Mountains, to the East is the unnamed eastern ocean. To the south and north is largely unknown.

Surrounding Areas: To the west is Estcarp. To the southeast is Karsten. To the northwest is Alizon. Somewhere to the north-east, on the coast are probably the settlements of the sea raiders. To the east is the sea and across the sea is the coast of the western continent and unknown lands, possibly The Waste.

Special Places:
1. The Valley of Green Silences with its pools of healing mud.
2. The lake and rivers of the Krogan.
3. The Dark Tower. (see: *Warlock of the Witch World* & *The Key of the Keplian*)
4. The forest of the Moss Wives. (see: *Warlock of the Witch World*, Milk from a Maiden's Breast & *The Weavers*)
5. Loskeetha's Garden of Stones, where she reads the Sands. (see: *Warlock of the Witch World*)
6. The Citadel of Hilarion rebuilt by the Adept after laying in ruins for centuries while he was trapped on another world. (see: *Sorceress of the Witch World*)
7. Near the Citadel of Hilarion, along the coast, are the lands of the Vupsall. (see: *Sorceress of the Witch World* and *The Scent of Magic*)
8. The burrows of the Thas (see: *Trey of Swords*).
9. The Valley of HaHarc which hold the ruins of the city of HaHarc where the tower of Iuchar once stood. (see: *Trey of Swords*)
10. In the mountains north-west of the Valley of Green Silences are the ruins of Zephar, former home of the evil Laidan. (see: *Trey of Swords*)
11. In a grove not far from Zephar lies Ninutra's Shrine. It is the place of training and home to the Mouth of Ninutra. (see: *Trey of Swords*)
12. North of the Dark Tower is the hidden Keplian Valley where Eleeri is slowly turning the Keplians to the Light. (see: *The Key of the Keplian*)
13. North-west of the Dark Tower and South-west of the Keplian Valley is Jeranny & Mayrin's village. (see: *The Key of the Keplian*)

Cities and Keeps
- Canyon Keep
- Duke Chastain's Holding
- The Citadel of Hilarion
- Dinzil's Dark Tower
- HaHarc

- Iuchar's Tower
- Jerrany's Keep
- Lynxholme
- Old Port

Towns and Villages
- Coelwyn -- *Fishing village* (Strait)
- Maddoc -- *A river town east of Green Valley* (Strait)

Geographic Features
- Garden of Stones
- Green Valley
- Gulf of Hilarion
- Hot Sgrings
- Lake of the Krogan
- Merfay Island
- Moss Forest
- Mount Holweg
- Mountain Pass
- Oceax Bay
- Strait of Storms
- Undermountain Caves
- Valley of the Sleepers

Ancient Battle Sites
- Emnin
- Jahalli
- Varhum
- Vock

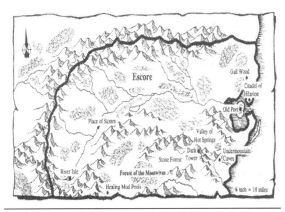

GURPS: Witch World Roleplaying Guide 1989 p.29

179

Varn

Varn was the last new country to be introduced in the [Witch World] series - in *Port of Dead Ships*. It is incorrectly called "Var" throughout _The Warding of Witch World_ but there are many spelling errors in that book.

Capital: Varn is a city state but there are tiny farming communities spread throughout the valley.

Government: The Vars race is lead by council of three men lead by the Speaker for the Seated One (a high priestess who wears a face covering cowl). The three councilors are probably in charge of the city, valley farmers/herders, and fishermen. The "Seated One" appears to be a seer priestess wrapped in bands like a mummy who holds a crystal ball of Power and sits on a throne in their temple.

Geography: Varn is a broad, nearly treeless valley surrounded by mountains with much grazing land for raising their own unique breed of sheep. The city was built on the slope rising up from their bay. The bay is guarded by treacherous reefs and a shore cliff on either side.

Surrounding Areas: To the North of Varn is the mountains which form the southern border of Karsten. On the coast, separating Varn and Karsten, is the "Point of the Hound" which juts out into the sea. To the east are more mountains which extend to the southern part of Escore. To the south are mountains which separate Varn from the mostly uninhabited lands where the evil, black cube gate which caused the *Port of Dead Ships* was located. Somewhere south of that is Salzarat, the former home to the Falconers race, only recently rediscovered (*Falcon Blood*). To the east is the ocean where there are many islands including the Isle of Usturt (*Spider Silk*), an island where the Kolder entered the Witch World (explored further in _Web of the Witch World_), as well as another island with a gate Simon & Jaelithe entered and were trapped in the machine world (_Three Against the Witch World_ & _Sorceress of the Witch World_). Beyond those is the shore of Sorn Fen on the western continent (*Legacy from Sorn Fen*).

Special Places:

1. The city of Varn is famous for it's glass work and the buildings of the city are vibrantly coloured.
2. The harbor is the main entrance to Varn though there may be mountain passes into the valley.

Deities and Old Ones

The division between Old Ones and deities is often indistinct. Some titles for Deities are: Eternal Ones or Hand of the Over Guardian. Shrines where they are worshipped or reside are called Fanes the priests or priestesses there are Those who Tend the Fanes.

Old Ones = Great Ones, Great Names, Those who Had Been Before. Their more-than-human intermediaries are Voices. The Old Ones' absence from human affairs since ancient times is known as the Long Rest. Their metal is silver, their gems opals, pearls, jade, and amber.

The Triune Goddess and Horned Man

- *Dians* = Moon Maiden. Gray eyes, black hair. Carries a silver bow and arrows. Wears a white tunic or robe and the New Moon wrought in silver over her brow. Austere and remote. Kurnous is her brother.
- *Gunnora* = Amber Lady Harvest Lady Evernourishing One Corn Woman Mother of Mares   (Kioga). Special protector of women and children. Neither she nor *Neave* like those who disturb the progress of Things As They Must Be. She is tall, dark, with full breasts and a narrow waist. Her eyes and gown are amber colored her symbol is a sheaf of ripe grain bound with a fruited vine. *Kurnous* is her Consort.
- *Raidhan* = The Crone. Black—robed Hag of the Dark Moon. *Kurnous* is her son.
- *Kurnous, The Horn Crowned Man* = He Who Hunts by ancient tradition, holds power only a few seasons, then his blood and flesh enrich the fields. Slanted eyes, pointed chin, amused expression, curling hair crowned with stag horns. Mail coat is green, brown, and blue. Often called upon by soldiers as well as hunters.

General List of Gods and Old Ones

- *Alafian* = He built an ancient way through The Waste and is still served by a Dryad there.   (Horn)
- *Archerydon* =   (HH) Female Old One of feathers and fire.   (Circle)
- *Archon* = The Dark Ones following him came south into Arvon.   (Horn)
- *Asbrakas* = The Waiter in the temple of Varn.   (Port)
- *Cuntif* = The evil balance of *Kurnous*.   (Horn)
- *Destree m'Regnant* = Voice of *Gunnora*. -- See Port
- *The Dog* = Gate Guardian. -- See Southeast Ak
- *Dussa* = Deity of the Krogan.
- *The Flame: Those Who Set the Flame* = Dalesfolk worship the Flame, symbol of creation, served by cloistered Houses of Dames (abbeys) and

Ladies of the Shrines. The most devout Dames wear silver hoops on their girdles, turning them like beads or wheels to accompany formal prayers.

- *Galkur* = Old One of the Dark -- See Gryg
- *Glydys* = An Old One Yonan called upon.   (Gate)
- *Ibycus* = Voice.   (Jpard)
- *Jonkara* -- See Falb
- *Landisl* = Old One of the Light, crested gryphon—man: avian face, paws for feet, taloned hands. (Gryg)
- *Matr* = A Sky-One, departed companion of *Landisl*.   (Gryg)
- *Mig* = Old One. -- See Circle.
- *Neave* = Goddess of truth and gentle peace. Rules the seasons and proper relationships. Guardian of the Forces of Things As They Must Be.
- *Ninutra* -- See Trey, Ware
- *Neevor* = Voice of *Landisl*. -- See CRYS.
- *Nornan* = Deity of Gorm.   (WW)
- *Qrd* =   (Tw) Dark Master served by Black Ones, birds with red eyes and red flesh about their bills.   (Horn)
- *Rllene* = Sky—One, departed companion of *Landisl*.   (Gryg)
- *Talann* = Her Moon Shrine is near Ghyll.   (Dsm)
- *Telgher* = *Landisl's* ally. -- See Gryg.
- *Volt* = Avian Old One revered by Torfolk. -- See WW.
- *Yahnon* = Old One, creator of a Gate gone rogue whose guardians were: *Laqit*, *Scalqah*, and *Theffen*.   (Port)
- *Yoer* = Sky—One departed companion of Landisl.   (Gryg)

People and Races

- *Alizonders* -- For descriptions see Mage & Falm
- *Dalesfolk* -- See Horn for origins.
- *Falconers* = Reddish brown hair, gold flecked eyes. Winged helms with masks. Uniforms bear falcon badges small undermodification marks denote individual troops. -- See Falb for origins Falm, FalLaw, Wtw, Southeast Ak for life styles and post—Turning developments.
- *Far North People* -- See Web, Ramp.
- *Flannan* =   (Esc, Est) Small avians. Sometimes used as messengers. Humanoid heads with jutting beaks. Arms beneath their wings, tiny hands, long, supple necks, clawed red feet. White feathers, except for their faces. Have very short attention spans.
- *Gray Ones* =   (Esc, Tw, Arv) Werewolves, usually of the Dark, though exceptions are known. Narrow heads, black lips, matted, brindled fur on their necks and shoulders. Yellow—red eyes.
- *Keplians* =   (Esc) Resemble powerful and beautiful horses. Of the Shadow can become either of the Dark or Light.

- *Kioga* =   (Arv) -- See Grye
- *Kolder* -- See Web (re uniforms, control belts) and Falm.
- *Krogan* =   (Esc, Kst) Humanoid amphibians, a result of experiments by Great Ones. They can exist briefly outside aquatic environment. Believe their life cycle is linked to Donta: See S'Ol. Webbed feet and fingers, gills, pale skin and hair eyes are deep green and have no whites. Wear waistcloths of scaled fabric and pouches made of shell halves. Krogan who marry outside the clan add "S'" to their names. For burial customs,-- See S'ol
- *Lizards* =   (Esc) Nearly man-sized. Green-gold jewel—scaled skin. Use front feet as hands. Domed, humanoid heads, wide, lipless mouths, long tongues. Distantly related to tree lizards.
- *Moss Wives* =   (Esc) Small, hunched, gray. Long, mosslike hair, gnarled hands, wrinkled faces, flattened noses, large eyes with thick, bushy lashes. Protruding stomachs, stumpy frames, withered- looking legs. Their homes   (nests) are walled with curtains of moss-grown vines. Shy usually friendly to humans.
- *Old Race* =   (Originated in Esc) Dark haired, pale skinned, slender, grey eyed, arched brows.
- *People of the Green Silences / Green People* =   (Esc) Ancient race dwelling in spell-protected Green Valley. Guardians of nature: use wind, water, earth, and air magic. Adapt to their surroundings' colors. Wall their houses with greenery and roof them in woven bird feathers Valley People cannot abide within stone walls or where only men live.
- *Renthans* =   (Esc) As large as horses. No manes topknots of fluff above a single red horn curving back in an arc. Coats: red roan with a creamy white underbody. Tails are small brushes they keep clipped tight to their haunches. Highly intelligent mind-speakers. Allies of the People of Green Silences.
- *Sarn Riders* =   (Esc) Servants of the Dark mounted on bony Keplians. They wear gloves, black, tight-fitting clothes, and thigh—length, hooded cloaks. Their eyes are greenish—yellow pits and their movements are jerky. Weapons: Rods emitting jagged flames.
- *Sulcar* = Tall, fair, big-boned traders and/or raiders. Called "sea-serpents", and live on serpent—prowed boats with their families. Bards chant them into battle. Their identifying crests are mythic creatures: birds, animals, reptiles.
- *Thas* =   (both continents) Subterranean race serving the Dark. Small covered with bristly, rootlike growths. They attack by undermining the earth and dragging victims into their vast burrows. Fear air and fire. Weapons: Ropes of roots envenomed spears.
- *Toads of Grimmerdale* -- See Tog and Wtw. Ancient race some members have degenerated and serve the Dark.

- *Tormen* = Dwell in the marsh between Estcarp and Alizon. Revere Volt his totems guard their house isle communities and fields. Their history is kept by "Rememberers" using "Remember Chants".
- Torfolk are small in stature, with large bones, long arms, short legs, fine, downy hair, and comely human faces. Are generally hostile to intruders. (WW, Web, Sas)
- *Var* -- See Port
- *Vrangs* =   (Esc) Eaglelike dwell in the heights. Have lizards' heads with glittering red scales and narrow, toothed jaws. Their bodies are covered by blue-gray feathers.
- *Vuqsalls* -- See Sorc
- *Were-Riders* -- See Yofu, p. 67, for origins and history. -- See Blood for were-Pack members and their change—forms.

Witch World Lithuania 2005

Customs - Rites of Passage

Birth

- Naming newborns = Done with a touch of water. "Look upon him, name him, that he may have life well set before him."   (Jpard) -- See also Three and Grye.

Puberty

- Rite of Manhood -- See Crys and *GEN INFO: OATHS*.
- Festival of Change = The Kioga coming-of—age ceremony.   (Grye)
- Maiden Day = For girls in Falconers' Women's villages.   (Wtw)

Marriage

- Axe marriage = By proxy bride is symbolically bedded beside an axe. This form includes a later right of bride refusal.   (Crys)
- Cup and Flame = Formal vows: Life Cup drunk and House Candle lit by bride and groom. At Bride Feast they eat from same plate.
- Fold Gather = Where High Hallack's nobility assemble to offer their eligible daughters for marriage.
- hand-fasting = Betrothal.
- maiden brides = wear blue.
- sworn troth = As binding as marriage.

Burials

- "Earth take that which is of earth. Water accept that of water. And that which is now freed, let it be free to follow the higher path."
- (Variant) "Let that which is of earth return to earth. Let the inner spark which is life return to That Which Sent It. May she who lives here be troubled no more and may She who Guards all womankind welcome this one into the House of Peace through the last of all gates."
- (For a stranger) "May your sleep be sweet, stranger, may your path be beyond smooth, may you come to your desiring and it give you peace." A white round stone is then placed on the grave's head.
- (For a warrior) "Honor his name forever." A bared sword is raised in salute to the warrior's funeral pyre.
- High Hallack burial = The dead are laid in the Field of Memory.
- Krogan burial -- See S'ol.
- Lelanin burial = The body's grave must be sealed by a priestess's words to prevent the spirit's rising. Grief is buried in a hole into which the mourner screams, then covers with a stone.
- Sulcar burials = Known as burn burials.
- Vupsall burials -- See Sorc for description.

Seasonal Customs

- earth tithe = Harvest Time feast bowl associated with Harvest Sacrifice.
- Harvest Homing Dance = Practiced in Estcarp.   (Sps)
- Fall Hunt ceremony
- Harvest Gift = Sent to an Arvon Clan Chief: wine and grain.
- Harvest Maid = The last stalks are woven into a human effigy which is toasted in cider, then impaled on a pitchfork atop the wain.
- First Day of Winter = At that time Dalesfolk burn straw wheels at that time to frighten off evil spirits.
- Mid—Winter Feast = One of four fateful nights of the year when powers are loosed.

- <u>Year's Turn Feast</u> =   (Regarded as pagan by the Abbeys not observed by the Dames.) Celebrants burn the Straw Man and Flax Maid women throw ivy in fire, the men holly, for good luck in the coming year.

Luck Wishes and Superstitions

- "<u>falcon-away</u>" = A sign used by superstitious Falconer women and children to ward off bad luck.   (Wtw)
- "Luck be with you and fortune your shield."
- One throws the stones to read for luck on the trail, etc.
- <u>War Departure wish</u> -- See Crys.
- <u>Fortune well</u> =   (Crys) In western Ithdale. When the full moon reflects on its waters, one casts in a pin and recites a spell rhyme for luck. The area is marked by numerous wish ribbons and straw and twig effigies.

Miscellaneous Customs

- <u>Hiring</u> = At market towns and fairs. Laborers seeking employment wear badges on their caps or bonnets to advertise their trades.
- <u>Merchant flags</u> = Raised over traders' tents and booths at fairs. Sulcar traders raise them when coming into the port.
- <u>head collecting</u> = A barbarian practice they believe it enslaves the ghosts of the slain.
- <u>visit veils</u> = Worn by Falconer women chosen to be impregnated.

Sayings and Expressions

- <u>Falconers'/Borderers' marching cadence</u> = Earth-sky—mountain—stone! Sword cuts to the bone!
- By...the Death of the Kolder   (Sps) = Simond's expression.
    - the Eyrie
    - the Fangs of(Zar)
    - the Favor of Likerwolf
    - Harith and Haron and the Blood of the Hawk Brood
    - the Heat of the Eternal Flame
    - the Horns of(Alizonian)
    - the Hunter's Cup
    - the Nine Words of Min
    - Reith and Nieve
    - the Sword Hand of Karthen the Fair
    - the Warmth of the Flame and the Flash of Gonder's Spell Sword
    - the Waves of Asper
- Sweet Gunnora
- Swordbrother Oath -- See Fallaw, <u>Terms and Expressions</u>.
- Volt guide us

Euphemisms

- Death = The Last gate, Last Road, Black Gate.
- Evernight; Victory of the Dark.
- Halls of the Valiant = the Falconers' Valhalla.

Expressions

- "A nest of Anda wasps..."
- "a stoat introduced into a house of hens..."
- "As long as the Flame Eternal burns upon any altar..."
- "As thin as Dame Carelda's washboard..."
- "As well try to empty Fos Tern with a kitchen ladle..."
- "By the Powers of Air, so shall it be."
- "I would take Gunnora's three oaths..."
- "if the Flame favors us..."
- "like all Demon Night opening..."   (Sulcar saying)
- "little dove, little love...." said to a child.   (Tog)
- "looked like a fetch out of an old tale..."
- "The queens of falcons be my witness..."
- "wisdom must balance all swords..."   (Estcarp Hillfolk saying)
- "Witch borne from Witch get. Witch she is, the pattern set."

Blessings

- (Anakue child blessing) "Let not his feet carry him near the Shadow. Let these hands work in the service of life and the Light, his mind remain clean and untainted. Grant him the strength of will to naysay any thought born of the Dark."   (Grye)
- (For killed grey) "Honor to the Great One of the herd. Our thanks to That Which Speak for the four-footed that we may eat. We take not save that which is freely given.   (Horn)
- "May the Right Hand of Lraken be your shield"   (Sulcar)
- "Good luck ride with you, to right, to left, at your back, and before." (Warl)
- "With the Fourth Blessing..." Neevor's blessing.
- "May the Great Flame abide about you, hedge you in."   (Trey)

Curses

- "May the Death of Kryphon of the Dart be upon you."   (Horn)
- "May the Rats of Nore forever gnaw him night and day."   (WW)

Religion and Beliefs

The Dales

- The Undying and One Flame
- Mount of Astron = a devotional reading required listening at many Dales' morning services.   (Tog)
- House spirits = family ceremonies as well as prayers take place before a small niche dedicated to the house's spirits.   (Amb)
- The Black Wain = This is said to carry away naughty children, or come for those doomed to die.   (Stillborn)
- Abbey Hours = Hour of the Fifth Flame Hour of Last Light Hour of Great Silence.   (Yofu)
- Those Who Tend the Fanes = Keepers of Shrines.
- A mirror kills demons.   (Yofu)

Sulcar

- Sign of Wottin = May be accompanied with a prayer for calm seas: Wind and wave! Mother Sea/ Lead us home/ Far the harbor/ Wild thy waves/ Still, by the power/ Sulcar saved!"   (Falb)
- "It lies between the fingers of the Old Woman," then spit over shoulder.
- A man will not fall in battle unless he hears his name called aloud while the clamor still rings.   (Warl)
- A man using a dead man's sword may be possessed in battle by his ghost, for good or evil.   (Warl)

Karsten

- Temple of Fortune = served by priests titled Reverend Voices   (WW)
- The Stone of Engis = Karstenians swear oaths by this.   (WW)

Arvon

- "The fabled Earth Center from which all life is said to have screamed." (Jpard)

Estcarp

- The Hand of the Over Guardian   (WW)

Escore

- White Brethren speculation = That a man who has not completed his task is reborn to finish it.   (Trey)
- Variant: One who dies with a task laid on him for good or ill clings to a shadow of life until the task is fulfilled.

- Cross two fingers when speaking of the dead to avoid their possible revenge-taking.   (Sorc)
- Paths gf Balemat = A primitive belief: An evil spirit awaits the dead whose rites were not properly carried out.   (Sorc)

Salutations

Salutes
- Men clap bare hands together, then raise right palm for friendly salute.
- A man brings his fist up to salute a war leader.   (Dss)
- Kioga: Palm pressed to forehead -- sign of respect.   (Grye)

Standard Greeting, with Variants
- To the giver of the feast, fair thanks. For the welcome of the gate, gratitude. To the ruler of this house, fair fortune and bright sun on the morrow.
- For the welcome of the gate, my thanks. For the feasting on the board, my pleasure and my good wishes. To the lord of this roof, fair fortune.
- To the house greeting, to those of the house good fortune. To the day a good dawn and sunset, to the endeavor good fortune without a break.
- Fair fortune to this holding and good morning to you.
- Good fortune to this house and the dwellers therein.
- To the farer on far roads the welcome of this roof, and may fortune favor your wandering.   (Dale welcome for a guest unknown personally to any lord.)
- Greeting to a sharer of the road.

Welcome and Guesting Cups, etc.
- High Hallack: A hosting horn   (the wine of hospitality) and a platter of welcome cakes is presented. The hostess then lays hand on a guest's wrist and leads him to table.
- The welcome cup enables the traveler to wash trail dust from his throat before he announces his name and business. A plate with bread, salt, and water seals the guesting bond.
- Estcarp: (A very old formula, in abeyance in wartime) "The House Of _____ , on which be the sun, the wind, and the good of wide harvest, opens gates to a geas—ordered man." Response: "Gates open to one swearing no threat against   (House name), man or clan, roof tree, field, flock, herd, or mount." The host's sword is then held out to the guest, point foremost he kneels and presses lips to it and repeats the response, opening with, "No threat from me against...." The guesting goblet is then offered.

- Guesting cup/goblet: Filled with a mixture of water, wine, and milk. Both host and guest drink. Then the guest sprinkles drops to right and left (house and land) and passes goblet back, to be handed around the host's household.
- Falconers' salutations: "Greeting, sword brother."
- "Between us there is peace. The Lord of Wings opens his Eyrie to the Captain of Estcarp."
- "I give you greeting, Brother. Was it fair, the hunting?" "It was fair, the hunting. Is the fire warm upon the hearth?" "The fire blazes and the board is laid. Will my Brother take his rest among my Brothers?" "Gladly would I rest."
- "Welcome, Hawk Blood, who kept well the faith."
- Tormarsh Salutations: "I give you greeting. May the blessing of Volt himself be with you."
- (To a Tor clan daughter who is with child.) "Fair day. Fair be your going, fair be your coming, firm your steps upon the crossing places, full your hands with good labor, your heart with warmth,
- your mind with thoughts which will serve you."
- Moss Forest: "Who are you who follow a trail through the mossland?" "No threat from me to the House of _____ and her sister, clan, or rooftree, harvest, flocks...."
- Krogan: "To Kofi of the river, greeting and peace from..."
- Sulcar: "I am Koityi Stymir, at your summoning..."
- Var: "Thrice blessing. Power calls to power, Light to light, even as Dark can call shadows. Peace is not yet won, but there is now a beginning." Response: "well to Varn."
- Vupsalls: "Fair morning, leader of men."
- "Mother of men, ruler of the Chief tent, be blessings and more good than can be held in the two hands of all on you."
- "Seeress, we seek." "They who seek may enter."
- "The Mother of Many does me honor...There shall be no forewalker or aftergoer between us."

Farewells

- High Hallack: "Go with the good will of the house."/"Go with the Peace." / "Go with the Will of the Flame."
- "Good fortune, sun bright and lasting to you."
- "May Our Lady of the Harvest Shrine guide your way."
- "For the feast, my thanks, for the roof, my blessing, for the future all good, as I take my road again."
- (Father—kin farewell, YEAR OF THE UNICORN): "As he who stands for all of you as father-kin, do I drink long years, fair life and easy passing, kin—favor, roof-fortune, child-holding. Thus it be ever."
- Estcarp: "Go with fortune."

- "Go in strength, watch well your footing, and keep always alert with eye and ear."
- "May your road be a fair one and may the sun shine upon it."
- "A fair road before you and a swift return."
- Falconer: "Be strong, warrior, and fly high. The Lord of Wings favor your hunting."
- "Go, winged warrior. We be of one breed with your master and there is peace between us."
- Alizonder: "I.wish you abundant hunting and the best of hounds for your pack.
- "Whatever you pursue, may your blade strike true."

Oaths

- Hands placed between those of the one to whom oath—taker swears, then pressed to forehead: "Lord, I am in your debt. Accept me as your liegeman, as is right."
- Rite of Manhood: (Crys) A kin—oath is sworn, then the father's gift-sword is accepted.
- Kioga Festival of Change: -- See CUSTOMS and Grye
- Oath of Bearing and Forebearing: (Crys) Spit at the subject's Eeet. Then, You have taken our kin—Lord. Therefore you stand in his place." (The burden of the speaker's support is the blood-price.)
- Falconers' Oath of Sword and Shield, Blood and Bread. See WW
- Swordbrother oath = See Fallaw, also Terms and Expressions.
- "I would take Gunnora's Three Oaths."   (Crys)
- "May I be slain by my own blade, struck with my own darts, if I ever meant any ill to those within the House of Dhulmat or to any man of Estcarp."   (Three)
- Koris swore upon the Axe of Volt when he promised to guard Jaelithe's triplets in her absence.

Truces

- Swords are exchanged to mark a truce. They also may be scabbarded with peace strings.
- Both hands held out, shoulder high, palm out: An age—old sign for truce. (Gryg)
- Fyndale Peace = Visiting heads of households laid bared hands on an Old Ones' gray stone pillar and swore to keep peace throughout the fair. (Amb)

Web of the Witch World UK 1978

Flora

- <u>angelica</u> = counteracts poison. -- See <u>Magic: Herbs</u>
- <u>agueweed</u> = feverwort. For coughs and fevers.   (Exl)
- <u>arrow tree</u> =   (Esc) Throws poisonous thorns.   (Gate)
- <u>ash tree</u> -- See <u>Magic: Herbs</u>
- <u>black willow</u> -- See <u>Magic: Herbs</u>
- <u>blue poppy</u> = Pain killer also for coughs and chest disorders. The seed pod's sap is stewed with sugar to make a syrup.   (Exl)
- <u>bounty bush</u> =   (Tw)   (Saltg)
- <u>bronze root</u> =   (HH) A cure for sneezing.   (Nighth)
- <u>bural</u> =   (HH) A root that is hard to pull free.   (Gryg)
- <u>carnation</u> -- See <u>Magic: Herbs</u>
- <u>carnelian fruits</u> =   (Ramp)
- <u>catmint</u> = For skin swellings, rashes, and small burns should be steeped, not boiled.   (Exl)
- <u>comfrey</u> = Good for healing wounds.   (Exl)
- <u>corfil</u> =   (TOR) Plant which yields a scarlet dye.
- <u>Dragon's Tongue</u> = Cleanses wound of putrid matter.
- <u>elder flower</u> = used in beauty creams.
- <u>elder wood</u> -- See <u>Magic: Herbs</u>
- <u>false sage</u> = beauty cream ingredient.
- <u>Fever-leaf vine</u> =   (Alz)
- <u>fogmot</u> =   (Esc) Grows on tree trunks edible.   (Gate)
- <u>fringe hazel</u> =   ("Double See Spit") Bark is an astringent, stops bleeding salves of it soothe pain.
- <u>frost flowers</u> =   (Exl)

- garlic -- See Magic: Herbs
- golden fruits =   (Ramp)
- huk-berries =   (Ware)
- hyssop = Good for insect bites.   (Exl)
- illbane -- See Magic: Herbs
- Insect-eaters =   (SoutheastAs) Plants growing on far southern shore (Port)
- ker-apples =   (HH) Of autumn.   (Tog)
- knitbone =   (Exl)
- langlorn -- See Magic: Herbs
- langmar -- See Web
- loguth =   (Tor, Est) Plants which produce fibers used in weaving.
- Lormt flowers =   (EST) Called "Noon and Midnight". Grow only near that ancient repository of knowledge.   (Exl)
- minz weed =   (HH) Addictive. It is chewed.   (Rodd)
- moly -- See Magic: Herbs
- moss = Used for bandages.
- mullein = beauty cream ingredient.
- nettles = boiled, they stop bleeding.
- pla-plums =   (Crys)
- primrose = beauty cream ingredient.
- rampion = Eases women's plight.   (Ramp)
- ranni vines = When they bud, spring is near.   (Godron's)
- red dead-man's hand = toxic seaweed; kills shellfish.
- redwort = Better for stimulating the heart than witch's thimble.
- rowan tree -- See Magic: Herbs
- saffron -- See Magic: Herbs
- salt -- See Magic: Herbs
- sandalwood -- See Magic: Herbs
- saxfrage = cures fever.
- selka =   (Arv) The Kioga make it into a refreshing juice.   (Grye)
- semroot = narcotic.   (Ramp)
- shred bark = makes a brown dye.   (Mage)
- silanti flowers = Grow on Karsten's coast.
- silver nettle = makes a bleach.   (Mage)
- star candles = Moss Forest flowers. -- See Warl
- star eyes =   (Esc) First flowers of spring.   (Sorc)
- stench vines -- See Warl
- smother root =   (Alz) A poison.
- stranglevine flowers =   (Alz) -- See Mage
- summer s last / first of spring =   (Est) Mountain Gate flowers.   (Oldt)
- tansen tree = Has fragrant blossoms. -- See Warl
- tresayne = Its leaves aid in healing.   (Green)

- valerian -- See Magic Herbs
- vervain -- See Magic: Herbs
- weed -- See Web
- witch's thimble = A heart stimulant.
- white heart -- See Zar
- white hedge berries =   (Alz)
- yarrow = an astringent.

Fauna

Mammals

- Alizonian Hounds -- See WW, Mage
- Aspt =   (Esc) Beaverlike animals same habits, but larger.   (Warl)
- assassin beast =   (Tor) -- See WW.
- Broc-boar =   (HH)   (Crys)
- blue-horned sheep =   (HH) -- See Mage
- deer
- dire-wolf =   (Alz) -- See Mage
- Donta =   (Kst) -- See S'ol
- Garth Howell mounts =   (Arv) -- See Song
- orex =   (Kst, Esc) -- See Ware
- Lormt pack =   (Est) Tri·horned canids. -- See Falh
- mountain leapers =   (Esc)   (Kep)
- mountain monster =   (Est)   (Torb)
- night-hunter =   (Kst) -- See Ware
- pards = both continents
- pronghorns
- rasti =   (Esc) Rodents three feet long, black, agile. Hunt and kill in packs.
- scavengers =   (Kst) -- See Ware
- seafoxes = Live on far northern islands. Thick—furred water dogs whose pelts are prized.   (Ramp)
- shriekers =   (Alz) Burrowing animals. -- See Mage
- snowbears =   (Esc)   (Kep)
- snowcats = Both continents. Larger than pards. Have beautiful thick gray—white fur. Renowned hunters.
- Torgians =   (Est; Esc) Much valued horse breed noted for speed and endurance. Duns with dark manes coats won't take a gloss.
- verbears =   (Kst; Esc) -- See Ware
- vuffle =   (Esc) -- See Warl: Expressions
- Vupsall Hounds =   (Esc) -- See Sorc
- Waste ponies -- See Gryg

Birds

- <u>hegitts</u> =   (HH) Sea birds. -- See Ramp
- <u>hooded crow</u> =   (Alz)
- <u>idylbirds</u> =   (HH)   (Ramp)
- <u>lanagoot</u> =   (HH)   (Isle)
- <u>rus</u> =   (Esc) Flying spies for Sarn Riders and others of the Dark. Long supple necks, small, beaky heads. Cry a whistling screech.

Reptiles

- <u>Merfay</u> =   (Esc) Turtlelike creatures. Scaly skin, webbed feet and hands, round heads, short necks. Friendly to Krogan.
- <u>Tor Lizard/ Wak-lizard</u> =   (Tor) -- See Web
- <u>tree lizards</u> =   (Esc) Live in treetop mazes.   (Three)

Water Creatures

- <u>Decca</u> -- See Seasd
- <u>fleckfish</u> =   (HH)   (Ramp)
- <u>fos-crab</u> =   (Esc)
- <u>pincushion fish</u> =   (HH)   (Ramp)
- <u>possel</u> =   (Esc) Shellfish. -- See Warl
- <u>quasfi</u> =   (Esc) Shellfish. -- See Warl, Strait.
- <u>taape fish</u> -- See Isle.

Insects, Arachnids, and Crustaceans

- <u>Anda wasps</u>
- <u>biting clouds/bitter motes</u> -- See Southeast Ak
- <u>light insects</u> =   (Tor, Esc) Used by Torfolk and Vupsalls. – See Sas, Sorc
- <u>rock crustacean</u> =   (ESC) Land-going lobster. -- See Gate
- <u>spider monster</u> =   (ESC) -- See Ware
- <u>web-riders</u> =   (ARV) -- See Song
- <u>zizt spiders</u> =   (Esc) -- See Sorc

Miscellaneous:

Terms

- <u>blank shield</u> = a mercenary for hire.
- <u>earth tithe</u> = the feast bowl at harvest time.
- <u>The Exile</u> = When those now dwelling in Arvon left the Dales, crossed the Waste, and entered their present land.
- <u>The Far Shore</u> = The Western Continent, to those of the Eastern.
- <u>The First Age of Arvon</u> = Before the Lost Lords warred.   (Jpard)
- <u>The Great Time of Trouble</u> = Period leading to the Last Struggle.

- Halls of the Valiant = The Falconers' Valhalla.
- Heal Craft
- The Last Struggle = Fought between Dark and Light in Arvon.
- Oath of Sword and Shield, Blood and Bread = A Falconer's bond of service, which may be extended to non-falconers. -- See Wwe
- Peace of the Highways = Safety for travelers not always honored in chaotic times.
- Road of Memory/Road of Sorrow = Taken by Arvon's exiles.
- sword taken = captured land.
- sword weight = tribute.
- Three Times Horning = A pogrom. -- See WW.
- Times = Ax time and sword time: humans. Wind and star time: Great Lords and Voices. Were-time and spell time: magic.   (Yofu)
- Warn sword = Used by a Herald to summon allies to war. He carries a carved wooden sword as a symbol, and each party joining the alliance adds a colored cord to its hilt.   (Warl)

Titles
- All Mother = Leader of the witches of Estcarp, post-Turning.   (Gate)
- The Four Great Weagons = Helm—Biter, Ice Tongue, Sword of Shadow, and the Tongue of Basir.   (Trey, Ware)
- The Four Lords = Of High Hallack, who allied to defeat the invaders: Imgry, Savron, Skirkar   (slain in battle), and Wintof.
- Gormvin = Title of the authorities and/or race employing/protecting the ancient race of Toads.   (Wtw)
- The Great Bargain = Struck between the Dales and the Weres: battle alliance in exchange for human brides.   (Yofu)
- Guardian = Leader of the witches, pre-Turning.
- Horn Leader =   (HH) A battlefield commission, in effect, a title given for bravery. Elys's brother received it.   (Dss)
- Master of Hounds = Warlord of the Alizonian ruler.   (Mage)
- The Seven Defenders of Arvon = Alon, Eydryth, Elys, Kerovan, Joisan, Hyana, and Trevon.   (Song)
- Venerators = Priests of Alizon.   (Mage)
- The War That Sealed the East = The previous Turning.   (Wtw)
- Watch Witch = Posted at Es Castle to listen for remote sendings.
- Wing Lord / Wing Master /Lord of Wings = Falconers' Leader.

Symbols and Badges of Authority
- Bard's ornament of profession -- See Song
- Heraldic Devices of High Hallack nobility = Basilisk, Gryphon, Phoenix, Salamander, Wyvern, etc.   (Crys, Yofu)

- Falconers' = Badge of a Wing Master: a falcon in flight. Badge of the Captain of a Company: a stooping falcon. Commandant's cloak of rank: black, lined with silver.   (Seak)
- Lord Hound's Mask = worn by Alizon's leader.   (Mage)

Conventional ~ Non-Magic Weapons
- Kolder = Submarines, tanks, airships, control-belts.
- Witch World Weapons = axe, bow and arrow, dagger, dart gun, flashing wands   (used by Sarn Riders) force lash/whip, pike, quarterstaff, spear, and sword.

Much Valued / Special Trade Goods
- foxsilk pelts
- Ithdale pearls
- Thunder Shield amber
- Var glass
- Woods: lamantine pinsal, redheart, spicy pine, and wence.

Beverages
- bloodwine = of Alizon.
- "life water" = raw ale.
- seamilk = wine of the far Northern Dales and isles.
- selka juice = A Kioga beverage.

Diseases
- Creeping plague
- Deep Chill

General Magic

N.B. = Any magical power misused or used selfishly may recoil on the spellcaster or drain her or him past the point of recovery.

Forms of Magic
- Banishment spell = "By the bone of death, the power of silver, the force of our desire -— thus do we loose one of three, never to be knotted together again." An arrow of light then was fired at Gillan, leaving her cold and abandoned   (Yofu).
- Barrow magic = May not be penetrated by the Dark.   (Horn)
- Binding spells and chants = Includes circle spells, spiral traps, horsebonding, etc.

- blood magic = Used to enhance the power of other spells, such as Gate opening.   (Warl, Crys, Song, Zar)
- chant song = Raises Power in the body and makes it flow outward.
- childbirth magic =   (1) Anghart aided Jaelithe with this during the triplets birth   (Three)   (2) Joisan used bespelled herbs to anoint a laboring woman's belly, palms, feet, and forehead with runes   (Grye).
- circle spell = A form of binding spell: Those to be imprisoned are circled three times widdershins, with a magic cry given at each circle's completion.
- compulsion spells =   (1) geas   (to break this courts disaster) (2) pull— spell   (3) summoning   (done three times, it forces the subject to obey).
- conversion chant = To return the Were-riders to their human forms: "By the Light, by the Cold Steel, by the Rowan, by the Candles of the Weres." (Blood)
- dream-weaving = Separates the witch's body and soul, each existing in a different world.
- Farseeing Magic = Scrying, or reading rune boards and stones.
- Foretelling = Examples: (1) Jaelithe's chant to foretell her triplets futures   (Three).   (2) Ninque read "pins on the Stone of Esinore" (Amb).
- Gate spell = Pentagram within a circle is drawn with blood, either the witch s own   (of the Light) or a sacrifice's   (Of the Dark) those to be transported stand on the star's points, facing inward.   (Crys, Song, Sorc)
- Gunnora's charm chant = "Life is breath, life is blood. By the seed and by the Leaf. By the Springtime in its flood. May this power bring relief." (Amb)
- Harvesting chant = Used when taking part of a living plant in order to work magic ensures that the power remains intact and does not recoil on the one doing the harvesting.   (Grye, Zar)
- Hunter's Magic = Men's magic: Pledging Kurnous with wine.
- illusion spells = Glamours shape—changing   (WW) cloaking   (Yofu) disappearances   (Crys).
- Moon Magic = Women's magic. Sometimes called High Moon magic. Includes Magic of Talaan   (Dsm). Often involves a Star Temple.
- Names / Words of Power = Ghithe: Old Tongue for "Light"   (Grye). Asmerillion   (Stillborn). Sytry   (Warl). Euthayan   (Three, etc.). Min's Nine Words   (See Nine, Circle). Ashlin Ceeara   (Kep). Hesturfljott Strjuka Jurtsprengur   (Stillborn). "By the Power of the Nine Great Names"   (stillborn). Svochos Enyahg   (Peacock).
- Power shaping = The ability to find Old Ones through their inanimate representations and thus steal their power.   (Circle)
- Power spell = "Earth, Air, Fire, and Water. By the Dawn of the East, the Moon White of the South, the Twilight of the West, the Black Midnight of

the North, by yew, hawthorn, rowan, by the Law of Knowledge, the Law of Name, the Law of True Falsehoods, the Law of Balance —- so do we move."   (Jpard)

- Power transfer = Moving objects from one plane to another each remains partly thought and continues to exist elsewhere in a different form.   (Horn)
- Protective spells = Examples: (1) "By the Flame, by the Sword wielded in just cause, by all that stands with the Light, we claim protection" (Nighth)   (2) placed at door of Elys's chamber to guard her and her unborn child. -- See Song
- recalling spell = To bring a separated spirit back to its body: "By the Ash, the Maul, the Blade that rusteth never, by the Clear Moon, the Light of Neave, the blood I have shed to He Whose Semblance I wear, by the virtue of Banebloom, and the Lash of Gorth, the Candles of the Weres, come you back"   (Yofu).
- Set spell = A gift accepted carries the spell with it if that is refused, the spell will rebound on the sender.
- Shape-changing and transformations = Require pentagram(s), a fire producing smoke, and chants. When the smoke ebbs, the change is complete.   (WW, Strait, JPARD, Strait, etc.)
- Spellbreaking = Examples: (1) circle widdershins against the sun three, seven, then nine times the spellbreaker yields some of his own power in this process   (Warl, Amb, GRYE).   (2) Circling deasil to break a spell is of the Light   (Song).   (3) Yaal's Serpent chant: "Aphar and Stolla, Worum awake!/ What was drunk, must be tongued./What was wrought, you must unmake!/ In the Name of _____"   (Amb). (4) To break evil vines' spell: "Blood to bind, blood to sow, blood to pay, so it is demanded"   (Zar).
- Spell Duel = A clash of the most powerful Adepts.
- Spell of the Hour = Used in ancient times to bind the Thas in their underground world it weakened over the eons   (Grye).
- sympathetic magic -- See (1) Game of Power   (WW) and (2) Destree's whittling magic of a model Scalgah   (Port).
- tracing/finding spells = Objects take on impressions of former owners or users that fact can be employed to seek them out and track them down. Examples: (1) Kaththea's scarf   (Warl)   (2) 0syra's Krogan xalta magic   (Port)   (3) Mayrin's hair ornament, given her by Romar, used to find him in the Tower.   (Kep).
- vanishing circle = Disappearance in smoke.   (Neevor in Crys)
- warding and protective spells = Examples: (1) A circle drawn with a wand, candles placed along equal points of the arc, and herbs scattered around its perimeter   (Grye).   (2) Fingers held in a vee,
- and the warder spits between them to left and right   (Three).

- water spell = "Wind and water, wind and water, wind to hasten, water to bear, sea to carry, fog to ensnare." Jaelithe chanted this over the chip boats and touched each with a fingernail, con-
- verting them into a phantom fleet to protect Sulcarkeep.   (WW)
- Were-Magic.

Magical Beings and Creatures
- Beasts of the Wood Lord -- See Ware
- Dark Lord's guardians -- See Oath-b
- Death Bringers -- See Horn
- eftan -- See Gate
- Lagit = Gate guardian. -- See Port
- Mountain monster -- See Falm
- Night Hound -- See Nighth
- Scalgah =-- See Port
- Shadow servant -- See Oath-b
- Silver Singers -- See Horn
- That Which Dwells Apart / That Which Abides = Of the Dark. -- See Three
- Theffen -- See Port
- Undermountain monster -- See Warl
- Varks -- See Horn
- web-riders -- See Song
- wenzal -- See Yofu
- Wings of Ord -- See Horn

Colors of Magic
From Jpard: Blue/blue-green = The Light.
Green Magic = Healer's Craft. Growing things.
Red = Power. Health. Physical strength. War.
Orange = Self-confidence and strong desire.
Yellow = Mind magic logic, philosophy, thaumaturgy.
Blue = Emotion, gods, prophecy, theurgy.
Indigo = Weather casting foretelling by stars.
Purple = Lust, hate, fear.
Violet = Pure power among spirits.
Brown = Woods, glades, and the animal world.
Black = The Dark.

Power colors   (Trey)
Blue = Safety.
Dull white! green! shot through with red = a trap.
Gray-green = a strong center of Dark Forces.

Magic Herbs

Those using herbs for good magic generally ask the blessing of a growing thing before taking a branch for a wand, a magical flower, or other botanical. This helps preserve the power.

- angelica = Herb of the sun in Leo. Protection against poison and evil magic. Used for amulets and in scented anointing oils. See Herrel's amulet, Blood Gillan's amulet, YofU.
- ash = For wands of the Light and effigies.
- basil = Of the Light. For amulets and protective spells.
- black willow = to heal fever. Brewed as a tisane with saffron and sandalwood and administered while praying to Gunnora.
- brony = For effigies.
- carnation = added to dragon's blood and diluted, this makes a strengthening cordial.
- dill = protection against evil used in combinations, amulets.
- dragon's blood -- see carnation.
- Dragon's Tongue = Seeks out and cleanses putrid matter from wounds.
- elder bush / wood = For Dark spells and wands, exorcisms, and banes.
- farkill = Evil narcotic. Raises blisters at a touch. Difficult even for illbane to heal.   (Gate)
- garlic = Protection against evil. Used in binding spells.
- hawthorn = of the Light.
- herb salves = Herbs mixed with thick grease and rubbed around the eyes and on one's ears and palms as protection.
- illbane = Repels sorcery. Twice as potent if harvested while still bedewed. Aids in healing. Also enables a witch to rove outside her body. (Futures)
- ivy leaf = protection against evil.
- langlorn = Has four trifid leaves. Clears the senses.
- mandrake = For fertility spells and poppets/effigies.
- moly = Breaks enchantments. Will only work once for the same individual.
- rosemary = Rosemary oil is protection against evil. The herb is also used in combination for spells and amulets.
- rowan = Protection against magic.
- saffron = Used in combination with black willow and sandalwood to cure childhood fevers.
- sandalwood -- See above.
- salt = Protective against evil. Used in binding spells.
- saxfrage = Cures fever.
- tarragon = Protective against evil used in amulets.
- trefoil = Good magic. Employed in combinations.
- valerian = Protective. Used in combination in amulets.
- vervain = Protective. Used in amulets and childbirth blessing.

- <u>white heart</u> = magical flower of a Waste tree.   (Zar)
- <u>yew</u> = of the Light.

Magical / Old Ones' Landmarks
- <u>An-Yak</u> = See Zar
- <u>Beacon Hut</u> = Of Old Ones. -- See Swou
- <u>Bleak Grove</u> = Arvon.   (Rite)
- <u>Blue Temple</u> = On border of the Dales and the Waste.   (Wolf)
- <u>The Broken Road</u> -- See Crys -- Began at edge of Waste.
- <u>Car Do Prawn</u> = Kethan's birthplace Arvon.   (Jpard)
- <u>Car De Dogan</u> = Maleron's Keep Arvon.   (Grye)
- <u>Cave of Immortality</u> = In the Waste.   (Rodd)
- <u>Cave of the Plumed Snake</u> = Dales. See Swseller.
- <u>Chairs of the Giants</u> = Northern Dales.   (Amb)
- <u>Circle of Silence</u> = Dales. Of Old Ones. -- See Circle
- <u>Circle of Toads</u> = Dales. Within Standing Stones.   (Tog)
- <u>Dame Cavern</u> = Estcarp. -- See Wtw
- <u>Darst</u> = Of Old Ones -- See Nighth
- <u>Dragonsback</u> = Dales. -- See Wolf
- <u>Elsenar's posterns</u> = In Lormt's cellar Southeast of Lormt in an ancient hunting lodge and in Castle Krevonel in Alizon City.   (Mage)
- <u>Fortress of the Redmantle</u> -- See Jpard
- <u>Garden of Loskeetha</u> = Escore. -- See Warl
- <u>Garth Howell</u> = School of sorcery, Arvon.   (Jpard, Song)
- <u>Great Falcon</u> -- See Falm
- <u>Grove near Rhystead Abbey</u> = Blue stone sanctuary.   (Were-f)
- <u>Great Star</u> = See Crys
- <u>Gunnorals Shrines</u> = Found throughout Dales, Arvon.   (Tog, Jpard)
- <u>Hall of the Henge</u> = On the White Road.   (Whiter)
- <u>Haunted Ruin</u> = Of the Shadow. -- See Jpard
- <u>Hawk's Claw</u> -- See Jpard
- <u>Hilarion's Citadel</u> = On Coastal Escore -- See Sorc
- <u>Hole of Volt</u> = On Karsten's western coast.   (WW)
- <u>The Horned One's Keep</u> =   (Horn)
- <u>Kar Garudwyn</u> = Landisl's Eyrie, Arvon.   (Grye)
- <u>Kathal Hall</u> -- See Zar
- <u>Linark</u> = A Moon Drawers' school, Arvon.   (Jpard)
- <u>Lure Well</u> = Arvon. -- See Grye
- <u>Moon Shrines</u> = Numerous sites examples found in Garnsdale and in Ithondale, near Ghyll.   (Horn, Dsm)
- <u>Narvok's Gate</u> = Western Ferndale.   (Mage)
- <u>Nexus</u> = See Gate
- <u>Ninth Meadow</u> = Gate near Mountain Gate in Southeast Estcarp.   (Oldt)

- The Pillar at Fyndale = Of Old Ones. Where Dales lords swore peace during Fyndale fair.   (Amb)
- Place of Light = In Varn.   (Port)
- Place of Power at Verlaine Keep = See WW.
- Quayth = Northern High Hallack.   (Amb)
- Ravensmoore = In the Waste. Of the Dark.   (Peacock)
- Reeth = Star Tower of Gillan, Herrel, and Aylinn.   (Jpard)
- Refuge of Wise Women = Witches' post—Turning sanctuary.   (Gate)
- Road of Dreams = The Waste.
- Road of the Old Ones = Ran to a damaged circle of standing stones occupied by Toads.   (Tog)
- Seely Shrine = In the Dales.   (Fortune's)
- Setting Up of the Kings = The resting place of Arvon's border guardians. (Grye)
- Skull Square = Karsten/Escore border. -- See Ware
- Sorn Fen = Of the Old Ones. Dales.   (Legacy)
- Spiral Mazes = Found on both continents.   (Examples: Dss, Three)
- Standing Stones = Both continents. Examples: -- see Gate, Tog, etc.
- Star Altars and Temples = Mainly western continent. One stood above the fishing village of Wark.   (Dss)
- Stone of Konnard = In the mountains south of Lormt. -- See Exl
- Stones of Sharnon = Dales. -- See Stones
- Sytry's Undermountain Tomb = Central Escore.   (Warl, Futures)
- Temple of the Five-Pointed Star = A Star Temple.   (Dss)
- Temple of the Skull = Escore. -- See Trey
- Tower of Iuchar = Escore. -- See Trey
- Trap Road = Arvon.   (Grye)
- Valley of Healing Mud = Escore.   (Three, Song, etc.)
- Valley of the Sleepers = In far eastern Escore. Source of the witches'_power.   (Gate)
- Varr = An ancient stronghold in the Waste.   (Zar)
- The Waiter's Hold = In the capital/port of Varn.   (Port)
- Waste Shrine -- See Crys
- The White Road = Leads into the Waste.   (Whiter)
- Zephar = Escore. -- See Trey

Spell of the Witch World UK 1977

Magical, Tools, Weapons and Artifacts

N.B. = References --— "See Crys", etc. -- will be found under <u>Magic</u> in that novel's or short story's index.

- <u>Amarrok's turguoise amulets</u> -- See Wolf.
- <u>Auridan's sword</u> -- See Swseller.
- <u>Aylinn's healing talisman</u> = See Jpard
- <u>bead circlets / bracelets</u> = Used for memory focusing.
- <u>blood</u> = Used to mark a pentagram for additional power in spellcasting or Gate opening. Evil magic uses another's or an animal's blood good magic uses the witch's <u>own</u> blood.
- <u>blue stones</u> = Found on both continents used for construction in ancient times by those of the Light the power is still effective.
- <u>Broc's sword</u> =   (Amb)
- <u>cat-head ring</u> = Joisan's. -- See "ring", Gyrg
- <u>compulsion mannikins/poppets</u> -- See Trey "Game of Power" in WW.
- The Crystal Gryphon -- See Crys and Gryg
- <u>detection metal</u> = Used by Jaelithe it blazed when anything of the Shadow was near.   (Sorc)
- <u>dream-weaving</u> = to separate body and soul for magic purposes.
- <u>Eleeri's stallion pendant</u> =   (Kep)
- <u>Esinore's stone</u> = Used in fortunetelling.   (Amb)
- <u>Essence of Life wine</u> -- See Lav
- <u>Elder's key</u> -- See Mage
- <u>Elsenar's magestone</u> = "Betrothal gift". -- See Mage
- <u>Elys's wand</u> -- See Swou
- <u>familiars</u> -- See Kaththea's   (Three) and <u>Targi's</u>   (Trey)

- Feathered Serpent = Found in Cave of Plumed Snake. -- See Swseller.
- Felde's talisman -- See Circle.
- Fooger Beast -- See Gate: "Nexus".
- Gate opening -- see GENERAL MAGIC: Gate Spell.
- Gillan's amulet -- See Yofu
- Green Fire = Warmed victims of evil cold.   (Oath-b)
- Helm Biter = One of the Four Great Weapons. Uruk's axe.
- herbs -- See MAGIC: HERBS.
- Herrel's amulet -- See Blood.
- hinder cord = Used to lame Herrel's mount.   (Yofu)
- Hunter's Cup -- See Horn
- Ice Tongue = One of the Four Great Weapons. Yonan's sword.
- Imrie's amulet -- See Que.
- Jervon's amulet -- See Dss, Swou
- Kerovan's wristlet -- See Crys
- Llan's Stone -- See Zar
- luck stones = thrown for forecasting or to tell directions.
- Maug's wand -- See Heir
- Merreth's locket = See Candle
- message rod -- See Web, Magic
- Mirror Gate -- See Know
- Ninutra's casket = See Ware
- Ninutra's record holder = See Ware
- Nolar's fragment of Stone of Konnard = See Exl
- Orel's amulet -- See Saltg
- pentagram(s) = Drawn with a wand. Candles placed on points   (and if called for in the spell, in the star's center) color of candles may determine type of magic and summoning is used. Shape-changing spells require a smoke-emitting brazier nearby. Gate openings and other powerful spells require blood placed on star's points.
- Plasper forces -- See Trey
- Quan-iron = Ancient blue—green metal of the Light. Used for weapons, amulets, Landisl's throne, to protect buildings, etc.
- rune boards/stones = to focus power and for forecasting.
- running water = Evil cannot cross it.
- Rymple's horseshoe -- See Candle
- screamer -- See Yofu
- scrying cup = Focus object used to foresee/farsee.   (Water of the Ninth Wave best for such purposes = Crys) -- See also Sorc, Dss
- Seeing Stone = Consulted by Jervon in his search for Elys.   (Song)
- Siege Perilous -- See WW, Tall.
- Sorn Fen ring -- See Legacy.

- <u>spiral traps</u> = compel ensorcelled prey to follow them inward to perpetual entrapment or death.   (Three, Candletrap)
- <u>spirit gongs</u> = Summon and focus power. Employed by Estcarp's witches and Sulcar seeresses   (who use them to draw favoring winds). Sound: low, brazen boom.
- <u>Sword of Shadow</u> = One of the Four Great Weapons wielded by Crytha.
- <u>Sytry's sword</u> -- See Warl, Futures.
- <u>That Which Runs the Ridges</u> -- See Grye   (Yofu)
- <u>Tongue of Basir</u> = One of the Four Great Weapons Nirel's sword.
- <u>Ursilla's bone whistle</u> -- See Jpard
- <u>Ursilla's wand</u> -- See Jpard
- <u>Vadim's amulet</u> -- See Sentinel
- <u>Vars' testing stone</u> -- See Port
- <u>wands</u> = Good magic: Ash and rowan. Evil magic   (and more powerful magic): Elder.
- <u>winged globes</u> -- See Grye
- <u>witch jewel</u> = Power focus attuned to a witch's personality in unique circumstances, can be transferred to a worthy heiress.   (Gate)
- <u>Ysmay's pendant</u> -- See Amb
- <u>Zvetta s talisman</u> -- See Seasd

Witch World UK 1978

Witch World by Mary Hanson-Roberts 1986 High-Hallack

Witch World by Mary Hanson-Roberts 1986 Escore

Timelines of Witch World
Version 1.0

This version of the timeline is that given in *GURPS: Witch World; Roleplaying in Andre Norton's Witch World*

Timeline V1.0	GURPS
	Refugees of the Old Race flee Escore erecting the Great Mountains separating Escore from Estcarp (Three Against the Witch World).
Approximately 600 years pass unrecorded.	
Year of the Cloven Hoof	The first Dalesmen come to High Hallack fleeing the disasters of their own world (Horn Crown).
Approximately 400 years pass.	
Year of the Serpent King	Kerovan is born in High Hallack (Crystal Gryphon, The).
Year of the Ringed Dove	Kerovan's sister Lisana is born in High Hallack (Crystal Gryphon, The).
Year of the Salamander	Almondia and Truan are shipwrecked off Wark
	Joisan is born in High Hallack (Crystal Gryphon, The).
Year of the Fire Arrow	
Year of the Bicorn	Elys and Elyn are born in High Hallack (Dragon Scale Silver).
Year of the Hill Giant	
Year of the Sea Calf	
Year of the Kestrel	
Year of the Yellow Dwarf	Dairine is cast ashore at Rannock, High Hallack (Spider Silk).
Year of the Mandrake	
Year of the Spitting Toad	Joisan and Kerovan are married by axe in High Hallack (Crystal Gryphon, The).
Year of the Horned Worm	
Year of the Gorgon	
Year of the Barrow-Wight	Simon Tregarth arrives in Estcarp through a Gate from Earth (Witch World).
	Sulcarkeep is destroyed (Witch World).
	Loyse of Verlaine marries Duke Yvian of Karsten by axe (Witch World).
Year of the Cameleopard	Simon Tregarth marries Jaelithe in Estcarp (Witch World).
	Duke Yvian of Karsten is killed (Web of the Witch World).
	Kyllan Tregarth is born on the last day of the year (Three Against the Witch World).
Year of the Crowned Swan	Kemoc and Kaththea Tregarth are born on the first day of the year (Three Against the Witch World).
Year of the Fire Troll	Koris of Gorm and Loyse of Verlaine are married in Estcarp (Three Against the Witch World).

	Dairine receives the gift of Touch-Sight in High Hallack (Spider Silk).
	Alizon invades High Hallack (Crystal Gryphon, The and Dragon Scale Silver).
Year of the Mosswife	Pagar begins his rise to power in Karsten (Three Against the Witch World).
Year of the Weldworm	The Sulcar come to the aid of High Hallack and begin harrying the coasts of Alizon (Crystal Gryphon, The).
	Dairine becomes apprenticed to the Weavers of Usturt (Spider Silk).
Year of the Swordsmith	The Sulcar carry their harrying action into Karsten
	Simon and Loyse are imprisoned in Tormarsh (Web of the Witch World).
	Simon and Jaelithe destroy the Kolder Gate (Web of the Witch World).
Year of the Leopard	Pagar's power base in Karsten grows unsteady (Three Against the Witch World).
	Gillan arrives in Norstead Abbey
	High Hallack rallies against the Alizon invasion (Crystal Gryphon, The).
Year of the Raven	Elys and Jervon dispel Ingaret's Curse in High Hallack (Dragon Scale Silver).
	Imgry becomes leader of the war forces in High Hallack (Gryphon in Glory).
Year of the Night Hound	Pagar begins to solidify his power in Karsten (Three Against the Witch World).
Year of the Gryphon	High Hallack makes the Pact with the Weres (Year of the Unicorn, Three Against the Witch World, Jargoon Pard, The and Gryphon in Glory).
Year of the Firedrake	
Year of the Hornet	High Hallack defeats the invaders from Alizon (Three Against the Witch World and Jargoon Pard, The).
Year of the Unicorn	Kyllan, Kemoc and Kaththea Tregarth rescue a Witch in Estcarp. Alerted to Kaththea's powers, the Council summons her for testing. Her parents refuse (Three Against the Witch World).
	Ysmay marries Hylle in High Hallack and journeys to Quayth (Amber Out of Quayth).
	Gillan and the Were Rider Herrel are married in High Hallack (Year of the Unicorn).
Year of the Red Boar	Ysmay frees Broc and Yaal; Hylle is overthrown in Quayth (Amber Out of Quayth).
	Aylinn is born in High Hallack (Jargoon Pard, The).
	Kethan is born in High Hallack (Jargoon Pard, The).
Year of the Fox Maiden	Simon Tregarth disappears from Estcarp (Three Against the Witch World).
Year of the Phoenix	Jaelithe Tregarth goes in search of Simon and disappears from Estcarp (Three Against the Witch World).
Year of the Hippogriff	Kyllan and Kemoc Tregarth ride with the Borderers of Estcarp against Karsten (Three Against the Witch World).
	Alon is born in Karsten (Ware Hawk).
Year of the Roc	Kaththea Tregarth is taken for training by The Council of Estcarp (Three Against the Witch World).
	Duke Pagar of Karsten suffers a defeat by the Borderers and subsequent setback (Three Against the Witch World).

Year of the Basilisk	Duke Pagar of Karsten rallies once more (<u>Three Against the Witch World</u>).
Year of the Black Adder	Kemoc Tregarth is wounded and goes to the Archives at Lormt (<u>Three Against the Witch World</u>).
	Koris is wounded and retires from leadership in Estcarp (<u>Three Against the Witch World</u> and <u>Warlock of the Witch World</u>).
Year of the Frost Giant	Simond is born to Koris and Loyse in Estcarp (<u>Sand Sister</u>).
Year of the Kobold	The Witches of Estcarp wreak the Turning — devastating the barrier ridge separating Karsten from Alizon — and Karsten is defeated (<u>Three Against the Witch World</u>).
	Kyllan and Kemoc Tregarth rescue Kaththea from the Council of Estcarp
	Kyllan Tregarth and Dahaun of the Green Silences are handfasted in Escore (<u>Three Against the Witch World</u>).
Year of the Snow Cat	Kyllan Tregarth returns to Estcarp to recruit settlers for Escore (<u>Three Against the Witch World</u>).
	Kemoc Tregarth and the Krogan maiden Orsya are handfasted (<u>Three Against the Witch World</u>).
	Kaththea Tregarth is lured away by the adept Dinzel and is rescued by Kemoc (<u>Warlock of the Witch World</u>).
	Kaththea Tregarth is lost in an avalanche en route from Escore to Estcarp. She is rescued by the Vupsall and taken deep into Escore (<u>Sorceress of the Witch World</u>).
Year of the Horned Hunter	Kaththea Tregarth becomes apprenticed to the Vupsall Wise Woman Utta (<u>Sorceress of the Witch World</u>).
	Kaththea Tregarth finds the Dark Tower and discovers the Gate into the Machine World (<u>Sorceress of the Witch World</u>).
	Kaththea Tregarth discovers Simon and Jaelithe in the Machine World, and they rescue the adept Hilarion from imprisonment (<u>Sorceress of the Witch World</u>).
Year of the Lamia	Kelsie arrives in Escore through a Gate from Earth (<u>Gate of the Cat, The</u>).
Year of the Chimera	Simon and Jaelithe Tregarth return to Estcarp from Escore (<u>Sorceress of the Witch World</u>).
Year of the Harpy	Tirtha of Hawkholme, Nirel the Falconer and the youth Alon adventure in Escore (<u>Ware Hawk</u>).
Year of the Orc	
Year of the Werewolf	
Year of the Thorn Cat	Kethan and Thaney are betrothed (<u>Jargoon Pard, The</u>).
Year of the Manticore	
Year of the Weld	
Year of the Hydra	
Year of the Triton	
Year of the Centaur	
Year of the Opinacus	
Year of the Sumurgh	
Year of the Remorhaz	
Year of the Elder Tree	
Year of the Wild Huntsman	

Year of the Troll-Dame	
Year of the Silversmith	
Year of the Bitter Herb	
Year of the Alfar	

Witch World Poland 2013

Witch World UK 1987

Timelines of Witch World
Version 1.1

This version of the timeline takes the GURPS: Timeline and corrects it for the information given in *Dragon Scale Silver* and *Spider Silk* - the changes are underlined as such.

V1.1	GURPS + Dragon Scale Silver & Spider Silk corrections
	Refugees of the Old Race flee Escore erecting the Great Mountains separating Escore from Estcarp (*Three Against the Witch World*).
Approximately 600 years pass unrecorded.	
Year of the Cloven Hoof	The first Dalesmen come to High Hallack fleeing the disasters of their own world (*Horn Crown*).
Approximately 400 years pass.	
Year of the Serpent King	Kerovan is born in High Hallack (*The Crystal Gryphon*).
Year of the Ringed Dove	Kerovan's sister Lisana is born in High Hallack (*The Crystal Gryphon*).
Year of the Salamander	Almondia and Truan are shipwrecked off Wark
	Joisan is born in High Hallack (*The Crystal Gryphon*).
Year of the Fire Arrow	
Year of the Sea Serpent	Elys and Elyn are born in High Hallack (*Dragon Scale Silver*).
Year of the Hill Giant	
Year of the Sea Calf	
Year of the Kestrel	
Year of the Yellow Dwarf	
Year of the Mandrake	
Year of the Spitting Toad	Joisan and Kerovan are married by axe in High Hallack (*The Crystal Gryphon*).
Year of the Horned Worm	
Year of the Gorgon	
Year of the Barrow-Wight	Simon Tregarth arrives in Estcarp through a Gate from Earth (*Witch World*).
	Sulcarkeep is destroyed (*Witch World*).
	Loyse of Verlaine marries Duke Yvian of Karsten by axe (*Witch World*).
Year of the Cameleopard	Simon Tregarth marries Jaelithe in Estcarp (*Witch World*).
	Duke Yvian of Karsten is killed (*Web of the Witch World*).
	Kyllan Tregarth is born on the last day of the year (*Three Against the Witch World*).
Year of the Crowned Swan	Kemoc and Kaththea Tregarth are born on the first day of the year (*Three Against the Witch World*).
Year of the Fire Troll	Koris of Gorm and Loyse of Verlaine are married in Estcarp (*Three Against the Witch World*).

	Alizon invades High Hallack (*The Crystal Gryphon*, *Dragon Scale Silver*).
Year of the Mosswife	Pagar begins his rise to power in Karsten (*Three Against the Witch World*).
Year of the Weld	The Sulcar come to the aid of High Hallack and begin harrying the coasts of Alizon (*The Crystal Gryphon*).
Year of the Swordsmith	The Sulcar carry their harrying action into Karsten
	Simon and Loyse are imprisoned in Tormarsh (*Web of the Witch World*).
	Simon and Jaelithe destroy the Kolder Gate (*Web of the Witch World*).
Year of the Leopard	Pagar's power base in Karsten grows unsteady (*Three Against the Witch World*).
	Gillan arrives in Norstead Abbey
	High Hallack rallies against the Alizon invasion (*The Crystal Gryphon*).
Year of the Raven	Elys and Jervon dispel Ingaret's Curse in High Hallack (*Dragon Scale Silver*).
	Imgry becomes leader of the war forces in High Hallack (*Gryphon in Glory*).
Year of the Night Hound	Pagar begins to solidify his power in Karsten (*Three Against the Witch World*).
Year of the Gryphon	High Hallack makes the Pact with the Weres (*Year of the Unicorn*, *Three Against the Witch World*, *The Jargoon Pard* and *Gryphon in Glory*).
Year of the Firedrake	
Year of the Hornet	High Hallack defeats the invaders from Alizon (*Three Against the Witch World* and *The Jargoon Pard*).
Year of the Unicorn	Kyllan, Kemoc and Kaththea Tregarth rescue a Witch in Estcarp. Alerted to Kaththea's powers, the Council summons her for testing. Her parents refuse (*Three Against the Witch World*).
	Ysmay marries Hylle in High Hallack and journeys to Quayth (*Amber Out of Quayth*).
	Gillan and the Were Rider Herrel are married in High Hallack (*Year of the Unicorn*).
Year of the Red Boar	Ysmay frees Broc and Yaal; Hylle is overthrown in Quayth (*Amber Out of Quayth*).
	Aylinn is born in High Hallack (*The Jargoon Pard*).
	Kethan is born in High Hallack (*The Jargoon Pard*).
Year of the Fox Maiden	Simon Tregarth disappears from Estcarp (*Three Against the Witch World*).
Year of the Phoenix	Jaelithe Tregarth goes in search of Simon and disappears from Estcarp (*Three Against the Witch World*).
Year of the Hippogriff	Kyllan and Kemoc Tregarth ride with the Borderers of Estcarp against Karsten (*Three Against the Witch World*).
	Alon is born in Karsten (*Ware Hawk*).
Year of the Roc	Kaththea Tregarth is taken for training by The Council of Estcarp (*Three Against the Witch World*).
	Duke Pagar of Karsten suffers a defeat by the Borderers and subsequent setback (*Three Against the Witch World*).
Year of the Basilisk	Duke Pagar of Karsten rallies once more (*Three Against the Witch World*).
Year of the Black Adder	Kemoc Tregarth is wounded and goes to the Archives at Lormt (*Three Against the Witch World*).

	Koris is wounded and retires from leadership in Estcarp (*Three Against the Witch World* and *Warlock of the Witch World*).
Year of the Frost Giant	Simond is born to Koris and Loyse in Estcarp (*Sand Sister*).
Year of the Kobold	The Witches of Estcarp wreak the Turning — devastating the barrier ridge separating Karsten from Alizon — and Karsten is defeated (*Three Against the Witch World*).
	Kyllan and Kemoc Tregarth rescue Kaththea from the Council of Estcarp
	Kyllan Tregarth and Dahaun of the Green Silences are handfasted in Escore (*Three Against the Witch World*).
	Dairine is cast ashore at Rannock, High Hallack (*Spider Silk*).
Year of the Snow Cat	Kyllan Tregarth returns to Estcarp to recruit settlers for Escore (*Three Against the Witch World*).
	Kemoc Tregarth and the Krogan maiden Orsya are handfasted (*Three Against the Witch World*).
	Kaththea Tregarth is lured away by the adept Dinzel and is rescued by Kemoc (*Warlock of the Witch World*).
	Kaththea Tregarth is lost in an avalanche en route from Escore to Estcarp. She is rescued by the Vupsall and taken deep into Escore (*Sorceress of the Witch World*).
Year of the Horned Hunter	Kaththea Tregarth becomes apprenticed to the Vupsall Wise Woman Utta (*Sorceress of the Witch World*).
	Kaththea Tregarth finds the Dark Tower and discovers the Gate into the Machine World (*Sorceress of the Witch World*).
	Kaththea Tregarth discovers Simon and Jaelithe in the Machine World, and they rescue the adept Hilarion from imprisonment (*Sorceress of the Witch World*).
Year of the Lamia	Kelsie arrives in Escore through a Gate from Earth (*The Gate of the Cat*).
Year of the Chimera	Simon and Jaelithe Tregarth return to Estcarp from Escore (*Sorceress of the Witch World*).
Year of the Harpy	Tirtha of Hawkholme, Nirel the Falconer and the youth Alon adventure in Escore (*Ware Hawk*).
Year of the Orc	
Year of the Werewolf	
Year of the Thorn Cat	Kethan and Thaney are betrothed (*The Jargoon Pard*).
Year of the Manticore	Dairine receives the gift of Touch-Sight in High Hallack (*Spider Silk*).
Year of the Weldworm	Dairine becomes apprenticed to the Weavers of Usturt (*Spider Silk*).
Year of the Hydra	
Year of the Triton	
Year of the Centaur	
Year of the Opinacus	
Year of the Sumurgh	
Year of the Remorhaz	
Year of the Elder Tree	
Year of the Wild Huntsman	
Year of the Troll-Dame	
Year of the Silversmith	
Year of the Bitter Herb	

Year of the Alfar	

Timelines of Witch World
Version 1.2

This version of the timeline takes the Previous Timeline and adds information from *Night Hound's Moon*, which states that the Year of the Night' Hound is followed by the Year of the Raven - the changes are underlined as such.

V1.2	Night Hound's Moon correction
Refugees of the Old Race flee Escore erecting the Great Mountains separating Escore from Estcarp (*Three Against the Witch World*).	
Approximately 600 years pass unrecorded.	
Year of the Cloven Hoof	The first Dalesmen come to High Hallack fleeing the disasters of their own world (*Horn Crown*).
Approximately 400 years pass.	
Year of the Serpent King	Kerovan is born in High Hallack (*The Crystal Gryphon*).
Year of the Ringed Dove	Kerovan's sister Lisana is born in High Hallack (*The Crystal Gryphon*).
Year of the Salamander	Almondia and Truan are shipwrecked off Wark
	Joisan is born in High Hallack (*The Crystal Gryphon*).
Year of the Fire Arrow	
Year of the Sea Serpent	Elys and Elyn are born in High Hallack (*Dragon Scale Silver*).
Year of the Hill Giant	
Year of the Sea Calf	
Year of the Kestrel	
Year of the Yellow Dwarf	
Year of the Mandrake	
Year of the Spitting Toad	Joisan and Kerovan are married by axe in High Hallack (*The Crystal Gryphon*).
Year of the Horned Worm	
Year of the Gorgon	
Year of the Barrow-Wight	Simon Tregarth arrives in Estcarp through a Gate from Earth (*Witch World*).
	Sulcarkeep is destroyed (*Witch World*).
	Loyse of Verlaine marries Duke Yvian of Karsten by axe (*Witch World*).
Year of the Cameleopard	Simon Tregarth marries Jaelithe in Estcarp (*Witch World*).
	Duke Yvian of Karsten is killed (*Web of the Witch World*).
	Kyllan Tregarth is born on the last day of the year (*Three Against the Witch World*).

Year of the Crowned Swan	Kemoc and Kaththea Tregarth are born on the first day of the year (*Three Against the Witch World*).
Year of the Fire Troll	Koris of Gorm and Loyse of Verlaine are married in Estcarp (*Three Against the Witch World*).
	Alizon invades High Hallack (*The Crystal Gryphon*, *Dragon Scale Silver*).
Year of the Mosswife	Pagar begins his rise to power in Karsten (*Three Against the Witch World*).
Year of the Weld	The Sulcar come to the aid of High Hal- lack and begin harrying the coasts of Alizon (*The Crystal Gryphon*).
Year of the Swordsmith	The Sulcar carry then- harrying action into Karsten
	Simon and Loyse are imprisoned in Tormarsh (*Web of the Witch World*).
	Simon and Jaelithe destroy the Kolder Gate (*Web of the Witch World*).
Year of the Leopard	Pagar's power base in Karsten grows unsteady (*Three Against the Witch World*).
	Gillan arrives in Norstead Abbey
	High Hallack rallies against the Alizon invasion (*The Crystal Gryphon*).
Year of the Night Hound	Elys and Jervon dispel Ingaret's Curse in High Hallack (*Dragon Scale Silver*).
	Imgry becomes leader of the war forces in High Ballade (*The Gryphon in Glory*).
Year of the Raven	Pagar begins to solidify his power in Karsten (*Three Against the Witch World*).
Year of the Gryphon	High Hallack makes the Pact with the Weres (*Year of the Unicorn*, *Three Against the Witch World*, *The Jargoon Pard* and *Gryphon in Glory*).
Year of the Firedrake	
Year of the Hornet	High Hallack defeats the invaders from Alizon (*Three Against the Witch World* and The Jargoon Pard).
Year of the Unicorn	Kyllan, Kemoc and Kaththea Tregarth rescue a Witch in Estcarp. Alerted to Kaththea's powers, the Council summons her for testing. Her parents refuse (*Three Against the Witch World*).
	Ysmay marries Hylle in High Hallack and journeys to Quayth (*Amber Out of Quayth*).
	Gillan and the Were Rider Herrel are married in High Hallack (*Year of the Unicorn*).
Year of the Red Boar	Ysmay frees Broc and Yaal; Hylle is overthrown in Quayth (*Amber Out of Quayth*).
	Aylinn is born in High Hallack (*The Jargoon Pard*).
	Kethan is born in High Hallack (*The Jargoon Pard*).
Year of the Fox Maiden	Simon Tregarth disappears from Estcarp (*Three Against the Witch World*).
Year of the Phoenix	Jaelithe Tregarth goes in search of Simon and disappears from Estcarp (*Three Against the Witch World*).
Year of the Hippogriff	Kyllan and Kemoc Tregarth ride with the Borderers of

	Estcarp against Karsten (*Three Against the Witch World*).
	Alon is born in Karsten (*Ware Hawk*).
Year of the Roc	Kaththea Tregarth is taken for training by The Council of Estcarp (*Three Against the Witch World*).
	Duke Pagar of Karsten suffers a defeat by the Borderers and subsequent setback (*Three Against the Witch World*).
Year of the Basilisk	Duke Pagar of Karsten rallies once more (*Three Against the Witch World*).
Year of the Black Adder	Kemoc Tregarth is wounded and goes to the Archives at Lormt (*Three Against the Witch World*).
	Koris is wounded and retires from leadership in Estcarp (*Three Against the Witch World* and *Warlock of the Witch World*).
Year of the Frost Giant	Simond is born to Koris and Loyse in Estcarp (*Sand Sister*).
Year of the Kobold	The Witches of Estcarp wreak the Turning — devastating the barrier ridge separating Karsten from Alizon — and Karsten is defeated (*Three Against the Witch World*).
	Kyllan and Kemoc Tregarth rescue Kaththea from the Council of Estcarp
	Kyllan Tregarth and Dahaun of the Green Silences are handfasted in Escore (*Three Against the Witch World*).
	Dairine is cast ashore at Rannock, High Hallack (*Spider Silk*).
Year of the Snow Cat	Kyllan Tregarth returns to Estcarp to recruit settlers for Escore (*Three Against the Witch World*).
	Kemoc Tregarth and the Krogan maiden Orsya are handfasted (*Three Against the Witch World*).
	Kaththea Tregarth is lured away by the adept Dinzel and is rescued by Kemoc (*Warlock of the Witch World*).
	Kaththea Tregarth is lost in an avalanche en route from Escore to Estcarp. She is rescued by the Vupsall and taken deep into Escore (*Sorceress of the Witch World*).
Year of the Horned Hunter	Kaththea Tregarth becomes apprenticed to the Vupsall Wise Woman Utta (*Sorceress of the Witch World*).
	Kaththea Tregarth finds the Dark Tower and discovers the Gate into the Machine World (*Sorceress of the Witch World*).
	Kaththea Tregarth discovers Simon and Jaelithe in the Machine World, and they rescue the adept Hilarion from imprisonment (*Sorceress of the Witch World*).
Year of the Lamia	Kelsie arrives in Escore through a Gate from Earth (*The Gate of the Cat*).
Year of the Chimera	Simon and Jaelithe Tregarth return to Estcarp from

	Escore (*Sorceress of the Witch World*).
Year of the Harpy	Tirtha of Hawkholme, Nirel the Falconer and the youth Alon adventure in Escore (*Ware Hawk*).
Year of the Orc	
Year of the Werewolf	
Year of the Thorn Cat	Kethan and Thaney are betrothed (*The Jargoon Pard*).
Year of the Manticore	Dairine receives the gift of Touch-Sight in High Hallack (*Spider Silk*).
Year of the Weldworm	Dairine becomes apprenticed to the Weavers of Usturt (*Spider Silk*).
Year of the Hydra	
Year of the Triton	
Year of the Centaur	
Year of the Opinacus	
Year of the Sumurgh	
Year of the Remorhaz	
Year of the Elder Tree	
Year of the Wild Huntsman	
Year of the Troll-Dame	
Year of the Silversmith	
Year of the Bitter Herb	
Year of the Alfar	

Web of the Witch World Poland 2013

Timelines of Witch World
Version 1.3

This version of the timeline takes the Previous Timeline and adds information from *The Magestone*, which introduces a year number (which eases things somewhat) and the short stories *To Rebuild the Eyrie* & *Falcon Magic* - the changes are underlined as such.

	V1.3	Magestone dates added + To Rebuild the Eyrie & Falcon Magic
	Refugees of the Old Race flee Escore erecting the Great Mountains separating Escore from Estcarp (*Three Against the Witch World*).	
	Approximately 600 years pass unrecorded.	
	Year of the Cloven Hoof	The first Dalesmen come to High Hallack fleeing the disasters of their own world (*Horn Crown*).
	Approximately 400 years pass.	
990	Year of the Blue-horned Ram	Mereth born – 40 years before invasion
1014	**Year of the Serpent King**	Kerovan is born in High Hallack (*The Crystal Gryphon*).
1015	**Year of the Ringed Dove**	Kerovan's sister Lisana is born in High Hallack (*The Crystal Gryphon*).
1016	**Year of the Salamander**	Almondia and Truan are shipwrecked off Wark
		Joisan is born in High Hallack (*The Crystal Gryphon*).
1017	**Year of the Fire Arrow**	
1018	**Year of the Sea Serpent**	Elys and Elyn are born in High Hallack (*Dragon Scale Silver*).
1019	**Year of the Hill Giant**	
1020	**Year of the Sea Calf**	
1021	**Year of the Kestrel**	
1022	**Year of the Yellow Dwarf**	
1023	**Year of the Mandrake**	
1024	**Year of the Spitting Toad**	Joisan and Kerovan are married by axe in High Hallack (*The Crystal Gryphon*).
1025	**Year of the Horned Worm**	
1026	**Year of the Gorgon**	
1027	**Year of the Barrow-Wight**	Simon Tregarth arrives in Estcarp through a Gate from Earth (*Witch World*).
		Sulcarkeep is destroyed (*Witch World*).
		Loyse of Verlaine marries Duke Yvian of Karsten by axe (*Witch World*).
		Kasarian born (*The Magestone*)
1028	**Year of the Cameleopard**	Simon Tregarth marries Jaelithe in Estcarp (*Witch World*).
		Duke Yvian of Karsten is killed (*Web of the Witch*

		World).
		Kyllan Tregarth is born on the last day of the year (*Three Against the Witch World*).
1029	**Year of the Crowned Swan**	Kemoc and Kaththea Tregarth are born on the first day of the year (*Three Against the Witch World*).
1030	**Year of the Fire Troll**	Koris of Gorm and Loyse of Verlaine are married in Estcarp (*Three Against the Witch World*).
		Alizon invades High Hallack (*The Crystal Gryphon*, *Dragon Scale Silver*).
1031	**Year of the Mosswife**	Pagar begins his rise to power in Karsten (*Three Against the Witch World*).
1032	**Year of the Weld**	The Sulcar come to the aid of High Hallack and begin harrying the coasts of Alizon (*The Crystal Gryphon*).
1033	**Year of the Swordsmith**	The Sulcar carry then- harrying action into Karsten
		Simon and Loyse are imprisoned in Tormarsh (*Web of the Witch World*).
		Simon and Jaelithe destroy the Kolder Gate (*Web of the Witch World*).
1034	**Year of the Leopard**	Pagar's power base in Karsten grows unsteady (*Three Against the Witch World*).
		Gillan arrives in Norstead Abbey
		High Hallack rallies against the Alizon invasion (*The Crystal Gryphon*).
1035	**Year of the Night Hound**	Elys and Jervon dispel Ingaret's Curse in High Hallack (*Dragon Scale Silver*).
		Imgry becomes leader of the war forces in High Ballade (*Gryphon in Glory*).
1036	**Year of the Raven**	Pagar begins to solidify his power in Karsten (*Three Against the Witch World*).
1037	**Year of the Gryphon**	High Hallack makes the Pact with the Weres (*Year of the Unicorn*, *Three Against the Witch World*, *The Jargoon Pard* and *Gryphon in Glory*).
1038	**Year of the Firedrake**	
1039	**Year of the Hornet**	High Hallack defeats the invaders from Alizon (*Three Against the Witch World* and *The Jargoon Pard*).
		Fall of Facellian, Baron of Alizon, replaced by Mallandor (*The Magestone*)
1040	**Year of the Unicorn**	Kyllan, Kemoc and Kaththea Tregarth rescue a Witch in Estcarp. Alerted to Kaththea's powers, the Council summons her for testing. Her parents refuse (*Three Against the Witch World*).
		Ysmay marries Hylle in High Hallack and journeys to Quayth (*Amber Out of Quayth*).
		Gillan and the Were Rider Herrel are married in High Hallack (*Year of the Unicorn*).
1041	**Year of the Red Boar**	Ysmay frees Broc and Yaal; Hylle is overthrown in Quayth (*Amber Out of Quayth*).
		Aylinn is born in High Hallack (*The Jargoon Pard*).

		Kethan is born in High Hallack (*The Jargoon Pard*).
1042	**Year of the Fox Maiden**	Simon Tregarth disappears from Estcarp (*Three Against the Witch World*).
1043	**Year of the Phoenix**	Jaelithe Tregarth goes in search of Simon and disappears from Estcarp (*Three Against the Witch World*).
1044	**Year of the Hippogriff**	Kyllan and Kemoc Tregarth ride with the Borderers of Estcarp against Karsten (*Three Against the Witch World*).
		Alon is born in Karsten (*Ware Hawk*).
1045	**Year of the Roc**	Kaththea Tregarth is taken for training by The Council of Estcarp (*Three Against the Witch World*).
		Duke Pagar of Karsten suffers a defeat by the Borderers and subsequent setback (*Three Against the Witch World*).
1046	**Year of the Basilisk**	Duke Pagar of Karsten rallies once more (*Three Against the Witch World*).
1047	**Year of the Black Adder**	Kemoc Tregarth is wounded and goes to the Archives at Lormt (*Three Against the Witch World*).
		Koris is wounded and retires from leadership in Estcarp (*Three Against the Witch World* and *Warlock of the Witch World*).
1048	**Year of the Frost Giant**	Simond is born to Koris and Loyse in Estcarp (*Sand Sister*).
1049	**Year of the Kobold**	The Witches of Estcarp wreak the Turning — devastating the barrier ridge separating Karsten from Alizon — and Karsten is defeated (*Three Against the Witch World*).
		Kyllan and Kemoc Tregarth rescue Kaththea from the Council of Estcarp
		Kyllan Tregarth and Dahaun of the Green Silences are handfasted in Escore (*Three Against the Witch World*).
		Dairine is cast ashore at Rannock, High Hallack (*Spider Silk*).
1050	**Year of the Snow Cat**	Kyllan Tregarth returns to Estcarp to recruit settlers for Escore (*Three Against the Witch World*).
		Kemoc Tregarth and the Krogan maiden Orsya are handfasted (*Three Against the Witch World*).
		Kaththea Tregarth is lured away by the adept Dinzel and is rescued by Kemoc (*Warlock of the Witch World*).
		Kaththea Tregarth is lost in an avalanche en route from Escore to Estcarp. She is rescued by the Vupsall and taken deep into Escore (*Sorceress of the Witch World*).
1051	**Year of the Horned Hunter**	Kaththea Tregarth becomes apprenticed to the Vupsall Wise Woman Utta (*Sorceress of the Witch*

		World).
		Kaththea Tregarth finds the Dark Tower and discovers the Gate into the Machine World (*Sorceress of the Witch World*).
		Kaththea Tregarth discovers Simon and Jaelithe in the Machine World, and they rescue the adept Hilarion from imprisonment (*Sorceress of the Witch World*).
1052	Year of the Lamia	Kelsie arrives in Escore through a Gate from Earth (*The Gate of the Cat*).
1053	Year of the Chimera	Simon and Jaelithe Tregarth return to Estcarp from Escore (*Sorceress of the Witch World*).
1054	Year of the Harpy	Tirtha of Hawkholme, Nirel the Falconer and the youth Alon adventure in Escore (*Ware Hawk*).
1055	Year of the Orc	Events of (*To Rebuild the Eyrie*)
1056	Year of the Werewolf	
1057	Year of the Thorn Cat	Kethan and Thaney are betrothed (*The Jargoon Pard*).
1058	Year of the Manticore	Dairine receives the gift of Touch-Sight in High Hallack (*Spider Silk*).
1059	Year of the Weldworm	Dairine becomes apprenticed to the Weavers of Usturt (*Spider Silk*).
1060	Year of the Hydra	
1061	Year of the Triton	
1062	Year of the Centaur	
1063	Year of the Opinacus	Events of (*Falcon Magic*?) Fall of Mallandor, Baron of Alizon, Norandor now Lord Baron
1064	Year of the Sumurgh	
1065	Year of the Remorhaz	
1066	Year of the Elder Tree	
1067	Year of the Wild Huntsman	
1068	Year of the Troll-Dame	
1069	Year of the Silversmith	
1070	Year of the Bitter Herb	
1071	Year of the Alfar	

Three Against the Witch World Poland 2014

Timelines of Witch World
Version 1.4

Year	Lorcan	V1.4	Lorcan's age from *Silver May Tarnish* added & Mosswife/Fire Troll order corrected
		Refugees of the Old Race flee Escore erecting the Great Mountains separating Escore from Estcarp (*Three Against the Witch World*).	
		Approximately 600 years pass unrecorded.	
		Year of the Cloven Hoof	The first Dalesmen come to High Hallack fleeing the disasters of their own world (*Horn Crown*).
		Approximately 400 years pass.	
990		Year of the Blue-horned Ram	Mereth born – 40 years before invasion
1014		Year of the Serpent King	Kerovan is born in High Hallack (*The Crystal Gryphon*).
1015		Year of the Ringed Dove	Kerovan's sister Lisana is born in High Hallack (*The Crystal Gryphon*).
1016		Year of the Salamander	Almondia and Truan are shipwrecked off Wark
			Joisan is born in High Hallack (*The Crystal Gryphon*).
1017		Year of the Pronghorn	
1018		Year of the Sea Serpent	Elys and Elyn are born in High Hallack (*Dragon Scale Silver*).

1019		Year of the Hill Giant	
1020		Year of the Sea Calf	
1021		Year of the Kestrel	
1022	0	Year of the Pard	
1023	1	Year of the Mandrake	
1024	2	Year of the Spitting Toad	Joisan and Kerovan are married by axe in High Hallack (*The Crystal Gryphon*).
1025	3	Year of the Horned Worm	
1026	4	Year of the Gorgon	
1027	5	Year of the Barrow-Wight	Simon Tregarth arrives in Estcarp through a Gate from Earth (*Witch World*).
			Sulcarkeep is destroyed (*Witch World*).
			Loyse of Verlaine marries Duke Yvian of Karsten by axe (*Witch World*).
			Kasarian born (*The Magestone*)
1028	6	Year of the Cameleopard	Simon Tregarth marries Jaelithe in Estcarp (*Witch World*).
			Duke Yvian of Karsten is killed (*Web of the Witch World*).
			Kyllan Tregarth is born on the last day of the year (*Three Against the Witch World*).
1029	7	Year of the Crowned Swan	Kemoc and Kaththea Tregarth are born on the first day of the year (*Three Against the Witch World*).
1030	8	Year of the Mosswife	Koris of Gorm and Loyse of Verlaine are married in Estcarp (*Three Against the Witch World*).
1031	9	Year of the Fire Troll	Alizon invades High Hallack (*The Crystal Gryphon, Dragon Scale Silver*).
			Pagar begins his rise to power in Karsten (*Three Against the Witch World*).
1032	10	Year of the Weld	The Sulcar come to the aid of High Hallack and begin harrying the coasts of Alizon (*The Crystal Gryphon*).
1033	11	Year of the Swordsmith	The Sulcar carry their harrying action into Karsten
			Simon and Loyse are imprisoned in Tormarsh (*Web of the Witch World*).
			Simon and Jaelithe destroy the Kolder Gate (*Web of the Witch World*).
1034	12	Year of the Leopard	Pagar's power base in Karsten grows unsteady (*Three Against the Witch World*).
			Gillan arrives in Norstead Abbey
			High Hallack rallies against the Alizon invasion (*The Crystal Gryphon*).
1035	13	Year of the Night Hound	Elys and Jervon dispel Ingaret's Curse in High Hallack (*Dragon Scale Silver*).
			Imgry becomes leader of the war forces in High Ballade (*Gryphon in Glory*).

1036	14	Year of the Raven	Pagar begins to solidify his power in Karsten (*Three Against the Witch World*).
1037	15	Year of the Gryphon	High Hallack makes the Pact with the Weres (*Year of the Unicorn*, *Three Against the Witch World*, *The Jargoon Pard* and *Gryphon in Glory*).
1038	16	Year of the Firedrake	
1039	17	Year of the Hornet	High Hallack defeats the invaders from Alizon (*Three Against the Witch World* and *The Jargoon Pard*).
			Fall of Facellian, Baron of Alizon, replaced by Mallandor (*The Magestone*)
1040	18	Year of the Unicorn	Kyllan, Kemoc and Kaththea Tregarth rescue a Witch in Estcarp. Alerted to Kaththea's powers, the Council summons her for testing. Her parents refuse (*Three Against the Witch World*).
			Ysmay marries Hylle in High Hallack and journeys to Quayth (*Amber Out of Quayth*).
			Gillan and the Were Rider Herrel are married in High Hallack (*Year of the Unicorn*).
1041		Year of the Red Boar	Ysmay frees Broc and Yaal; Hylle is overthrown in Quayth (*Amber Out of Quayth*).
			Aylinn is born in High Hallack (*The Jargoon Pard*).
			Kethan is born in High Hallack (*The Jargoon Pard*).
1042		Year of the Fox Maiden	Simon Tregarth disappears from Estcarp (*Three Against the Witch World*).
1043		Year of the Phoenix	Jaelithe Tregarth goes in search of Simon and disappears from Estcarp (*Three Against the Witch World*).
1044		Year of the Hippogriff	Kyllan and Kemoc Tregarth ride with the Borderers of Estcarp against Karsten (*Three Against the Witch World*).
			Alon is born in Karsten (*Ware Hawk*).
1045		Year of the Roc	Kaththea Tregarth is taken for training by The Council of Estcarp (*Three Against the Witch World*).
			Duke Pagar of Karsten suffers a defeat by the Borderers and subsequent setback (*Three Against the Witch World*).
1046		Year of the Basilisk	Duke Pagar of Karsten rallies once more (*Three Against the Witch World*).
1047		Year of the Black Adder	Kemoc Tregarth is wounded and goes to the Archives at Lormt (*Three Against the Witch World*).
			Koris is wounded and retires from leadership in Estcarp (*Three Against the Witch World* and *Warlock of the Witch World*).
1048		Year of the Frost Giant	Simond is born to Koris and Loyse in Estcarp

			(*Sand Sister*).
1049		**Year of the Kobold**	The Witches of Estcarp wreak the Turning — devastating the barrier ridge separating Karsten from Alizon — and Karsten is defeated (*Three Against the Witch World*).
			Kyllan and Kemoc Tregarth rescue Kaththea from the Council of Estcarp
			Kyllan Tregarth and Dahaun of the Green Silences are handfasted in Escore (*Three Against the Witch World*).
			Dairine is cast ashore at Rannock, High Hallack (*Spider Silk*).
1050		**Year of the Snow Cat**	Kyllan Tregarth returns to Estcarp to recruit settlers for Escore (*Three Against the Witch World*).
			Kemoc Tregarth and the Krogan maiden Orsya are handfasted (*Three Against the Witch World*).
			Kaththea Tregarth is lured away by the adept Dinzel and is rescued by Kemoc (*Warlock of the Witch World*).
			Kaththea Tregarth is lost in an avalanche en route from Escore to Estcarp. She is rescued by the Vupsall and taken deep into Escore (*Sorceress of the Witch World*).
1051		**Year of the Horned Hunter**	Kaththea Tregarth becomes apprenticed to the Vupsall Wise Woman Utta (*Sorceress of the Witch World*).
			Kaththea Tregarth finds the Dark Tower and discovers the Gate into the Machine World (*Sorceress of the Witch World*).
			Kaththea Tregarth discovers Simon and Jaelithe in the Machine World, and they rescue the adept Hilarion from imprisonment (*Sorceress of the Witch World*).
1052		**Year of the Lamia**	Kelsie arrives in Escore through a Gate from Earth (*The Gate of the Cat*).
1053		**Year of the Chimera**	Simon and Jaelithe Tregarth return to Estcarp from Escore (*Sorceress of the Witch World*).
1054		**Year of the Harpy**	Tirtha of Hawkholme, Nirel the Falconer and the youth Alon adventure in Escore (*Ware Hawk*).
1055		**Year of the Orc**	Events of (*To Rebuild the Eyrie*)
1056		**Year of the Werewolf**	
1057		**Year of the Thorn Cat**	Kethan and Thaney are betrothed (*The Jargoon Pard*).
1058		**Year of the Manticore**	Dairine receives the gift of Touch-Sight in High Hallack (*Spider Silk*).
1059		**Year of the Weldworm**	Dairine becomes apprenticed to the Weavers of Usturt (*Spider Silk*).
1060		**Year of the Hydra**	

1061		Year of the Triton	
1062		Year of the Centaur	
1063		Year of the Opinacus	Events of (*Falcon Magic*?) Fall of Mallandor, Baron of Alizon, Norandor now Lord Baron
1064		Year of the Sumurgh	Events of (*The Magestone*?)
1065		Year of the Remorhaz	
1066		Year of the Elder Tree	
1067		Year of the Wild Huntsman	
1068		Year of the Troll-Dame	
1069		Year of the Silversmith	
1070		Year of the Bitter Herb	
1071		Year of the Alfar	

Timelines of Witch World
Ciara's Song

As has been mentioned on the page for *Ciara's Song* the timeline seems out of whack compared to other timelines. This is intended as a direct comparison to show where these inconsistencies lie.

~ Having asked Lyn McConchie why the timeline discrepancies exist, her reply was: "This is down in a way to the publisher who decided they didn't need the 'intermission' that I wrote between books one and two. This was a dozen or so pages skimming over the intervening generation, and with it gone and nothing altered in book two, it left that time problem. I suggested that I rewrite, but they didn't want to wait and as I'd long since signed the contract they simply brought the book out." ~ (December 04, 2019)

Ciara's Age	Event(s)	Other	Horning	Triplets[1]
9	Thrice Horning[2]	Witch World places it in the winter of this year.[3]	0	
10	Midsummer of the this year brings news of Yvian's death.[4] She turns ten sometime later.[5]	The events of *Web of the Witch World* take place some six months after those of *Witch World*. It's stated that Web starts in midsummer. This would mean a message would have to travel very quickly to reach them by the same midsummer.	1	
11	There is news of Alizon fighting overseas[6]	In many books, this is the Year of the Fire Troll.[7]	2	
12			3	
13		Kyllan is born at the last day of this year. In *Three Against the Witch World* it is mentioned that after her last child is born Jaelithe passes into a form of trance which lasts several months. "By the end of our birth year Pagar was strong	4	

		enough to risk battle against a confederation of rivals. And four months later he was proclaimed Duke, even along the border. "		
14		Kemoc and Kaththea are born on the first day of this year. "**It was heading into another year** when the Lady Jaelithe at last aroused...when the Seneschal Koris and his lady wife, the Lady Loyse, came to South Keep at the **waning of the year** to make merry, since the almost ceaseless war had been brought to an uneasy truce and for the first time in years there was no flame nor fast riding along either border...but that was only a short breathing space."[8]	5	0
15			6	1
16			7	2
17			8	3
18	Ciara turns 18[9] and she and Trovagh are married[10]	This is said to be the Year of the Pronghorn[11] In *Silver May Tarnish* the year of the Pronghorn is some thirteen years *before* the Year of the Fire Troll.[12]	9	4
19			10	5
20			11	6
21	Ciara gives birth to Kirin.[13]		12	7
22			13	8
23			14	9
24			15	10
25	Ciara gives birth to a daughter.[14] Around this time Pagar of Geen begins his rise.	Triplets are 11. Pagar began his rise the same year Kemoc and Kaththea are born. If her timeline matched that of *Three Against the Witch World* she'd only be 13.	16	11
26			17	12[15]
27			18	13
28			19	14[16]
29			20	15
30	Pagar is crowned duke of Kars.[17] Pagar is 33 when he launches a campaign to reclaim Verlaine and he also starts raiding the border of Estcarp[18]	In *Three Against the Witch World* "For it was four months into the new year when the threat of Pagar came into being... By the end of our birth year Pagar was strong enough to risk battle against a confederation of rivals. And four months later he was proclaimed Duke, even along the border." It is in this same year he begins border raiding against Estcarp. In	21	16

		retaliation Hostovrul of the Sulcar leads twenty ships to attack Karsten, even attacking the city of Kars. This attack leaves Pagar's hold on Karsten weakened so that shortly after Pagar's half-brother challenges his rule.[19]		
31			22	17[20]
32			23	18
33			23	19[21]
34			24	20
35	Ciara's daughter would be 10.[22]	The Turning	25[23]	21
36				
37				
38				
39				
40				
41	Ciara's daughter marries (age 16)[24]			
42	Kirin probably marries Aisha.[25]			
43				
44				
45				
46				
47	Trader Tanrae and Ciara's daughter die, the latter under suspicious circumstance and the former in a raid that was more than it seemed.[26] It is not indicated how many years exactly have passed since Ciara's daughter was married.			
48	Sersgarth has been abandoned[27] a month later a new family moves in[28] Later that year they buy Elmsgarth and Kirion is born[29]			
49				
50				
51	Keelan is born.			
52				
53				
54				
55				
56				
57	It has been ten years since Ciara's daughter died and she finds out Kirion wants to ride			

	to war with Pagar.[30] Aisling is born[31] The Turning happens this year.[32]			
58				
59				
60				
61				
62				
63				
64				
65				
66				
67				
68	In the year Aisling turns 11, Kirion starts taking an interest in Power.[33] Keelan goes to Aiskeep[34]			
69	Keelan's 18th birthday comes in early spring of this year. It is also when Kirion attempts to gain entry to Aiskeep to further his research but he is rebuffed. Keelan formally asks to stay at Aiskeep.			
70	Kirion raises Shandro to be duke and tries to stir up hatred against those with Old Race blood in order to extract revenge against his own family. He changes course when he realizes this will make himself a target.			
71				
72				
73	Kirion attempts to force Aisling (now 16) into a marriage she doesn't want to Ruart. It is in this year that Shosho (during the summer) gets pregnant at age 4 and later gives birth to Wind Dancer. Aisling is kidnapped after her refusal and held by Ruart and Kirion. She manages to escape.			
74	Kirion and Ruart resume their efforts to get Aisling for their own purposes. In winter of this year Aiskeep is under siege and Elanor dies. Aisling decides to leave for Estcarp but Ciara tells her about her			

	dream of Escore. She first goes to Geavon then to Temon where Ruart catches her, but he and Temon die. Aisling passes through some kind of gate and meets Neevor in Escore.			
75				
76				
77	Aisling returns to Karsten under a geas to remove Shandro and Kirion from power. In summer, Franzo leads a siege due to many deaths in the Coast Clan thanks to Shandro and Kirion. This is also when the events of *The Gate of the Cat* are mentioned (page 128 of the hard cover).[35]			
78	In spring of this year, Franzo makes a second siege of Kars. Shandro and Kirion die and Aisling and Hadrann are formally betroth.[35]			

Footnotes:

1. Most of the continuity errors are in relation to events of *Three Against the Witch World*, so this column and the previous will keep track of the years since the Horning (which occurs in winter) and the ages of the Triplets - using Kemoc's and Kaththea's at the beginning of the year.

2. p. 6

3. p. 146

4. p. 45

5. p. 58

6. p. 60

7. The Year of the Fire Troll seems to be four years after the events of *Witch World* based on the text of *Three Against the Witch World* that places the Turning nearly 25 years after the Horning (and the triplets are 21) and a reference in *The Crystal Gryphon* to some "grievous defeat" that happened to the Sulcar two years prior to the Year of the Moss Wife (the year before the Fire Troll).

8. This is very confusing since the crowning of Pagar happens at the end of their birth year and it is stated that four months into the new raiding starts, yet this indicates that a whole year passes without any border raids or other issues.

9. p. 102

10. p. 106

11. Since the same author wrote this book and *Silver May Tarnish* it may be reasonably assumed that the reference here (which is the only reference to a Dales year) is to deliberately tie the two. However, it would more likely be the *Year of the Unicorn*, which takes place eight years after the Year of the Fire Troll. The Year of the Fire Troll would almost have to take place when Ciara is 12 due to the way the timeline for the war in the Dales works out.

12. In *Year of the Unicorn*, it is mentioned initially that the fighting in High Hallack had a handful of years of peace possibly in an attempt to make it similar to World War I

and World War II, though there was 21 years between those two wars. It could more easily refer to the years of the Falcon, Raven, and Night Hound - sometime after the small victories in Leopard and before the wereriders joined in full in *Gryphon in Glory* when the Hounds could have been stymied.

13. p. 110
14. p. 110
15. Kemoc and Kyllan go on first foray against Pagar at age 12.
16. Simon disappears and some months later Jaelithe followed.
17. p. 111
18. pgs. 111-112
19. There is absolutely no way to reconcile this.
20. Pagar suffers a major defeat but Kaththea is taken by the Witches.
21. Kemoc is wounded and goes to Lormt
22. Interestingly Aisling is almost 11 when Kirion visits. If her unnamed daughter had been the one to adventure instead of Aisling, things could have worked out for the timeline much better. Then again, if her daughter had been born in the year of the Turning, Ciara would have to have been born about a year after the Horning.
23. Since *Three Against the Witch World* has the Turning take place in late summer, and it is four years since Kaththea was taken at age 17, Kyllan must have turned 21 at the end of the previous year while Kemoc and Kaththea turned 21 at the beginning of this one. It is also "nearly" 25 years since the Horning - exactly 25 would be at the beginning of winter this year.
24. p. 114
25. p. 114
26. p. 115
27. p. 118
28. p. 119
29. p. 120, p. 127, p. 143
30. p. 120
31. p. 143
32. p. 135
33. p. 153
34. p. 153
35. *The Duke's Ballad*

Warlock of the Witch World Poland 2014

Warlock of the Witch World UK 1988

Timeline by the Years

This timeline is based, as much as possible, on events mentioned in various **Witch World** books, novels, and short stories as they first start appearing in *Year of the Unicorn*. This timeline also attempts to incorporate both the GURPS: Roleplaying Guide as well as Andre Norton's own list of years compiled by Juanita Coulson.

There are some years and events that contradict earlier ones within the books and, especially, in the GURPS years. Even Coulson's Index sometimes conflict with events. When resolving contradictions, the timeline will have this order of precedence: 1) publication order of the Norton books[1] 2) Norton books before anthology books[2] 3) GURPS years before Coulson's Index.[3]

Years marked with an asterisk are those mentioned in at least one published story. All others will either be GURPS: years or Coulson's Index. [4]

NOTE: The "Coulson Index" has been split up and incorporated into this tome.

Note: Due to the way of computers this table is set up different than the original. When the wikidots page is updated it automatically renumbers and addresses the footnotes. This site does not. The original table currently has 180 footnotes, this is very difficult to keep updated for every time a footnote is added or changed we have to manually reset all the other footnotes. Therefore we broke the footnotes up into more manageable groups. If you find this format difficult to read, please go to the elwher.wikidot.com/timeline-years webpge.

Footnotes: for the beginning of this timeline

1. If a book published in 1989, for instance, contradicted a book published in 1969, the 1969 book would have precedence.

2. Both Year of the Pard and Year of the Yellow Dwarf are supposed to be ten years before the Year of the Moss Wife. Because Year of the Pard appears in a book published by Andre Norton (even though the short story containing the Year of the Dwarf was published before), the Year of the Pard will have precedence.

3. While normally the author's notes would be given precedence, some years have slashes that makes it confusing to tell what order they are supposed to be in.

4. Interestingly, though the GURPS and Coulson Index diverge a great deal, the following years appear in the same order in both sets: Serpent King, Ringed Dove, Salamander, Fire Arrow, Bicorn, Hill Giant, Sea Calf, Kestrel; Raven, Night Hound, Gryphon, Fire Drake, Hornet, Unicorn, Red Boar; Lamia, Chimera, Harpy, Orc, Werewolf; Roc, Phoenix, Hippogriff, Basilisk, Black Adder, Frost Giant; Weld, Hydra, Triton, Centaur, Opinicus, Simurgh, Remorhaz.

5. These years are mentioned in *Port of Dead Ships*. It is the Year 6810 in *Port of Dead Ships*, but it is unclear what Dales year it is; the order here is the best guess. Since Simon and Jaelithe are back it is, at least, sometime after *Sorceress of the Witch World*

6. In *Ciara's Song*, Ciara goes from a young girl during the Horning to a grandmother by the Turning. This simply won't work since only 25 years have passed between the Horning and the Turning. Further, a lot of events mentioned in *Three Against the Witch World* get placed at different intervals in Song. This column shows where the timeline varies. Considering the same author wrote both *Silver May Tarnish* and *Ciara's Song* and the Year of the Pronghorn is mentioned in both, it can reasonably be assumed they are cotemperal and this column reflects how events would occur if the two books are internally consistent.

7. Having asked Lyn McConchie why the timeline discrepancies exist, her reply was: "This is down in a way to the publisher who decided they didn't need the 'intermission' that I wrote between books one and two. This was a dozen or so pages skimming over the intervening generation, and with it gone and nothing altered in book two, it left that time problem. I suggested that I rewrite, but they didn't want to wait and as I'd long since signed the contract they simply brought the book out." ~ (December 04, 2019)

Founding Years of Varn [5]	Year Since the Betrayal	Dale Year	Event(s)	Ciara's Timeline [6 & 7]
circa 5752	Year of the Betrayal	Year of the ???	Shorrosh and Elsenar bring in the Alizonders from their home world. Elsenar weds lady Kylanina. Alizon City created; Lormt erected. The First Turning. Shorrosh reveals himself as a Dark Adept and Elsenar seals the Gate to the Alizonder home world with Shorrosh trapped on the other side. The Master Gate is attempted at Lormt but fails. Elsenar attempts a postern to Arvon but it is first broken by the energies of the failed Master Gate, then later rerouted by the Dark Adept Narvok. Elsenar is subsequently trapped, severed spirit from body, until released by Kasarian. [a1] Presumably Es City is founded around this time too.	
circa 5753	1	Year of the ???	Krevonel, son of Elsenar and Kylanina born.	
circa 6352	circa 600	Year of the Cloven Hoof [a2]	The first Dalesmen come to High Hallack through their own Gate. They are caused to forget why they left their homeworld, however. Events of *Horn Crown* take place	
circa 6376-6576	circa 625-825	Year of the???	The first Karstenians arrive in what will become Karsten. [a3]	
circa 6651-6676	circa 900-925	Year of the???	The Falconers arrive seeking sanctuary in Estcarp. [a4]; Sometime between now and when Mereth is born, Sulcarkeep is built. [a5]	

a1. *The Magestone*

a2. GURPS: years or Coulson's Index

a3. On p.165 of *Witch World* Ingvald mentions that the new race in Karsten and the Old Race have been more or less at peace for ten generations. Assuming a generation is 20-25 years then this would have been 200-250 years ago. It is possible to assume even longer since the Old Race live much longer: Utta in *Sorceress of the Witch World* has lived through six different consorts up to Ifeng, and was likely an adult by the time she met her first consort, so she's probably at least 140 years old at the time of her death, and she could easily be much older. For purposes here, I'm assuming it's been no less than 200 years and no more than 400.

a4. On p.116 of *Witch World* Koris mentions it's been 'a hundred years or more' since the Falconers first came from overseas and settled in the mountains between Estcarp and Karsten. Of course, in this story they are not fleeing Jonkara but rather an overthrow by barbarian invaders.

a5. On p.53 of *Witch World* Magnis Osberic mentions Sulcarkeep was built in his great-grandfather's day. Since Magnis's son Anner is fully grown Magnis himself is likely in his 30's or 40's at the time he destroys Sulcarkeep. Depending on how old each of his ancestors were there could be between 60-90 years of time (if the ages were 20-30) beforehand. In any case, it is certainly built by the time Mereth is born.

6738	987	Year of the Blue-Horned Ram* [b1]	Mereth is born.	
6739	988	Year of the ???		
6740	989	Year of the ???		
6741	990	Year of the ???		
6742	991	Year of the ???		
6743	992	Year of the ???		
6744	993	Year of the ???		
6745	994	Year of the ???		
6746	995	Year of the ???		
6747	996	Year of the ???		Trovagh is born [b2]
6748	997	Year of the ???		Ciara is born [b3]
6749	998	Year of the ???		
6750	999	Year of the ???		
6751	1000	Year of the ???		
6752	1001	Year of the ???		
6753	1002	Year of the ???		
6754	1003	Year of the ???		
6755	1004	Year of the ???		
6756	1005	Year of the ???		
6757	1006	Year of the ???		Ciara is 9 and the Horning occurs [b5]
6758	1007	Year of the ???	Mereth turns 20. Earlier this year her mother dies. [b4]	Ciara is 10 [b6]
6759	1008	Year of the ???	Hlymer born [b7]; Lorcan's brother Merrion is born.	
6760	1009	Year of the ???		
6761	1010	Year of the Serpent King [b8]	Kerovan born [b9]; Sif born	

b1. Mentioned in *The Magestone*

b2. *Ciara's Song*

b3. *Ciara's Song*

b4. *Ciara's Song* This is an issue since in *Three Against the Witch World* it is nearly 25 years since the Horning when the Turning takes place and the Triplets are 21. If Ciara's timeline were correct, however, it would be almost 44 years from Horning to the Turning. While the 44 years gives Ciara time to become a grandmother, the 25 would not.

b5. *The Magestone*

b6. *Ciara's Song*

b7. On p8 of *The Crystal Gryphon* it mentions that Lady Tephana's son was "in his second year" the year Kerovan was born.

b8. Both GURPS: years or Coulson's Index begin the 'regular' listing of years with the Serpent King.

b9. *Of the Shaping of Ulm's Heir* / *Heir Apparent*

6762	1011	Year of the Ringed Dove	Kerovan's sister Lisana is born; Lorcan's brother Anla is born.	
6763	1012	Year of the Salamander* [c1]	Joisan born; *Dragon Scale Silver* begins when Almondia and Truan arrive in Wark, High Hallack; Alys born	
6764	1013	Year of the Sea Serpent* [c2]	Elyn and Elys born; Gillan may be born [c11]	
6765	1014	Year of the Fire Arrow [c3]		
6766	1015	Year of the Pronghorn* [c4]	Coughing sickness kills two of Lorcan's siblings	Ciara is 18 [c5]
6767	1016	Year of the Yellow Dwarf* [c6]		
6768	1017	Year of the Pard* [c7]	Lorcan born.	
6769	1018	Year of the Bicorn		
6770	1019	Year of the Hill Giant		Ciara (22) gives birth to her son Kirin. [c8]
6771	1020	Year of the Spitting Toad* [c9]	Kerovan (10) and Joisan (8) ax-wed	
6772	1021	Year of the Winged Bull* [c10]	According to *Port of Dead Ships* shortly before Kolder invade Gorm	

c1. Mentioned in *Dragon Scale Silver*

c2. Mentioned in *Dragon Scale Silver*

c3. It would be possible to insert this year between that of the Salamander and Sea Serpent. See the discussion section of *Dragon Scale Silver*

c4. Mentioned in *Silver May Tarnish* and *Ciara's Song*

c5. In *Ciara's Song* it is mentioned that Ciara and Trovagh are married when she is 18, but it also mentions she turns 18 in the Year of the Pronghorn. Given the same author wrote the two books in which this year appears, it is not unreasonable to assume she meant them to be correlated, especially since the Year of the Pronghorn is the *only* year specifically mentioned by name in *Ciara's Song*.

c6. Mentioned in *Sea Serpents of Domnudale*. Technically it takes place ten years before the Year of the Moss wife, placing it as the same as the Year of the Pard.

c7. Mentioned in *Silver May Tarnish*

c8. *Ciara's Song*

c9. Mentioned in *The Crystal Gryphon*

c10. Mentioned in *Port of Dead Ships*

c11. She believes herself no younger than 18 and no older than 20, so if this is true she's born sometime between the beginning of this year and the end of the Year of the Pronghorn.

6773	1022	Year of the Horned Worm [d1]	According to *The Magestone* the Kolder invade Gorm (p.154); Mereth 34-35.	
6774	1023	Year of the Sea Calf		Ciara (26) gives birth to her daughter. [d2]
6775	1024	Year of the Kestrel [d3]		
6776	1025	Year of the Mandrake [d4]	*Witch World* could take place [d5]; This is the earliest possible year the Horning can take place in order for it to be "nearly twenty-five years" since the event by the time the Turning occurs in *Three Against the Witch World* and for all other things to be consistent. It's not impossible for it to have happened two years later, though, since 23 is nearly 25.	In *Ciara's Song* it mentions this is about the time Pagar starts his raids on Estcarp and the Sulcar sack Kars. Pagar is mentioned as being 33.

d1. From GURPS. Norton's notes have a Year of the Horn Worm. In both timelines these years follow that of the Winged Bull.

d2. In *Ciara's Song* it mentions this is about when Pagar of Geen starts his campaigning, which doesn't work with the timeline for several reasons.

d3. In both GURPS: years or Coulson's Index the Kestrel follows the Seacalf. However, the Sea Calf usually follows the Hill Giant, which doesn't work out.

d4. In GURPS the year after the Mandrake is the Spitting Toad while in Norton's notes it's both the Kobold and the Wyvern (the Year of the Mandrake gets listed twice).

d5. In *The Crystal Gryphon* Joisan mentions that two years prior to the Year of the Moss Wife the Sulcars had suffered some grievous defeat. The only thing this can likely refer to is the fall of Sulcarkeep. However, this doesn't quite fit in with the invasion of the Dales due to the length of time between the destruction of the Kolder and the start of the War in the Dales.

6777	1026	Year of the Crowned Swan* [e1]	*Web of the Witch World* could take place. [e2]; Kerovan is 16 and Joisan is 14 [e3]; Merreth born and left at the abby. [e4]	
6778	1027	Year of the Moss Wife* [e5]	Simon Tregarth enters the Witch World [e6]; Sulcarkeep falls to Kolder forces; The Horning takes place early winter this year. [e7]; All other events of *Witch World* take place [e8]; Simon Tregarth and Jaelithe probably married at the end of this year [e9]; Spies of Alizon begin snooping around the Dales [e10]; Lorcan 10 [e11]; Una of Seakeep born [e12]; Doubt proposes to Mereth (age 39 or	

			40} [e13]	
6779	1028	Year of the Fire Troll* [e14]	War in Dales begins [e15]; Gillan (between 10-12) brought over on an Alizon vessel for unknown reasons [e16]; Events of *Web of the Witch World* take place [e17]; Kasarian is 5 or is born [e18]; Kyllan Tregarth is born on the last day of the year.	

e1. Mentioned in *The Crystal Gryphon*

e2. This presents one major issue - between the destruction of the Kolder gate this year and the beginning of the War on the Dales (which uses Kolder weapons) there's almost a two year gap. While Kolder tactics don't tend to make a lot of sense, unless they had a multi-year supply of weapons and fuel it's hard to see how the invasion would work, unless they assumed it'd only take a short time to win. Even then, other than a handful in Alizon, there's none left by the time the War began

e3. *The Crystal Gryphon*

e4. *Candletrap*

e5. Mentioned in *The Crystal Gryphon* and *Silver May Tarnish*

e6. Simon is mentioned as having been in Estcarp weeks when Magnis arrives seeking aid.

e7. There's both mention of winter-killed grass in the place Jaelithe is at and later winter-pressed stack of hay in False Hawk, though there's no mention of snow or particularly cold temperatures.

e8. After the destruction of Sulcarkeep all other events seem to occur within the same year.

e9. It is midsummer when __Web of the Witch World__ begins and mentions later that "half a year ago Simon would have witnessed but not understood the torments which tore the younger man now" p.245 Annals of the Witch World

e10. __The Crystal Gryphon__

e11. __Silver May Tarnish__

e12. __Seakeep__

e13. Mentioned in __The Magestone__

e14. Mentioned in several books

e15. __The Crystal Gryphon__ chapter 6, __Dragon Scale Silver__

e16.. In __Year of the Unicorn__ Gillan is unsure as to her actual age but believes herself to be between 18-20 and mentions it being eight years since she was brought to the Norstead Abby. With her Power, however, it's pretty odd she's not trained as a Witch, since that generally begins when girls are around 6. However, she only can remember being taken over for some purpose and nothing beforehand.

e17. Simon remembers his warning against delving too closely into the Kolder artifacts as being months ago. Jaelithe could have become pregnant in the Month of Willowcarp, and thus would be a month pregnant with the triplets - not showing at all and maybe not suspecting yet - in the midsummer Month of the Golden Lacewing. However, the reference in __The Crystal Gryphon__ to the defeat the Sulcar had two years prior to the Year of the Moss Wife (the year that it's mentioned in Joisan's narrative) would have to be changed to 'this year'.

e18. In *Magestone* Kasarian mentions being five when the war with the Dales began, but he is 22 at the time of the Turning. Since the Tregarth triples are 21 at the time of the Turning he cannot be more than a year older than them. Either he is born in this year or he is 27 years old at the time of the Turning.

6780	1029	Year of the Leopard* [f1]	Kemoc and Kaththea Tregarth born the first day of the year [f2]; Elyn (15 or 16) joins the war,	In *Ciara's Song* it is mentioned that this is the year Pagar's supposed half

			Elys and the people of Wark travel inland (spring) and it would also be their first summer in exile [f3]; *Wolfhead* could take place this year [f4]; Well into this year, the Dales make their first, small victories [f5]; Pagar strong enough to take on his rivals by the end of the year. [f6]	brother is killed but others rise to replace him.
6781	1030	Year of the Falcon [f7]	Sif (20) returns to Ulys to rescue Alys (17) [f8]; Four months into the year Pagar proclaimed Duke of Karsten; In the summer of this year Pagar is border raiding against Estcarp. In retaliation Hostovrul of the Sulcar leads twenty ships to attack Karsten, even attacking the city of Kars. This attack leaves Pagar's hold on Karsten weakened so that shortly after Pagar's half-brother challenges his rule. [f9]; This would be the second summer of the people of Wark's exile. [f10]	

f1. Mentioned in *The Crystal Gryphon*, *Year of the Unicorn*

f2. *Three Against the Witch World*

f3. *Dragon Scale Silver*

f4. In any case it takes place after the start of the War and before the Year of the Gryphon

f5. *The Crystal Gryphon* chapter 7, *Year of the Unicorn*

f6. *Three Against the Witch World*

f7. Mentioned in Coulson's Index. It is used here because GURPS puts the Year of the Leopard next to the Year of the Raven which won't work.

f8. *Rampion*

f9. *Three Against the Witch World*

f10. *Dragon Scale Silver*

6782	1031	Year of the Raven* [g1]	Simond may be born [g2]; This would be the third summer of the people of Wark's exile - when they finally find refuge. [g3]; *Night Hound's Moon* takes place at the end of this year and the beginning of the next. [g4]	
6783	1032	Year of the Night Hound* [g5]	Events similar to those of *Port of Dead Ships* take place in Varn; Kerovan goes back to Ulmsdale to see how it fares - he is attacked along the way, finds his father dead and Lady Telphana in charge. She, Rogear, Hlymer, and Lisana all	

			plot to deal with Power, to the undoing of Ulmsdale; Cyart, Math, and Toross die and Ithdale is overrun; Kerovan meets Joisan and most of *The Crystal Gryphon* takes place [g6]; People of Wark's first midsummer since finding refuge. [g7]	
6784	1033	Year of the Gryphon* [g8]	Covenant made with the Were Riders in the spring of this year. Specifically, Kerovan meets the Wereriders in the Waste. [g9]; *Gryphon in Glory* takes place [g10]; People of Wark's second midsummer since finding refuge. When Elys meets Jervon and he tells her of the covenant with the Wereriders in the spring of this year [g11]; Near the end of fall this year, Elys defeats the Curse of Ingaret and rescues her brother Elyn with the help of Jervon. [g12]; Past-Abbess Malwinna dies in winter of this year. [g13]	

g1. Mentioned in *Night Hound's Moon*

g2. The Year of the Frost Giant is when the GURPS timeline places Simond's birth, but this would be sixteen years before the earliest possible year for *Sand Sister* to take place - and both Simond and Tursla seem to be around 16 in the story.

g3. *Dragon Scale Silver*

g4. GURPS places the Year of the Raven immediately after the Year of the Leopard, but the story does not mention the war in the Dales specifically, though it does mention 'violent skirmishes' when Kennard was 5 (and he's around 12 in the story). Dales are known to have fought before the War, but both Norton's notes and the GURPS timelines place this year as if it's part of the war, so it's placed here.

g5. Mentioned in *Night Hound's Moon*

g6. While Kerovan mentions that they were well within the Year of the Leopard before they saw any gains, the only way that events in Crystal can happen some months before those in *Gryphon in Glory* is if they happen this year, even though the set-up of Crystal seems to imply the Years of Fire Troll, Leopard, and Gryphon all occur one after another. However, *Gryphon's Eyrie* takes place three years after *Gryphon in Glory* and it is clearly the Year of the Unicorn. Similarly, *Dragon Scale Silver*
makes it clear that there would be three years unaccounted for if this were the case.

g7. *Dragon Scale Silver*

g8. Mentioned in *Year of the Unicorn* and *Dragon Scale Silver*

g9. *Gryphon in Glory*, *Year of the Unicorn*, *Dragon Scale Silver* Note that Elys and Jervon meet Joisan (before she's taken by the Thas) and then Kerovan shortly after he treats with the Wereriders, despite them not actually meeting until summer of this year, let alone being near the Waste.

g10. In the book it's mentioned that the events of *The Crystal Gryphon* are months in the past. Kerovan would be 22 or 23 depending on when his birthday occurs. Joisan would be 20 (since this is spring) but 21 by the end of the year.

g11. *Dragon Scale Silver*

g12. *Dragon Scale Silver*

g13. *Year of the Unicorn*

6785	1034	Year of the Fire Drake* [h1]	If *Were-Wrath* takes place in the Witch World, this is probably when it takes place. Tirath may have met Herwydin the fens; Khemrys may be born. [h2]	
6786	1035	Year of the Hornet* [h3]	Alizon forces are beaten [h4]; Pagar has defeated his half brother and other forces [h5]; Kasarian is 12 [h12]; Lord Baron Facellion is overthrown and killed, Mallandor is placed as Lord Baron [h6]. Brixia, Marbon & Dwed travel into the The Waste free the ancient city An-Yak from *Zarsthor's Bane*. Elys & Jervon fight an ancient god in The Waste with the *Sword of Unbelief*. Hertha raped by Daleman in the aftermath of the Invasion and seeks out *The Toads of Grimmerdale*. Before the first day of the Year of the Unicorn, twelve and one brides are given to the Were Riders as payment in the Great Bargain; Gillan believes herself to be no younger than 18 and no older than 20. [h13]	
6787	1036	Year of the Unicorn* [h7]	On the first day of the year the Were Riders and their new brides enter Arvon. Events of *Year of the Unicorn* take place; Fyndale fair may be resumed this year. [h8]; Hertha's baby girl Elfanor born and Hertha seals the circle of the Toads in *Changeling*. *Gryphon's Eyrie* takes place this year. [h9]; Ysmay marries Hylle in High Hallack and journeys to Quayth where she frees Broc and Yaal. Hylle is overthrown on Midwinter Day [h10]; Lorcan 18 and Meive 15 Years old at end of Year of the Unicorn. [h11]	

h1. Mentioned in *Year of the Unicorn*

h2. *Were-Flight*

h3. Mentioned in *Year of the Unicorn*

h4. *Year of the Unicorn*

h5. *Three Against the Witch World*

h6. *The Magestone*

h7. Mentioned in *Year of the Unicorn*

h8. *The Sword Seller* mentions the fair resumed shortly after the end of the war. *How* shortly is not stated, but it's not unreasonable to guess it would have been as soon as feasible. It's entirely possible that the fair could have been resumed as soon the Year of the Hornet - though that would probably push things a bit.

h9. Kerovan is 25 or 26 and Joisan is 23 (she'll be 24 in the fall).

h10. *Amber Out of Quayth*

h11. "But two days after my eighteenth birthday, at the End of the Year of the Unicorn, I rode South." - Lorcan on page 47 of *Silver May Tarnish*. If Lorcan turns 10 at the end of the Year of the Moss Wife, he ought to turn 19 this year.

h12. This works with him being 5 when the War started but not with him being 22 in the Year of the Kobold (he should be 27).

h13. *Year of the Unicorn*

6788	1037	Year of the Red Boar* [i1]	Kethan and Aylinn born and switched at the Shrine of Gunnora at the beginning of this year [i2]; Hyana may be born to Kerovan and Joisan [i3]; *Legacy from Sorn Fen* probably takes place around here. [i4]; Much of *Silver May Tarnish* happens this year [i5]	
6789	1038	Year of the Hippogriff* [i6]	Eydryth born, Alon may also be born; Levas and Elesha wed in spring while Lorcan and Meive wed in summer. Lord Silas and his people arrive in summer and settle in Merrowdale. Meive is pregnant by the end of the year and will give birth before the summer of the next year. [i7]	
6790	1039	Year of the Roc	Around this time *Ully the Piper* probably takes place. The child of Meive and Lorcan is born summer of this year. [i8]	Ciara's daughter turns 16 and is wed. [i9]
6791	1040	Year of the Basilisk	Events of *The Sword Seller* take place [i10]	Kirin and Aisha are wed and Pagar resumes raiding Estcarp. [i11]
6792	1041	Year of the Black Adder	Kyllan, Kemoc and Kaththea are 12. Kyllan and Kemoc go on their first foray. The three rescue a Witch in need from Karstinian forces. [i12]	At some point, Ciara's daughter dies and trader Tanrae is slain, though it may not be exactly this year. Similarly at some point Kirion is born [i13]

i1. Mentioned in *The Jargoon Pard*

i2. *The Jargoon Pard*

i3. Joisan mentions in *Gryphon's Eyrie* that she expects to deliver around midwinter, which is generally shown as towards the end of the year, as in *Amber Out of Quayth*, so Hyana could have been born near the end of the Year of the Unicorn instead.

i4. It takes place after the war, but the context makes it sound like it's not *too* far after.

i5. Lorcan is captured by bandits in spring, in late spring of this year, Meive (now 16) saves Lorcan from bandits (p.90). They begin wandering the Dales looking for people to repopulate Honeycoombe. In summer of this year Meive and Lorcan visit Tildale. By near the end of the year there are now twenty-four in Honeycoombe. It is this winter that Hogeth decides to come after Lorcan, but he and his army are killed.

i6. Mentioned in *Songsmith*

i7. *Silver May Tarnish* Note that Lorcan mentions it is spring again when he and Meive visit Tildale, putting a year between, but this contradicts the flow of the book: Lorcan is captured in early spring, freed by Meive in late spring, they both visit Tildale in summer and stay about ten days. It is about a week after they leave Tildale that they save the few remaining survivors of Drosdale. Ten days after they hire Levas and his men, they arrive at Merrowdale and a day after in Honeycoombe - so about two months of traveling altogether. It is late summer by the time they get back to Honeycoombe. They spend time there except when Meive goes out looking for more supplies and people, until winter arrives. It probably is early in the next year that Hogeth arrives, since it's after false spring, but Lorcan and Meive do not spend any intervening winter outside Honeycoombe.

i8. *Silver May Tarnish*

i9. *Ciara's Song* Ciara would be 42.

i10. Not counting the year of the Unicorn, this would be the fourth year. Counting it, the story would have been last year. *Amber Out of Quayth* mentions it being hot when the fair took place, so likely in summer of this year (or last).

i11. *Ciara's Song*

i12. *Three Against the Witch World*

i13. *Ciara's Song*

6793	1042	Year of the Frost Giant [i1]	Simon Tregarth vanishes at sea while exploring islands suspected of Kolder activity. Jaelithe moves to Estford and shuts herself up for months. When she emerges she calls her children to her and uses them to help her find Simon. Shortly after this she rides out and vanishes as well. She made Koris swear on Volt's Axe to protect her children from the wiles of the Counsel. [i2]	
6794	1043	Year of the Phoenix [i3]	Kethan (6) goes to the Youth's Tower [i4]; Firdun born [i5]	
6795	1044	Year of the Horned Hunter* [i6]	The story *Candletrap* takes place; Mereth is traveling to Lormt over sea. [i7]	Keelan may be born. (He is three years younger than Kirion in any case.) [i8]
6796	1045	Year of the Lamia* [i9]		
6797	1046	Year of the Chimera* [i10]	Kaththea (17) taken by the Witches, Koris wounded and can no longer wield Volt's Axe [i11]	

j1. GURPS places Simond's birth in this year, but it seems unlikely that Koris and Loyse would have waited this long before having a kid. It's not impossible, though, since they may have had

244

trouble conceiving and there's nothing in the timeline to prevent it from being this late.

j2. _Three Against the Witch World_

j3. Though both GURPS and the notes place this year before that of the Hippogriff, Eydryth is only one year younger than Hyana and 13 in the Year of the Werewolf.

j4. _The Jargoon Pard_

j5. _Songsmith_

j6. Mentioned in _The Magestone_.

j7. In _The Magestone_ the Turning is mentioned as having taken place two years prior (p.5). Given that the Tregarth Triplets must be 21 in the year of the turning, and that their birth cannot take place until after _Web of the Witch World_, it seems more likely that Mereth should be traveling in the Year of the Horned Cat.

j8. _Ciara's Song_

j9. Mentioned in _The Jargoon Pard_, _The Magestone_

j10. Mentioned in _The Jargoon Pard_

j11. _Three Against the Witch World_

6798	1047	Year of the Sphinx* [k1]	_Sand Sister_ may take place [k2]	
6799	1048	Year of the Harpy* [k3]	Khemrys turns 16 [k4]; Elys and the unborn Trevon hidden by forces of the Dark; Eydryth 10, Firdun 5; Trevon would have been born [k5]; Kemoc (19) wounded and goes to Lormt. [k6]; Most events of _Were-Flight_ takes place at the end of this year and the beginning of the next.	
6800	1049	Year of the Orc* [k7]		
6801	1050	Year of the Kobald* [k8]	Year of the Second Turning; 23-25 years since the Horning [k9]; Pagar tries to invade Estcarp; Kyllan and Kemoc rescue Kaththea and all three escape to Escore [k10]; _Three Against the Witch World_, _Warlock of the Witch World_, and the beginning portion of _Sorceress of the Witch World_ all take place this year as does _Trey of Swords_ [k11]; Trey takes place concurrently with Warlock [k12]; according to _The Magestone_ Kasarian is 22 [k13]; _Exile_ takes place during this year, shortly after the Turning; According to _Spider Silk_ Dairene is saved from the sea appearing to be age 6 or 7; Una of Seakeep may be married to Ferrick and shortly after a sickness sweeps over the Dales [k14]; Aisling is born this year [k15];	According to _Ciara's Song_ Aisling would be born this year - it is also the year of the Turning. The year itself is not mentioned, but Kirion is 9 and Keelan is 6 when Aisling is born. Ciara would be 52.

			Kerovan is 40, Joisan is 38.	

k1. Mentioned in *Were-Flight*. *The Jargoon Pard* seems to imply this would be the Year of the Chimera instead "for we had behind us such as the Years of the Lamia, the Chimera, the Harpy and the Orc. There were signs that the golden peace of my childhood was fading, though the why of this puzzled all who thought about the matter. " (p.44). Though this implies they occur in this order, there's no reason they couldn't occur in some other order nor that there could not be years in-between. In any case, Kethan would be 10 this year.

k2. This is the earliest possible year the story can take place, since when Simond goes into Tor Marsh it is known that his father lost the ability to wield Volt's Axe. We don't know how old either Simond or Tursla is, except that Tursla is old enough to get pregnant. (p.54) Tursla is likely around 16 and Simond seems about the same age. In any case, since both Simond and Tursla are in *The Warding of Witch World* their meeting has to take place sometime earlier than the events of that book.

k3. Mentioned in *The Jargoon Pard*, *Were-Flight*

k4. p.414 *Were-Flight*. Note that it's only been 14 years since her birth, though. This means she either had to be born about a year before the Year of the Gryphon (which would contradict her father being separated from his fellows in the War) or she ought to turn 16 in the Year of the Kobold.

k5. *Songsmith*

k6. *Three Against the Witch World*

k7. Mentioned in *The Jargoon Pard*, *Were-Flight*

k8. Mentioned in *Spider Silk*

k9. Depending on when Witch World is placed.

k10. *Three Against the Witch World* - it is also mentioned in Three that this is nearly 25 years after the Horning. Considering the triplets are 21, the Horning cannot have taken place more than four years before they were born. Indeed *Web of the Witch World* is at least six months after *Witch World* and there's no indication that Jaelithe is even pregnant at that time.

k11. Three also covers their childhood in some detail. Warlock takes place a few weeks after the end of Three, and Sorceress begins about midwinter. While the events in Escore in both Three and Warlock take about two or three weeks each, Sorceress takes place over a month (40 days by her counting) before Kaththea enters the machine world and returns with Simon and Jaelithe a couple months later.

k12. Barring the weird time stuff in the Sword of Lost Battles (*Trey of Swords*)

k13. "They [Gratch and Guborian] both returned to Alizon City when I was twenty, but they carefully stayed out of Mallandor's way until two years later, when Estcarp's Witches worked their foulest magic, tearing at the very roots of their southern bordering mountains to foil Karsten's impending invasion (p.23)." This does not work with either the original GURPS or any other timeline. If Kasarian is meant to be 24/25 in the book (which takes place in the third year after the Turning) then his other ages would have to be adjusted to accommodate this. Otherwise Kasarian ought to be older.

k14. p. 221 "only a few short weeks later [after Una's marriage]... a sickness which had swept over all the continent with breathless speed and varying effects. To some Dales and some people, it brought but a few days of more or less mild illness. To others it was devastating." p. 222 "For several years all went well." -after the disease hit. *Seakeep*. Since *Falcon Hope* explicitly says it is eight years after the turning and it seems to be later in the same year that events of Seakeep take place, this seems to be the best year for the wedding and disease. It's unlikely they'd have married next year considering that Kethan and Thaney weren't due to the year name, but they could also be married in the Year of the Horned Cat. It's not likely they were married the previous year since it'd make the years past nearer a decade. Una would be 23 this year.

k15. *Ciara's Song*

Founding	Year	Dale Year	Event(s)	Ciara's Timeline [6]

Years of Varn [5]	Since the Betrayal			
6802	1051	Year of the Werewolf* [I1]	Simon, Jaelithe, and Hilarion all return to the Witch World from their exile in very early spring this year [I2];Kethan (14) and Thaney are betrothed and would be married except for year name; Most of *The Jargoon Pard* takes place around fall this year; Eydryth is 13; Alon is supposedly adopted by Hilarion and Kaththea this year [I3]; Monso is foaled [I4]; Jervon Power blasted at the Cyclops scry stone [I5]	
6803	1052	Year of the Horned Cat* [I6]	Elona and Keris may be born to Kyllan and Dahaun [I7]; Mereth is 65; *The Gate of the Cat* likely takes place this year [I8]; Early events of *The Magestone* are supposed to occur [I9]; 30 years since the Kolder invaded Gorm. [I10]	
6804	1053	Year of the Fox Maiden	Eleeri may enter the Witch World. [I11] *Ware Hawk* takes place in spring of this year. [I12] Alon is at least 12 this year and comes to Escore [I13]; Events of *To Rebuild the Eyrie* may take place this year [I14]; Eirran 18 and Yareth no older than 20. [I15]; Later events of *The Magestone* are supposed to take place this year. [I16]	

I1. Mentioned in *The Jargoon Pard*

I2. *Sorceress of the Witch World*

I3. Given the events of *Ware Hawk* Alon could not have been adopted this year since he was not yet in Escore.

I4. Not only won't this work with the timeline, given what is covered in *The Key of the Keplian* it seems impossible that either male or female Keplian would take a normal horse to mate without a lot of mental coercion!

I5. *Songsmith*

I6. Mentioned in *The Jargoon Pard*. The GURPS has a Year of the Thorn Cat, which might be the same year misremembered.

I7. Though it's mentioned on p.158 of *Songsmith* that they seem only five years younger than Eydryth, this simply won't work. This year, though, would be a logical one for their birth since they'd both be 13 by *The Warding of Witch World*, though they could have also been born as early as late spring or early summer of last year too.

I8. In any case Simon is in Escore even if Jaelithe's whereabouts are unknown, so it can't have happened before early spring of the previous year

I9. From the Month of the Fire Thorn to the 4th/5th day of the Month of the Ice Dragon where the year switches. Note that the book also says it goes from the year of the Horned Hunter to the year of the Lamina which just doesn't work at all.

I10. Mereth mention this (p.154) but also that she is 75 [p.103], so there's some weirdness in the timeline. The 30 years from the invasion of Gorm works perfectly, but Mereth would be 65 this year. Also, no matter what, Jenys/Mouse has to be born after the Turning and has to be 6 going on 7, so minimally Falcon Magic cannot occur before spring of 1057 and more likely is in spring of 1058. However, the book keeps referring to the Turning having occurred two years ago, going on three, and the raid in the spring the previous year to get young witches for the Kolder with one of those witches being Jenys/Mouse.

I11. Although *The Key of the Keplian* says it is over thirty years since the Turning. This is not consistent with the time that *The Warding of Witch World* is placed. Of course, this year isn't over thirty years since the Horning, either, but since Eleeri goes from being almost sixteen to nearly twenty-one in the book, and she and the Keplains are in *Warding*, she must arrive at least five years prior to the events of *Warding*.

I12. On the first page, it mentions there have been three years of harsh winters and on page 7 we learn the hiring fair takes place in early spring. On page 22 it mentions that Koris rules over Estcarp with Simon and Jaelithe. Crytha, Yonan, and Uruk appear late in the book, and Crytha has control over the Sword of Shadows, so it takes place after both *Trey of Swords* and *Sorceress of the Witch World*.

I13. On page 122 Alon admits he does not know how old he is, but that he can count at least twelve years since he and Yachne arrived. However, he looks hardly half that age.

I14. It's after the Turning and before the birth of Jenys/Mouse in any case.

I15. *To Rebuild the Eyrie*

I16. Starting Moon of the Knife/Month of the Ice Dragon and going into the 4th day of the Moon of the Fever Leaf/5th day month of the Willow Carp.

6805	1054	Year of the Gorgon	Jenys/Mouse is born this year. [m1] The first child of Hilarion and Kaththea born [m2]	
6806	1055	Year of the Manticore	Mereth is 68; This would be 30 years from the Horning. [m3]	
6807	1056	Year of the Barrow-Wight	The second child of Hilarion and Kaththea may be born; Sulcar visit Rannock six years after the Year of the Kobold [m4]	
6808	1057	Year of the Cameoleopard	Eydryth is 19; events of *Songsmith* take place; Ingvarna teaches Dairine to "see" with her fingers the year after Ortis's visit [m5]; This is also possibly the year *Falcon Blood* takes place in. [m6]	
6809	1058	Year of the Weldworm* [m7]	Events of *Were-Hunter* may take place. [m8]; events of *Knowledge* take place in spring; the events of *Seakeep* take place [m9]; According to *Spider Silk* Dairine passes into "young womanhood" (she'd be 14 or 15), Ingvarna dies, Captain Ortis returns and Dairine is taken to Usurt, learns to weave better, regains her sight. [m10]; The events of *Falcon Law* may take	

			place. [m11]; Eleeri, Jerrany, and Mayrin rescue Romar from the Dark Tower. The Keplian are now able to stand for the Light again. The Dark Tower is ruined and may be destroyed. [m12]; The events of *Falcon Hope* take place near the end of the year [m13]; This would be 30 years since the War in the Dales and 33 years after the Horning.	

m1. Since she's 6 going on 7 in the spring of *Falcon Magic*.

m2. *Songsmith* mentions that Hilarion and Kaththea have two children two years apart: "several years after I [Alon] came to live with them [Hilarion and Kaththea] they had a child of their own...then, two years later, another" pp. 124-125. Alon goes on to mention that he was nearly full grown at the time of the second birthing and so left. While it is true Alon will be at least 15 by the time the second birth occurs (more likely 18 since he's seems to be about the same age as Eydryth), there's simply no way for him to have been with them more than about a year by the time the first birth occurs.

m3. Though both *Songsmith* and *The Key of the Keplian* are supposed to take place 30 years after the Turning, 30+ years after the Horning actually works out much better timeline-wise.

m4. *Spider Silk*

m5. *Spider Silk*

m6. The story takes place after the Turning in any case.

m7. Mentioned in *Spider Silk*. This would be sixteen years from the Year of the Frost Giant, so *Sand Sister* could take place this year. Note that in both GURPS and Norton this is the Year of the Weld.

m8. Glenda is over 18 but it's never clear by how much, and she estimates she's the same age as Harwin. Since Harwin is the third child of Kildas and Harl he can't have been born before the Year of the Hippogriff (assuming his two older siblings are twins and he was born a year after them). However, it's more likely that they were each born a year apart at least. Kethan and Aylinn would be 21 this year.

m9. *Seakeep* starts in late spring (p.217) and continues over the course of a couple months - going through at least early fall "A storm comes, one of the sea's mighty gales, though it is very early in the season for those, and most of our harvest is still in stacks upon the fields." (p.306) Though there are a number of other, smaller, crops not yet ready for harvest. (p.308) It *might* take place the year before since *Falcon Hope* mentions Una having to wait until fall so she could join Talarch at Lormt (and if it were already fall she wouldn't have to wait), but given that it's near-winter in Falcon Hope it could be the same year.

m10. *Spider Silk*

m11. The story clearly references the events of Falcon Blood and so must occur after, even if other stories contradict this by making the area of the former Eyrie uninhabitable.

m12. *The Key of the Keplian*

m13. It's mentioned that it's been eight years since the turning. The events of this story start around the end of fall or beginning of winter when Una is able to travel to help Tarlach in Lormt. (p.184) The attempted invasion by the Sultanites probably takes about a month and a half to two months (in any case takes at least two to three weeks to get from Seakeep to Linna, and the same to return).

6810	1059	Year of the Swordsman	*Port of Dead Ships* takes place in fall of this year. [n1]	
6811	1060	Year of the Thorn Cat		

6812	1061	Year of the Snow Cat [n2]	Events of *Falcon Magic* would take place spring this year. [n3]; Mallandor is killed and Norandor is now Lord Baron in Alizon; the second child of Eirran and Yareth is born later this year. [n4]	When Aisling is almost 11, Kirion visits and challenges her to a race. After she beats him (and he humiliates himself) he attempts to kill her and she uses Power to defend herself. Later Kirion remembers this and starts to learn about various ways of Power. He also spends his time making Keelan miserable, which causes him to move to Aiskeep. Sometime later this year Shosho the cat is born and Keelan is given her to take care of. [n5]
6813	1062	Year of the Weld [n6]	Mereth is 75 [n7]; Events of *The Magestone* would take place at the end of this year and the beginning of the next. [n8].	Keelan's 18th birthday comes in early spring of this year. It is also when Kirion attempts to gain entry to Aiskeep to further his research but he is rebuffed. Keelan formally asks to stay at Aiskeep. [n9]

n1. This is the earliest year it can take place since on page 20 Koris mentions there is talk of Falconer's establishing a new Eyrie overseas as per *Seakeep* and *Falcon Hope*. However, it could easily take place in any of the following years prior to *Warding*. It's been 34 years since Simon entered the Witch World, so his surprise at 50 passing in ours is justified.

n2. Both GURPS and Norton place the order of years as Kobold, Snow Cat, and Horned Hunter, but this won't work.

n3. *The Magestone* refers to the abduction of the witch children (which includes Jenys/Mouse) taking place the year before and Jenys is six going on seven.

n4. *Falcon Magic*

n5. *Ciara's Song*

n6. Weld is a plant (also known as dyer's rocket, dyer's weed, woold, and yellow weed) of the mignonette family that produces yellow dye.

n7. In *The Magestone* Mereth says she is 75 (p.103). While this works with other statements (she's been a trader nearly 60 years on page 4) it won't work out with the Turning having been only two years ago when, in reality it must be closer to twelve. However, this does resolve the issue regarding Mouse who is almost seven at the time the raid occurred.

n8. This won't agree with the insistence that the Turning was only two years ago. Kasarian would be 34 (on page 45 Mereth thinks Kasarian is barely 30, so that matches), the Tregarth triplets would be 33, and Elona and Keris would be about 10. It also works with other books in the three anthologies of *Storms of Victory*, *Flight of Vengeance*, and *On Wings of Magic*.

n9. *Ciara's Song*

6814	1063	Year of the Hydra	To keep track of things, by this point Duratan (38) and Nolar (33) have some kind of relationship going on [o1] and Derren of Karsten is married to Anylse [o2]; Simon, Jaelithe, Koris,	Kirion raises Shandro to be duke and tries to stir up hatred against those with Old Race blood in order to extract revenge against his own family. He changes

			and Loyse are ruling Estcarp [o3]; Mereth is 76; Kerovan 52-53, Joisan 50 (51 in the fall); Elyn and Elys 49; Gillan 45-47; Lorcan 45 and Meive 43; Una of Seakeep 36; Jerrany, Kasarian 35 [o4]; Tirtha and Nirel are probably 38 [o5]; Kyllan, Kemoc and Kaththea are 34; Romar and Mayrin 32; Simond and Tursla are probably around 32 [o6]; Yareth 30 and Eirran 28; Elfanor (daughter of Hertha) 27; Eleeri, Hyana, Kethan and Aylinn 26; Eydryth 25; Harwin and Glinda 24 [o7]; First child of Meive and Lorcan 23; Alon is at least 22 [o8]; Firdun 20; Dairene 19-20; Trevon 15; Elona and Keris 11; Jenys/Mouse, The first child of Hilarion and Kaththea 9; The second child of Hilarion and Kaththea 7; Second child of Eirran and Yareth will be 2 at the end of this year. [o9]	course when he realizes this will make himself a target. [o10]
6815	1064	Year of the Triton		
6816	1065	Year of the Centaur	This may be the year that the events of *The Warding of Witch World* take place. [o11]	

o1. Seen in the introduction and interludes of *On Wings of Magic* and Kasarian refers to Nolar as Duratan's mate in *The Magestone*, so they could even be married.

o2. p.405 *On Wings of Magic*

o3. The ages of these four are hard to know. Jaelithe in particular could be almost any age since the Old Race live so long. Note that Simon's age is a curious factor since he joined the army in 1939 and was in occupied Germany (which lasted from 1945 until 1955). Assuming he was 18 when he joined he would be between 24-34 when court marshaled, spent a year in jail and another seven on the run before meeting Dr. Petronius and thus making him between 32-42 at the start of *Witch World*. He *ought* to be between 70-80 by now, but seems to be physically in his prime still. Even accounting for the nine lost years in the Machine World, he ought to physically be between 61-71. Koris and Loyse are likely 56, assuming they were 18 at the time of the first book (it's been 38 years since then)

o4. As per usual his age could be 40 if he's actually five when the invasion began.

o5. Much like Duratan, Tirtha was born before the Horning, though it's hard to know how much before.

o6. There's no way to know for certain but it's unlikely they're much less than 30.

o7. This is an estimate - they could be a couple years younger. Glenda is over 18 in *Were-Hunter* and Harwin seems about the same age. Since Harwin is the third child of Kildas and Harl he was likely born at least two years after Kethan was.

o8. *Songsmith* seems to put him and Eydryth at the same age, which is possible since he only remembers 12 years. Other aspects of that story are more questionable given the timeline.

o9. For possible discussion/speculation: Do Duratan and Nolar, Derren and Anylse, and or Eleeri and Romar have kids? They're all certainly old enough to. For that matter, Nirel and Tirath could have kids too and the fact that Kasarian doesn't have a mate by now is pretty baffling (though not so strange if *The Magestone* were supposed to be almost ten years ago when he would have been 25). Una and Tarlach certainly ought to have at least one child (age 4 or 5) by now as well. Does Kemoc move into Lormt with Orsya? It'd be odd if he didn't since he's only been advertising it to everyone he meets!

o10. *Ciara's Song*

o11. Since both *Songsmith* and *The Key of the Keplian* are supposed to take place thirty years after the Turning (and this is only 15), references to the thirty years into the future need to be ignored for the most part. It does work if Keris is supposed to be near his teens.

6817	1066	Year of the Opinicus [p1]	*Earthborne* may take place. [p2]	Kirion attempts to force Aisling (now 16) into a marriage she doesn't want to Ruart. It is in this year that Shosho (during the summer) gets pregnant at age 4 and later gives birth to Wind Dancer. Aisling is kidnapped after her refusal and held by Ruart and Kirion. She manages to escape. [p3]
6818	1067	Year of the Simurgh [p4]		Kirion and Ruart resume their efforts to get Aisling for their own purposes. In winter of this year Aiskeep is under siege and Elanor dies. Aisling decides to leave for Estcarp but Ciara tells her about her dream of Escore. She first goes to Geavon then to Temon where Ruart catches her, but he and Temon die. Aisling passes through some kind of gate and meets Neevor in Escore. [p5]
6819	1068	Year of the Remorhaz [p6]		
6820	1069	Year of the Elder Tree		
6821	1070	Year of the Wild Huntsman		Aisling returns to Karsten under a geas to remove Shandro and Kirion from power. In summer, Franzo leads a siege due to many deaths in the Coast Clan thanks to Shandro and Kirion. This is also when the events of *The Gate of the Cat* are mentioned (page 128 of the hard cover). [p7]
6822	1071	Year of the Troll-Dame		In spring of this year, Franzo makes a second

				siege of Kars. Shandro and Kirion die and Aisling and Hadrann are formally betroth. [p8]
6823	1072	Year of the Silversmith		
6824	1073	Year of the Bitter Herb		
6825	1074	Year of the Alfar [p9]		
6826	1075	Year of the Air Spirit [p10]		
6827	1076	Year of the Swordsmith		
6828	1077	Year of the Gargoyle		
6829	1078	Year of the Wyvern		
6830	1079	Year of the Horn Worm		
6831	1080	Year of the Dragon Horse	Thirty years after the Turning. Events of *The Key of the Keplian* take place; The events of *Songsmith* are also supposed to occur this year. [p11]	
6832	1081	Year of the Nix		
6833	1082	Year of the Pookaworm		

p1. Misspelled Opinacus in GURPS.

p2. The story mentions both the Warding and the Turning. It also mentions that the two fallen towers of Lormt have been restored. Mereth would be 79 this year.

p3. *Ciara's Song*

p4. Misspelled as Sumurgh in GURPS. The Simurgh is a benevolent female creature of Iranian origin, usually depicted as a huge peacock with the claws of a lion and a head that is either canine or human.

p5. *Ciara's Song*

p6. This creature first appeared in Dungeons and Dragons in 1976. It resembles a gigantic blue centipede but which bends around the middle so that the lower segments have legs and the upper have webbed spikes that resemble a cobra's 'hood'. There are multiple red gem-like areas along its back (two per segment) that emit heat.

p7. *The Duke's Ballad*

p8. *The Duke's Ballad*

p9. Last year in GURPS

p10. This year, as well as all the following, are from Coulter's Index alone.

p11. Again, this is a problem given some ages and characters in *The Warding of Witch World*

Sorceress of the Witch World Poland 2014

GURPS: Years Defined

[*GURPS: Witch World; Roleplaying in Andre Norton's Witch World*] (1989) Published by Steve Jackson Games Inc., written by Sasha Miller and Ben W. Miller, Edited by Sharleen Lambard ~ cover by Toni Taylor

Each year in the Witch World bears a name rather than a number and — unlike the Chinese calendar — the names are not repeated. This system originated with the Dalesmen and was brought to the Eastern Continent by the Sulcar traders. It is now followed by nearly all the inhabitants of the Witch World.

The Book of Years, which lists year names for thousands of years, was written by the Bard-Sages of High Hallack. They claim to have learned, not created, the names, and made a record.

The following lists years from the **Year of the Serpent King** to the **Year of the Alfar** in chronological order. This is a complete list for this period, including many names that have not yet appeared in Witch World novels or stories.

Year unnamed
Refugees of the Old Race flee Escore, erecting the Great Mountains separating Escore from Estcarp ~ *Three Against the Witch World*.
Approximately 600 years pass unrecorded.

Year of the Cloven Hoof
The first Dalesmen come to High Hallack, fleeing the disasters of their own world ~ *Horn Crown*.
Approximately 400 years pass.[1]

Year of the Serpent King
Kerovan is born in High Hallack ~ *The Crystal Gryphon*.[2]

Year of the Ringed Dove
Kerovan's sister Lisana is born in High Hallack ~ *The Crystal Gryphon*.

Year of the Salamander
Almondia and Truan are shipwrecked off Wark, High Hallack ~ *Dragon Scale Silver*.
Joisan is born in High Hallack ~ *The Crystal Gryphon*.
Year of the Fire Arrow
Year of the Bicorn
Elys and Elyn are born in High Hallack ~ *Dragon Scale Silver*.[3]
Year of the Hill Giant
Year of the Sea Calf
Year of the Kestrel
Year of the Yellow Dwarf
Dairine is cast ashore at Rannock, High Hallack ~ *Spider Silk*.[4]
Year of the Mandrake
Year of the Spitting Toad
Joisan and Kerovan are married by axe in High Hallack ~ *The Crystal Gryphon*.
Year of the Winged Bull
Year of the Horned Worm
Year of the Gorgon
Year of the Barrow-Wight
Simon Tregarth arrives in Estcarp through a Gate from Earth ~ *Witch World*.
Sulcarkeep is destroyed ~ *Witch World*.
Loyse of Verlaine marries Duke Yvian of Karsten by axe ~ *Witch World*.
Year of the Cameleopard
Simon Tregarth marries Jaelithe in Estcarp ~ *Witch World*.
Duke Yvian of Karsten is killed ~ *Web of the Witch World*.
Kyllan Tregarth is born on the last day of the year ~ *Three Against the Witch World*.
Year of the Crowned Swan
Kemoc and Kaththea Tregarth are born on the first day of the year ~ *Three Against the Witch World*.
Year of the Fire Troll
Koris of Gorm and Loyse of Verlaine are married in Estcarp ~ *Three Against the Witch World*.
Dairine receives the gift of Touch-Sight in High Hallack ~ *Spider Silk*.[5]
Alizon invades High Hallack ~ *The Crystal Gryphon*, *Dragon Scale Silver*.
Year of the Mosswife[6]
Pagar begins his rise to power in Karsten ~ *Three Against the Witch World*.
Year of the Weldworm
The Sulcar come to the aid of High Hallack and begin harrying the coasts of Alizon ~ *The Crystal Gryphon*.
Dairine becomes apprenticed to the Weavers of Usturt ~ *Spider Silk*.[7]
Year of the Swordsman
The Sulcar carry their harrying action into Karsten, raiding the city of Kars ~ *Three Against the Witch World*.
Simon and Loyse are imprisoned in Tormarsh ~ *Web of the Witch World*.
Simon and Jaelithe destroy the Kolder Gate ~ *Web of the Witch World*.
Year of the Leopard
Pagar's power base in Karsten grows unsteady ~ *Three Against the Witch World*.
Gillan arrives in Norstead Abbey, High Hallack ~ *Year of the Unicorn*.
High Hallack rallies against the Alizon invasion ~ *The Crystal Gryphon*.
Year of the Raven
Elys and Jervon dispel Ingaret's Curse in High Hallack ~ *Dragon Scale Silver*.
Imgry becomes leader of the war forces in High Hallack ~ *Gryphon in Glory*.
Year of the Night Hound
Pagar begins to solidify his power in Karsten ~ *Three Against the Witch World*.
Year of the Gryphon
High Hallack makes the Pact with the Weres ~ *Year of the Unicorn*, *Three Against the Witch World*, *The Jargoon Pard* and *Gryphon in Glory*.

Year of the Firedrake

Year of the Hornet

High Hallack defeats the invaders from Alizon ~ *Three Against the Witch World* and *The Jargoon Pard*.[8]

Year of the Unicorn

Kyllan, Kemoc and Kaththea Tregarth rescue a Witch in Estcarp. Alerted to Kaththea's powers, the Council summons her for testing. Her parents refuse ~ *Three Against the Witch World*.

Ysmay marries Hylle in High Hallack and journeys to Quayth ~ *Amber Out of Quayth*.[9]

Gillan and the Were Rider Herrel are married in High Hallack ~ *Year of the Unicorn*.[10]

Year of the Red Boar[11]

Ysmay frees Broc and Yaal; Hylle is overthrown in Quayth ~ *Amber Out of Quayth*.[12]

Aylinn is born in High Hallack ~ *The Jargoon Pard*.[13]

Kethan is born in High Hallack ~ *The Jargoon Pard*.[14]

Year of the Fox Maiden

Simon Tregarth disappears from Estcarp ~ *Three Against the Witch World*.

Year of the Phoenix

Jaelithe Tregarth goes in search of Simon and disappears from Estcarp ~ *Three Against the Witch World*.

Year of the Hippogriff

Kyllan and Kemoc Tregarth ride with the Borderers of Estcarp against Karsten ~ *Three Against the Witch World*.

Alon is born in Karsten ~ *Ware Hawk*.

Year of the Roc

Kaththea Tregarth is taken for training by The Council of Estcarp ~ *Three Against the Witch World*.

Duke Pagar of Karsten suffers a defeat by the Borderers and subsequent setback ~ *Three Against the Witch World*.

Year of the Basilisk

Duke Pagar of Karsten rallies once more ~ *Three Against the Witch World*.

Year of the Black Adder

Kemoc Tregarth is wounded and goes to the Archives at Lormt ~ *Three Against the Witch World*.

Koris is wounded and retires from leadership in Estcarp ~ *Three Against the Witch World* and *Warlock of the Witch World*.

Year of the Frost Giant

Simond is born to Koris and Loyse in Estcarp ~ *Sand Sister*.

Year of the Kobold

The Witches of Estcarp wreak the Turning - devastating the barrier ridge separating Karsten from Alizon - and Karsten is defeated ~ *Three Against the Witch World*.[15]

Kyllan and Kemoc Tregarth rescue Kaththea from the Council of Estcarp, and the Three flee over the mountains to Escore ~ *Three Against the Witch World*.

Kyllan Tregarth and Dahaun of the Green Silences are handfasted in Escore ~ *Three Against the Witch World*.

Year of the Snow Cat

Kyllan Tregarth returns to Estcarp to recruit settlers for Escore ~ *Three Against the Witch World*.

Kemoc Tregarth and the Krogan maiden Orsya are handfasted ~ *Three Against the Witch World*.

Kaththea Tregarth is lured away by the adept Dinzel and is rescued by Kemoc ~ *Warlock of the Witch World*.[16]

Kaththea Tregarth is lost in an avalanche en route from Escore to Estcarp. She is rescued by the Vupsall and taken deep into Escore ~ *Sorceress of the Witch World*.

Year of the Horned Hunter

Kaththea Tregarth becomes apprenticed to the Vupsall Wise Woman Utta ~ *Sorceress of the Witch World*.

Kaththea Tregarth finds the Dark Tower and discovers the Gate into the Machine World ~ *Sorceress of the Witch World*.

Kaththea Tregarth discovers Simon and Jaelithe in the Machine World, and they rescue the adept Hilarion from imprisonment ~ *Sorceress of the Witch World*.

Year of the Lamia

Kelsie arrives in Escore through a Gate from Earth ~ *The Gate of the Cat*.[17]

Year of the Chimera

Simon and Jaelithe Tregarth return to Estcarp from Escore ~ *Sorceress of the Witch World*.

Year of the Harpy

Tirtha of Hawkholme, Nirel the Falconer and the youth Alon adventure in Escore ~ *Ware Hawk*.[18]

Year of the Orc

Year of the Werewolf

Year of the Thorn Cat

Kethan and Thaney are betrothed ~ *The Jargoon Pard*.

Year of the Manticore

Year of the Weld

Year of the Hydra

Year of the Triton

Year of the Centaur

Year of the Opinacus

Year of the Sumurgh

Year of the Remorhaz

Year of the Elder Tree

Year of the Wild Huntsman

Year of the Troll-Dame

Year of the Silversmith

Year of the Bitter Herb

Year of the Alfar

Footnotes:

1. Sometime during these years, *One Spell Wizard* takes place in High Hallack.

2. The details of Kerovan's birth are revealed in *Of the Shaping of Ulm's Heir* & *Heir Apparent*. Sometime around here, *Dream Smith* may take place.

3. This is incorrect. It is named the "Year of the Sea Serpent" in *Dragon Scale Silver*.

4. This is incorrect, both in time and location. Rannock is in Estcarp on the shore south of the Tor Marsh. This story takes place around The Turning. In fact, this where the name of the year when The Turning occurred, the Year of the Kobold, was first mentioned.

5. This is incorrect. See the previous Note.

6. The Year of the Moss Wives is mentioned as before the Fire Troll in *The Crystal Gryphon* as well as in *Silver May Tarnish*.

7. This is incorrect, see Footnote #4.

8. Also this year, Hertha is raped by a Dalesman in the aftermath of the war and she seeks her revenge in *The Toads of Grimmerdale*, Elys & Jervon fight an ancient god in *Sword of Unbelief* and Brixia undoes *Zarsthor's Bane*.

9. Early in this year, Hertha gives birth to her daughter Elfanor and seals the circle of the Toads in *Changeling*. Also this year, Kerovan & Joisan enter Arvon and Joisan discovers she is pregnant and due to deliver around Midwinter of this year in *Gryphon's Eyrie*.

10. This happened on the first day of the year.

11. Also during this year the events of *Ully the Piper* and *Legacy from Sorn Fen*.

12. This actually happened on the last day of the *Year of the Unicorn*.

13. This is incorrect, she's born in Arvon.

<u>14</u>. This is incorrect, he is born in <u>Arvon</u>.

<u>15</u>. The name from this year came from *Spider Silk*.

<u>16</u>. The book *Trey of Swords* takes place just before Kaththea is lured away by Dinzel during <u>*Warlock of the Witch World*</u>.

<u>17</u>. This was published after <u>*Sorceress of the Witch World*</u> & <u>*Ware Hawk*</u>, why it was placed before is very odd.

<u>18</u>. This was published before *The Gate of the Cat*, why it was placed after is very odd.

Sorceress of the Witch World UK 1988

Months of Witch World

In *The Magestone* the Years since the Betrayal are introduced as the Alizonder way of tracking time. These years are placed alongside the year names of the Dales and so make keeping track of events and ages somewhat easier. Along with the Years since the Betrayal both Alizonder and Dale months are introduced and reinforced. Here is a rough listing of the months and their order based on the contexts of different books.

In Coulson's Index there are list of both <u>months</u> and <u>years</u> I have included these below marking them with an asterisks.

Order in year	Dales Calendar[1]	Days in month	Season	Alizon Calendar	Days in month	Season	Real World [2]
1	Month of the Snow Bird	28	Winter	First Whelping Moon	28	Winter	(Jan./Feb.)
2	Month of the Hawk[3]	28	Spring	Moon of the Dire Wolf	28	Winter	(Mid Feb. into March)

3	Month of the Crooknecked Fern	28	Spring	Moon of Cordosh	28	Spring	(March / April)
4	Month of the Fringed Violet	28	Spring	Moon of the Spotted Viper	28	Spring	(April into May)
5	Month of Willowcarp[4]	28	Summer[5]	Moon of the Fever Leaf	28	Spring	(May into June)
6	Month of the Golden Lacewing*[6]	29	Summer	Moon of the Split-Tusked Boar*	28	Summer	(June / July)
7	Month of the Silver Crowned Bee*	28	Summer	Moon of the Torgian Foals *	28	Summer	(July / August)
8	Month of the Anda Wasp*	28	Autumn?[7]	The Second Whelping Moon[8]	28	Summer	(August)
9	Month of the Shredbark Tree[9]	28	Autumn	Moon of the Hooded Crow*	28	Summer/Autumn?	(Sept.)
10	Month of the Crested Owl*	28	Autumn	Moon of the Bloodwine*	28	Autumn	(Sept. / Oct.)
11	Month of the Firethorn[10]	28	Autumn	Moon of the Dart Venom *	28	Autumn	(Nov.)
12	Month of Peryton[11]	28	Autumn/Winter?	The Hunger Moon*	28	Autumn/Winter?	(Dec.)
13	Month of the Ice Dragon	28	Winter	Moon of the Knife	29	Winter	(Jan.)

Sorcerer's Notes:

The months mentioned in *The Magestone* have at least 26 days in them (p.210, 217, 227). If the *Witch World* has about 365 days the year could be divided into twelve 30-day months (with extra days in some) or thirteen 28-day months with one month having one extra day. *The Magestone* seems to imply that both Dales and Alizon calendars have thirteen months based on how the days line up in the book. A list of months in the Discussion section shows how this would work out.

Kasarian arrives in Es Port on the Seventeenth Day of the Month of the Snow Bird (p. 249). "Morfew suggested the *Storm Seeker* would likely require four to six weeks for its passage...We therefore calculated that Kasarian should have arrived at Vennesport late in the Month of the Hawk or early in the Month of the Crooknecked Fern" (p. 250). This means that the Month of the Snow Bird, Hawk, Crooknecked Fern, and Fringed Violet must follow one another in that order.

The spring season for the Dales/Estcarp starts a month earlier than it does in Alizon: "I awoke, they told me, the following day, which the Lormt folk termed the Second Day of the Month of the Fringed Violet, the last Moon of their Spring Season. I was taken aback. [12] Morfew ensured me that it was indeed the First Day of the Moon of the

259

Spotted Viper, the second of our three moons of the Spring Season." (*The Magestone* pp. 242-243) Since Alizon is further north this makes some sense.

In *The Magestone* Mereth is traveling oversea in the Month of the Firethorn (p. 1). "Then, nearly two months ago, in the Month of the Shredbark Tree, Dame Gwersa's letter reached me at Venesport" (p. 5). Kasarian leaves Lormt for Es City on the Third Day of the First Whelping Moon (p.215) and arrives there on the Thirteenth Day of the same month. Though this journey takes time due to snow, it is likely that Mereth, being old, would have taken a similarly slow course to reach Lormt. It is later mentioned that it takes Kasarian some thirty-four days to reach Venesport by ship (p.226). Those at Lormt also expect the voyage to take four to six week by sea (p. 250). Since Mereth does not give the exact day in her first journal entry, it is hard to tell exactly how long it takes her to reach Lormt. Her first journal entry there is on the 4th and 5th Days of the Ice Dragon - though it cannot yet be the Year of the Lamia since in previous books (*The Crystal Gryphon*) the Month of the Snowbird is the first month of the year. In any case her journey is likely to take four to six weeks by sea and possibly another couple overland. If she left around the middle of the month of the Firethorn it could have taken her the rest of that month and all the next before she reached Lormt.

Both the Dales and Alizon have a thirteen month system.[13] Below are the months and days as mentioned in *The Magestone*. Those days that are not specifically mentioned have asterisks by them. This mainly applies to those days in months not covered or days near the end of the month - if a passage mentions it is the twenty-sixth day of the month but no other days before it, it is a safe bet the other twenty-five days exist.

1st Month
Month of the Snow Bird/First Whelping Moon
1/28th day of the Moon of the Knife*
2/1
3/2
4/3
5/4
6/5
7/6
8/7
9/8
10/9
11/10
12/11
13/12
14/13
15/14
16/15
17/16
18/17
19/18 <= Kasarian sails from Es Port (p. 223)
20/19*
21/20*
22/21*
23/22*
24/23*
25/24*
26/25*
27/26*
28/27*

2nd Month

Month of the Hawk/Moon of the Dire Wolf
1/28th day of the First Welping Moon*
2/1
3/2
4/3
5/4
6/5
7/6
8/7
9/8
10/9
11/10
12/11
13/12
14/13
15/14
16/15
17/16
18/17
19/18
20/19
21/20
22/21
23/22
24/23
25/24 <= Kasarian arrives in Vennesport in the Dales after about 34 days at sea by his tally. (p. 226)
26/25
27/26 <= Kasarian leaves Vennesport to Trevamper (p. 228)
28/27*

3rd Month
Month of the Crooknecked Fern/Moon of Chordosh
1/28th day Moon of the Dire Wolf *
2/1
3/2
4/3
5/4
6/5
7/6
8/7
9/8
10/9
11/10
12/11
13/12
14/13
15/14
16/15
17/16
18/17
19/18
20/19
21/20
22/21
23/22

24/23

25/24 <= Kasarian arrives at the cave Elsenar is trapped in by his counting of days.
(p.231)

26/25

27/26*

28/27* <= Jonja detects Kasarian is in mortal peril on the last day of the Month of the
Crooknecked Fern (p. 250 *The Magestone*). He is facing Elsenar and the stone (p. 251).[14]

4th Month
Month of the Fringed Violet/Moon of the Spotted Viper
1/28th day of the Moon of Chordosh
2/1 <= returns to Lormt after trip through magical postern. (p. 251)
3/2 <= Kasarian returns to Alizon via the postern in Lormt (p. 270)
4/3
5/4
6/5
7/6
8/7
9/8*
10/9*
11/10*
12/11*
13/12*
14/13*
15/14*
16/15*
17/16*
18/17*
19/18*
20/19*
21/20*
22/21*
23/22*
24/23*
25/24*
26/25*
27/26*
28/27*

5th Month
Month of the Willowcarp/Moon of the Fever Leaf
1/28th day of the Moon of the Spotted Viper
2/1
3/2*
4/3*
5/4*
6/5*
7/6*
8/7*
9/8*
10/9*
11/10*
12/11*
13/12*
14/13*
15/14*

16/15*
17/16*
18/17*
19/18*
20/19*
21/20*
22/21*
23/22*
24/23*
25/24*
26/25*
27/26*
28/27*

6th Month
Month of the Golden Lacewing*/Moon of the Split-tusked Boar
1/28th day of the Moon of the Fever Leaf*
2/1*
3/2*
4/3*
5/4*
6/5*
7/6*
8/7*
9/8*
10/9*
11/10*
12/11*
13/12*
14/13*
Midsummer Day/14*
15/15*
16/16*
17/17*
18/18*
19/19*
20/20*
21/21*
22/22*
23/23*
24/24*
25/25*
26/26*
27/27*
28/28*

7th Month
Month of the Silver Crowned Bee/Moon of the Torgian Foals
1/1*
2/2*
3/3*
4/4*
5/5*
6/6*
7/7*
8/8*

9/9*
10/10*
11/11*
12/12*
13/13*
14/14*
15/15*
16/16*
17/17*
18/18*
19/19*
20/20*
21/21*
22/22*
23/23*
24/24*
25/25*
26/26*
27/27*
28/28*

8th Month
Month of the Anda Wasp/The Second Whelping Moon
1/1*
2/2*
3/3*
4/4*
5/5*
6/6*
7/7*
8/8*
9/9*
10/10*
11/11*
12/12*
13/13*
14/14*
15/15*
16/16*
17/17*
18/18*
19/19*
20/20*
21/21*
22/22*
23/23*
24/24*
25/25*
26/26*
27/27*
28/28*

9th Month
Month of the Shredbark Tree/Moon of the Hooded Crow
1/1*
2/2*

3/3*
4/4*
5/5*
6/6*
7/7*
8/8*
9/9*
10/10*
11/11*
12/12*
13/13*
14/14*
15/15*
16/16*
17/17*
18/18*
19/19*
20/20*
21/21*
22/22*
23/23*
24/24*
25/25*
26/26*
27/27*
28/28*

10th Month
Month of the Crested Owl/Moon of the Bloodvine
1/1*
2/2*
3/3*
4/4*
5/5*
6/6*
7/7*
8/8*
9/9*
10/10*
11/11*
12/12*
13/13*
14/14*
15/15*
16/16*
17/17*
18/18*
19/19*
20/20*
21/21*
22/22*
23/23*
24/24*
25/25*
26/26*
27/27*

28/28*

11th Month
Month of the Firethorn/Moon of the Dart Venom
1/1*
2/2*
3/3*
4/4*
5/5*
6/6*
7/7*
8/8*
9/9*
10/10*
11/11*
12/12*
13/13*
14/14*
15/15*
16/16*
17/17*
18/18*
19/19*
20/20*
21/21*
22/22*
23/23*
24/24*
25/25*
26/26*
27/27*
28/28*

12th Month
Month of the Peryton/The Hunger Moon
1/1*
2/2*
3/3*
4/4*
5/5*
6/6*
7/7*
8/8*
9/9*
10/10*
11/11*
12/12*
13/13*
14/14*
15/15*
16/16*
17/17*
18/18*
19/19*
20/20*
21/21*

22/22*
23/23*
24/24*
25/25*
26/26*
27/27*
28/28*

13th Month
Month of the Ice Dragon/Moon of the Knife
1/1
2/2
3/3
4/4
5/5
6/6
7/7
8/8
9/9
10/Veneration Day
11/10
12/11
13/12
14/13
15/14
16/15
17/16
18/17
19/18
20/19
21/20
22/21
23/22*
24/23*
25/24*
26/25*
27/26*
28/27*

Footnotes:
1. In the Coulson Index it's specifically Dales/Estcarp, but Arvon has the same year names as the Dales, so it seems likely they'd share the months too. While folks in Escore never seem to mention years or months much, given it was the original home to the Old Race it seems likely that it too would share in this system.

2. as indicated by Norton

3. The Month of the Hawk first appeared on page 62 of _The Crystal Gryphon_ and it seems to immediately follow the Month of the Snow Bird. For some reason in both _Wolfhead_ and _Were-Flight_ there is mention made of a Month of the Frost Sprite following the Month of the Snow Bird, which contradicts this. In _Sorceress of the Witch World_ Kaththea mentions, when they return to Escore through Hilarion's Gate, that it was now the Month of Chrysalis on p235. Kaththea: 'Then I, too, learned the surprises time can deal: I had entered here in the coldest grasp of winter, but I came out now into the warmth and sun of spring—the month of Chrysalis, still too early for the sowing of fields, and yet a time when the new blood and first joys of spring stir in one, bringing a kind of restlessness and inner excitement. Still, to my reckoning, I had only been away days, not weeks!' This may not be a continuity error since it's possible for

Estcarp to have its own names for months, but given that those in Lormt tend to use the Dales names, it seems unlikely that there's a developed, separate calendar system. Since it's warmer weather but still too early for plowing, the Month of Chrysalis must be the first spring month, probably similar in weather to March on Earth.

4. The month of the Willow Carp seems to directly follow the Month of the Fringed Violet. Duratan and Jonja leave for Es City on the Eight day of the Month of the Fringed Violet (p. 270), stay five days there (p. 271), and return on the Second Day of the Month of the Willow Carp. It is a slow ten-day journey to Es City in winter [Kasarian leaves Lormt for Es City on the Third Day of the First Whelping Moon (p.215) and arrives there on the Thirteenth Day of the same month] and even if they were in haste they might have only been able to shave off a few days both ways. In any case it's unlikely they spent a whole month on the road. At most their journey lasted 22 days, at least five of which were spent meeting with the Witches.

5. "Late on the Second Day of the Month of the Willow Carp, Duratan and Jonja splashed through Lormt's gate during the first Summer rain." (p. 271)

6. In _Songsmith_ Eydryth mentions she was born in the Month of the Gryfalcon so, with all but four months accounted for except in the notes, it should be one of these.

7. The notes indicate that in the Dales Midsummer Day is set apart between the 14th and 15th days of Golden Lacewing. Since that month would be the second of the three summer months, it follows that the Anda Wasp is likely an autumnal month - though it's probably still very warm through most of it. That said, this gives the Dales about five months of autumnal weather. Now this is certainly possible, but so far it seems like the weather for the Dales and Alizon more or less corresponds to weather in the temperate regions of our world, so it presents some problems with the months as expressed given Peryton is presented as the last month of autumn in _Port of Dead Ships_. If it were to be more or less even in terms of seasons, then the order here ought to be 8 - Shedbark Tree [autumn], 9 - Crested Owl [autumn], 10 - Firethorn [autumn], 11 - Peryton [autumn]. Even if Peryton is a month of more wintry weather towards the end to have three full months of winter, the twelfth month has to be a fully winter one (which "the Frost Sprite" would be a perfect name for).

8. I'm not marking this with an asterisks since it's mentioned there are two whelping moons in _The Magestone_: p. 147 "...to fetch my hound pup Moonbeam, who had been whelped early, between the year's two regular Whelping Moons."

9. Both this month and that of the Firethorn are mentioned in _The Magestone_ and as being two months apart.

10. The notes indicate that this is the eleventh month of the year.

11. In _Port of Dead Ships_ the last month of autumn is called the "month of Peryton".

12. It's less than clear why Kasarian is taken aback, though. By his own count of days he's arrived at the site very late into the Moon of Cordosh - a mere five days before the Moon of the Spotted Viper - and he knows his tally of days could be off a bit, though maybe he didn't expect to lose almost an entire week.

13. The Celtic Calendar has a thirteen month system as well, based on sacred trees. Since quite a lot of real-world things end up in Witch World, it's very likely that Andre based at least her Dales calendar on this. For reference, the months are: Birch Moon: December 24 - January 20, Rowan Moon: January 21 - February 17, Ash Moon: February 18 - March 17, Alder Moon: March 18 - April 14, Willow Moon: April 15 - May 12, Hawthorn Moon: May 13 - June 9, Oak Moon: June 10 - July 7, Holly Moon: July 8 - August 4, Hazel Moon: August 5 - September 1, Vine Moon: September 2 - September 29, Ivy Moon: September 30 - October 27, Reed Moon: October 28 - November 23, and Elder Moon: November 24 - December 23. This is further borne out in the notes themselves which have some real world months notated next to them and seem to follow this pattern except in a couple places.

14. Given that Kasarian was unsure exactly how many days he'd actually been at sea due to storms: "We had spent thirty-four days at sea, by my judgement, for during the worst of the storms, it had been difficult to determine when day ended and night began" (p. 226 _The Magestone_) it is more likely this is the day he actually arrives at the

cave since Jonja and the others at Lormt were not affected by the storms and so their accounting of days is going to be more accurate.

Character Ages

Given the constancy problems, the chart below lists how old some of the characters ought to be in a given year. In some cases, like Gillan, Elys, and Jervon, this is a best guess based on text in the books. In the case of Kasarian two different ages age given due to the irreconcilable statements that he was five when the war began in the Dales and twenty-two when the Turning occurred. This is irreconcilable because he would then be only a year older than Kyllan, Kemoc, and Kaththea. Since *Web of the Witch World* mentions that Simon had been in love with Jaelithe half a year or less at the time of the events the Triplets were not likely even conceived, much less born. Since the Kolder Gate was closed in *Web of the Witch World* it could not have happened much sooner than the end of the Year of the Fire Troll or early in the Year of the Leopard, since the Year of the Leopard is mentioned in *The Crystal Gryphon* as being the year that the first victories against Alizon were being made, as well as the fact that the supplies of Kolder weapons seemed limited. The Kolder nest was also wiped out during the events of *Web of the Witch World* making it unlikely that any shattered fragments of Kolder would risk the wrath of the Alizonder barons if their scheme should fail.

First Generation:

		Jaelithe[1]	Simon	Koris	Loyse	Kerovan	Lisana	Jervon	Joisan	Elys, Elyn	Gillan	Lorcan	Meive
1010	Year of the Serpent King	17	17	3	3	0							
1011	Year of the Ringed Dove	18	18	4	4	1	0	0					
1012	Year of the Bicorn	19	19	5	5	2	1	1	0				
1013	Year of the Salamander	20	20	6	6	3	2	2	1	0			
1014	Year of the Sea Serpent	21	21	7	7	4	3	3	2	1			
1015	Year of the Pronghorn	22	22	8	8	5	4	4	3	2			
1016	Year of the Kestral	23	23	9	9	6	5	5	4	3	0		
1017	Year of the Pard	24	24	10	10	7	6	6	5	4	1	0	
1018	Year of the Yellow Dwarf	25	25	11	11	8	7	7	6	5	2	1	
1019	Year of the Mandrake	26	26	12	12	9	8	8	7	6	3	2	0
1020	Year of the Spitting Toad	27	27	13	13	10	9	9	8	7	4	3	1
1021	Year of the Winged Bull	28	28	14	14	11	10	10	9	8	5	4	2

1022	Year of the Horned Worm	29	29	15	15	12	11	11	10	9	6	5	3
1023	Year of the Gorgon	30	30	16	16	13	12	12	11	10	7	6	4
1024	Year of the Barrow-Wight	31	31	17	17	14	13	13	12	11	8	7	5
1025	Year of the Cameoleopard	32	32[2]	18[3]	18[4]	15	14	14	13	12	9	8	6
1026	Year of the Crowned Swan	33	33	19	19	16	15	15	14	13	10	9	7
1027	Year of the Moss Wife	34	34	20	20	17	16	16	15	14	11	10	8
1028	Year of the Fire Troll	35	35	21	21	18	17	17	16	15	12	11	9
1029	Year of the Leopard	36	36	22	22	19	18	18	17	16	13	12	10
1030	Year of the Sword Smith	37	37	23	23	20	-	19	18	17	14	13	11
1031	Year of the Raven	38	38	24	24	21	-	20	19	18	15	14	12
1032	Year of the Night Hound	39	39	25	25	22	-	21	20	19	16	15	13
1033	Year of the Gryphon	40	40	26	26	23	-	22	21	20	17	16	14
1034	Year of the Fire Drake	41	41	27	27	24	-	23	22	21	18	17	15
1035	Year of the Hornet	42	42	28	28	25	-	24	23	22	19	18	16
1036	Year of the Unicorn	43	43	29	29	26	-	25	24	23	20	19	17
1037	Year of the Red Boar	44	44	30	30	27	-	26	25	24	21	20	18
1038	Year of the Hippogriff	45	45	31	31	28	-	27	26	25	22	21	19
1039	Year of the Roc	46	46	32	32	29	-	28	27	26	23	22	20
1040	Year of the Basilisk	47	47	33	33	30	-	29	28	27	24	23	21
1041	Year of the Black Adder	48	48	34	34	31	-	30	29	28	25	24	22
1042	Year of the Frost Giant	49	49	35	35	32	-	31	30	29	26	25	23
1043	Year of the Fox Maiden	50*[5]	50*	36	36	33	-	32	31	30	27	26	24
1044	Year of the Snow Cat	50*	50*	37	37	34	-	33	32	31	28	27	25
1045	Year of the	50*	50*	38	38	35	-	34	33	32	29	28	26

5	Horned Hunter											
1046	Year of the Lamia	50*	50*	39	39	36	-	35	34	33	30	29	27
1047	Year of the Chimera	50*	50*	40	40	37	-	36	35	34	31	30	28
1048	Year of the Harpy	50*	50*	41	41	38	-	37	36	35	32	31	29
1049	Year of the Orc	50*	50*	42	42	39	-	38	37	36	33	32	30
1050	Year of the Kobald	50*	50*	43	43	40	-	39	38	37	34	33	31
1051	Year of the Werewolf	50*	50*	44	44	41	-	40	39	38	35	34	32
1052	Year of the Horned Cat	50*	50*[6]	45	45	42	-	41	40	39	36	35	33
1053	Year of the Manticore	51	51	46	46	43	-	42	41	40	37	35	34
1054	Year of the Weld	52	52	47	47	44	-	43	42	41	38	36	35
1055	Year of the Hydra	53	53	48	48	45	-	44	43	42	39	37	36
1056	Year of the Triton	54	54	49	49	46	-	45	44	43	40	38	37
1057	Year of the Centaur	55	55	50	50	47	-	46	45	44	41	39	38
1058	Year of the Weldworm	56	56	51	51	48	-	47	46	45	42	40	39
1059	Year of the Sumurgh	57	57	52	52	49	-	48	47	46	43	41	40
1060	Year of the Remorhaz	58	58	53	53	50	-	49	48	47	44	42	41
1061	Year of the Elder Tree	59	59	54	54	51	-	50	49	48	45	43	42
1062	Year of the Wild Hunt	60	60	55	55	52	-	51	50	49	46	44	43
1063	Year of the Troll-Dame	61	61	56	56	53	-	52	51	50	47	45	44
1064	Year of the Silversmith	62	62	57	57	54	-	53	52	51	48	46	45
1065	Year of the Bitter Herb	63	63	58	58	55	-	54	53	50	49	47	46
1066	Year of the Alfar	64	64	59	59	56	-	55	54	53	50	48	47
1067	Year of the ???	65	65	60	60	57	-	56	55	54	51	49	48
1068	Year of the ???	66	66	61	61	58	-	57	56	55	52	50	49
1069	Year of the ???	67	67	62	62	59	-	58	57	56	53	51	50
1070	Year of the	68	68	63	63	60	-	59	58	57	54	52	51

0	???												
1071	Year of the ???	69	69	64	64	61	-	60	59	58	55	53	52
1072	Year of the ???	70	70	65	65	62	-	61	60	59	56	54	53
1073	Year of the ???	71	71	66	66	63	-	62	61	60	57	55	54
1074	Year of the ???	72	72	67	67	64	-	63	62	61	58	56	55
1075	Year of the ???	73	73	68	68	65	-	64	63	62	59	57	56
1076	Year of the ???	74	74	69	69	66	-	65	64	63	60	58	57
1077	Year of the ???	75	75	70	70	67	-	66	65	64	61	59	58
1078	Year of the ???	76	76	71	71	68	-	67	66	65	62	60	59
1079	Year of the ???	77	77	72	72	69	-	68	67	66	63	61	60
1080	Year of the ???	78	78	73	73	70	-	69	68	67	64	62	61

Second Generation:

		Kasarian	Una	Kyllan[7], Kemoc, Kaththea	Khemrys	Simund, Trusla[8]	Kethan, Aylinn, Hyana	Eleeri	Eydryth, Alon	Firdun	Trevon
1023	Year of the Gorgon	0									
1024	Year of the Barrow-Wight	1									
1025	Year of the Cameoleopard	2									
1026	Year of the Crowned Swan	3									
1027	Year of the Moss Wife	4	0								
1028	Year of the Fire Troll	5/0	1								
1029	Year of the Leopard	6/1	2	0							
1030	Year of the Sword Smith	7/2	3	1							
1031	Year of the Raven	8/3	4	2							
1032	Year of the Night Hound	9/4	5	3							
103	Year of the	10/5	6	4							

272

3	Gryphon										
1034	Year of the Fire Drake	11/6	7	5	0						
1035	Year of the Hornet	12/7	8	6	1						
1036	Year of the Unicorn	13/8	9	7	2	0					
1037	Year of the Red Boar	14/9	10	8	3	1	0	0			
1038	Year of the Hippogriff	15/10	11	9	4	2	1	1	0		
1039	Year of the Roc	16/11	10	12	5	3	2	2	1		
1040	Year of the Basilisk	17/12	13	11	6	4	3	3	2		
1041	Year of the Black Adder	18/13	14	12	7	5	4	4	3		
1042	Year of the Frost Giant	19/14	15	13	8	6	5	5	4		
1043	Year of the Fox Maiden	20/15	16	14	9	7	6	6	5	0	
1044	Year of the Snow Cat	21/16	17	15	10	8	7	7	6	1	
1045	Year of the Horned Hunter	22/17	18	16	11	9	8	8	7	2	
1046	Year of the Lamia	23/18	19	17	12	10	9	9	8	3	
1047	Year of the Chimera	24/19	20	18	13	11	10	10	9	4	
1048	Year of the Harpy	25/20	21	19	14	12	11	11	10	5	*9
1049	Year of the Orc	26/21	22	20	15	13	12	12	11	6	
1050	Year of the Kobald	27/22	23	21	16	14	13	13	12	7	
1051	Year of the Werewolf	28/23	24	22	17	15	14	14	13	8	
1052	Year of the Horned Cat	29/24	25	23	18	16	15	15	14	9	
1053	Year of the Manticore	30/25	26	24	19	17	16	16	15	10	
1054	Year of the Weld	31/26	27	25	20	18	17	17	16	11	
1055	Year of the Hydra	32/27	28	26	21	19	18	18	17	12	
1056	Year of the Triton	33/28	29	27	22	20	19	19	18	13	
1057	Year of the Centaur	34/29	30	28	23	21	20	20	19	14	0
1058	Year of the	35/30	31	29	24	22	21	21	20	15	1

8	Opinicus										
1059	Year of the Sumurgh	36/31	32	30	25	23	22	22	21	16	2/11*10
1060	Year of the Remorhaz	37/32	33	31	26	24	23	23	22	17	12
1061	Year of the Elder Tree	38/33	34	32	27	25	24	24	23	18	13
1062	Year of the Wild Hunt	39/34	35	33	28	26	25	25	24	19	14
1063	Year of the Troll-Dame	40/35	36	34	29	27	26	26	25	20	15
1064	Year of the Silversmith	41/36	37	35	30	28	27	27	26	21	16
1065	Year of the Bitter Herb	42/37	38	36	31	29	28	28	27	22	17
1066	Year of the Alfar	43/38	39	37	32	30	29	29	28	23	18
1067	Year of the ???	44/39	40	38	33	31	30	30	29	24	19
1068	Year of the ???	45/40	41	39	34	32	31	31	30	25	20
1069	Year of the ???	46/41	42	40	35	33	32	32	31	26	21
1070	Year of the ???	47/42	43	41	36	34	33	33	32	27	22
1071	Year of the ???	48/43	44	42	37	35	34	34	33	28	23
1072	Year of the ???	49/44	45	43	38	36	35	35	34	29	24
1073	Year of the ???	50/45	46	44	39	37	36	36	35	30	25
1074	Year of the ???	51/46	47	45	40	38	37	37	36	31	26
1075	Year of the ???	52/47	48	46	41	39	38	38	37	32	27
1076	Year of the ???	53/48	49	47	42	40	39	39	38	33	28
1077	Year of the ???	54/49	50	48	43	41	40	40	39	34	29
1078	Year of the ???	55/50	51	49	44	42	41	41	40	35	30
1079	Year of the ???	56/51	52	50	45	43	42	42	41	36	31
1080	Year of the ???	57/52	53	51	46	44	43	43	42	37	32

Third Generation:

		Elona and Keris: Mouse/Jenys11	The first child of Hilarion and Kaththea	The second child of Hilarion and Kaththea
1052	Year of the	0		

	Horned Cat			
1053	Year of the Manticore	1		
1054	Year of the Weld	2	0	
1055	Year of the Hydra	3	1	
1056	Year of the Triton	4	2	0
1057	Year of the Centaur	5	3	1
1058	Year of the Opinicus	6	4	2
1059	Year of the Sumurgh	7	5	3
1060	Year of the Remorhaz	8	6	4
1061	Year of the Elder Tree	9	7	5
1062	Year of the Wild Hunt	10	8	6
1063	Year of the Troll-Dame	11	9	7
1064	Year of the Silversmith	12	10	8
1065	Year of the Bitter Herb	13	11	9
1066	Year of the Alfar	14	12	10
1067	Year of the ???	15	13	11
1068	Year of the ???	16	14	12
1069	Year of the ???	17	15	13
1070	Year of the ???	18	16	14
1071	Year of the ???	19	17	15
1072	Year of the ???	20	18	16
1073	Year of the ???	21	19	17
1074	Year of the ???	22	20	18
1075	Year of the ???	23	21	19
1076	Year of the ???	24	22	20
1077	Year of the ???	25	23	21
1078	Year of the ???	26	24	22
1079	Year of the ???	27	25	23
1080	Year of the ???	28	26	24

Footnotes:

1. There is no way to even hazard a guess as to Jaelithe's age, but since she and Simon are the parents of the next generation, she is included on this table with the estimate that she and Simon are probably around the same age.

2. Simon is older than 25. He enlisted on March 10, 1939 (presumably at 18) and rose

in rank fairly quickly. He served in the Allied occupation of Germany (post 1945). It's not clear when the black market deal had happened, but it could have been in 1946 when Simon was 25. He's been on the run for seven years at the time of his meeting with Petronius. See: *Witch World*

3. Koris is mentioned as being 'a boy who had only recently come into manhood' when Simon first meets him.

4. She seems to be about the same age as Koris.

5. Jaelithe follows Simon into another world. Time there passes much more slowly than in the *Witch World* so that several years are only a few days. See: *Sorceress of the Witch World*

6. When Simon and Jaelithe return to the *Witch World* they do not age to what they would be if they had not left. See: *Sorceress of the Witch World*

7. Kyllan is born at the last day of the year and thus, technically, a year older than Kemoc and Kaththea. For sake of simplicity they are listed as the same age in the table.

8. The ages of these two are a best guess.

9. Trevon should have been born this year but, due to the enchantment placed on Elys, he was not born until nine years later when Elys was freed.

10. in *The Warding of Witch World* it is mentioned that Trevon has rapidly aged to what his proper age would be if he'd been born in his proper year.

11. We really don't know much about Jenys's grandparents but she's about the same age as Elona and Keris and so included here.

When Were the Tregarth Children Born?

The birth of the Tregarth triplets shortly after the end of *Web of the Witch World* could have happened at the turning of the Year of the Leopard and here's why:

On p70 of *The Crystal Gryphon* Kerovan narrates, 'It would seem, though, that their supply of such fearsome weapons as they used in the first assaults—those metal monsters—was limited.' 'We took prisoners, and from some of those learned that the weapons we had come to fear the most were not truly of Alizon at all, but had been supplied by another people no engaged in war on the eastern continent where Alizon lay. And the reason for the invasion here was to prepare the way in time for these mightier strangers. The men of Alizon, for all their arrogance, seemed fearful of these others whose weapons they had early used, and they theatened us with some terrible vengeance when the strangers had finished their own present struggle and turned their full attention on us.'

It must take weeks (at least!) to cross the ocean from the eastern to western continents by ship. In fact Joisan narrates in *The Crystal Gryphon*, p45: 'News from overseas is long old before it reaches us. But we had heard many times that the eastern lands were locked in a struggle for power between nation and nation. Now and then there was mention of a country, a city, or even some warlord or leader whose deeds reached us in such a garbled form they were already well on the way to becoming a tale more fancy than fact.' It is likely the grunt troops of Alizon captured by the Dalesmen would not have the cutting edge latest news either. It is possible the Kolder Gate might even have been destroyed in the Year of the Fire Troll and that this information is due to a combination of the delay in receiving the latest news and propaganda to keep up the Alizonder troops' morale.

Joisan then goes on to inform us 'The Sulcarmen had suffered some grievous defeat of their own two years since in the eastern waters.' The only thing this can possibly refer to is the Fall of Sulcarkeep. Really, that's the only thing that could affect the entire Sulcar race to keep them from their usual trading with High Hallack.

In the *Annals of the Witch World* omnibus it mentions in (*Web of the Witch World*) that "Simon knew again the doubts which had moved him months earlier when he had stood before the Council of Guardians and had given the opinion they had asked for: leave the things found at Gorm alone..." This is obviously a reference to the events at the end of *Witch World*

In chapter VII, p. 245 of the same book it seems that Jaelithe and Simon have been married less than half a year: "Could he blame Koris for this present single-mindedness which was like to imperil their whole cause? Objectively, yes. A half year ago Simon would have witnessed but not understood the torment which tore the younger man now." Since the events of *Web of the Witch World* result in the Kolder Gate being closed the triplets aren't going to be born at this time since their parents have had a relationship barely six months. It's unlikely Jaelith is even pregnant at this time, unless she has just conceived. There's certainly nothing in the book to indicate she's approaching her second trimester. Because of this it can be inferred that the events of *Web of the Witch World* take place about half a year after the end events of *Witch World*.

In the hardback edition of *The Jargoon Pard* there seems to be a reference to the Turning on page 57: "There has been a great warring throughout our world. The Dales have battled ruthless invaders and, after a long term of years, driven them forth again. Overseas those of our cousinhood have also been embroiled in a struggle that has left them near beaten into the ground. This war they won, but in the winning, they made such an effort with the Power that for generations they will not be able to summon much to their service again." *The Jargoon Pard* seems to take place entirely within the Year of the Werewolf, when Kethan is 14. It is impossible to know how long ago the Turning happened at this point but in any case it would place the Year of the Kobald before the Year of the Werewolf.

The Tregarth Triplets are at least 21 by the time of the Turning. Chapter II, *Lost Lands of the Witch World* omnibus page 31: (*Three Against the Witch World*) "He [Pagar] met defeat in the spring of the year we counted seventeen winters behind us" it is that year that Kaththea is taken by the Witches and Koris is so wounded he can no longer wield the Axe of Volt (pp. 32 -33). Pg 37: "It was the beginning of the second year after Kaththea was taken that the road to Lormt opened for Kemoc, but not in a fashion we would have wished." Thus the three would be 19. In chapter III (pg. 38) "But it would seem Pagar had no wish to drink cup-brotherhood with Facellian of Alizon". "However, it was that very act [putting the Power to concentrated use] which they determined upon the second year after Kemoc left us." This would mean the three are now 21. The Turning takes place that summer. If the news of the Turning spread relatively quickly (and it's entirely likely it would) those of Arvon could have heard of it by the end of the year or beginning of the next (and since they are Power-adept themselves they could even have sensed it).

		Kyllan[1], Kemoc, Kaththea	Kethan, Aylinn, Hyana	Eydryth, Alon	Firdun	Eastern continent Event
1010	Year of the Serpent King					
1011	Year of the Ringed Dove			.		
1012	Year of the Bicorn					
1013	Year of the Salamander					Something prompts Truan and Almondia to flee Estcarp
1014	Year of the Sea Serpent					
1015	Year of the Pronghorn					
1016	Year of the Kestral					

1017	Year of the Pard				
1018	Year of the Yellow Dwarf				
1019	Year of the Mandrake				
1020	Year of the Spitting Toad				
1021	Year of the Winged Bull				
1022	Year of the Horned Worm				According to *The Magestone* the Kolder invade Gorm (p.154)
1023	Year of the Gorgon				
1024	Year of the Barrow-Wight				Simon Tregarth may enter the Witch World
1025	Year of the Cameoleopard				Sulcarkeep may fall, the Horning may take place late this year or early the next
1026	Year of the Crowned Swan				
1027	Year of the Moss Wife				
1028	Year of the Fire Troll				The events of *Web of the Witch World* probably take place late this year.
1029	Year of the Leopard	0			
1030	Year of the Sword Smith	1			
1031	Year of the Raven	2			
1032	Year of the Night Hound	3			
1033	Year of the Gryphon	4			
1034	Year of the Fire Drake	5			
1035	Year of the Hornet	6			
1036	Year of the Unicorn	7			
1037	Year of the Red Boar	8	0		
1038	Year of the Hippogriff	9	1	0	
1039	Year of the Roc	10	2	1	
1040	Year of the Basilisk	11	3	2	
1041	Year of the	12	4	3	

	Black Adder				
1042	Year of the Frost Giant	13	5	4	
1043	Year of the Fox Maiden	14	6	5	0	Simon Tregarth disappears while investigating some suspicious islands. Jaelithe follows after him a few months later.
1044	Year of the Snow Cat	15	7	6	1	
1045	Year of the Horned Hunter	16	8	7	2	
1046	Year of the Lamia	17	9	8	3	Kaththea taken by the Witches.
1047	Year of the Chimera	18	10	9	4	
1048	Year of the Harpy	19	11	10	5	Kemoc wounded and goes to Lormt
1049	Year of the Orc	20	12	11	6	
1050	Year of the Kobald	21	13	12	7	The Turning occurs; much of *Three Against the Witch World* after the Turning likely takes place.
1051	Year of the Werewolf	22	14	13	8	The events of *Warlock of the Witch World* likely take place
1052	Year of the Horned Cat	23	15	14	9	The early events of *Sorceress of the Witch World* likely take place.
1053	Year of the Manticore	24	16	15	10	Most of the main events of *The Magestone* take place. In the book it is the Year of the Lamia, but this does not mesh well with the age of the Tregarth triplets at the time of the Turning and the events leading to the closing of the Kolder Gate; The end events of *Sorceress of the Witch World* likely take place.
1054	Year of the Weld	25	17	16	11	
1055	Year of the Hydra	26	18	17	12	
1056	Year of the Triton	27	19	18	13	
1057	Year of the Centaur	28	20	19	14	
1058	Year of the Opinicus	29	21	20	15	
1059	Year of the Sumurgh	30	22	21	16	
1060	Year of the Remorhaz	31	23	22	17	
1061	Year of the Elder Tree	32	24	23	18	

1062	Year of the Wild Hunt	33	25	24	19	
1063	Year of the Troll-Dame	34	26	25	20	
1064	Year of the Silversmith	35	27	26	21	
1065	Year of the Bitter Herb	36	28	27	22	
1066	Year of the Alfar	37	29	28	23	

Sorcerer's Notes:

Andre doesn't go into detail about how long it takes to travel across the Witch World by walking, by horse or by ship. There must be weeks of time, months even between the events in *Witch World* and *Web of the Witch World* even though the narrative flow makes it seem like they all just take place within a short time. However, in *Falcon Hope* there is a reference that it takes at least two months to travel from Lormt to High Hallack.

Even with that said, the placement of the destruction of the Kolder Gate in the Year of the Leopard is to make the shortest amount of time between the fall of Sulcarkeep (the year before Crowned Swan) and the point where the Hounds run out of Kolder weapons. We learn in *Gryphon in Glory* that Galkur was the reason the Kolder sent the Hounds into High Hallack in the first place. Even after their Gate was destroyed, other sources imply that there were still Kolder surviving in Alizon after that. With their Gate destroyed, they were no longer able to supply the Hounds with weapons, ammunition and supplies but the Kolder were still a power to be reckoned with. Also, Galkur was manipulating the Hounds with his dark powers which kept them heading for the Waste up until the Year of the Gryphon when he was defeated by Kerovan, Joisan, Neevor, etc. After that, the Hounds were driven out of High Hallack with the help of the Were-Riders.

Actually, in *Three Against the Witch World* chapter 15 Kyllan says, "I had hopes only of the Old Race uprooted in the south. A few, very few, of the refugees from Karsten had been absorbed into Estcarp. The rest roved restlessly along the border, taking grim vengeance for the massacre of their blood. It had been close to twenty-five years since that happening, yet they would not forget nor really make one with Estcarp dwellers." which places The Turning 24 years (and some months?) after The Horning. Which means they were born 3 years (and a few months?) after the Horning if they were 21 the year of the Turning. -MD

Footnotes:

1. Kyllan is born at the last day of the year and thus, technically, a year older than Kemoc and Kaththea. For sake of simplicity they are listed as the same age in the table.

Witch World Map by Barbi Johnson - ACE Gift Box Set 1970

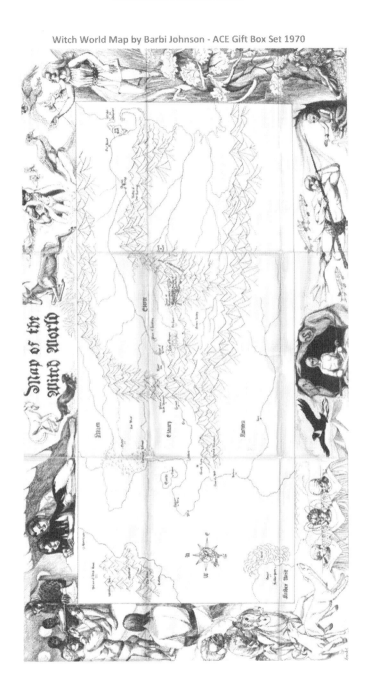

Index of Volume I WW Saga

Image Credits of Volume I WW Saga

Page 01   Andre Norton in her Office, Winter Park, Florida 1990s – From the Estate of Andre Norton

Page 06   Andre Norton in her Office, Altamonte, Florida 1980 – From the Estate of Andre Norton

Page 13   **The Many Worlds of Andre Norton** ~ (1974) Edited by Roger Elwood, Published by Chilton, HC, 0-801-95927-6, LCCN 74010980, $6.95, 208pg ~ cover by Charles Geer

Page 30   **Dread Companion** ~ (1998) Published in Poland; by Amber, 83-716-9822-4, 208pg ~ translated by Jacek Kozerski ~ cover by Steve Crisp ~ Polish title Pani Krainy Mgieł ~~ NOT a Witch World Title

Page 31   **Witch World** ~ (1977) Published by Gregg Press, HC, 0-839-82355-X, LCCN 77023209, $7.95, 222pg ~ As Witch World 1: Witch World ~ Dust Jacket and Text Art by Jack Gaughan, Frontmatter by Alice Phalen, Endpaper Maps by Barbi Johnson, Introduction and Chronology by Sandra Miesel

Page 43   *Witch World Titles* – Image found on Internet approx. 2008

Page 54   **Witch World** ~ (1974) Published by ACE, PB, #89702 $0.95 222pg - covers by J.H. Breslow

Page 56   **The Crystal Gryphon** ~ (1976) Published by Peacock, PB, 0-140-47083-2, £0.75, 248pg - 1979 £0.80 ~ UK printing ~ cover by David Smee

Page 57   *Masters of Fantasy* (2006) Edited by Bill Fawcett and Brian Thomsen, Published by BAEN, PB, 1-416-50927-5, $7.99, 563pg ~ cover by Jeff Easley ~ Contains *Earthborne*

Page 58   **Horn Crown** ~ (1981) Published by SFBC, HC, $2.95, 211pg ~ cover by Jack Woolhiser

Page 60   **Zarsthor's Bane** ~ (1978) Published by ACE, PB, 0-441-95490-1 , $1.95, 204pg - covers by Manuel Sanjulian, illustrated by Evan TenBroeck Steadman

Page 61   **Tales of the Witch World 1** ~ (1989) Published by Pan, TP, 0-330-30674-X, 978-0-330-30674-4, £3.99, 343pg ~ UK printing ~ cover by Brian Smallwood, maps by John M. Ford

Page 61   **Three Against the Witch World** ~ ((1987) Published by Gollancz, PB, 0-575-03998-1, £2.50, 191pg ~ UK printing ~ cover by Mike Posen

Page 63   **Storms of Victory** ~ (1991) Published by TOR, HC, 0-312-93171-9, LCCN 90049030, $19.95, 432pg ~ cover by Dennis A. Nolan, maps by John M. Ford

Page 64   **Tales of the Witch World 2** ~ (1989) Published by Pan, TP, 0-330-30809-2, 978-0-330-30809-0, £3.99, 370pg ~ UK printing ~ cover by Geoff Andrews, maps by John M. Ford

Page 65   **Sorceress of the Witch World** ~ (1987) Published by ACE, PB, #77558 $2.75 280pg 8th print - cover by John Pound ~~ Cropped to show just the artwork

Page 73   *Three Against the Witch World* ~ (1986) Published by ACE, PB, #80808 $2.75 251pg - cover by John Pound ~~ Cropped to show just the artwork

Page 81   *Witch World* ~ (1984) Published by ACE, PB, #89707-X $2.50 282pg - cover by John Pound ~~ Cropped to show just the artwork

Page 89   *Year of the Unicorn* ~ (1989) Published by ACE, PB, #95255-5 $3.50 281pg - cover by John Pound ~~ Cropped to show just the artwork

Page 94   Jalithe Tregath ~ Sketch by Sally C. Fink ~ From one of Andre's Scrapbooks

Page 95   Simon Trgarth ~ Sketch by Sally C. Fink ~ From one of Andre's Scrapbooks

Page 102   *Web of the Witch World* ~ (1983) Published by ACE, PB, #87877-6 $2.50 190pg - cover by John Pound, maps by Jack Gaughan ~~ Cropped to show just the artwork

Page 106   *Trey of Swords* ~ (1986) Published by ACE, PB, #82346 1986 $2.75 180pg - cover by John Pound ~~ Cropped to show just the artwork

Page 121   Map ~ From GURPS: Witch World Roleplaying Guide 1989 p.28

Page 131   Map ~ From GURPS: Witch World Roleplaying Guide 1989 p.28

Page 135   Map ~ From 1998 & 1999 Flight of Vengeance and Storms of Victory cover by Lubos Makarsky – Czechoslovakia

Page 142   *The Warding of Witch World* ~ (1996) Published by Warner Aspect, HC, 0-446-51991-X, LCCN 96007266, $22.95, 560pg ~ cover and map by John M. Ford

Page 146   Map ~ From GURPS: Witch World Roleplaying Guide 1989 p.17

Page 147   Map ~ From GURPS: Witch World Roleplaying Guide 1989 p.30

Page 158   *Trey of Swords* ~ (1979) Published by (Universal) Star Books, PB, 0-352-30376-X, £0.75p, 192pg ~ UK printing ~ cover by Rodney Mathews

Page 158   *Gryphon in Glory* ~ (1991) Published in Warsaw, Poland; by Amber, 83-850-7993-9, 239pg ~ translation by Elżbieta Dagny-Ryńska ~ cover by Boris Vallejo ~ Polish title **Gryf w Chwale** [Griffin in Glory]

Page 159   Map ~ From GURPS: Witch World Roleplaying Guide 1989 p.33

Page 166   Map ~ From GURPS: Witch World Roleplaying Guide 1989 p.31

Page 168   Map ~ From GURPS: Witch World Roleplaying Guide 1989 p.25

Page 169   *The Magestone* ~ (1996) Published by Warner Aspect, PB, 0-446-60222-1, $5.50, 276pg ~ cover and map by John M. Ford

Page 170   Map ~ From GURPS: Witch World Roleplaying Guide 1989 p.26

Page 171   Map ~ From GURPS: Witch World Roleplaying Guide 1989 p.23

Page 173   Map ~ From GURPS: Witch World Roleplaying Guide 1989 p.22

Page 174   Map ~ From GURPS: Witch World Roleplaying Guide 1989 p.19

Page 177   Map ~ From GURPS: Witch World Roleplaying Guide 1989 p.18

Page 179   Map ~ From GURPS: Witch World Roleplaying Guide 1989 p.29

Page 184   ***Witch World*** ~ (2005) Published in Kaunus, Lithuania; by Eridanas, 99-869-7111-X, 224pg ~ translation by John Bulovas ~ cover by Luis Royo ~ Lithuanian title **Raganų pasaulis** [The world of witches] ~ limited to 1000 copies

Page 192   ***Web of the Witch World*** ~ (1978) Published by Universal (Tandem), PB, 0-426-05020-7, £0.75, 192pg ~ UK printing ~ cover by Rodney Matthews, map by Jack Gaughan

Page 204   ***Spell of the Witch World*** ~ (1978) Published by Universal, PB, 0-426-18534-X, £0.75 ~ UK printing ~ cover by Rodney Matthews

Page 206   ***Witch World*** ~ (1978) Published by Universal (Tandem), PB, 0-426-05012-6, £0.75, 224pg ~ UK printing ~ cover by Rodney Matthews, map by Jack Gaughan

Page 207   Map ~ Witch World by Mary Hanson-Roberts 1986 High-Hallack ~ Released by the Andre Norton Ltd.

Page 207   Map ~ Witch World by Mary Hanson-Roberts 1986 Escore ~ Released by the Andre Norton Ltd.

Page 211   ***Witch World*** ~ (2013) Published in Warsaw, Poland; by Nasza Księgarnia, 978-83-10-11794-6, PB, 338pg ~ translation by Ewa Witecka ~ Polish title **Świat Czarownic** [Witch World]

Page 211   ***Witch World*** ~ (1987) Published by Gollancz, PB, 0-575-03995-7, £2.50, 222pg ~ UK printing ~ Cover by Mark Harrison

Page 219   ***Web of the Witch World*** ~ (2013) Published in Warsaw, Poland; by Nasza Księgarnia, 978-8-31011-795-3, PB, 288pg ~ translation by Ewa Witecka ~ Polish title **Świat Czarownic w pułapce** [The world of witches trapped]

Page 224   ***Three Against the Witch World*** ~ (2014) Published in Warsaw, Poland; by Nasza Księgarnia, 978-83-10-11796-0, PB, 288pg ~ translation by Ewa Witecka ~ Polish title **Troje przeciw Światu Czarownic** [Three Against the Witch World]

Page 234   ***Warlock of the Witch World*** ~ (2014) Published in Warsaw, Poland; by Nasza Księgarnia, 978-83-10-11797-7, PB, 320pg ~ translation by Ewa Witecka ~ Polish title **Czarodziej ze Świata Czarownic** [Magician from the world of Witches]

Page 235   ***Warlock of the Witch World*** ~ (1988) Published by Gollancz, PB, 0-575-03997-3, £2.50, 220pg ~ UK printing ~ cover by Michael Posen

Page 256   ***Sorceress of the Witch World*** ~ (2014) Published in Warsaw, Poland; by Nasza Księgarnia, 978-83-10-11798-4, PB, 320pg ~ translation by Ewa Witecka ~ Polish title **Czarodziejka ze Świata Czarownic** [Sorceress from the World of Witches]

Page 261   ***Sorceress of the Witch World*** ~ (1988) Published by Gollancz, PB, 0-575-04000-9, £2.95, 222pg ~ UK printing ~ cover by Michael Posen

Page 284   Witch World Map by Barbi Johnson – ACE Gift Box Set 1970

Index of Volume II WW Stories

Printed in Poland
by Amazon Fulfillment
Poland Sp. z o.o., Wrocław
16 August 2022

453f8ed7-7064-4b75-8c3c-5838b9b58fbdR01